THE NOVELS
AND RELATED WORKS OF

CHARLES BROCKDEN BROWN

BICENTENNIAL EDITION

VOLUME IV

EDGAR HUNTLY

Previous Volumes in the Bicentennial Edition

Wieland; or The Transformation. An American Tale with *Memoirs of Carwin the Biloquist*

Ormond; or The Secret Witness

Arthur Mervyn; or Memoirs of the Year 1793. First and Second Parts

CHARLES BROCKDEN BROWN

EDGAR HUNTLY

or

MEMOIRS OF A SLEEP-WALKER

Bicentennial Edition

KENT STATE UNIVERSITY PRESS

The preparation of this volume was made possible (in part) by grants from the Program for Editions, and its publication was assisted by a grant from the Publications Program, of the National Endowment for the Humanities, an independent Federal agency.

CENTER FOR
SCHOLARLY EDITIONS
AN APPROVED EDITION
MODERN LANGUAGE
ASSOCIATION OF AMERICA

Library of Congress Cataloging in Publication Data

Brown, Charles Brockden, 1771–1810.
    Edgar Huntly, or, Memoirs of a sleep-walker.

    (The Novels and related works of Charles Brockden
Brown ; v. 4)
        I. Title.   II. Title: Memoirs of a sleep-walker.
III. Series: Brown, Charles Brockden, 1771–1810.
Novels ; v. 4.
PZ3.B814 Nr 5, vol. 4   [PS1134]   813'.2s [813'.2] 84-4376
ISBN 0-87338-305-2

EDITORS

FOREWORD

This volume contains a critical edition of Charles Brockden Brown's *Edgar Huntly*, the third of his novels to be
published in 1799 and the first to deal with the American
wilderness. The basis of the text is the first edition,
printed and published by Hugh Maxwell in Philadelphia
late in the year, but the "Fragment" printed independently
in Brown's *Monthly Magazine* earlier in 1799 supplies some
readings in Chapters 17–20. The Historical Essay, which
follows the text, covers matters of composition, publication, historical background, and literary evaluation, and
the Textual Essay discusses the transmission of the text,
choice of copy-text, and editorial policy. A general textual
statement for the entire edition appears in Volume I of the
series.

Our work has required the gracious assistance of insitu-
tions and individuals who allowed us to make use of first
editions and other material. For the loan of early editions
and other copies used for collation, we wish to thank the
following:

Robert S. Fraser and Howard C. Rice, Jr., *Princeton
University Library*; James Gregory and James J. Heslin,
The New York Historical Society; Marcus McCorison, Fre-
derick E. Bauer, Jr., and James E. Mooney, *American
Antiquarian Society*; Richard Ryan and John W. Boyd,
Ohio University Library; Julius P. Barclay and Joan St. C.
Crane, *The University of Virginia Library*; William H.

Loos and Jane D. Van Arsdale, *Buffalo and Erie County Public Library*; Nathaniel H. Puffer, Delores Altemus, and Stuart Dick, *University of Delaware Library*; Maud D. Cole and Francis O. Mattson, *The New York Public Library*; Kenneth A. Lohf and Hugh MacDonald, *Butler Library, Columbia University*; Deena D. Frazier and Jean Burnham, *New York Society Library*; Lawrence F. London and Harry Bergholz, *University of North Carolina Library*; Edwin Wolf II, Anne P. Hennessey, Susan Mainwaring, and Lillian Tonkin, *The Library Company of Philadelphia*; William Matheson and Robert H. Land, *Library of Congress*; Carey S. Bliss, *Huntington Library*; Carolyn E. Jakeman and Elizabeth Droppers, *Houghton Library, Harvard University*; Martha C. Slotten and Yates M. Forbis, *Dickinson College Library*.

Particular gratitude is due to Pamela Burr, one of Brown's descendants, and to William J. Marshall, *University of Kentucky Library*; Charles W. Mann, *Pattee Library, Pennsylvania State University*; and Donald A. Sinclair, *A. S. Alexander Library, Rutgers University*.

The editors also wish to express their appreciation to the following for responding to inquiries:

Ann L. Wadsworth, *Library of the Boston Athenaeum*; Karen S. Lennon and Matt P. Lowman, *The Newberry Library*; Ellen M. Oldham, *Boston Public Library*; Donald Gallup and Dorothy W. Bridgwater, *Yale University Library*; John L. Sharpe and Florence Blakely, *Perkins Library, Duke University*; Theodore Grieder, *Elmer Holmes Bobst and Fales Libraries, New York University*; Josiah Q. Bennett and Edward P. Rich, *Lilly Library, Indiana University*; Gretchen Lagana, *Memorial Library, University of Wisconsin*; Neda M. Westlake and Lyman W. Riley, *University of Pennsylvania*; and Amy Lighthill, *Boston Museum of Fine Arts*.

In appreciation of their continued support and aid in facilitating the work of the Bibliographical and Textual Center, we would like to thank the following members of the Kent State University administration, library, and

English Department: Brage Golding, Michael Schwartz, Rudolph O. Buttlar, Eugene Wenninger, Carol Toncar, Hyman Kritzer, Dean Keller, the late Helen Peoples, Linda Neloms, Michael R. Cole, Robert Bamberg, Sanford Marovitz, Bruce Harkness, Wayne Kvam, and Lee Stockdale.

We also wish to express our thanks to our graduate research assistants Vicki Hendricks, the late Larry Swank, Diane Kushnar, Marc Leeds, Lorie Roth, Ramona Stamm, Elizabeth Ford, John Holmes, and John Lent, and to our staff and student assistants: Mary E. Dush, Roberta Trowbridge, Gypsy Clark, Mary Austin, Maureen Austin, Kathy Bajenski, Barbara Ward Barker, Saundra Brown, Marie Compston, Sylvia DeCapite, Celeste Doubek, Julie Fishman, Thomas Fries, Jim Gartner, Marcy Ginsberg, Mike Heard, Lynn Homewood, Darlene Jordan, Deb Knudsen, Kathy Krach, Vanessa Long, Debbie Moore, Valerie Mosely, Jane Nisset, Nadine Norton, Maryan Pawlowski, Lynda Stewart, J. C. Givens, Mark Calvey, Mark Keating, and David Weymiller.

Special thanks go to Richard D. Rust, of the University of North Carolina, for his helpful counsel and to Lucy and Donald Ringe for their aid.

Kent, Ohio   S.J.K.
April 1982   S.W.R.

CONTENTS

TISH-CO-HAN
A DELAWARE CHIEF

EDGAR HUNTLY;

or,

MEMOIRS OF A SLEEP-WALKER

TO THE PUBLIC

THE flattering reception that has been given, by the public, to Arthur Mervyn, has prompted the writer to solicit a continuance of the same favour, and to offer to the world a new performance.

America has opened new views to the naturalist and politician, but has seldome furnished themes to the moral painter. That new springs of action, and new motives to curiosity should operate; that the field of investigation, opened to us by our own country, should differ essentially from those which exist in Europe, may be readily conceived. The sources of amusement to the fancy and instruction to the heart, that are peculiar to ourselves, are equally numerous and inexhaustible. It is the purpose of this work to profit by some of these sources; to exhibit a series of adventures, growing out of the condition of our country, and connected with one of the most common and most wonderful diseases or affections of the human frame.

One merit the writer may at least claim; that of calling forth the passions and engaging the sympathy of the reader, by means hitherto unemployed by preceding authors. Puerile superstition and exploded manners; Gothic castles and chimeras, are the materials usually employed for this end. The incidents of Indian hostility, and the perils of the western wilderness, are far more suitable; and, for a native of America to overlook these, would admit of no apology. These, therefore, are, in part, the ingredients of this tale, and these he has been ambitious of depicting in vivid and faithful colours. The success of his efforts must be estimated by the liberal and candid reader.

C.B.B.

John Vanderlyn
The Death of Jane McCrea (ca. 1803)
Courtesy of Wadsworth Atheneum, Hartford, Connecticut

EDGAR HUNTLY;
OR, MEMOIRS OF A SLEEP-WALKER.

CHAPTER I

I SIT down, my friend, to comply with thy request. At
length does the impetuosity of my fears, the transports of my wonder permit me to recollect my promise and perform it. At length am I somewhat delivered
from suspence and from tremors. At length the drama is
brought to an imperfect close, and the series of events,
that absorbed my faculties, that hurried away my attention, has terminated in repose.

Till now, to hold a steadfast pen was impossible; to
disengage my senses from the scene that was passing or
approaching; to forbear to grasp at futurity; to suffer so
much thought to wander from the purpose which
engrossed my fears and my hopes, could not be.

Yet am I sure that even now my perturbations are
sufficiently stilled for an employment like this? That the
incidents I am going to relate can be recalled and
arranged without indistinctness and confusion? That
emotions will not be re-awakened by my narrative,
incompatible with order and coherence? Yet when I shall
be better qualified for this task I know not. Time may
take away these headlong energies, and give me back my
ancient sobriety: but this change will only be effected by
weakening my remembrance of these events. In proportion as I gain power over words, shall I lose dominion
over sentiments. In proportion as my tale is deliberate
and slow, the incidents and motives which it is designed

to exhibit will be imperfectly revived and obscurely pourtrayed.

O! why art thou away at a time like this? Wert thou present, the office to which my pen is so inadequate would easily be executed by my tongue. Accents can scarcely be too rapid, or that which words should fail to convey, my looks and gestures would suffice to communicate. But I know thy coming is impossible. To leave this spot is equally beyond my power. To keep thee in ignorance of what has happened would justly offend thee. There is no method of informing thee except by letter, and this method, must I, therefore, adopt.

How short is the period that has elapsed since thou and I parted, and yet how full of tumult and dismay has been my soul during that period! What light has burst upon my ignorance of myself and of mankind! How sudden and enormous the transition from uncertainty to knowledge! —

But let me recall my thoughts: let me struggle for so much composure as will permit my pen to trace intelligible characters. Let me place in order the incidents that are to compose my tale. I need not call on thee to listen. The fate of Waldegrave was as fertile of torment to thee as to me. His bloody and mysterious catastrophe equally awakened thy grief, thy revenge, and thy curiosity. Thou wilt catch from my story every horror and every sympathy which it paints. Thou wilt shudder with my forboding and dissolve with my tears. As the sister of my friend, and as one who honours me with her affection, thou wilt share in all my tasks and all my dangers.

You need not be reminded with what reluctance I left you. To reach this place by evening was impossible, unless I had set out early in the morning, but your society was too precious not to be enjoyed to the last moment. It was indispensable to be here on Tuesday, but my duty required no more than that I should arrive by sun-rise on that day. To travel during the night, was productive of no formidable inconvenience. The air was likely to be frosty and sharp, but these would not incommode one who

6

walked with speed. A nocturnal journey in districts so romantic and wild as these, through which lay my road, was more congenial to my temper than a noon-day ramble.

By night-fall I was within ten miles of my uncle's house. As the darkness increased, and I advanced on my way, my sensations sunk into melancholy. The scene and the time reminded me of the friend whom I had lost. I recalled his features, and accents, and gestures, and mused with unutterable feelings on the circumstances of his death.

My recollections once more plunged me into anguish and perplexity. Once more I asked, who was his assassin? By what motives could he be impelled to a deed like this? Waldegrave was pure from all offence. His piety was rapturous. His benevolence was a stranger to remisness or torpor. All who came within the sphere of his influence experienced and acknowledged his benign activity. His friends were few, because his habits were timid and reserved, but the existence of an enemy was impossible.

I recalled the incidents of our last interview, my importunities that he should postpone his ill-omened journey till the morning, his inexplicable obstinacy; his resolution to set out on foot, during a dark and tempestuous night, and the horrible disaster that befel him.

The first intimation I received of this misfortune, the insanity of vengeance and grief into which I was hurried, my fruitless searches for the author of this guilt, my midnight wanderings and reveries beneath the shade of that fatal Elm, were revived and re-acted. I heard the discharge of the pistol, I witnessed the alarm of Inglefield, I heard his calls to his servants, and saw them issue forth, with lights and hasten to the spot whence the sound had seemed to proceed. I beheld my friend, stretched upon the earth, ghastly with a mortal wound, alone, with no traces of the slayer visible, no tokens by which his place of refuge might be sought, the motives of his enmity or his instruments of mischief might be detected.

I hung over the dying youth, whose insensibility forbade him to recognize his friend, or unfold the cause of his destruction. I accompanied his remains to the grave, I tended the sacred spot where he lay, I once more exercised my penetration and my zeal in pursuit of his assassin. Once more my meditations and exertions were doomed to be disappointed.

I need not remind thee of what is past. Time and reason seemed to have dissolved the spell which made me deaf to the dictates of duty and discretion. Remembrances had ceased to agonize, to urge me to headlong acts, and foster sanguinary purposes. The gloom was half dispersed and a radiance had succeeded sweeter than my former joys.

Now, by some unseen concurrence of reflections, my thoughts reverted into some degree of bitterness. Methought that to ascertain the hand who killed my friend, was not impossible, and to punish the crime was just. That to forbear inquiry or withold punishment was to violate my duty to my God and to mankind. The impulse was gradually awakened that bade me once more to seek the Elm; once more to explore the ground; to scrutinize its trunk. What could I expect to find? Had it not been an hundred times examined? Had I not extended my search to the neighbouring groves and precipices? Had I not pored upon the brooks, and pryed into the pits and hollows, that were adjacent to the scene of blood?

Lately I had viewed this conduct with shame and regret; but in the present state of my mind, it assumed the appearance of conformity with prudence, and I felt myself irresistably prompted to repeat my search. Some time had elapsed since my departure from this district. Time enough for momentous changes to occur. Expedients that formerly were useless, might now lead instantaneously to the end which I sought. The tree which had formerly been shunned by the criminal, might, in the absence of the avenger of blood, be incautiously approached. Thoughtless or fearless of my return, it was possible that he might, at this moment, be detected hovering near the scene of his offences.

Nothing can be pleaded in extenuation of this relapse into folly. My return, after an absence of some duration, into the scene of these transactions and sufferings, the time of night, the glimmering of the stars, the obscurity in which external objects were wrapped, and which, consequently, did not draw my attention from the images of fancy, may, in some degree, account for the revival of those sentiments and resolutions which immediately succeeded the death of Waldegrave, and which, during my visit to you, had been suspended.

You know the situation of the Elm, in the midst of a private road, on the verge of Norwalk, near the habitation of Inglefield, but three miles from my uncle's house. It was now my intention to visit it. The road in which I was travelling, led a different way. It was requisite to leave it, therefore, and make a circuit through meadows and over steeps. My journey would, by these means, be considerably prolonged, but on that head I was indifferent, or rather, considering how far the night had already advanced, it was desirable not to reach home till the dawn.

I proceeded in this new direction with speed. Time, however, was allowed for my impetuosities to subside, and for sober thoughts to take place. Still I persisted in this path. To linger a few moments in this shade; to ponder on objects connected with events so momentous to my happiness, promised me a mournful satisfaction. I was familiar with the way, though trackless and intricate, and I climbed the steeps, crept through the brambles, leapt the rivulets and fences with undeviating aim, till at length I reached the craggy and obscure path, which led to Inglefield's house.

In a short time, I descried through the dusk the widespread branches of the Elm. This tree, however faintly seen, cannot be mistaken for another. The remarkable bulk and shape of its trunk, its position in the midst of the

9

way, its branches spreading into an ample circumference, made it conspicuous from afar. My pulse throbbed as I approached it.

My eyes were eagerly bent to discover the trunk and the area beneath the shade. These, as I approached, gradually became visible. The trunk was not the only thing which appeared in view. Somewhat else, which made itself distinguishable by its motions, was likewise noted. I faultered and stopt.

To a casual observer this appearance would have been unnoticed. To me, it could not but possess a powerful significance. All my surmises and suspicions, instantly returned. This apparition was human, it was connected with the fate of Waldegrave, it led to a disclosure of the author of that fate. What was I to do? To approach unwarily would alarm the person. Instant flight would set him beyond discovery and reach.

I walked softly to the road-side. The ground was covered with rocky masses, scattered among shrub-oaks and dwarf-cedars, emblems of its sterile and uncultivated state. Among these it was possible to elude observation and yet approach near enough to gain an accurate view of this being.

At this time, the atmosphere was somewhat illuminated by the moon, which, though it had already set, was yet so near the horizon, as to benefit me by its light. The shape of a man, tall and robust, was now distinguished. Repeated and closer scrutiny enabled me to perceive that he was employed in digging the earth. Something like flannel was wrapt round his waist and covered his lower limbs. The rest of his frame was naked. I did not recognize in him any one whom I knew.

A figure, robust and strange, and half naked, to be thus employed, at this hour and place, was calculated to rouse up my whole soul. His occupation was mysterious and obscure. Was it a grave that he was digging? Was his purpose to explore or to hide? Was it proper to watch him at a distance, unobserved and in silence, or to rush upon him and extort from him by violence or menaces, an explanation of the scene?

Before my resolution was formed, he ceased to dig. He cast aside his spade and sat down in the pit that he had dug. He seemed wrapt in meditation; but the pause was short, and succeeded by sobs, at first low, and at wide intervals, but presently louder and more vehement. Sorely charged was indeed that heart whence flowed these tokens of sorrow. Never did I witness a scene of such mighty anguish, such heart-bursting grief.

What should I think? I was suspended in astonishment. Every sentiment, at length, yielded to my sympathy. Every new accent of the mourner struck upon my heart with additional force, and tears found their way spontaneously to my eyes. I left the spot where I stood, and advanced within the verge of the shade. My caution had forsaken me, and instead of one whom it was duty to persecute, I beheld, in this man, nothing but an object of compassion.

My pace was checked by his suddenly ceasing to lament. He snatched the spade, and rising on his feet began to cover up the pit with the utmost diligence. He seemed aware of my presence, and desirous of hiding something from my inspection. I was prompted to advance nearer and hold his hand, but my uncertainty as to his character and views, the abruptness with which I had been ushered into this scene, made me still hesitate; but though I hesitated to advance, there was nothing to hinder me from calling.

What, ho! said I. Who is there? What are you doing?

He stopt, the spade fell from his hand, he looked up and bent forward his face towards the spot where I stood. An interview and explanation were now methought unavoidable. I mustered up my courage to confront and interrogate this being.

He continued for a minute in his gazing and listening attitude. Where I stood I could not fail of being seen, and yet he acted as if he saw nothing. Again he betook himself to his spade, and proceeded with new diligence to fill up the pit. This demeanour confounded and bewildered me. I had no power but to stand and silently gaze upon his motions.

The pit being filled, he once more sat upon the ground, and resigned himself to weeping and sighs with more vehemence than before. In a short time the fit seemed to have passed. He rose, seized the spade, and advanced to the spot where I stood.

Again I made preparation as for an interview which could not but take place. He passed me, however, without appearing to notice my existence. He came so near as almost to brush my arm, yet turned not his head to either side. My nearer view of him, made his brawny arms and lofty stature more conspicuous; but his imperfect dress, the dimness of the light, and the confusion of my own thoughts, hindered me from discerning his features. He proceeded with a few quick steps, along the road, but presently darted to one side and disappeared among the rocks and bushes.

My eye followed him as long as he was visible, but my feet were rooted to the spot. My musing was rapid and incongruous. It could not fail to terminate in one conjecture, that this person was *asleep*. Such instances were not unknown to me, through the medium of conversation and books. Never, indeed, had it fallen under my own observation till now, and now it was conspicuous and environed with all that could give edge to suspicion, and vigour to inquiry. To stand here was no longer of use, and I turned my steps toward my uncle's habitation.

CHAPTER II

I HAD food enough for the longest contemplation. My steps partook, as usual, of the vehemence of my thoughts, and I reached my uncle's gate before I believed myself to have lost sight of the Elm. I looked up and discovered the well-known habitation. I could not endure that my reflections should so speedily be interrupted. I, therefore, passed the gate, and stopped not till I had reached a neighbouring summit, crowned with chestnut-oaks and poplars.

Here I more deliberately reviewed the incidents that had just occurred. The inference was just, that the man, half-clothed and digging, was a sleeper: But what was the cause of this morbid activity? What was the mournful vision that dissolved him in tears, and extorted from him tokens of inconsolable distress? What did he seek, or what endeavour to conceal in this fatal spot? The incapacity of sound sleep denotes a mind sorely wounded. It is thus that atrocious criminals denote the possession of some dreadful secret. The thoughts, which considerations of safety enables them to suppress or disguise during wakefulness, operate without impediment, and exhibit their genuine effects, when the notices of sense are partly excluded, and they are shut out from a knowledge of their intire condition.

This is the perpetrator of some nefarious deed. What but the murder of Waldegrave could direct his steps

13

hither? His employment was part of some fantastic drama in which his mind was busy. To comprehend it, demands penetration into the recesses of his soul. But one thing is sure; an incoherent conception of his concern in that transaction, bewitches him hither. This it is that deluges his heart with bitterness and supplies him with ever-flowing tears.

But whence comes he? He does not start from the bosom of the earth, or hide himself in airy distance. He must have a name and a terrestrial habitation. It cannot be at an immeasurable distance from the haunted Elm. Inglefield's house is the nearest. This may be one of its inhabitants. I did not recognize his features, but this was owing to the dusky atmosphere and to the singularity of his garb. Inglefield has two servants, one of whom was a native of this district, simple, guileless and incapable of any act of violence. He was, moreover devoutly attached to his sect. He could not be the criminal.

The other was a person of a very different cast. He was an emigrant from Ireland, and had been six months in the family of my friend. He was a pattern of sobriety and gentleness. His mind was superior to his situation. His natural endowments were strong, and had enjoyed all the advantage of cultivation. His demeanour was grave, and thoughtful, and compassionate. He appeared not untinctured with religion, but his devotion, though unostentatious, was of a melancholy tenor.

There was nothing in the first view of his character calculated to engender suspicion. The neighbourhood was populous. But as I conned over the catalogue, I perceived that the only foreigner among us was Clithero. Our scheme was, for the most part, a patriarchal one. Each farmer was surrounded by his sons and kinsmen. This was an exception to the rule. Clithero was a stranger, whose adventures and character, previously to his coming hither, were unknown to us. The Elm was surrounded by his master's domains. An actor there must be, and no one was equally questionable.

14

The more I revolved the pensive and reserved deportment of this man, the ignorance in which we were placed respecting his former situation, his possible motives for abandoning his country and chusing a station so much below the standard of his intellectual attainments, the stronger my suspicions became. Formerly, when occupied with conjectures relative to the same topic, the image of this man did not fail to occur; but the seeming harmlessness of his ordinary conduct, had raised him to a level with others, and placed him equally beyond the reach of suspicion. I did not, till now, advert to the recentness of his appearance among us, and to the obscurity that hung over his origin and past life. But now these considerations appeared so highly momentous, as almost to decide the question of his guilt.

But how were these doubts to be changed into absolute certainty? Henceforth this man was to become the subject of my scrutiny. I was to gain all the knowledge, respecting him, which those with whom he lived, and were the perpetual witnesses of his actions, could impart. For this end I was to make minute inquiries, and to put seasonable interrogatories. From this conduct I promised myself an ultimate solution of my doubts.

I acquiesced in this view of things with considerable satisfaction. It seemed as if the maze was no longer inscrutable. It would be quickly discovered who were the agents and instigators of the murder of my friend.

But it suddenly occurred to me, For what purpose shall I prosecute this search? What benefit am I to reap from this discovery? How shall I demean myself when the criminal is detected? I was not insensible, at that moment, of the impulses of vengeance, but they were transient. I detested the sanguinary resolutions that I had once formed. Yet I was fearful of the effects of my hasty rage, and dreaded an encounter, in consequence of which, I might rush into evils which no time could repair, nor penitence expiate.

But why, said I, should it be impossible to arm myself

15

with firmness? If forbearance be the dictate of wisdom, cannot it be so deeply engraven on my mind as to defy all temptation, and be proof against the most abrupt surprise? My late experience has been of use to me. It has shewn me my weakness and my strength. Having found my ancient fortifications insufficient to withstand the enemy, what should I learn from thence but that it becomes me to strengthen and enlarge them?

No caution indeed can hinder the experiment from being hazardous. Is it wise to undertake experiments by which nothing can be gained, and much may be lost? Curiosity is vicious, if undisciplined by reason, and inconducive to benefit.

I was not, however, to be diverted from my purpose. Curiosity, like virtue, is its own reward. Knowledge is of value for its own sake, and pleasure is annexed to the acquisition, without regard to any thing beyond. It is precious even when disconnected with moral inducements and heart-felt sympathies, but the knowledge which I sought by its union with these was calculated to excite the most complex and fiery sentiment in my bosom.

Hours were employed in revolving these thoughts. At length I began to be sensible of fatigue, and returning home, explored the way to my chamber without molesting the repose of the family. You know that our doors are always unfastened, and are accessible at all hours of the night.

My slumbers were imperfect, and I rejoiced when the morning light permitted me to resume my meditations. The day glided away, I scarcely know how, and as I had rejoiced at the return of morning, I now hailed, with pleasure, the approach of night.

My uncle and sisters having retired, I betook myself, instead of following their example, to the *Chesnut-hill*. Concealed among its rocks, or gazing at the prospect, which stretched so far and so wide around it, my fancy has always been accustomed to derive its highest enjoyment from this spot. I found myself again at leisure to recall the scene which I had witnessed during the last night, to imagine its connection with the fate of Waldegrave, and to plan the means of discovering the secret that was hidden under these appearances.

Shortly, I began to feel insupportable disquiet at the thoughts of postponing this discovery. Wiles and stratagems were practicable, but they were tedious and of dubious success. Why should I proceed like a plotter? Do I intend the injury of this person? A generous purpose will surely excuse me from descending to artifices. There are two modes of drawing forth the secrets of another, by open and direct means and by circuitous and indirect. Why scruple to adopt the former mode? Why not demand a conference, and state my doubts, and demand a solution of them, in a manner worthy of a beneficent purpose? Why not hasten to the spot? He may be, at this moment, mysteriously occupied under this shade. I may note his behaviour; I may ascertain his person, if not by the features that belong to him, yet by tracing his footsteps when he departs, and pursuing him to his retreats.

I embraced this scheme, which was thus suggested, with eagerness. I threw myself, with headlong speed, down the hill and pursued my way to the Elm. As I approached the tree, my palpitations increased, though my pace slackened. I looked forward with an anxious glance. The trunk of the tree was hidden in the deepest shade. I advanced close up to it. No one was visible, but I was not discouraged. The hour of his coming was, perhaps, not arrived. I took my station at a small distance, beside a fence, on the right hand.

An hour elapsed before my eyes lighted on the object of which they were in search. My previous observation had been roving from one quarter to another. At last, it dwelt upon the tree. The person whom I before described was seated on the ground. I had not perceived him before, and the means by which he placed himself in this situation had escaped my notice. He seemed like one, whom an

17

effort of will, without the exercise of locomotion, had transported hither, or made visible. His state of disarray, and the darkness that shrouded him, prevented me, as before, from distinguishing any peculiarities in his figure or countenance.

I continued watchful and mute. The appearances already described took place, on this occasion, except the circumstance of digging in the earth. He sat musing for a while, then burst into sighs and lamentations.

These being exhausted, he rose to depart. He stalked away with a solemn and deliberate pace. I resolved to tread, as closely as possible, in his footsteps, and not to lose sight of him till the termination of his career.

Contrary to my expectation, he went in a direction opposite to that which led to Inglefield's. Presently, he stopped at bars, which he cautiously removed, and, when he had passed through them, as deliberately replaced. He then proceeded along an obscure path, which led across stubble fields, to a wood. The path continued through the wood, but he quickly struck out of it, and made his way, seemingly at random, through a most perplexing undergrowth of bushes and briars.

I was, at first, fearful that the noise, which I made behind him, in trampling down the thicket, would alarm him; but he regarded it not. The way that he had selected, was always difficult; sometimes considerable force was requisite to beat down obstacles; sometimes, it led into a deep glen, the sides of which were so steep as scarcely to afford a footing; sometimes, into fens, from which some exertions were necessary to extricate the feet, and sometimes, through rivulets, of which the water rose to the middle.

For some time I felt no abatement of my speed or my resolution. I thought I might proceed, without fear, through breaks and dells, which my guide was able to penetrate. He was perpetually changing his direction. I could form no just opinion as to my situation or distance from the place at which we had set out.

I began at length to be weary. A suspicion, likewise, suggested itself to my mind, whether my guide did not perceive that he was followed, and thus prolonged his journey in order to fatigue or elude his pursuer. I was determined, however, to baffle his design. Though the air was frosty, my limbs were bedewed with sweat and my joints were relaxed with toil, but I was obstinately bent upon proceeding.

At length a new idea occurred to me. On finding me indefatigable in pursuit, this person might resort to more atrocious methods of concealment. But what had I to fear? It was sufficient to be upon my guard. Man to man, I needed not to dread his encounter.

We, at last, arrived at the verge of a considerable precipice. He kept along the edge. From this height, a dreary vale was discoverable, embarrassed with the leafless stocks of bushes, and encumbered with rugged and pointed rocks. This scene reminded me of my situation. The desert tract called Norwalk, which I have often mentioned to you, my curiosity had formerly induced me to traverse in various directions. It was in the highest degree, rugged, picturesque and wild. This vale, though I had never before viewed it by the glimpses of the moon, suggested the belief that I had visited it before. Such an one I knew belonged to this uncultivated region. If this opinion were true, we were at no inconsiderable distance from Inglefield's habitation. Where, said I, is this singular career to terminate?

Though occupied with these reflections, I did not slacken my pursuit. The stranger kept along the verge of the cliff, which gradually declined till it terminated in the valley. He then plunged into its deepest thickets. In a quarter of an hour he stopped under a projecture of the rock which formed the opposite side of the vale. He then proceeded to remove the stalks, which, as I immediately perceived, concealed the mouth of a cavern. He plunged into the darkness, and in a few moments, his steps were heard no more!

Hitherto my courage had supported me, but here it failed. Was this person an assassin, who was acquainted with the windings of the grotto, and who would take advantage of the dark, to execute his vengeance upon me, who had dared to pursue him to these forlorn retreats; or was he maniac, or walker in his sleep? Whichever supposition were true, it would be rash in me to follow him. Besides, he could not long remain in these darksome recesses, unless some fatal accident should overtake him.

I seated myself at the mouth of the cave, determined patiently to wait till he should think proper to emerge. This opportunity of rest was exceedingly acceptable after so toilsome a pilgrimage. My pulse began to beat more slowly, and the moisture that incommoded me ceased to flow. The coolness which, for a little time, was delicious, presently increased to shivering, and I found it necessary to change my posture, in order to preserve my blood from congealing.

After I had formed a path before the cavern's mouth, by the removal of obstructions, I employed myself in walking to and fro. In this situation I saw the moon gradually decline to the horizon, and, at length, disappear. I marked the deepenings of the shade, and the mutations which every object successively underwent. The vale was narrow, and hemmed in on all sides by lofty and precipitous cliffs. The gloom deepened as the moon declined, and the faintness of star-light was all that preserved my senses from being useless to my own guidance.

I drew nearer the cleft at which this mysterious personage had entered. I stretched my hands before it, determined that he should not emerge from his den without my notice. His steps would, necessarily, communicate the tidings of his approach. They could not move without a noise which would be echoed to, on all sides, by the abruptnesses by which this valley was surrounded. Here, then, I continued till the day began to dawn, in momentary expectation of the stranger's reappearance.

My attention was at length excited by a sound that

seemed to issue from the cave. I imagined that the sleeper was returning, and prepared therefore to seize him. I blamed myself for neglecting the opportunities that had already been afforded, and was determined that another should not escape. My eyes were fixed upon the entrance. The rustling increased, and presently an animal leapt forth, of what kind I was unable to discover. Heart-struck by this disappointment, but not discouraged, I continued to watch, but in vain. The day was advancing apace. At length the sun arose, and its beams glistened on the edges of the cliffs above, whose sapless stalks and rugged masses were covered with hoar-frost. I began to despair of success, but was unwilling to depart, until it was no longer possible to hope for the return of this extraordinary personage. Whether he had been swallowed up by some of the abysses of this grotto, or lurked near the entrance, waiting my departure, or had made his exit at another and distant aperture, was unknown to me.

Exhausted and discouraged, I prepared, at length, to return. It was easy to find my way out of this wilderness by going forward in one direction, regardless of impediments and cross-paths. My absence I believed to have occasioned no alarm to my family, since they knew not of my intention to spend the night abroad. Thus unsatisfactorily terminated this night's adventures.

CHAPTER III

THE ensuing day was spent, partly in sleep, and partly in languor and disquietude. I incessantly ruminated on the incidents of the last night. The scheme that I had formed was defeated. Was it likely that this unknown person would repeat his midnight visits to the Elm? If he did, and could again be discovered, should I resolve to undertake a new pursuit, which might terminate abortively, or in some signal disaster? But what proof had I that the same rout would be taken, and that he would again inter himself alive in the same spot? Or, if he did, since his reappearance would sufficiently prove that the cavern was not dangerous, and that he who should adventure in, might hope to come out again in safety, why not enter it after him? What could be the inducements of this person to betake himself to subterranean retreats? The basis of all this region is *limestone*; a substance that eminently abounds in rifts and cavities. These, by the gradual decay of their cementing parts, frequently make their appearance in spots where they might have been least expected. My attention has often been excited by the hollow sound which was produced by my casual footsteps, and which shewed me that I trod upon the roof of caverns. A mountain-cave and the rumbling of an unseen torrent, are appendages of this scene, dear to my youthful imagination. Many of romantic structure were found within the precincts of Norwalk.

These I had industriously sought out; but this had hitherto escaped my observation, and I formed the resolution of sometime exploring it. At present I determined to revisit the Elm, and dig in the spot where this person had been employed in a similar way. It might be that something was here deposited which might exhibit this transaction in a new light. At the suitable hour, on the ensuing night, I took my former stand. The person again appeared. My intention to dig was to be carried into effect on condition of his absence, and was, consequently, frustrated.

Instead of rushing on him, and breaking at once the spell by which his senses were bound, I concluded, contrary to my first design, to wait his departure, and allow myself to be conducted whithersoever he pleased. The track into which he now led me was different from the former one. It was a maze, oblique, circuitous, upward and downward, in a degree which only could take place in a region so remarkably irregular in surface, so abounding with hillocks and steeps, and pits and brooks as *Solebury*. It seemed to be the sole end of his labours to bewilder or fatigue his pursuer, to pierce into the deepest thickets, to plunge into the darkest cavities, to ascend the most difficult heights, and approach the slippery and tremulous verge of the dizziest precipices.

I disdained to be outstripped in this career. All dangers were overlooked, and all difficulties defied. I plunged into obscurities, and clambered over obstacles, from which, in a different state of mind, and with a different object of pursuit, I should have recoiled with invincible timidity. When the scene had passed, I could not review the perils I had undergone without shuddering.

At length my conductor struck into a path which, compared with the ruggedness of that which we had lately trodden, was easy and smooth. This track led us to the skirt of the wilderness, and at no long time we reached an open field, when a dwelling appeared, at a small distance, which I speedily recognized to be that belonging to

23

Inglefield. I now anticipated the fulfilment of my predictions. My conductor directed his steps towards the barn, into which he entered by a small door.

How were my doubts removed! This was no other than Clithero Edny. There was nothing in his appearance incompatible with this conclusion. He and his fellow servant occupied an apartment in the barn as a lodging room. This arduous purpose was accomplished, and I retired to the shelter of a neighbouring shed, not so much to repose myself after the fatigues of my extraordinary journey, as to devise farther expedients.

Nothing now remained but to take Clithero to task; to repeat to him the observations of the two last nights; to unfold to him my conjectures and suspicions; to convince him of the rectitude of my intentions, and to extort from him a disclosure of all the circumstances connected with the death of Waldegrave, which it was in his power to communicate.

In order to obtain a conference, I resolved to invite him to my uncle's, to perform a certain piece of work for me under my own eyes. He would, of course, spend the night with us, and in the evening I would make an opportunity of entering into conversation with him.

A period of the deepest deliberation was necessary to qualify myself for performing suitably my part in this projected interview. I attended to the feelings that were suggested in this new state of my knowledge. I found reason to confide in my newly acquired equanimity. Remorse, said I, is an ample and proper expiation for all offences. What does vengeance desire but to inflict misery? If misery come, its desires are accomplished. It is only the obdurate and exulting criminal that is worthy of our indignation. It is common for pity to succeed the bitterest suggestions of resentment. If the vengeful mind be delighted with the spectacle of woes of its own contriving, at least its canine hunger is appeased, and thenceforth, its hands are inactive.

On the evening of the next day, I paid a visit to Inglefield. I wished to impart to him the discoveries that I had made, and to listen to his reflections on the subject. I likewise desired to obtain all possible information from the family respecting the conduct of Clithero.

My friend received me with his usual kindness. Thou art no stranger to his character; thou knowest with what paternal affection I have ever been regarded by this old man; with what solicitude the wanderings of my reason and my freaks of passion, have been noted and corrected by him. Thou knowest his activity to save the life of thy brother, and the hours that have been spent by him, in aiding my conjectures as to the cause of his death, and inculcating the lessons of penitence and duty.

The topics which could not but occur at such a meeting, were quickly discussed, and I hastily proceeded to that subject which was nearest my heart. I related the adventures of the two preceding nights, and mentioned the inference to which they irresistably led.

He said that this inference coincided with suspicions he had formed, since our last interview, in consequence of certain communications from his house-keeper. It seems the character of Clithero, had, from the first, exercised the inquisitiveness of this old lady. She had carefully marked his musing and melancholy deportment. She had tried innumerable expedients for obtaining a knowledge of his past life, and particularly of his motives for coming to America. These expedients, however profound and addressful, had failed. He took no pains to elude them. He contented himself with turning a deaf ear to all indirect allusions and hints, and, when more explicitly questioned, with simply declaring that he had nothing to communicate worthy of her notice.

During the day he was a sober and diligent workman. His evenings he spent in incommunicative silence. On sundays, he always rambled away, no one knew whither, and without a companion. I have already observed that he and his fellow servant occupied the same apartment in the barn. This circumstance was not unattended to by

Miss Inglefield. The name of Clithero's companion was Ambrose. This man was copiously interrogated by his mistress, and she found him by no means so refractory as the other.

Ambrose, in his tedious and confused way, related that soon after Clithero and he had become bed-fellows, the former was considerably disturbed by restlessness and talking in his sleep. His discourse was incoherent. It was generally in the tone of expostulation, and appeared to be intreating to be saved from some great injury. Such phrases as these, "have pity"; "have mercy," were frequently intermingled with groans, and accompanied with weeping. Sometimes he seemed to be holding conferences with some one, who was making him considerable offers on condition of his performing some dangerous service. What he said, in his own person, and in answer to his imaginary tempter, testified the utmost reluctance.

Ambrose had no curiosity on the subject. As this interruption prevented him at first from sleeping, it was his custom to put an end to the dialogue, by awakening his companion, who betrayed tokens of great alarm and dejection. On discovering how he had been employed, he would solicitously inquire what were the words that he had uttered; but Ambrose's report was seldom satisfactory, because he had attended to them but little, and because he begrudged every moment in which he was deprived of his accustomed repose.

Whether Clithero had ceased from this practice, or habit had reconciled his companion to the sounds, they no longer occasioned any interruption to his slumber.

No one appeared more shocked than he at the death of Waldegrave. After this event his dejection suddenly increased. This symptom was observed by the family, but none but the house-keeper took the trouble to notice it to him, or build conjectures on the incident. During nights, however, Ambrose experienced a renewal of his ancient disturbances. He remarked that Clithero, one night, had disappeared from his side. Ambrose's range of reflection

26

was extremely narrow. Quickly falling asleep, and finding his companion beside him when he awoke, he dismissed it from his mind.

On several ensuing nights he awakened in like manner,
and always found his companion's place empty. The repetition of so strange an incident at length incited him to
mention it to Clithero. The latter was confounded at this
intelligence. He questioned Ambrose with great anxiety
as to the particulars of this event, but he could gain no
satisfaction from the stupid inattention of the other. From
this time there was a visible augmentation of his sadness.
His fits of taciturnity became more obstinate, and a
deeper gloom sat upon his brow.

There was one other circumstance, of particular importance, mentioned by the house-keeper. One evening some
one on horseback, stopped at this gate. He rattled at the
gate, with an air of authority, in token of his desire that
some one would come from the house. Miss Inglefield
was employed in the kitchen, from a window of which she
perceived who it was that made the signal. Clithero happened, at the same moment, to be employed near her.
She, therefore, desired him to go and see whom the stranger wanted. He laid aside his work and went. The conference lasted above five minutes. The length of it excited in
her a faint degree of surprise, inducing her to leave her
employment, and pay an unintermitted attention to the
scene. There was nothing, however, but its duration that
rendered it remarkable.

Clithero at length entered, and the traveller proceeded.
The countenance of the former betrayed a degree of perturbation which she had never witnessed before. The
muscles of his face was distorted and tremulous. He
immediately sat down to his work, but he seemed, for
some time, to have lost all power over his limbs. He
struggled to avoid the sight of the lady, and his gestures,
irresolute, or misdirected, betokened the deepest dismay.
After some time, he recovered, in some degree, his self-
possession; but, while the object was viewed through a

27

new medium, and the change existed only in the imagination of the observer, a change was certainly discovered.

These circumstances were related to me by Inglefield and corroborated by his house-keeper. One consequence inevitably flowed from them. The sleep-walker, he who had led me through so devious a tract, was no other than Clithero. There was, likewise, a strong relation between this person and him who stopped at the gate. What was the subject of discourse between them? In answer to Miss Inglefield's interrogatories, he merely said that the traveller inquired whither the road led, which at a small distance forward, struck out of the principal one. Considering the length of the interview it was not likely that this was the only topic.

My determination to confer with him in private acquired new force from these reflections. Inglefield assented to my proposal. His own affairs would permit the absence of his servant for one day. I saw no necessity for delay, and immediately made my request to Clithero. I was fashioning an implement, I told him, with respect to which I could not wholly depend upon my own skill. I was acquainted with the dexterity of his contrivances, and the neatness of his workmanship. He readily consented to assist me on this occasion. Next day he came. Contrary to my expectation, he prepared to return home in the evening. I urged him to spend the night with us; but no: It was equally convenient, and more agreeable to him, to return.

I was not aware of this resolution. I might, indeed, have foreseen, that, being conscious of his infirmity, he would desire to avoid the scrutiny of strangers. I was painfully disconcerted, but it occurred to me, that the best that could be done, was to bear him company, and seize some opportunity, during this interval, of effecting my purpose. I told him, that since he would not remain, I cared not if, for the sake of recreation, and of a much more momentous purpose, I went along with him. He tacitly, and without apparent reluctance, consented to my scheme, and accordingly, we set off together. This was an awful crisis. The time had now come, that was to dissipate my uncertainty. By what means should I introduce a topic so momentous and singular? I had been qualified by no experience for rightly conducting myself on so critical an emergency. My companion preserved a mournful and inviolable silence. He afforded me no opening, by which I might reach the point in view. His demeanour was sedate, while I was almost disabled, by the confusion of my thoughts, to utter a word.

It was a dreadful charge that I was about to insinuate. I was to accuse my companion of nothing less than murder. I was to call upon him for an avowal of his guilt. I was to state the grounds of my suspicions, and desire him to confute, or confirm them. In doing this, I was principally stimulated by an ungovernable curiosity; yet, if I intended not the conferring of a benefit, I did not, at least, purpose the infliction of evil. I persuaded myself, that I was able to exclude from my bosom, all sanguinary or vengeful impulses; and that, whatever should be the issue of this conversation, my equanimity would be unsubdued.

I revolved various modes of introducing the topic, by which my mind was engaged. I passed rapidly from one to another. None of them were sufficiently free from objection, to allow me to adopt it. My perplexity became, every moment, more painful, and my ability to extricate myself, less.

In this state of uncertainty, so much time elapsed, that the Elm at length appeared in sight. This object had somewhat of a mechanical influence upon me. I stopped short, and seized the arm of my companion. Till this moment, he appeared to have been engrossed by his own reflections, and not to have heeded those emotions, which must have been sufficiently conspicuous in my looks.

This action recalled him from his reverie. The first idea that occurred to him, when he had noticed my behaviour, was, that I was assailed by some sudden indisposition.

What is the matter, said he, in a tone of anxiety: Are you not well?

Yes, replied I, perfectly well; but stop a moment; I have something to say to you.

To me? answered he, with surprise.

Yes, said I, let us turn down this path, pointing at the same time, to that along which I had followed him the preceding night.

He now partook, in some degree, of my embarrassment.

Is there any thing particular? said he, in a doubting accent. There he stopped.

Something, I answered, of the highest moment. Go with me down this path. We shall be in less danger of interruption.

He was irresolute and silent, but seeing me remove the bars and pass through them, he followed me. Nothing more was said till we entered the wood. I trusted to the suggestions of the moment. I had now gone too far to recede, and the necessity that pressed upon me, supplied me with words. I continued.

This is a remarkable spot. You may wonder why I have led you to it. I ought not to keep you in suspence. There is a tale connected with it, which I am desirous of telling you. For this purpose I have brought you hither. Listen to me.

I then recapitulated the adventures of the two preceding nights. I added nothing, nor retrenched any thing. He listened in the deepest silence. From every incident, he gathered new cause of alarm. Repeatedly he wiped his face with his handkerchief, and sighed deeply. I took no verbal notice of these symptoms. I deemed it incumbent on me to repress nothing. When I came to the concluding circumstance, by which his person was identified, he heard me, without any new surprise. To this narrative, I subjoined the inquiries that I had made at Inglefield's, and the result of those inquiries. I then continued in these words.

You may ask why I subjected myself to all this trouble? The mysteriousness of these transactions would have naturally suggested curiosity in any one. A transient passenger would probably have acted as I have done. But I had motives peculiar to myself. Need I remind you of a late disaster? That it happened beneath the shade of this tree? Am I not justified in drawing certain inferences from your behaviour? What they are, I leave you to judge. Be it your task, to confute, or confirm them. For this end I have conducted you hither.

My suspicions are vehement. How can they be otherwise? I call upon you to say whether they be just.

The spot where we stood was illuminated by the moon, that had now risen, though all around was dark. Hence his features and person were easily distinguished. His hands hung at his side. His eyes were downcast, and he was motionless as a statue. My last words seemed scarcely to have made any impression on his sense. I had no need to provide against the possible suggestions of revenge. I felt nothing but the tenderness of compassion. I continued, for some time, to observe him in silence, and could discover no tokens of a change of mood. I could not forbear, at last, to express my uneasiness at the fixedness of his features and attitude.

Recollect yourself. I mean not to urge you too closely. This topic is solemn, but it need not divest you of the fortitude becoming a man.

The sound of my voice startled him. He broke from me, looked up, and fixed his eyes upon me with an expression of affright. He shuddered and recoiled as from a spectre. I began to repent of my experiment. I could say nothing suitable to this occasion. I was obliged to stand a silent and powerless spectator, and to suffer this paroxysm to subside of itself. When its violence appeared to be somewhat abated, I resumed.

I can feel for you. I act not thus, in compliance with a temper that delights in the misery of others. The explanation that I have solicited is no less necessary for your sake than for mine. You are no stranger to the light in which I viewed this man. You have witnessed the grief which his fate occasioned, and the efforts that I made to discover, and drag to punishment his murderer. You heard the execrations that I heaped upon him, and my vows of eternal revenge. You expect that, having detected the offender, I will hunt him to infamy and death. You are mistaken. I consider the deed as sufficiently expiated.

I am no stranger to your gnawing cares. To the deep and incurable despair that haunts you, to which your waking thoughts are a prey, and from which sleep cannot secure you. I know the enormity of your crime, but I know not your inducements. Whatever they were, I see the consequences with regard to yourself. I see proofs of that remorse which must ever be attendant on guilt.

This is enough. Why should the effects of our misdeeds be inexhaustible? Why should we be debarred from a comforter? An opportunity of repairing our errors may, at least, be demanded from the rulers of our destiny.

I once imagined, that he who killed Waldegrave inflicted the greatest possible injury on me. That was an error, which reflection has cured. Were futurity laid open to my view, and events, with their consequences unfolded, I might see reason to embrace the assassin as my best friend. Be comforted.

He was still incapable of speaking; but tears came to his relief. Without attending to my remonstrances, he betrayed a disposition to return. I had, hitherto, hoped for some disclosure, but now feared that it was designed to be withheld. He stopped not till we reached Inglefield's piazza. He then spoke, for the first time, but in an hollow and tremulous voice.

You demand of me a confession of crimes. You shall have it. Some time you shall have it. When it will be, I cannot tell. Something must be done, and shortly.

He hurried from me into the house, and after a pause, I turned my steps homewards. My reflections, as I proceeded, perpetually revolved round a single point. These were scarcely more than a repetition, with slight variations, of a single idea.

When I awoke in the morning, I hied, in fancy, to the wilderness. I saw nothing but the figure of the wanderer before me. I traced his footsteps anew, retold my narrative, and pondered on his gestures and words. My condition was not destitute of enjoyment. My stormy passions had subsided into a calm, portentous and awful. My soul was big with expectation. I seemed as if I were on the eve of being ushered into a world, whose scenes were tremendous, but sublime. The suggestions of sorrow and malice had, for a time, taken their flight, and yielded place to a generous sympathy, which filled my eyes with tears, but had more in it of pleasure than of pain. That Clithero was instrumental to the death of Waldegrave, that he could furnish the clue, explanatory of every bloody and mysterious event, that had hitherto occurred, there was no longer the possibility of doubting. He, indeed, said I, is the murderer of excellence, and yet it shall be my province to emulate a father's clemency, and restore this unhappy man to purity, and to peace.

Day after day passed, without hearing any thing of Clithero. I began to grow uneasy and impatient. I had gained so much, and by means so unexpected, that I could more easily endure uncertainty, with respect to what remained to be known. But my patience had its limits. I should, doubtless, have made use of new means to accelerate this discovery, had not his timely appearance made them superfluous.

Sunday being at length arrived, I resolved to go to Inglefield's, seek an interview with his servant, and urge him, by new importunities, to confide to me the secret. On my way thither, Clithero appeared in sight. His visage was pale and wan, and his form emaciated and shrunk. I was astonished at the alteration, which the lapse of a week had made in his appearance. At a small distance I mistook him for a stranger. As soon as I perceived who it was, I greeted him with the utmost friendliness. My civilities made little impression on him, and he hastened to inform me, that he was coming to my uncle's, for the purpose of meeting and talking with me. If I thought proper, we would go into the wood together: and find some spot, where we might discourse at our leisure, and be exempt from interruption.

You will easily conceive with what alacrity I accepted his invitation. We turned from the road into the first path, and proceeded in silence, till the wildness of the surrounding scenery informed us, that we were in the heart of Norwalk. We lighted on a recess, to which my companion appeared to be familiar, and which had all the advantages of solitude, and was suitable to rest. Here we stopped. Hitherto my companion had displayed a certain degree of composure. Now his countenance betokened a violent internal struggle. It was a considerable time before he could command his speech. When he had so far effected the conquest of his feelings, he began.

CHAPTER IV

YOU call upon me for a confession of my offences. What a strange fortune is mine! That an human being, in the present circumstances, should make this demand, and that I should be driven, by an irresistable necessity to comply with it! That here should terminate my calamitous series! That my destiny should call upon me to lie down and die, in a region so remote from the scene of my crimes; at a distance, so great, from all that witnessed and endured their consequences!

You believe me to be an assassin. You require me to explain the motives that induced me to murder the innocent. While this is your belief, and this the scope of your expectations, you may be sure of my compliance. I could resist every demand but this.

For what purpose have I come hither? Is it to relate my story? Shall I calmly sit here, and rehearse the incidents of my life? Will my strength be adequate to this rehearsal? Let me recollect the motives that governed me, when I formed this design. Perhaps, a strenuousness may be imparted by them, which, otherwise, I cannot hope to obtain. For the sake of those, I consent to conjure up the ghost of the past, and to begin a tale that, with a fortitude like mine, I am not sure that I shall live to finish.

You are unacquainted with the man before you. The inferences which you have drawn, with regard to my designs, and my conduct, are a tissue of destructive errors. You, like others, are blind to the most momentous consequences of your own actions. You talk of imparting consolation. You boast the benificence of your intentions. You set yourself to do me a benefit. What are the effects of your misguided zeal, and random efforts? They have brought my life to a miserable close. They have shrouded the last scene of it in blood. They have put the seal to my perdition.

My misery has been greater than has fallen to the lot of mortals. Yet it is but beginning. My present path, full as it is of asperities, is better than that into which I must enter, when this is abandoned. Perhaps, if my pilgrimage had been longer, I might, at some future day, have lighted upon hope. In consequence of your interference, I am forever debarred from it. My existence is henceforward to be invariable. The woes that are reserved for me, are incapable alike of alleviation or intermission.

But I came not hither to recriminate. I came not hither to accuse others but myself. I know the retribution that is appointed for guilt like mine. It is just. I may shudder at the foresight of my punishment and shrink in the endurance of it; but I shall be indebted for part of my torment to the vigour of my understanding, which teaches me that my punishment is just. Why should I procrastinate my doom and strive to render my burthen more light? It is but just that it should crush me. Its procrastination is impossible. The stroke is already felt. Even now I drink of the cup of retribution. A change of being cannot aggravate my woe. Till consciousness itself be extinct, the worm that gnaws me will never perish.

Fain would I be relieved from this task. Gladly would I bury in oblivion the transactions of my life: but no. My fate is uniform. The dæmon that controuled me at first is still in the fruition of power. I am entangled in his fold, and every effort that I make to escape only involves me in deeper ruin. I need not conceal, for all the consequences of disclosure are already experienced. I cannot endure a groundless imputation, though to free me from it, I must create and justify imputations still more atrocious. My story may at least be brief. If the agonies of remembrance must be awakened afresh, let me do all that in me lies to shorten them.

I was born in the county of Armagh. My parents were of the better sort of peasants, and were able to provide me with the rudiments of knowledge. I should doubtless have trodden in their footsteps, and have spent my life in the cultivation of their scanty fields, if an event had not happened, which, for a long time, I regarded as the most fortunate of my life; but which I now regard as the scheme of some infernal agent and as the primary source of all my calamities.

My father's farm was a portion of the demesne of one who resided wholly in the metropolis, and consigned the management of his estates to his stewards and retainers. This person married a lady, who brought him great accession of fortune. Her wealth was her only recommendation in the eyes of her husband, whose understanding was depraved by the prejudices of luxury and rank, but was the least of her attractions in the estimate of reasonable beings.

They passed some years together. If their union were not a source of misery to the lady, she was indebted for her tranquility to the force of her mind. She was, indeed, governed, in every action of her life by the precepts of duty, while her husband listened to no calls but those of pernicious dissipation. He was immersed in all the vices that grow out of opulence and a mistaken education.

Happily for his wife his career was short. He was enraged at the infidelity of his mistress, to purchase whose attachment, he had lavished two thirds of his fortune. He called the paramour, by whom he had been supplanted, to the field. The contest was obstinate, and terminated in the death of the challenger.

This event freed the lady from many distressful and humiliating obligations. She determined to profit by her newly acquired independence, to live thenceforward conformable to her notions of right, to preserve and improve, by schemes of economy, the remains of her fortune, and to employ it in the diffusion of good. Her plans made it necessary to visit her estates in the distant provinces.

During her abode in the manor of which my father was a vassal, she visited his cottage. I was at that time a child. She was pleased with my vivacity and promptitude, and determined to take me under her own protection. My parents joyfully acceded to her proposal, and I returned with her to the capital.

She had an only son of my own age. Her design, in relation to me, was, that I should be educated with her child, and that an affection, in this way, might be excited in me towards my young master, which might render me, when we should attain to manhood, one of his most faithful and intelligent dependents. I enjoyed, equally with him, all the essential benefits of education. There were certain accomplishments, from which I was excluded, from the belief that they were unsuitable to my rank and station. I was permitted to acquire others, which, had she been actuated by true discernment, she would, perhaps, have discovered to be far more incompatible with a servile station. In proportion as my views were refined and enlarged by history and science, I was likely to contract a thirst of independence, and an impatience of subjection and poverty.

When the period of childhood and youth was past, it was thought proper to send her son, to improve his knowledge and manners, by a residence on the continent. This young man was endowed with splendid abilities. His errors were the growth of his condition. All the expedients that maternal solicitude and wisdom could suggest, were employed to render him an useful citizen. Perhaps this wisdom was attested by the large share of excellence which he really possessed; and, that his character was not unblemished, proved only, that no exertions could preserve him from the vices that are inherent in wealth and rank, and which flow from the spectacle of universal depravity.

As to me, it would be folly to deny, that I had benefited by my opportunities of improvement. I fulfilled the expectation of my mistress, in one respect. I was deeply imbued with affection for her son, and reverence for herself. Perhaps the force of education was evinced in those particulars, without reflecting any credit on the directors of it. Those might merit the name of defects, which were regarded by them as accomplishments. My unfavorable qualities, like those of my master, were imputed to my condition, though, perhaps, the difference was advantageous to me, since the vices of servitude are less hateful than those of tyranny.

It was resolved that I should accompany my master in his travels, in quality of favourite domestic. My principles, whatever might be their rectitude, were harmonious and flexible. I had devoted my life to the service of my patron. I had formed conceptions of what was really conducive to his interest, and was not to be misled by specious appearances. If my affection had not stimulated my diligence, I should have found sufficient motives in the behaviour of his mother. She condescended to express her reliance on my integrity and judgment. She was not ashamed to manifest, at parting, the tenderness of a mother, and to acknowledge that, all her tears were not shed on her son's account. I had my part in the regrets that called them forth.

During our absence, I was my master's constant attendant. I corresponded with his mother, and made the conduct of her son the principal theme of my letters. I deemed it my privilege, as well as duty, to sit in judgment on his actions, to form my opinions without regard to selfish considerations, and to avow them whenever the avowal tended to benefit. Every letter which I wrote, particularly those in which his behaviour was freely criticised, I allowed him to peruse. I would, on no account, connive at, or participate in the slightest irregularity. I knew the duty of my station, and assumed no other controul than that which resulted from the avoiding of deceit, and the open expression of my sentiments. The youth was of a noble spirit, but his firmness was wavering. He yielded to temptations which a censor less rigorous than I would have regarded as venial, or, perhaps laudable. My duty required me to set before him the consequences of his actions, and to give impartial and timely information to his mother.

He could not brook a monitor. The more he needed reproof, the less supportable it became. My company became every day less agreeable, till at length, there appeared a necessity of parting. A seperation took place, but not as enemies. I never lost his respect. In his representations to his mother, he was just to my character and services. My dismission was not allowed to injure my fortune, and his mother considered this event merely as a new proof of the inflexible consistency of my principles.

On this change in my situation, she proposed to me to become a member of her own family. No proposal could be more acceptable. I was fully acquainted with the character of this lady, and had nothing to fear from injustice and caprice. I did not regard her with filial familiarity, but my attachment and reverence would have done honour to that relation. I performed for her the functions of a steward. Her estates in the city were put under my direction. She placed boundless confidence in my discretion and integrity, and consigned to me the payment, and in some degree, the selection and government of her servants. My station was a servile one, yet most of the evils of servitude were unknown to me. My personal ease and independence were less infringed than that of those who are accounted the freest members of society. I derived a sort of authority and dignity from the receipt and disbursement of money. The tenants and debtors of the lady were, in some respects, mine. It was, for the most part, on my justice and lenity that they depended for their treatment. My lady's household establishment was large and opulent. Her servants were my inferiors and menials. My leisure was considerable, and my emoluments large enough to supply me with every valuable instrument of improvement or pleasure.

These were reasons why I should be contented with my lot. These circumstances alone would have rendered it more eligible than any other, but it had additional, and far more powerful recommendations, arising from the character of Mrs. Lorimer, and from the relation in which she allowed me to stand to her.

How shall I enter upon this theme? How shall I expatiate upon excellencies, which it was my fate to view in their genuine colours, to adore with an immeasurable and inextinguishable ardour, and which, nevertheless, it was my hateful task to blast and destroy? Yet I will not be spared. I shall find in the rehearsal, new incitements to sorrow. I deserve to be supreme in misery, and will not be denied the full measure of a bitter retribution.

No one was better qualified to judge of her excellencies. A casual spectator might admire her beauty, and the dignity of her demeanour. From the contemplation of those, he might gather motives for loving or revering her. Age was far from having withered her complexion, or destroyed the evenness of her skin; but no time could rob her of the sweetness and intelligence which animated her features. Her habitual beneficence was bespoken in every look. Always in search of occasions for doing good, always meditating scenes of happiness, of which she was the author, or of distress, for which she was preparing relief, the most torpid insensibility was, for a time, subdued, and the most depraved smitten by charms, of which, in another person, they would not perhaps have been sensible.

A casual visitant might enjoy her conversation, might applaud the rectitude of her sentiments, the richness of her elocution, and her skill in all the offices of politeness. But it was only for him, who dwelt constantly under the same roof, to mark the inviolable consistency of her actions and opinions, the ceaseless flow of her candour, her cheerfulness, and her benevolence. It was only for one who witnessed her behaviour at all hours, in sickness and in health, her management of that great instrument of evil and good, money, her treatment of her son, her menials, and her kindred, rightly to estimate her merits.

The intercourse between us was frequent, but of a peculiar kind. My office in her family required me often to see her, to submit schemes to her considerations, and receive her directions. At these times she treated me in a manner, in some degree, adapted to the difference of rank, and the inferiority of my station, and yet widely dissimilar from that, which a different person would have adopted, in the same circumstances. The treatment was not that of an equal and a friend, but still more remote was it from that of a mistress. It was merely characterised by affability and condescention, but as such it had no limits.

She made no scruple to ask my council in every pecuniary affair, to listen to my arguments, and decide conformably to what, after sufficient canvassings and discussions, should appear to be right. When the direct occasions of our interview were dismissed, I did not of course withdraw. To detain or dismiss me was indeed at her option, but, if no engagement interfered, she would enter into general conversation. There was none who could with more safety to herself have made the world her confessor; but the state of society in which she lived, imposed certain limitations on her candour. In her intercourse with me there were fewer restraints than on any other occasion. My situation had made me more intimately acquainted with domestic transactions, with her views respecting her son, and with the terms on which she thought proper to stand with those whom old acquaintance or kindred gave some title to her good offices. In addition to all those motives to a candid treatment of me, there were others which owed their efficacy to her maternal regard for me, and to the artless and unsuspecting generosity of her character.

Her hours were distributed with the utmost regularity, and appropriated to the best purposes. She selected her society without regard to any qualities but probity and talents. Her associates were numerous, and her evening conversations embellished with all that could charm the senses or instruct the understanding. This was a chosen field for the display of her magnificence, but her grandeur was unostentatious, and her gravity unmingled with hautiness. From these my station excluded me, but I was compensated by the freedom of her communications in the intervals. She found pleasure in detailing to me the incidents that passed on those occasions, in rehearsing conversations and depicting characters. There was an uncommon portion of dramatic merit in her recitals, besides valuable and curious information. One uniform effect was produced in me by this behaviour. Each day, I thought it impossible for my attachment to receive any new accessions, yet the morrow was sure to produce some new emotion of respect or of gratitude, and to set the unrivalled accomplishments of this lady in a new and more favourable point of view. I contemplated no change in my condition. The necessity of change, whatever were the alternative, would have been a subject of piercing regret. I deemed my life a cheap sacrifice in her cause. No time would suffice to discharge the debt of gratitude that was due to her. Yet it was continually accumulating. If an anxious thought ever invaded my bosom it arose from this source.

It was no difficult task faithfully to execute the functions assigned to me. No merit could accrue to me from this source. I was exposed to no temptation. I had passed the feverish period of youth. No contagious example had contaminated my principles. I had resisted the allurements of sensuality and dissipation incident to my age. My dwelling was in pomp and splendour. I had amassed sufficient to secure me, in case of unforeseen accidents, in the enjoyment of competence. My mental resources were not despicable, and the external means of intellectual gratification were boundless. I enjoyed an unsullied reputation. My character was well known in that sphere which my lady occupied, not only by means of her favourable report, but in numberless ways in which it was my fortune to perform personal services to others.

CHAPTER V

MRS. LORIMER had a twin brother. Nature had impressed the same image upon them, and had modelled them after the same pattern. The resemblance between them was exact to a degree almost incredible. In infancy and childhood they were perpetually liable to be mistaken for each other. As they grew up nothing to a superficial examination appeared to distinguish them but the sexual characteristics. A sagacious observer would, doubtless, have noted the most essential differences. In all those modifications of the features which are produced by habits and sentiments, no two persons were less alike. Nature seemed to have intended them as examples of the futility of those theories, which ascribe every thing to conformation and instinct, and nothing to external circumstances; in what different modes the same materials may be fashioned, and to what different purposes the same materials may be applied. Perhaps the rudiments of their intellectual character as well as of their form, were the same; but the powers, that in one case, were exerted in the cause of virtue, were, in the other, misapplied to sordid and flagitious purposes.

Arthur Wiatte, that was his name, had ever been the object of his sister's affection. As long as he existed she never ceased to labour in the promotion of his happiness. All her kindness was repaid by a stern and inexorable hatred. This man was an exception to all the rules which govern us in our judgments of human nature. He exceeded in depravity all that has been imputed to the arch-foe of mankind. His wickedness was without any of those remorseful intermissions from which it has been supposed that the deepest guilt is not entirely exempt. He seemed to relish no food but pure unadulterated evil. He rejoiced in proportion to the depth of that distress of which he was the author.

His sister, by being placed most within the reach of his enmity, experienced its worst effects. She was the subject on which, by being acquainted with the means of influencing her happiness, he could try his malignant experiments with most hope of success. Her parents being high in rank and wealth, the marriage of their daughter was, of course, an object of anxious attention. There is no event on which our felicity and usefulness more materially depends, and with regard to which, therefore, the freedom of choice and the exercise of our own understanding ought to be less infringed, but this maxim is commonly disregarded in proportion to the elevation of our rank and extent of our property.

The lady made her own election, but she was one of those who acted on a comprehensive plan, and would not admit her private inclination to dictate her decision. The happiness of others, though founded on mistaken views, she did not consider as unworthy of her regard. The choice was such as was not likely to obtain the parental sanction, to whom the moral qualities of their son-in-law, though not absolutely weightless in the balance, were greatly inferior to the considerations of wealth and dignity.

The brother set no value on any thing but the means of luxury and power. He was astonished at that perverseness which entertained a different conception of happiness from himself. Love and friendship he considered as groundless and chimerical, and believed that those delusions, would, in people of sense, be rectified by experience; but he knew the obstinacy of his sister's attachment to these phantoms, and that to bereave her of the good they promised was the most effectual means of rendering her miserable. For this end he set himself to thwart her wishes. In the imbecility and false indulgence of his parents he found his most powerful auxiliaries. He prevailed upon them to forbid that union which wanted nothing but their concurrence, and their consent to endow her with a small portion of their patrimony to render completely eligible. The cause was that of her happiness and the happiness of him on whom she had bestowed her heart. It behoved her, therefore, to call forth all her energies in defence of it, to weaken her brother's influence on the minds of her parents, or to win him to be her advocate. When I reflect upon her mental powers, and the advantages which should seem to flow from the circumstance of pleading in the character of daughter and sister, I can scarcely believe that her attempts miscarried. I should have imagined that all obstacles would yield before her, and particularly in a case like this, in which she must have summoned all her forces, and never have believed that she had struggled sufficiently.

Certain it is that her lot was fixed. She was not only denied the husband of her choice, but another was imposed upon her, whose recommendations were irresistible in every one's apprehension but her own. The discarded lover was treated with every sort of contumely. Deceit and violence were employed by her brother to bring his honour, his liberty, and even his life into hazard. All these iniquities produced no considerable effect on the mind of the lady. The machinations to which her love was exposed, would have exasperated him into madness, had not her most strenuous exertions been directed to appease him.

She prevailed on him at length to abandon his country, though she thereby merely turned her brother's depravity into a new channel. Her parents died without consciousness of the evils they inflicted, but they experienced a bitter retribution in the conduct of their son. He was the darling and stay of an ancient and illustrious house, but his actions reflected nothing but disgrace upon his ancestry, and threatened to bring the honours of their line to a period in his person. At their death the bulk of their patrimony devolved upon him. This he speedily consumed in gaming and riot. From splendid, he descended to meaner vices. The efforts of his sister to recall him to virtue were unintermitted and fruitless. Her affection for him he converted into a means of prolonging his selfish gratifications. She decided for the best. It was no argument of weakness that she was so frequently deceived. If she had judged truly of her brother, she would have judged not only without example, but in opposition to the general experience of mankind. But she was not to be forever deceived. Her tenderness was subservient to justice. And when his vices had led him from the gaming table to the highway, when seized at length by the ministers of law, when convicted and sentenced to transportation, her intercession was solicited, when all the world knew that pardon would readily be granted to a supplicant of her rank, fortune, and character, when the criminal himself, his kindred, his friends, and even indifferent persons implored her interference, her justice was inflexible: She knew full well the incurableness of his depravity; that banishment was the mildest destiny that would befall him; that estrangement from ancient haunts and associates was the condition from which his true friends had least to fear.

Finding intreaties unavailing, the wretch delivered himself to the suggestions of his malice, and he vowed to be bloodily revenged on her inflexibility. The sentence was executed. That character must indeed be monstrous from which the execution of such threats was to be dreaded. The event sufficiently shewed that our fears on this head were well grounded. This event, however, was at a great distance. It was reported that the fellons, of whom he was one, mutinied on board the ship in which they had been embarked. In the affray that succeeded it was said that he was killed.

Among the nefarious deeds which he perpetrated was to be numbered the seduction of a young lady, whose heart was broken by the detection of his perfidy. The fruit of this unhappy union was a daughter. Her mother died shortly after her birth. Her father was careless of her destiny. She was consigned to the care of an hireling, who, happily for the innocent victim, performed the maternal offices for her own sake, and did not allow the want of a stipulated recompence to render her cruel or neglectful.

This orphan was sought out by the benevolence of Mrs. Lorimer and placed under her own protection. She received from her the treatment of a mother. The ties of kindred, corroborated by habit, was not the only thing that united them. That resemblance to herself, which had been so deplorably defective in her brother, was completely realized in his offspring. Nature seemed to have precluded every difference between them but that of age. This darling object excited in her bosom more than maternal sympathies. Her soul clung to the happiness of her *Clarice*, with more ardour than to that of her own son. The latter was not only less worthy of affection, but their separation necessarily diminished their mutual confidence.

It was natural for her to look forward to the future destiny of *Clarice*. On these occasions she could not help contemplating the possibility of a union between her son and niece. Considerable advantages belonged to this scheme, yet it was the subject of hope rather than the scope of a project. The contingencies were numerous and delicate on which the ultimate desirableness of this union depended. She was far from certain that her son would be worthy of this benefit, or that, if he were worthy, his propensities would not select for themselves a different object. It was equally dubious whether the young lady would not think proper otherwise to dispose of her affections. These uncertainties could be dissipated only by time. Meanwhile she was chiefly solicitous to render them virtuous and wise.

49

As they advanced in years, the hopes that she had formed were annihilated. The youth was not exempt from egregious errors. In addition to this, it was manifest that the young people were disposed to regard each other in no other light than that of brother and sister. I was not unapprised of her views. I saw that their union was impossible. I was near enough to judge of the character of Clarice. My youth and intellectual constitution made me peculiarly susceptible to female charms. I was her play-fellow in childhood, and her associate in studies and amusements at a maturer age. This situation might have been suspected of a dangerous tendency. This tendency, however, was obviated by motives of which I was, for a long time, scarcely conscious.

I was habituated to consider the distinctions of rank as indelible. The obstructions that existed, to any wish that I might form, were like those of time and space, and as, in their own nature, insuperable.

Such was the state of things previous to our setting out upon our travels. Clarice was indirectly included in our correspondence. My letters were open to her inspection, and I was sometimes honoured with a few complimentary lines under her own hand. On returning to my ancient abode, I was once more exposed to those sinister influences which absence had, at least, suspended. Various suitors had, meanwhile, been rejected. Their character, for the most part, had been such as to account for her refusal, without resorting to the supposition of a lurking or unavowed attachment.

On our meeting she greeted me in a respectful but dignified manner. Observers could discover in it nothing not corresponding to that difference of fortune which subsisted between us. If her joy, on that occasion, had in it some portion of tenderness, the softness of her temper, and the peculiar circumstances in which we had been placed, being considered, the most rigid censor could find no occasion for blame or suspicion.

A year passed away, but not without my attention

being solicited by something new and inexplicable in my own sensations. At first I was not aware of their true cause; but the gradual progress of my feelings left me not long in doubt as to their origin. I was alarmed at the discovery, but my courage did not suddenly desert me. My hopes seemed to be extinguished the moment that I distinctly perceived the point to which they led. My mind had undergone a change. The ideas with which it was fraught were varied. The sight, or recollection of Clarice, was sure to occasion my mind to advert to the recent discovery, and to revolve the considerations naturally connected with it. Some latent glows and secret trepidations were likewise experienced, when, by some accident, our meetings were abrupt or our interviews unwitnessed; yet my usual tranquility was not as yet sensibly diminished. I could bear to think of her marriage with another without painful emotions, and was anxious only that her choice should be judicious and fortunate.

My thoughts could not long continue in this state. They gradually became more ardent and museful. The image of Clarice occurred with unseasonable frequency. Its charms were enhanced by some nameless and indefinable additions. When it met me in the way I was irresistibly disposed to stop and survey it with particular attention. The pathetic cast of her features, the deep glow of her cheek, and some catch of melting music, she had lately breathed, stole incessantly upon my fancy. On recovering from my thoughtful moods, I sometimes found my cheeks wet with tears, that had fallen unperceived, and my bosom heaved with involuntary sighs.

These images did not content themselves with invading my wakeful hours; but, likewise, incroached upon my sleep. I could no longer resign myself to slumber with the same ease as before. When I slept, my visions were of the same impassioned tenor.

There was no difficulty in judging rightly of my situation. I knew what it was that duty exacted from me. To remain in my present situation was a chimerical project.

That time and reflection would suffice to restore me to myself was a notion equally falacious. Yet I felt an insupportable reluctance to change it. This reluctance was owing, not wholly or chiefly to my growing passion, but to the attachment which bound me to the service of my lady. All my contemplations had hitherto been modelled on the belief of my remaining in my present situation during my life. My mildest anticipations had never fashioned an event like this. Any misfortune was light in comparison with that which tore me from her presence and service. But should I ultimately resolve to separate, how should I communicate my purpose? The pain of parting would scarcely be less on her side than on mine. Could I consent to be the author of disquietude to her? I had consecrated all my faculties to her service. This was the recompence which it was in my power to make for the benefits that I had received. Would not this procedure bear the appearance of the basest ingratitude? The shaddow of an imputation like this was more excruciating than the rack.

What motive could I assign for my conduct? The truth must not be told. This would be equivalent to supplicating for a new benefit. It would more become me to lessen than increase my obligations. Among all my imaginations on this subject, the possibility of a mutual passion never occurred to me. I could not be blind to the essential distinctions that subsist among men. I could expatiate, like others, on the futility of ribbonds and titles, and on the dignity that was annexed to skill and virtue; but these, for the most part, were the incoherences of speculation, and in no degree influenced the stream of my actions, and practical sentiments. The barrier that existed in the present case, I deemed insurmountable. This was not even the subject of doubt. In disclosing the truth, I should be conceived to be soliciting my lady's mercy and intercession; but this would be the madness of presumption. Let me impress her with any other opinion than that I go in search of the happiness that I have lost under her roof.

Let me save her generous heart from the pangs which this persuasion would infallibly produce.

I could form no stable resolutions. I seemed unalterably convinced of the necessity of separation, and yet could not execute my design. When I had wrought up my mind to the intention of explaining myself on the next interview, when the next interview took place my tongue was powerless. I admitted any excuse for postponing my design, and gladly admitted any topic, however foreign to my purpose.

It must not be imagined that my health sustained no injury from this conflict of my passions. My patroness perceived this alteration. She inquired with the most affectionate solicitude, into the cause. It could not be explained. I could safely make light of it, and represented it as something which would probably disappear of itself, as it originated without any adequate cause. She was obliged to acquiesce in my imperfect account.

Day after day passed in this state of fluctuation. I was conscious of the dangers of delay, and that procrastination, without rendering the task less necessary, augmented its difficulties. At length, summoning my resolution, I demanded an audience. She received me with her usual affability. Common topics were started; but she saw the confusion and trepidation of my thoughts, and quickly relinquished them. She then noticed to me what she had observed, and mentioned the anxiety which these appearances had given her. She reminded me of the maternal regard which she had always manifested towards me, and appealed to my own heart whether any thing could be said in vindication of that reserve with which I had lately treated her, and urged me as I valued her good opinion, to explain the cause of a dejection *that was too visible*.

To all this I could make but one answer: Think me not, Madam, perverse or ungrateful. I came just now to apprise you of a resolution that I had formed. I cannot explain the motives that induce me. In this case, to lie to you would be unpardonable, and since I cannot assign my true motives, I will not mislead you by false representations. I came to inform you of my intention to leave your service, and to retire with the fruits of your bounty, to my native village, where I shall spend my life, I hope, in peace.

Her surprise at this declaration was beyond measure. She could not believe her ears. She had not heard me rightly. She compelled me to repeat it. Still I was jesting. I could not possibly mean what my words imported.

I assured her, in terms still more explicit, that my resolution was taken and was unalterable, and again intreated her to spare me the task of assigning my motives.

This was a strange determination. What could be the grounds of this new scheme? What could be the necessity of hiding them from her? This mystery was not to be endured. She could by no means away with it. She thought it hard that I should abandon her at this time, when she stood in particular need of my assistance and advice. She would refuse nothing to make my situation eligible. I had only to point out where she was deficient in her treatment of me and she would endeavour to supply it. She was willing to augment my emoluments in any degree that I desired. She could not think of parting with me; but, at any rate, she must be informed of my motives.

It is an hard task, answered I, that I have imposed upon myself. I foresaw its difficulties, and this foresight has hitherto prevented me from undertaking it; but the necessity by which I am impelled, will no longer be withstood. I am determined to go; but to say why, is impossible. I hope I shall not bring upon myself the imputation of ingratitude; but this imputation, more intolerable than any other, must be borne, if it cannot be avoided but by this disclosure.

Keep your motives to yourself, said she. I have too good an opinion of you to suppose that you would practice concealment without good reason. I merely desire you to remain where you are. Since you will not tell me why you take up this new scheme, I can only say that it is impossible there should be any advantage in this scheme. I will not hear of it I tell you. Therefore, submit to my decree with a good grace.

Notwithstanding this prohibition I persisted in declaring that my determination was fixed, and that the motives that governed me would allow of no alternative.

So, you will go, will you, whether I will or no? I have no power to detain you? You will regard nothing that I can say?

Believe me, madam, no resolution ever was formed after a more vehement struggle. If my motives were known, you would not only cease to oppose, but would hasten my departure. Honour me so far with your good opinion, as to believe that, in saying this, I say nothing but the truth, and render my duty less burthensome by cheerfully acquiescing in its dictates.

I would, replied my lady, I could find somebody that has more power over you than I have. Whom shall I call in to aid me in this arduous task?

Nay, dear madam, if I can resist your intreaties, surely no other can hope to succeed.

I am not sure of that, said my friend, archly: there is one person in the world whose supplications, I greatly suspect, you would not withstand.

Whom do you mean? said I, in some trepidation.

You will know presently. Unless I can prevail upon you, I shall be obliged to call for assistance.

Spare me the pain of repeating that no power on earth can change my resolution.

That's a fib, she rejoined, with increased archness. You know it is. If a certain person intreat you to stay, you will easily comply. I see I canno* hope to prevail by my own strength. That is a mortifying consideration, but we must not part, that is a point settled. If nothing else will do, I must go and fetch my advocate. Stay here a moment.

I had scarcely time to breathe, before she returned, leading in Clarice. I did not yet comprehend the meaning of this ceremony. The lady was overwhelmed with sweet confusion. Averted eyes and reluctant steps, might have explained to me the purpose of this meeting, if I had believed that purpose to be possible. I felt the necessity of new fortitude, and struggled to recollect the motives that had hitherto sustained me.

There, said my patroness, I have been endeavouring to persuade this young man to live with us a little longer. He is determined, it seems, to change his abode. He will not tell why, and I do not care to know, unless I could shew his reasons to be groundless. I have merely remonstrated with him on the folly of his scheme, but he has proved refractory to all I can say. Perhaps your efforts may meet with better success.

Clarice said not a word. My own embarrassment equally disabled me from speaking. Regarding us both, for some time, with a benign aspect, Mrs. Lorimer resumed, taking an hand of each and joining them together.

I very well know what it was that suggested this scheme. It is strange that you should suppose me so careless an observer as not to note, or not to understand your situation. I am as well acquainted with what is passing in your heart as you yourself are, but why are you so anxious to conceal it? You know less of the adventurousness of love than I should have suspected. But I will not trifle with your feelings.

You, Clithero, know the wishes that I once cherished. I had hoped that my son would have found, in this darling child, an object worthy of his choice, and that my girl would have preferred him to all others. But I have long since discovered that this could not be. They are nowise suited to each other. There is one thing in the next place desirable, and now my wishes are accomplished. I see that you love each other, and never, in my opinion, was a passion more rational and just. I should think myself the worst of beings if I did not contribute all in my power to your happiness. There is not the shadow of objection to your union. I know your scruples, Clithero, and am sorry to see that you harbour them for a moment. Nothing is more unworthy of your good sense.

I found out this girl long ago. Take my word for it, young man, she does not fall short of you in the purity and tenderness of her attachment. What need is there of tedious preliminaries? I will leave you together, and hope you will not be long in coming to a mutual understanding. Your union cannot be completed too soon for my wishes. Clarice is my only and darling daughter. As to you Clithero, expect henceforth that treatment from me, not only to which your own merit intitles you, but which is due to the husband of my daughter. — With these words she retired and left us together.

Great God! deliver me from the torments of this remembrance. That a being by whom I was snatched from penury and brutal ignorance, exalted to some rank in the intelligent creation, reared to affluence and honour, and thus, at last, spontaneously endowed with all that remained to complete the sum of my felicity, that a being like this — but such thoughts must not yet be — I must shut them out, or I shall never arrive at the end of my tale. My efforts have been thus far successful. I have hitherto been able to deliver a coherent narrative. Let the last words that I shall speak afford some glimmering of my better days. Let me execute without faltering the only task that remains for me.

CHAPTER VI

HOW propitious, how incredible was this event! I could scarcely confide in the testimony of my senses. Was it true that Clarice was before me, that she was prepared to countenance my presumption, that she had slighted obstacles which I had deemed insurmountable, that I was fondly beloved by her, and should shortly be admitted to the possession of so inestimable a good? I will not repeat the terms in which I poured forth, at her feet, the raptures of my gratitude. My impetuosity soon extorted from Clarice, a confirmation of her mother's declaration. An unrestrained intercourse was thenceforth established between us. Dejection and languor gave place, in my bosom, to the irradiations of joy and hope. My flowing fortunes seemed to have attained their utmost and immutable height.

Alas! They were destined to ebb with unspeakably greater rapidity, and to leave me, in a moment, stranded and wrecked.

Our nuptials would have been solemnised without delay, had not a melancholy duty interferred. Clarice had a friend in a distant part of the kingdom. Her health had long been the prey of a consumption. She was now evidently tending to dissolution. In this extremity she intreated her friend to afford her the consolation of her presence. The only wish that remained was to die in her arms.

This request could not but be willingly complied with. It became me patiently to endure the delay that would thence arise to the completion of my wishes. Considering the urgency and mournfulness of the occasion, it was impossible for me to murmur, and the affectionate Clarice would suffer nothing to interfere with the duty which she owed to her dying friend. I accompanied her on this journey, remained with her a few days, and then parted from her to return to the metropolis. It was not imagined that it would be necessary to prolong her absence beyond a month. When I bade her farewell, and informed her on what day I proposed to return for her, I felt no decay of my satisfaction. My thoughts were bright and full of exultation. Why was not some intimation afforded me of the snares that lay in my path? In the train laid for my destruction, the agent had so skilfully contrived that my security was not molested by the faintest omen.

I hasten to the crisis of my tale. I am almost dubious of my strength. The nearer I approach to it, the stronger is my aversion. My courage, instead of gathering force as I proceed, decays. I am willing to dwell still longer on preliminary circumstances. There are other incidents without which my story would be lame. I retail them because they afford me a kind of respite from horrors, at the thought of which every joint in my frame trembles. They must be endured, but that infirmity may be forgiven, which makes me inclined to procrastinate my suffering.

I mentioned the lover whom my patroness was compelled, by the machinations of her brother, to discard. More than twenty years had passed since their separation. His birth was mean and he was without fortune. His profession was that of a surgeon. My lady not only prevailed upon him to abandon his country, but enabled him to do this by supplying his necessities from her own purse. His excellent understanding was, for a time, obscured by passion; but it was not difficult for my lady ultimately to obtain his concurrence to all her schemes. He saw and adored the rectitude of her motives, did not disdain to accept her gifts, and projected means for maintaining an epistolary intercourse during their separation.

Her interest procured him a post in the service of the East-India company. She was, from time to time, informed of his motions. A war broke out between the Company and some of the native powers. He was present at a great battle in which the English were defeated. She could trace him by his letters and by other circumstances thus far, but here the thread was discontinued, and no means which she employed could procure any tidings of him. Whether he was captive, or dead, continued, for several years, to be merely matter of conjecture.

On my return to Dublin, I found my patroness engaged in conversation with a stranger. She introduced us to each other in a manner that indicated the respect which she entertained for us both. I surveyed and listened to him with considerable attention. His aspect was noble and ingenuous, but his sun-burnt and rugged features bespoke a various and boisterous pilgrimage. The furrows of his brow were the products of vicissitude and hardship, rather than of age. His accents were fiery and energetic, and the impassioned boldness of his address, as well as the tenor of his discourse, full of allusions to the past, and regrets that the course of events had not been different, made me suspect something extraordinary in his character.

As soon as he left us, my lady explained who he was. He was no other than the object of her youthful attachment, who had, a few days before, dropped among us as from the skies. He had a long and various story to tell. He had accounted for his silence by enumerating the incidents of his life. He had escaped from the prisons of Hyder, had wandered on foot, and under various disguises, through the northern district of Hindoostaun. He was sometimes a scholar of Benares, and sometimes a disciple of the Mosque. According to the exigencies of the times, he was a pilgrim to Mecca or to Jagunaut. By a long, circuitous, and perilous route, he at length arrived at the Turkish capital. Here he resided for several years, deriving a precarious subsistence from the profession of a surgeon. He was obliged to desert this post, in consequence of a duel between two Scotsmen. One of them had embraced the Greek religion, and was betrothed to the daughter of a wealthy trader of that nation. He perished in the conflict, and the family of the lady not only procured the execution of his antagonist, but threatened to involve all those who were known to be connected with him in the same ruin.

His life being thus endangered, it became necessary for him to seek a new residence. He fled from Constantinople with such precipitation as reduced him to the lowest poverty. He had traversed the Indian conquests of Alexander, as a mendicant. In the same character, he now wandered over the native country of Philip and Philopoemen. He passed safely through multiplied perils, and finally, embarking at Salonichi, he reached Venice. He descended through the passes of the Apennine into Tuscany. In this journey he suffered a long detention from banditti, by whom he was waylaid. In consequence of his harmless deportment, and a seasonable display of his chirurgical skill, they granted him his life, though they, for a time restrained him of his liberty, and compelled him to endure their society. The time was not misemployed which he spent immured in caverns and carousing with robbers. His details were eminently singular and curious, and evinced the acuteness of his penetration, as well the steadfastness of his courage.

After emerging from these wilds, he found his way along the banks of the Arno to Leghorn. Thence he procured a passage to America, whence he had just returned, with many additions to his experience, but none to his fortune.

This was a remarkable event. It did not at first appear how far its consequences would extend. The lady was, at present, disengaged and independent. Though the pas-

sion which clouded her early prosperity was extinct, time
had not diminished the worth of her friend, and they were
far from having reached that age when love becomes chimerical and marriage folly. A confidential intercourse was
immediately established between them. The bounty of
Mrs. Lorimer soon divested her friend of all fear of poverty. At any rate, said she, he shall wander no further, but
shall be comfortably situated for the rest of his life. All his
scruples were vanquished by the reasonableness of her
remonstrances and the vehemence of her solicitations.

A cordial intimacy grew between me and the newly
arrived. Our interviews were frequent, and our communications without reserve. He detailed to me the result of
his experience, and expatiated without end on the history
of his actions and opinions. He related the adventures of
his youth, and dwelt upon all the circumstances of his
attachment to my patroness. On this subject I had heard
only general details. I continually found cause, in the
course of his narrative, to revere the illustrious qualities of
my lady, and to weep at the calamities to which the infernal malice of her brother had subjected her.

The tale of that man's misdeeds, amplified and dra-
matised, by the indignant eloquence of this historian,
oppressed me with astonishment. If a poet had drawn
such a portrait I should have been prone to suspect the
soundness of his judgment. Till now I had imagined that
no character was uniform and unmixed, and my theory of
the passions did not enable me to account for a propensity
gratified merely by evil, and delighting in shrieks and
agony for their own sake.

It was natural to suggest to my friend, when expatiating on this theme, an inquiry as to how far subsequent
events had obliterated the impressions that were then
made, and as to the plausibility of reviving, at this more
auspicious period, his claims on the heart of his friend.
When he thought proper to notice these hints, he gave me
to understand that time had made no essential alteration
in his sentiments in this respect, that he still fostered an

hope, to which every day added new vigour, that whatever was the ultimate event, he trusted in his fortitude to sustain it, if adverse, and in his wisdom to extract from it the most valuable consequences, if it should prove prosperous.

The progress of things was not unfavourable to his hopes. She treated his insinuations and professions with levity; but her arguments seemed to be urged, with no other view than to afford an opportunity of confutation; and, since there was no abatement of familiarity and kindness, there was room to hope that the affair would terminate agreeably to his wishes.

CHAPTER VII

CLARICE, meanwhile, was absent. Her friend seemed, at the end of a month, to be little less distant from the grave than at first. My impatience would not allow me to wait till her death. I visited her, but was once more obliged to return alone. I arrived late in the city, and being greatly fatigued, I retired almost immediately to my chamber.

On hearing of my arrival, Sarsefield hastened to see me. He came to my bed-side, and such, in his opinion, was the importance of the tidings which he had to communicate, that he did not scruple to rouse me from a deep sleep. . . .

At this period of his narrative, Clithero stopped. His complexion varied from one degree of paleness to another. His brain appeared to suffer some severe constriction. He desired to be excused, for a few minutes, from proceeding. In a short time he was relieved from this paroxysm, and resumed his tale with an accent tremulous at first, but acquiring stability and force as he went on.

On waking, as I have said, I found my friend seated at my bed-side. His countenance exhibited various tokens of alarm. As soon as I perceived who it was, I started, exclaming, What is the matter?

He sighed. Pardon, said he, this unseasonable intrusion. A light matter would not have occasioned it. I have waited, for two days past, in an agony of impatience, for your return. Happily, you are, at last, come. I stand in the utmost need of your council and aid.

Heaven defend! cried I. This is a terrible prelude. You may, of course, rely upon my assistance and advice. What is it that you have to propose?

Tuesday evening, he answered, I spent here. It was late before I returned to my lodgings. I was in the act of lifting my hand to the bell, when my eye was caught by a person standing close to the wall, at the distance of ten paces. His attitude was that of one employed in watching my motions. His face was turned towards me, and happened, at that moment, to be fully illuminated by the rays of a globe-lamp that hung over the door. I instantly recognized his features. I was petrified. I had no power to execute my design, or even to move, but stood, for some seconds gazing upon him. He was, in no degree, disconcerted by the eagerness of my scrutiny. He seemed perfectly indifferent to the consequences of being known. At length he slowly turned his eyes to another quarter, but without changing his posture, or the sternness of his looks. I cannot describe to you the shock which this encounter produced in me. At last I went into the house, and have ever since been excessively uneasy.

I do not see any ground for uneasiness.

You do not then suspect who this person is?

No. . . .

It is Arthur Wiatte. . . .

Good heaven! It is impossible. What, my lady's brother?

The same. . . .

It cannot be. Were we not assured of his death? That he perished in a mutiny on board the vessel in which he was embarked for transportation?

Such was rumour, which is easily mistaken. My eyes cannot be deceived in this case. I should as easily fail to recognize his sister, when I first met her, as him. This is the man; whether once dead or not, he is, at present, alive, and in this city.

But has any thing since happened to confirm you in this opinion?

Yes, there has. As soon as I had recovered from my first surprise, I began to reflect upon the measures proper to be taken. This was the identical Arthur Wiatte. You know his character. No time was likely to change the principles of such a man, but his appearance sufficiently betrayed the incurableness of his habits. The same sullen and atrocious passions were written in his visage. You recollect the vengeance which Wiatte denounced against his sister. There is every thing to dread from his malignity. How to obviate the danger, I know not. I thought, however, of one expedient. It might serve a present purpose, and something better might suggest itself on your return.

I came hither early the next day. Old Gowan the porter is well acquainted with Wiatte's story. I mentioned to him that I had reason to think that he had returned. I charged him to have a watchful eye upon every one that knocked at the gate, and that if this person should come, by no means to admit him. The old man promised faithfully to abide by my directions. His terrors, indeed, were greater than mine, and he knew the importance of excluding Wiatte from these walls.

Did you not inform my lady of this?

No. In what way could I tell it to her? What end could it answer? Why should I make her miserable? But I have not done. Yesterday morning Gowan took me aside, and informed me that Wiatte had made his appearance, the day before, at the gate. He knew him, he said, in a moment. He demanded to see the lady, but the old man told him she was engaged, and could not be seen. He assumed peremtory and haughty airs, and asserted that his business was of such importance as not to endure a moment's delay. Gowan persisted in his first refusal. He retired with great reluctance, but said he should return to-morrow, when he should insist upon admission to the presence of the lady. I have inquired, and find that he has not repeated his visit. What is to be done?

I was equally at a loss with my friend. This incident was so unlooked for. What might not be dreaded from the monstrous depravity of Wiatte? His menaces of vengeance against his sister still rung in my ears. Some means of eluding them were indispensable. Could law be resorted to? Against an evil like this, no legal provision had been made. Nine years had elapsed since his transportation. Seven years was the period of his exile. In returning, therefore, he had committed no crime. His person could not be lawfully molested. We were justified, merely, in repelling an attack. But suppose we should appeal to law, could this be done without the knowledge and concurrence of the lady? She would never permit it. Her heart was incapable of fear from this quarter. She would spurn at the mention of precautions against the hatred of her brother. Her inquietude would merely be awakened on his own account.

I was overwhelmed with perplexity. Perhaps if he were sought out, and some judgment formed of the kind of danger to be dreaded from him, by a knowledge of his situation and views, some expedient might be thence suggested.

But how should his haunts be discovered? This was easy. He had intimated the design of applying again for admission to his sister. Let a person be stationed near at hand, who, being furnished with an adequate description of his person and dress, shall mark him when he comes, and follow him, when he retires, and shall forthwith impart to us the information on that head which he shall be able to collect.

My friend concurred in this scheme. No better could, for the present, be suggested. Here ended our conference.

I was thus supplied with a new subject of reflection. It was calculated to fill my mind with dreary forbodings. The future was no longer a scene of security and pleasure.

It would be hard for those to partake of our fears, who did not partake of our experience. The existence of Wiatte, was the canker that had blasted the felicity of my patroness. In his reappearance on the stage, there was something portentous. It seemed to include in it, consequences of the utmost moment, without my being able to discover what these consequences were.

That Sarsefield should be so quickly followed by his Arch-foe; that they started anew into existence, without any previous intimation, in a manner wholly unexpected, and at the same period. It seemed as if there lurked, under those appearances, a tremendous significance, which human sagacity could not uncover. My heart sunk within me when I reflected that this was the father of my Clarice. He by whose cruelty her mother was torn from the injoyment of untarnished honour, and consigned to infamy and an untimely grave: He by whom herself was abandoned in the helplessness of infancy, and left to be the prey of obdurate avarice, and the victim of wretches who traffic in virgin innocence: Who had done all that in him lay to devote her youth to guilt and misery. What were the limits of his power? How may he exert the parental prerogatives?

To sleep, while these images were haunting me, was impossible. I passed the night in continual motion. I strode, without ceasing, across the floor of my apartment. My mind was wrought to an higher pitch than I had ever before experienced. The occasion, accurately considered, was far from justifying the ominous inquietudes which I then felt. How then should I account for them?

Sarsefield probably enjoyed his usual slumber. His repose might not be perfectly serene, but when he ruminated on impending or possible calamities, his tongue did not cleave to his mouth, his throat was not parched with unquenchable thirst, he was not incessantly stimulated to employ his superfluous fertility of thought in motion. If I trembled for the safety of her whom I loved, and whose safety was endangered by being the daughter of this miscreant, had he not equal reason to fear for her whom he also loved, and who, as the sister of this ruffian, was encompassed by the most alarming perils? Yet he probably was calm while I was harassed by anxieties.

Alas! The difference was easily explained. Such was the beginning of a series ordained to hurry me to swift destruction. Such were the primary tokens of the presence of that power by whose accursed machinations I was destined to fall. You are startled at this declaration. It is one to which you have been little accustomed. Perhaps you regard it merely as an effusion of phrenzy. I know what I am saying. I do not build upon conjectures and surmises. I care not indeed for your doubts. Your conclusion may be fashioned at your pleasure. Would to heaven that my belief were groundless, and that I had no reason to believe my intellects to have been perverted by diabolical instigations.

I could procure no sleep that night. After Sarsefield's departure I did not even lie down. It seemed to me that I could not obtain the benefits of repose otherwise than by placing my lady beyond the possibility of danger.

I met Sarsefield the next day. In pursuance of the scheme which had been adopted by us on the preceding evening, a person was selected and commissioned to watch the appearance of Wiatte. The day passed as usual with respect to the lady. In the evening she was surrounded by a few friends. Into this number I was now admitted. Sarsefield and myself made a part of this company. Various topics were discussed with ease and sprightliness. Her societies were composed of both sexes, and seemed to have monopolized all the ingenuity and wit that existed in the metropolis.

After a slight repast the company dispersed. This separation took place earlier than usual on account of a slight indisposition in *Mrs. Lorimer*. Sarsefield and I went out together. We took that opportunity of examining our agent, and receiving no satisfaction from him, we dismissed him, for that night, enjoining him to hold himself in readiness for repeating the experiment to-morrow. My friend directed his steps homeward, and I proceeded to execute a commission, with which I had charged myself.

A few days before, a large sum had been deposited in the hands of a banker, for the use of my lady. It was the amount of a debt which had lately been recovered. It was lodged here for the purpose of being paid on demand of her or her agents. It was my present business to receive this money. I had deferred the performance of this engagement to this late hour, on account of certain preliminaries which were necessary to be adjusted.

Having received this money, I prepared to return home. The inquietude which had been occasioned by Sarsefield's intelligence, had not incapacitated me from performing my usual daily occupations. It was a theme, to which, at every interval of leisure from business or discourse, I did not fail to return. At those times I employed myself in examining the subject on all sides; in supposing particular emergencies, and delineating the conduct that was proper to be observed on each. My daily thoughts were, by no means, so fear-inspiring as the meditations of the night had been.

As soon as I left the banker's door, my meditations fell into this channel. I again reviewed the recent occurrences, and imagined the consequences likely to flow from them. My deductions were not, on this occasion, peculiarly distressful. The return of darkness had added nothing to my apprehensions. I regarded Wiatte merely as one against whose malice it was wise to employ the most vigilant precautions. In revolving these precautions nothing occurred that was new. The danger appeared without unusual aggravations, and the expedients that offered themselves to my choice, were viewed with a temper not more sanguine or despondent than before.

In this state of mind I began and continued my walk. The distance was considerable between my own habitation and that which I had left. My way lay chiefly through populous and well frequented streets. In one part of the way, however, it was at the option of the passenger either to keep along the large streets, or considerably to shorten the journey, by turning into a dark, crooked, and narrow lane. Being familiar with every part of this metropolis, and deeming it advisable to take the shortest and obscurest road, I turned into the alley. I proceeded without interruption to the next turning. One night officer, distinguished by his usual ensigns, was the only person who passed me. I had gone three steps beyond when I perceived a man by my side. I had scarcely time to notice this circumstance, when an hoarse voice exclaimed, "Damn ye villain, ye're a dead man!"

At the same moment a pistol flashed at my ear, and a report followed. This, however, produced no other effect, than, for a short space, to overpower my senses. I staggered back, but did not fall.

The ball, as I afterwards discovered, had grazed my forehead, but without making any dangerous impression. The assassin, perceiving that his pistol had been ineffectual, muttered, in an enraged tone, — This shall do your business — At the same time, he drew a knife forth from his bosom.

I was able to distinguish this action by the rays of a distant lamp, which glistened on the blade. All this passed in an instant. The attack was so abrupt that my thoughts could not be suddenly recalled from the confusion into which they were thrown. My exertions were mechanical. My will might be said to be passive, and it was only by retrospect and a contemplation of consequences, that I became fully informed of the nature of the scene.

If my assailant had disappeared as soon as he had discharged the pistol, my state of extreme surprise might have slowly given place to resolution and activity. As it was, my sense was no sooner struck by the reflection from the blade, than my hand, as if by spontaneous energy, was thrust into my pocket. I drew forth a pistol —

He lifted up his weapon to strike, but it dropped from his powerless fingers. He fell and his groans informed me that I had managed my arms with more skill than my adversary. The noise of this encounter soon attracted spectators. Lights were brought and my antagonist discovered bleeding at my feet. I explained, as briefly as I was able, the scene which they witnessed. The prostrate person was raised by two men, and carried into a public house, nigh at hand.

I had not lost my presence of mind. I, at once, perceived the propriety of administering assistance to the wounded man. I dispatched, therefore, one of the bystanders for a surgeon of considerable eminence, who lived at a small distance, and to whom I was well known. The man was carried into an inner apartment and laid upon the floor. It was not till now that I had a suitable opportunity of ascertaining who it was with whom I had been engaged. I now looked upon his face. The paleness of death could not conceal his well known features. It was Wiatte himself who was breathing his last groans at my feet! . . .

The surgeon, whom I had summoned, attended; but immediately perceived the condition of his patient to be hopeless. In a quarter of an hour he expired. During this interval, he was insensible to all around him. I was known to the surgeon, the landlord and some of the witnesses. The case needed little explanation. The accident reflected no guilt upon me. The landlord was charged with the care of the corse till the morning, and I was allowed to return home, without further impediment.

72

CHAPTER VIII

TILL now my mind had been swayed by the urgencies of this occasion. Those reflections were excluded, which rushed tumultuously upon me, the moment I was at leisure to receive them. Without foresight of a previous moment, an entire change had been wrought in my condition.

I had been oppressed with a sense of the danger that flowed from the existence of this man. By what means the peril could be annihilated, and we be placed in security from his attempts, no efforts of mind could suggest. To devise these means, and employ them with success, demanded, as I conceived, the most powerful sagacity and the firmest courage. Now the danger was no more. The intelligence in which plans of mischief might be generated, was extinguished or flown. Lifeless were the hands ready to execute the dictates of that intelligence. The contriver of enormous evil, was, in one moment, bereft of the power and the will to injure. Our past tranquility had been owing to the belief of his death. Fear and dismay had resumed their dominion when the mistake was discovered. But now we might regain possession of our wonted confidence. I had beheld with my own eyes the lifeless corpse of our implacable adversary. Thus, in a moment, had terminated his long and flagitious career. His restless indignation, his malignant projects, that had so long occupied the stage, and been so fertile of calamity, were now at an end!

73

In the course of my meditations, the idea of the death of this man had occurred, and it bore the appearance of a desirable event. Yet it was little qualified to tranquilise my fears. In the long catalogue of contingencies, this, indeed, was to be found; but it was as little likely to happen as any other. It could not happen without a series of anterior events paving the way for it. If his death came from us, it must be the theme of design. It must spring from laborious circumvention and deep laid stratagems.

No. He was dead. I had killed him. What had I done? I had meditated nothing. I was impelled by an unconscious necessity. Had the assailant been my father the consequence would have been the same. My understanding had been neutral. Could it be? In a space so short, was it possible that so tremendous a deed had been executed? Was I not deceived by some portentous vision? I had witnessed the convulsions and last agonies of Wiatte. He was no more, and I was his destroyer!

Such was the state of my mind for some time after this dreadful event. Previously to it I was calm, considerate, and self-collected. I marked the way that I was going. Passing objects were observed. If I adverted to the series of my own reflections, my attention was not seized and fastened by them. I could disengage myself at pleasure, and could pass, without difficulty, from attention to the world within, to the contemplation of that without.

Now my liberty, in this respect, was at an end. I was fettered, confounded, smitten with excess of thought, and laid prostrate with wonder! I no longer attended to my steps. When I emerged from my stupor, I found that I had trodden back the way which I had lately come, and had arrived within sight of the banker's door. I checked myself, and once more turned my steps homeward.

This seemed to be an hint for entering into new reflections. The deed, said I, is irretreivable. I have killed the brother of my patroness, the father of my love.

This suggestion was new. It instantly involved me in terror and perplexity. How shall I communicate the tidings? What effect will they produce? My lady's sagacity is obscured by the benevolence of her temper. Her brother was sordidly wicked. An hoary ruffian, to whom the language of pity was as unintelligible as the gabble of monkeys. His heart was fortified against compunction, by the atrocious habits of forty years: he lived only to interrupt her peace, to confute the promises of virtue, and convert to rancour and reproach the fair fame of fidelity.

He was her brother still. As an human being, his depravity was never beyond the health-restoring power of repentance. His heart, so long as it beat, was accessible to remorse. The singularity of his birth had made her regard this being as more intimately her brother, than would have happened in different circumstances. It was her obstinate persuasion that their fates were blended. The rumour of his death she had never credited. It was a topic of congratulation to her friends, but of mourning and distress to her. That he would one day reappear upon the stage, and assume the dignity of virtue, was a source of consolation with which she would never consent to part.

Her character was now known. When the doom of exile was pronounced upon him, she deemed it incumbent on her to vindicate herself from aspersions founded on misconceptions of her motives in refusing her interference. The manuscript, though unpublished, was widely circulated. None could resist her simple and touching eloquence, nor rise from the perusal without resigning his heart to the most impetuous impulses of admiration, and enlisting himself among the eulogists of her justice and her fortitude. This was the only monument, in a written form, of her genius. As such it was engraven on my memory. The picture that it described was the perpetual companion of my thoughts.

Alas! It had, perhaps, been well for me if it had been buried in eternal oblivion. I read in it the condemnation of my deed, the agonies she was preparing to suffer, and the indignation that would overflow upon the author of so signal a calamity.

I had rescued my life by the sacrifice of his. Whereas I should have died. Wretched and precipitate coward! What had become of my boasted gratitude? Such was the zeal that I had vowed to her. Such the services which it was the business of my life to perform. I had snatched her brother from existence. I had torn from her the hope which she so ardently and indefatigably cherished. From a contemptible and dastardly regard to my own safety I had failed in the moment of trial, and when called upon by heaven to evince the sincerity of my professions.

She had treated my professions lightly. My vows of eternal devotion she had rejected with lofty disinterestedness. She had arraigned my impatience of obligation as criminal, and condemned every scheme I had projected for freeing myself from the burthen which her beneficence had laid upon me. The impassioned and vehement anxiety with which, in former days, she had deprecated the vengeance of her lover against Wiatte, rung in my ears. My senses were shocked anew by the dreadful sounds "Touch not my brother. Wherever you meet with him, of whatever outrage he be guilty, suffer him to pass in safety. Despise me: abandon me: kill me. All this I can bear even from you, but spare, I implore you, my unhappy brother. The stroke that deprives him of life will not only have the same effect upon me, but will set my portion in everlasting misery."

To these supplications I had been deaf. It is true I had not rushed upon him unarmed, intending no injury nor expecting any. Of that degree of wickedness I was, perhaps, incapable. Alas! I have immersed myself sufficiently deep in crimes. I have trampled under foot every motive dear to the heart of honour. I have shewn myself unworthy the society of men.

Such were the turbulent suggestions of that moment. My pace slackened. I stopped and was obliged to support myself against a wall. The sickness that had seized my heart penetrated every part of my frame. There was but one thing wanting to complete my distraction. . . . My lady, said I, believed her fate to be blended with that of Wiatte. Who shall affirm that the persuasion is a groundless one? She had lived and prospered, notwithstanding the general belief that her brother was dead. She would not hearken to the rumour. Why? Because nothing less than indubitable evidence would suffice to convince her? Because the counter-intimation flowed from an infallible source? How can the latter supposition be confuted? Has she not predicted the event?

The period of terrible fulfilment has arrived. The same blow that bereaved *him* of life, has likewise ratified her doom.

She has been deceived. It is nothing more, perhaps, than a fond imagination. . . . It matters not. Who knows not the cogency of faith? That the pulses of life are at the command of the will? The bearer of these tidings will be the messenger of death. A fatal sympathy will seize her. She will shrink, and swoon, and perish at the news!

Fond and short-sighted wretch! This is the price thou hast given for security. In the rashness of thy thought thou said'st, Nothing is wanting but his death to restore us to confidence and safety. Lo! the purchase is made. Havock and despair, that were restrained during his life, were let loose by his last sigh. Now only is destruction made sure. Thy lady, thy Clarice, thy friend, and thyself, are, by this act, involved in irretreivable and common ruin!

I started from my attitude. I was scarcely conscious of any transition. The interval was fraught with stupor and amazement. It seemed as if my senses had been hushed in sleep, while the powers of locomotion were unconsciously exerted to bear me to my chamber. By whatever means the change was effected, there I was. . . .

I have been able to proceed thus far. I can scarcely believe the testimony of my memory that assures me of this. My task is almost executed, but whence shall I obtain strength enough to finish it? What I have told is light as gossamer, compared with the insupportable and crushing horrors of that which is to come. Heaven, in token of its vengeance, will enable me to proceed. It is fitting that my scene should thus close.

My fancy began to be infected with the errors of my understanding. The mood into which my mind was plunged was incapable of any propitious intermission. All within me was tempestuous and dark. My ears were accessible to no sounds but those of shrieks and lamentations. It was deepest midnight, and all the noises of a great metropolis were hushed. Yet I listened as if to catch some strain of the dirge that was begun. Sable robes, sobs and a dreary solemnity encompassed me on all sides. I was haunted to despair by images of death, imaginary clamours, and the train of funeral pageantry. I seemed to have passed forward to a distant era of my life. The effects which were to come were already realized. The foresight of misery created it, and set me in the midst of that hell which I feared.

From a paroxysm like this the worst might reasonably be dreaded, yet the next step to destruction was not suddenly taken. I paused on the brink of the precipice, as if to survey the depth of that phrensy that invaded me; was able to ponder on the scene, and deliberate, in a state that partook of calm, on the circumstances of my situation. My mind was harrassed by the repetition of one idea. Conjecture deepened into certainty. I could place the object in no light which did not corroborate the persuasion that, in the act committed, I had ensured the destruction of my lady. At length my mind, somewhat relieved from the tempest of my fears, began to trace and analize the consequences which I dreaded.

The fate of Wiatte would inevitably draw along with it that of his sister. In what way would this effect be produced? Were they linked together by a sympathy whose influence was independent of sensible communication? Could she arrive at a knowledge of his miserable end by other than verbal means? I had heard of such extraordinary co-partnerships in being and modes of instantaneous intercourse among beings locally distant. Was this a new instance of the subtlety of mind? Had she already endured his agonies, and like him already ceased to breathe?

Every hair bristled at this horrible suggestion. But the force of sympathy might be chimerical. Buried in sleep, or engaged in careless meditation, the instrument by which her destiny might be accomplished, was the steel of an assassin. A series of events, equally beyond the reach of foresight, with those which had just happened, might introduce, with equal abruptness, a similar disaster. What, at that moment, was her condition? Reposing in safety in her chamber, as her family imagined. But were they not deceived? Was she not a mangled corse? Whatever were her situation, it could not be ascertained, except by extraordinary means, till the morning. Was it wise to defer the scrutiny till then? Why not instantly investigate the truth?

These ideas passed rapidly through my mind. A considerable portion of time and amplification of phrase are necessary to exhibit, verbally, ideas contemplated in a space of incalculable brevity. With the same rapidity I conceived the resolution of determining the truth of my suspicions. All the family, but myself, were at rest. Winding passages would conduct me, without danger of disturbing them, to the hall from which double staircases ascended. One of these led to a saloon above, on the east side of which was a door that communicated with a suit of rooms, occupied by the lady of the mansion. The first was an antichamber, in which a female servant usually lay. The second was the lady's own bed-chamber. This was a sacred recess, with whose situation, relative to the other apartments of the building, I was well acquainted, but of which I knew nothing from my own examination, having never been admitted into it.

Thither I was now resolved to repair. I was not deterred by the sanctity of the place and hour. I was insensible to all consequences but the removal of my doubts. Not that my hopes were balanced by my fears. That the same tragedy had been performed in her chamber and in the street, nothing hindered me from believing with as much cogency as if my own eyes had witnessed it, but the reluctance with which we admit a detestable truth.

To terminate a state of intolerable suspense, I resolved to proceed forthwith to her chamber. I took the light and paced, with no interruption, along the galleries. I used no precaution. If I had met a servant or robber, I am not sure that I should have noticed him. My attention was too perfectly engrossed to allow me to spare any to a casual object. I cannot affirm that no one observed me. This, however, was probable from the distribution of the dwelling. It consisted of a central edifice and two wings, one of which was appropriated to domestics, and the other, at the extremity of which my apartment was placed, comprehended a library, and rooms for formal, and social, and literary conferences. These, therefore, were deserted at night, and my way lay along these. Hence it was not likely that my steps would be observed.

I proceeded to the hall. The principal parlour was beneath her chamber. In the confusion of my thoughts I mistook one for the other. I rectified, as soon as I detected my mistake. I ascended, with a beating heart, the staircase. The door of the antichamber was unfastened. I entered, totally regardless of disturbing the girl who slept within. The bed which she occupied was concealed by curtains. Whether she were there, I did not stop to examine. I cannot recollect that any tokens were given of wakefulness or alarm. It was not till I reached the door of her own apartment that my heart began to falter.

It was now that the momentousness of the question I was about to decide, rushed with its genuine force, upon my apprehension. Appaled and aghast, I had scarcely power to move the bolt. If the imagination of her death was not to be supported, how should I bear the spectacle of wounds and blood? Yet this was reserved for me. A few paces would set me in the midst of a scene, of which I was the abhorred contriver. Was it right to proceed? There were still the remnants of doubt. My forebodings might possibly be groundless. All within might be safety and serenity. A respite might be gained from the execution of an irrevocable sentence. What could I do? Was not any thing easy to endure in comparison with the agonies of suspense? If I could not obviate the evil I must bear it, but the torments of suspense were susceptible of remedy.

I drew back the bolt, and entered with the reluctance of fear, rather than the cautiousness of guilt. I could not lift my eyes from the ground. I advanced to the middle of the room. Not a sound like that of the dying saluted my ear. At length, shaking off the fetters of hopelesness, I looked up. . . .

I saw nothing calculated to confirm my fears. Every where there reigned quiet and order. My heart leaped with exultation. Can it be, said I, that I have been betrayed with shadows? . . . But this is not sufficient. . . .

Within an alcove was the bed that belonged to her. If her safety were inviolate, it was here that she reposed. What remained to convert tormenting doubt into ravishing certainty? I was insensible to the perils of my present situation. If she, indeed, were there, would not my intrusion awaken her? She would start and perceive me, at this hour, standing at her bed-side. How should I account for an intrusion so unexampled and audacious? I could not communicate my fears. I could not tell her that the blood with which my hands were stained had flowed from the wounds of her brother.

My mind was inaccessible to such considerations. They did not even modify my predominant idea. Obstacles like these, had they existed, would have been trampled under foot.

Leaving the lamp, that I bore, on the table, I approached the bed. I slowly drew aside the curtain and beheld her tranquilly slumbering. I listened, but so profound was her sleep that not even her breathings could be overheard. I dropped the curtain and retired.

How blissful and mild were the illuminations of my

bosom at this discovery. A joy that surpassed all utterance succeeded the fierceness of desperation. I stood, for some moments, wrapt in delightful contemplation. Alas! It was a luminous but transient interval. The madness, to whose black suggestions it bore so strong a contrast, began now to make sensible approaches on my understanding.

True, said I, she lives. Her slumber is serene and happy. She is blind to her approaching destiny. Some hours will at least be rescued from anguish and death. When she wakes the phantom that soothed her will vanish. The tidings cannot be withheld from her. The murderer of thy brother cannot hope to enjoy thy smiles. Those ravishing accents, with which thou hast used to greet me, will be changed. Scouling and reproaches, the invectives of thy anger and the maledictions of thy justice will rest upon my head.

What is the blessing which I made the theme of my boastful arrogance? This interval of being and repose is momentary. She will awake but only to perish at the spectacle of my ingratitude. She will awake only to the consciousness of instantly impending death. When she again sleeps she will wake no more. I her son, I, whom the law of my birth doomed to poverty and hardship, but whom her unsolicited beneficence snatched from those evils, and endowed with the highest good known to intelligent beings, the consolations of science and the blandishments of affluence; to whom the darling of her life, the offspring in whom are faithfully preserved the lineaments of its angelic mother, she has not denied! . . . What is the recompense that I have made? How have I discharged the measureless debt of gratitude to which she is entitled? Thus! . . .

Cannot my guilt be extenuated? Is there not a good that I can do thee? Must I perpetrate unmingled evil? Is the province assigned me that of an infernal emissary, whose efforts are concentred in a single purpose and that purpose a malignant one? I am the author of thy calamities. Whatever misery is reserved for thee, I am the source whence it flows. Can I not set bounds to the stream? Cannot I prevent thee from returning to a consciousness which, till it ceases to exist, will not cease to be rent and mangled?

Yes. It is in my power to screen thee from the coming storm: to accelerate thy journey to rest. I will do it. . . .

The impulse was not to be resisted. I moved with the suddenness of lightning. Armed with a pointed implement that lay . . . it was a dagger. As I set down the lamp, I struck the edge. Yet I saw it not, or noticed it not till I needed its assistance. By what accident it came hither, to what deed of darkness it had already been subservient, I had no power to inquire. I stepped to the table and seized it.

The time which this action required was insufficient to save me. My doom was ratified by powers which no human energies can counterwork. . . . Need I go farther? Did you entertain any imagination of so frightful a catastrophe? I am overwhelmed by turns with dismay and with wonder. I am prompted by turns to tear my heart from my breast, and deny faith to the verdict of my senses.

Was it I that hurried to the deed? No. It was the dæmon that possessed me. My limbs were guided to the bloody office by a power foreign and superior to mine. I had been defrauded, for a moment, of the empire of my muscles. A little moment for that sufficed.

If my destruction had not been decreed why was the image of Clarice so long excluded? Yet why do I say long? The fatal resolution was conceived, and I hastened to the execution, in a period too brief for more than itself to be viewed by the intellect.

What then? Were my hands embrued in this precious blood? Was it to this extremity of horror that my evil genius was determined to urge me? Too surely this was his purpose; too surely I was qualified to be its minister.

I lifted the weapon. Its point was aimed at the bosom of the sleeper. The impulse was given. . . .

At the instant a piercing shriek was uttered behind me,

and a stretched-out hand, grasping the blade, made it swerve widely from its aim. It descended, but without inflicting a wound. Its force was spent upon the bed.

O! for words to paint that stormy transition! I loosed my hold of the dagger. I started back, and fixed eyes of frantic curiosity on the author of my rescue. He that interposed to arrest my deed, that started into being and activity at a moment so pregnant with fate, without tokens of his purpose or his coming being previously imparted, could not, methought, be less than divinity.

The first glance that I darted on this being corroborated my conjecture. It was the figure and the lineaments of Mrs. Lorimer. Negligently habited in flowing and brilliant white, with features bursting with terror and wonder, the likeness of that being who was stretched upon the bed, now stood before me.

All that I am able to conceive of angel was comprised in the moral constitution of this woman. That her genius had overleaped all bounds, and interposed to save her, was no audacious imagination. In the state in which my mind then was no other belief than this could occupy the first place.

My tongue was tied. I gazed by turns upon her who stood before me, and her who lay upon the bed, and who, awakened by the shriek that had been uttered, now opened her eyes. She started from her pillow, and, by assuming a new and more distinct attitude, permitted me to recognize *Clarice herself!*

Three days before, I had left her, beside the bed of a dying friend, at a solitary mansion in the mountains of Donnegal. Here it had been her resolution to remain till her friend should breathe her last. Fraught with this persuasion; knowing this to be the place and hour of repose of my lady, hurried forward by the impetuosity of my own conceptions, deceived by the faint gleam which penetrated through the curtain and imperfectly irradiated features which bore, at all times, a powerful resemblance to those of Mrs. Lorimer, I had rushed to the brink of this terrible precipice!

Why did I linger on the verge? Why, thus perilously situated, did I not throw myself headlong? The steel was yet in my hand. A single blow would have pierced my heart, and shut out from my remembrance and foresight the past and the future.

The moment of insanity had gone by, and I was once more myself. Instead of regarding the act which I had meditated as the dictate of compassion or of justice, it only added to the sum of my ingratitude, and gave wings to the whirlwind that was sent to bear me to perdition.

Perhaps I was influenced by a sentiment which I had not leisure to distribute into parts. My understanding was, no doubt, bewildered in the maze of consequences which would spring from my act. How should I explain my coming hither in this murderous guise, my arm lifted to destroy the idol of my soul, and the darling child of my patroness? In what words should I unfold the tale of Wiatte, and enumerate the motives that terminated in the present scene? What penalty had not my infatuation and cruelty deserved? What could I less than turn the dagger's point against my own bosom?

A second time, the blow was thwarted and diverted. Once more this beneficent interposer held my arm from the perpetration of a new iniquity. Once more frustrated the instigations of that dæmon, of whose malice a mysterious destiny had consigned me to be the sport and the prey.

Every new moment added to the sum of my inexpiable guilt. Murder was succeeded, in an instant, by the more detestable enormity of suicide. She, to whom my ingratitude was flagrant in proportion to the benefits of which she was the author, had now added to her former acts, that of rescuing me from the last of mischiefs.

I threw the weapon on the floor. The zeal which prompted her to seize my arm, this action occasioned to subside, and to yield place to those emotions which this spectacle was calculated to excite. She watched me in silence, and with an air of ineffable solicitude. Clarice, governed by the instinct of modesty, wrapt her bosom and face in the bed-clothes, and testified her horror by vehement, but scarcely articulate exclamations.

I moved forward, but my steps were random and tottering. My thoughts were fettered by reverie, and my gesticulations destitute of meaning. My tongue faltered without speaking, and I felt as if life and death were struggling within me for the mastery.

My will, indeed, was far from being neutral in this contest. To such as I, annihilation is the supreme good. To shake off the ills that fasten on us by shaking off existence, is a lot which the system of nature has denied to man. By escaping from life, I should be delivered from this scene, but should only rush into a world of retribution, and be immersed in new agonies.

I was yet to live. No instrument of my deliverance was within reach. I was powerless. To rush from the presence of these women, to hide me forever from their scrutiny, and their upbraiding, to snatch from their minds all traces of the existence of Clithero, was the scope of unutterable longings.

Urged to flight by every motive of which my nature was susceptible, I was yet rooted to the spot. Had the pause been only to be interrupted by me, it would have lasted forever.

At length, the lady, clasping her hands and lifting them, exclaimed, in a tone melting into pity and grief:

Clithero! what is this? How came you hither and why?

I struggled for utterance: I came to murder you. Your brother has perished by my hands. Fresh from the commission of this deed, I have hastened hither, to perpetrate the same crime upon you.

My brother! replied the lady, with new vehemence, O! say not so! I have just heard of his return from Sarsefield and that he lives.

He is dead, repeated I, with fierceness: I know it. It was I that killed him.

Dead! she faintly articulated. And by thee Clithero? O! cursed chance that hindered thee from killing me also!

Dead! Then is the omen fulfilled! Then am I undone! Lost forever!

Her eyes now wandered from me, and her countenance sunk into a wild and rueful expression. Hope was utterly extinguished in her heart, and life forsook her at the same moment. She sunk upon the floor pallid and breathless. . . .

How she came into possession of this knowledge I know not. It is possible that Sarsefield had repented of concealment, and, in the interval that passed between our separation and my encounter with Wiatte, had returned, and informed her of the reappearance of this miscreant.

Thus then was my fate consummated. I was rescued from destroying her by a dagger, only to behold her perish by the tidings which I brought. Thus was every omen of mischief and misery fulfilled. Thus was the enmity of Wiatte, rendered efficacious, and the instrument of his destruction, changed into the executioner of his revenge.

Such is the tale of my crimes. It is not for me to hope that the curtain of oblivion will ever shut out the dismal spectacle. It will haunt me forever. The torments that grow out of it, can terminate only with the thread of my existence, but that I know full well will never end. Death is but a shifting of the scene, and the endless progress of eternity, which, to the good, is merely the perfection of felicity, is, to the wicked, an accumulation of woe. The self-destroyer is his own enemy; this has ever been my opinion. Hitherto it has influenced my action. Now, though the belief continues, its influence on my conduct is annihilated. I am no stranger to the depth of that abyss, into which I shall plunge. No matter. Change is precious for its own sake.

Well: I was still to live. My abode must be somewhere fixed. My conduct was henceforth the result of a perverse and rebellious principle. I banished myself forever from my native soil. I vowed never more to behold the face of my Clarice, to abandon my friends, my books, all my wonted labours, and accustomed recreations.

I was neither ashamed nor afraid. I considered not in what way the justice of the country would affect me. It merely made no part of my contemplations. I was not embarrassed by the choice of expedients, for trammeling up the visible consequences and for eluding suspicion. The idea of abjuring my country, and flying forever from the hateful scene, partook, to my apprehension, of the vast, the boundless, and strange: of plunging from the height of fortune to obscurity and indigence, corresponded with my present state of mind. It was of a piece with the tremendous and wonderful events that had just happened.

These were the images that haunted me, while I stood speechlessly gazing at the ruin before me. I heard a noise from without, or imagined that I heard it. My reverie was broken, and my muscular power restored. I descended into the street, through doors of which I possessed one set of keys, and hurried by the shortest way beyond the precincts of the city. I had laid no plan. My conceptions, with regard to the future, were shapeless and confused. Successive incidents supplied me with a clue, and suggested, as they rose, the next step to be taken.

I threw off the garb of affluence, and assumed a beggar's attire. That I had money about me for the accomplishment of my purposes was wholly accidental. I travelled along the coast, and when I arrived at one town, knew not why I should go further; but my restlessness was unabated, and change was some relief. I at length arrived at Belfast. A vessel was preparing for America. I embraced eagerly the opportunity of passing into a new world. I arrived at Philadelphia. As soon as I landed I wandered hither, and was content to wear out my few remaining days in the service of Inglefield.

I have no friends. Why should I trust my story to another? I have no solicitude about concealment; but who is there who will derive pleasure or benefit from my rehearsal? And why should I expatiate on so hateful a theme? Yet now have I consented to this. I have confided in you the history of my disasters. I am not fearful of the use that you may be disposed to make of it. I shall quickly set myself beyond the reach of human tribunals. I shall relieve the ministers of law from the trouble of punishing. The recent events which induced you to summon me to this conference, have likewise determined me to make this disclosure.

I was not aware, for some time, of my perturbed sleep. No wonder that sleep cannot soothe miseries like mine: that I am alike infested by memory in wakefulness and slumber. Yet I was anew distressed at the discovery that my thoughts found their way to my lips, without my being conscious of it, and that my steps wandered forth unknowingly and without the guidance of my will.

The story you have told is not incredible. The disaster to which you allude did not fail to excite my regret. I can still weep over the untimely fall of youth and worth. I can no otherwise account for my frequenting this shade than by the distant resemblance which the death of this man bore to that of which I was the perpetrator. This resemblance occurred to me at first. If time were able to weaken the impression which was produced by my crime, this similitude was adapted to revive and inforce them.

The wilderness, and the cave to which you followed me, were familiar to my sunday rambles. Often have I indulged in audible griefs on the cliffs of that valley. Often have I brooded over my sorrows in the recesses of that cavern. This scene is adapted to my temper. Its mountainous asperities supply me with images of desolation and seclusion, and its headlong streams lull me into temporary forgetfulness of mankind.

I comprehend you. You suspect me of concern in the death of Waldegrave. You could not do otherwise. The conduct that you have witnessed was that of a murderer. I will not upbraid you for your suspicions, though I have bought exemption from them at an high price.

CHAPTER IX

THERE ended his narrative. He started from the spot where he stood, and, without affording me any opportunity of replying or commenting, disappeared amidst the thickest of the wood. I had no time to exert myself for his detention. I could have used no arguments for this end, to which it is probable he would have listened. The story I had heard was too extraordinary, too completely the reverse of all my expectations, to allow me to attend to the intimations of self-murder which he dropped.

The secret, which I imagined was about to be disclosed, was as inscrutable as ever. Not a circumstance, from the moment when Clithero's character became the subject of my meditations, till the conclusion of his tale, but served to confirm my suspicion. Was this error to be imputed to credulity? Would not any one, from similar appearances, have drawn similar conclusions? Or is there a criterion by which truth can always be distinguished? Was it owing to my imperfect education that the inquietudes of this man were not traced to a deed performed at the distance of a thousand leagues, to the murder of his patroness and friend?

I had heard a tale which apparently related to scenes and persons far distant, but though my suspicions have appeared to have been misplaced, what should hinder but that the death of my friend was, in like manner, an act of momentary insanity and originated in a like spirit of mistaken benevolence?

But I did not consider this tale merely in relation to myself. My life had been limited and uniform. I had communed with romancers and historians, but the impression made upon me by this incident was unexampled in my experience. My reading had furnished me with no instance, in any degree, parallel to this, and I found that to be a distant and second-hand spectator of events was widely different from witnessing them myself and partaking in their consequences. My judgement was, for a time, sunk into imbecility and confusion. My mind was full of the images unavoidably suggested by this tale, but they existed in a kind of chaos, and not otherwise, than gradually, was I able to reduce them to distinct particulars, and subject them to a deliberate and methodical inspection.

How was I to consider this act of Clithero? What a deplorable infatuation! Yet it was the necessary result of a series of ideas mutually linked and connected. His conduct was dictated by a motive allied to virtue. It was the fruit of an ardent and grateful spirit.

The death of Wiatte could not be censured. The life of Clithero was unspeakably more valuable than that of his antagonist. It was the instinct of self-preservation that swayed him. He knew not his adversary in time enough, to govern himself by that knowledge. Had the assailant been an unknown ruffian, his death would have been followed by no remorse. The spectacle of his dying agonies would have dwelt upon the memory of his assassin like any other mournful sight, in the production of which he bore no part.

It must at least be said that his will was not concerned in this transaction. He acted in obedience to an impulse which he could not controul, nor resist. Shall we impute guilt where there is no design? Shall a man extract food for self-reproach from an action to which it is not enough to say that he was actuated by no culpable intention, but that he was swayed by no intention whatever? If consequences arise that cannot be foreseen, shall we find no refuge in the persuasion of our rectitude and of human frailty? Shall we deem ourselves criminal because we do not enjoy the attributes of deity? Because our power and our knowledge are confined by impassable boundaries?

But whence arose the subsequent intention? It was the fruit of a dreadful mistake. His intents were noble and compassionate. But this is of no avail to free him from the imputation of guilt. No remembrance of past beneficence can compensate for this crime. The scale, loaded with the recriminations of his conscience, is immovable by any counter-weight.

But what are the conclusions to be drawn by dispassionate observers? Is it possible to regard this person with disdain or with enmity? The crime originated in those limitations which nature has imposed upon human faculties. Proofs of a just intention are all that are requisite to exempt us from blame. He is thus in consequence of a double mistake. The light in which he views this event is erroneous. He judges wrong and is therefore miserable.

How imperfect are the grounds of all our decisions! Was it of no use to superintend his childhood, to select his instructors and examples, to mark the operations of his principles, to see him emerging into youth, to follow him through various scenes and trying vicissitudes, and mark the uniformity of his integrity? Who would have predicted his future conduct? Who would not have affirmed the impossibility of an action like this?

How mysterious was the connection between the fate of Wiatte and his sister! By such circuitous, and yet infallible means, were the prediction of the lady and the vengeance of the brother accomplished! In how many cases may it be said, as in this, that the prediction was the cause of its own fulfilment? That the very act, which considerate observers, and even himself, for a time, imagined to have utterly precluded the execution of Wiatte's menaces, should be that inevitably leading to it? That the execution should be assigned to him, who, abounding in abhor-rence, and in the act of self-defence, was the slayer of the menacer?

As the obstructor of his designs, Wiatte way-laid and assaulted Clithero. He perished in the attempt. Were his designs frustrated? . . . No. It was thus that he secured the gratification of his vengeance. His sister was cut off in the bloom of life and prosperity. By a refinement of good fortune, the voluntary minister of his malice had entailed upon himself exile without reprieve and misery without end.

But what chiefly excited my wonder was the connection of this tale with the destiny of Sarsefield. This was he whom I have frequently mentioned to you as my precep-tor. About four years previous to this era, he appeared in this district without fortune or friend. He desired, one evening, to be accomodated at my uncle's house. The conversation turning on the objects of his journey, and his present situation, he professed himself in search of lucra-tive employment. My uncle proposed to him to become a teacher, there being a sufficient number of young people in this neighbourhood to afford him occupation and sub-sistence. He found it his interest to embrace this proposal.

I, of course, became his pupil, and demeaned myself in such a manner as speedily to grow into a favourite. He communicated to us no part of his early history, but informed us sufficiently of his adventures in Asia and Italy, to make it plain that this was the same person alluded to by Clithero. During his abode among us his conduct was irreproachable. When he left us, he mani-fested the most poignant regret, but this originated chiefly in his regard to me. He promised to maintain with me an epistolary intercourse. Since his departure, how-ever, I had heard nothing respecting him. It was with unspeakable regret that I now heard of the disappoint-ment of his hopes, and was inquisitive respecting the measures which he would adopt in his new situation. Per-haps he would once more return to America, and I should again be admitted to the enjoyment of his society. This event I anticipated with the highest satisfaction.

At present, the fate of the unhappy Clithero was the subject of abundant anxiety. On his suddenly leaving me, at the conclusion of his tale, I supposed that he had gone upon one of his usual rambles, and that it would terminate only with the day. Next morning a message was received from Inglefield inquiring if any one knew what had become of his servant. I could not listen to this message with tranquility. I recollected the hints that he had given of some design upon his life, and admitted the most dreary forebodings. I speeded to Inglefield's. Clithero had not returned, they told me, the preceding evening. He had not apprized them of any intention to change his abode. His boxes, and all that composed his slender property, were found in their ordinary state. He had expressed no dissatisfaction with his present condition.

Several days passed, and no tidings could be procured of him. His absence was a topic of general speculation, but was a source of particular anxiety to no one but myself. My apprehensions were surely built upon sufficient grounds. From the moment that we parted, no one had seen or heard of him. What mode of suicide he had selected, he had disabled us from discovering, by the impenetrable secrecy in which he had involved it.

In the midst of my reflections upon this subject, the idea of the wilderness occurred. Could he have executed his design in the deepest of its recesses? These were unvisited by human footsteps, and his bones might lie for ages in this solitude without attracting observation. To seek them where they lay, to gather them together and provide for them a grave, was a duty which appeared incumbent on me, and of which the performance was connected with a thousand habitual sentiments and mixed pleasures.

Thou knowest my devotion to the spirit that breathes its inspiration in the gloom of forests and on the verge of streams. I love to immerse myself in shades and dells, and hold converse with the solemnities and secrecies of nature

94

in the rude retreats of Norwalk. The disappearance of Clithero had furnished new incitements to ascend its cliffs and pervade its thickets, as I cherished the hope of meeting in my rambles, with some traces of this man. But might he not still live? His words had imparted the belief that he intended to destroy himself. This catastrophe, however, was far from certain. Was it not in my power to avert it? Could I not restore a mind thus vigorous, to tranquil and wholesome existence? Could I not subdue his perverse disdain and immeasurable abhorrence of himself? His upbraiding and his scorn were unmerited and misplaced. Perhaps they argued phrensy rather than prejudice; but phrensy, like prejudice, was curable. Reason was no less an antidote to the illusions of insanity like his, than to the illusions of error.

I did not immediately recollect that to subsist in this desert was impossible. Nuts were the only fruits it produced, and these were inadequate to sustain human life. If it were haunted by Clithero, he must occasionally pass its limits and beg or purloin victuals. This deportment was too humiliating and flagitious to be imputed to him. There was reason to suppose him smitten with the charms of solitude, of a lonely abode in the midst of mountainous and rugged nature; but this could not be uninterruptedly enjoyed. Life could be supported only by occasionally visiting the haunts of men, in the guise of a thief or a mendicant. Hence, since Clithero was not known to have reappeared, at any farm-house in the neighbourhood, I was compelled to conclude, either that he had retired far from this district, or that he was dead.

Though I designed that my leisure should chiefly be consumed in the bosom of Norwalk, I almost dismissed the hope of meeting with the fugitive. There were indeed two sources of my hopelessness on this occasion. Not only was it probable that Clithero had fled far away, but, should he have concealed himself in some nook or cavern, within these precincts, his concealment was not to be traced. This arose from the nature of that sterile region.

It would not be easy to describe the face of this district, in a few words. Half of Solebury, thou knowest, admits neither of plough nor spade. The cultivable space lies along the river, and the desert, lying on the north, has gained, by some means, the apellation of Norwalk. Canst thou imagine a space, somewhat circular, about six miles in diameter, and exhibiting a perpetual and intricate variety of craggy eminences and deep dells?

The hollows are single, and walled around by cliffs, ever varying in shape and height, and have seldom any perceptible communication with each other. These hollows are of all dimensions, from the narrowness and depth of a well, to the amplitude of one hundred yards. Winter's snow is frequently found in these cavities at midsummer. The streams that burst forth from every crevice, are thrown, by the irregularities of the surface, into numberless cascades, often disappear in mists or in chasms, and emerge from subterranean channels, and, finally, either subside into lakes, or quietly meander through the lower and more level grounds.

Wherever nature left a flat it is made rugged and scarcely passable by enormous and fallen trunks, accumulated by the storms of ages, and forming, by their slow decay, a moss-covered soil, the haunt of rabbets and lizards. These spots are obscured by the melancholy umbrage of pines, whose eternal murmurs are in unison with vacancy and solitude, with the reverberations of the torrents and the whistling of the blasts. Hiccory and poplar, which abound in the low-lands, find here no fostering elements.

A sort of continued vale, winding and abrupt, leads into the midst of this region and through it. This vale serves the purpose of a road. It is a tedious maze, and perpetual declivity, and requires, from the passenger, a cautious and sure foot. Openings and ascents occasionally present themselves on each side, which seem to promise you access to the interior region, but always terminate, sooner or later, in insuperable difficulties, at the verge of a precipice, or the bottom of a steep.

Perhaps no one was more acquainted with this wilderness than I, but my knowledge was extremely imperfect. I had traversed parts of it, at an early age, in pursuit of berries and nuts, or led by a roaming disposition. Afterwards the sphere of my rambles was enlarged and their purpose changed. When Sarsefield came among us, I became his favourite scholar and the companion of all his pedestrian excursions. He was fond of penetrating into these recesses, partly from the love of picturesque scenes, partly to investigate its botanical and mineral productions, and, partly to carry on more effectually that species of instruction which he had adopted with regard to me, and which chiefly consisted in moralizing narratives or synthetical reasonings. These excursions had familiarized me with its outlines and most accessible parts; but there was much which, perhaps, could never be reached without wings, and much the only paths to which I might forever overlook.

Every new excursion indeed added somewhat to my knowledge. New tracks were pursued, new prospects detected, and new summits were gained. My rambles were productive of incessant novelty, though they always terminated in the prospect of limits that could not be overleaped. But none of these had led me wider from my customary paths than that which had taken place when in pursuit of Clithero. I had faint remembrance of the valley, into which I had descended after him, but till then I had viewed it at a distance, and supposed it impossible to reach the bottom but by leaping from a precipice some hundred feet in height. The opposite steep seemed no less inaccessible, and the cavern at the bottom was impervious to any views which my former positions had enabled me to take of it.

My intention to re-examine this cave and ascertain whither it led, had, for a time, been suspended by different considerations. It was now revived with more energy than ever. I reflected that this had formerly been haunted by Clithero, and might possibly have been the scene of the desperate act which he had meditated. It might at least conceal some token of his past existence. It might lead into spaces hitherto unvisited, and to summits from which wider landscapes might be seen.

One morning I set out to explore this scene. The road which Clithero had taken was laboriously circuitous. On my return from the first pursuit of him, I ascended the cliff in my former footsteps, but soon lighted on the beaten track which I had already described. This enabled me to shun a thousand obstacles, which had lately risen before me, and opened an easy passage to the cavern.

I once more traversed this way. The brow of the hill was gained. The ledges of which it consisted, afforded sufficient footing, when the attempt was made, though viewed at a distance they seemed to be too narrow for that purpose. As I descended the rugged stair, I could not but wonder at the temerity and precipitation with which this descent had formerly been made. It seemed as if the noon-day-light and the tardiest circumspection would scarcely enable me to accomplish it, yet then it had been done with headlong speed, and with no guidance but the moon's uncertain rays.

I reached the mouth of the cave. Till now I had forgotten that a lamp or a torch might be necessary to direct my subterranean footsteps. I was unwilling to defer the attempt. Light might possibly be requisite, if the cave had no other outlet. Somewhat might present itself within to the eyes, which might forever elude the hands, but I was more inclined to consider it merely as an avenue, terminating in an opening on the summit of the steep, or on the opposite side of the ridge. Caution might supply the place of light, or, having explored the cave as far as possible at present, I might hereafter return, better furnished for the scrutiny.

CHAPTER X

W ITH these determinations, I proceeded. The
entrance was low, and compelled me to resort
to hands as well as feet. At a few yards from the
mouth the light disappeared, and I found myself
immersed in the dunnest obscurity. Had I not been persuaded that another had gone before me, I should have
relinquished the attempt. I proceeded with the utmost
caution, always ascertaining, by out-stretched arms, the
height and breadth of the cavity before me. In a short
time the dimensions expanded on all sides, and permitted
me to resume my feet.

I walked upon a smooth and gentle declivity. Presently
the wall, on one side, and the ceiling receded beyond my
reach. I began to fear that I should be involved in a maze,
and should be disabled from returning. To obviate this
danger it was requisite to adhere to the nearest wall, and
conform to the direction which it should take, without
straying through the palpable obscurity. Whether the ceiling was lofty or low, whether the opposite wall of the
passage was distant or near, this, I deemed no proper
opportunity to investigate.

In a short time, my progress was stopped by an abrupt
descent. I set down the advancing foot with caution,
being aware that I might at the next step encounter a
bottomless pit. To the brink of such an one I seemed now
to have arrived. I stooped, and stretched my hand forward and downward, but all was vacuity.

Here it was needful to pause. I had reached the brink of a cavity whose depth it was impossible to ascertain. It might be a few inches beyond my reach, or hundreds of feet. By leaping down I might incur no injury, or might plunge into a lake or dash myself to pieces on the points of rocks.

I now saw with new force the propriety of being furnished with a light. The first suggestion was to return upon my footsteps, and resume my undertaking on the morrow. Yet, having advanced thus far, I felt reluctance to recede without accomplishing my purposes. I reflected likewise that Clithero had boldly entered this recess, and had certainly come forth at a different avenue from that at which he entered.

At length it occurred to me, that though I could not go forward, yet I might proceed along the edge of this cavity. This edge would be as safe a guidance, and would serve as well for a clue by which I might return, as the wall which it was now necessary to forsake.

Intense dark is always the parent of fears. Impending injuries cannot in this state be descried, nor shunned, nor repelled. I began to feel some faltering of my courage and seated myself, for a few minutes, on a stoney mass which arose before me. My situation was new. The caverns I had hitherto met with, in this desert, were chiefly formed of low-browed rocks. They were chambers, more or less spacious, into which twi-light was at least admitted; but here it seemed as if I was surrounded by barriers that would forever cut off my return to air and to light.

Presently I resumed my courage and proceeded. My road appeared now to ascend. On one side I seemed still upon the verge of a precipice, and, on the other, all was empty and waste. I had gone no inconsiderable distance, and persuaded myself that my career would speedily terminate. In a short time, the space on the left hand, was again occupied, and I cautiously proceeded between the edge of the gulf and a rugged wall. As the space between them widened I adhered to the wall.

I was not insensible that my path became more intricate and more difficult to retread in proportion as I advanced. I endeavoured to preserve a vivid conception of the way which I had already passed, and to keep the images of the left, and right-hand wall, and the gulf, in due succession in my memory.

The path which had hitherto been considerably smooth, now became rugged and steep. Chilling damps, the secret trepidation which attended me, the length and difficulties of my way, enhanced by the ceaseless caution and the numerous expedients which the utter darkness obliged me to employ, began to overpower my strength. I was frequently compelled to stop and recruit myself by rest. These respites from toil were of use, but they could not enable me to prosecute an endless journey, and to return was scarcely a less arduous task than to proceed.

I looked anxiously forward in the hope of being comforted by some dim ray, which might assure me that my labours were approaching an end. At last this propitious token appeared, and I issued forth into a kind of chamber, one side of which was open to the air and allowed me to catch a portion of the checquered sky. This spectacle never before excited such exquisite sensations in my bosom. The air, likewise, breathed into the cavern, was unspeakably delicious.

I now found myself on the projecture of a rock. Above and below the hill-side was nearly perpendicular. Opposite, and at the distance of fifteen or twenty yards, was a similar ascent. At the bottom was a glen, cold, narrow and obscure. The projecture, which served as a kind of vestibule to the cave, was connected with a ledge, by which, though not without peril and toil, I was conducted to the summit.

This summit was higher than any of those which were interposed between itself and the river. A large part of this chaos of rocks and precipices was subjected, at one view, to the eye. The fertile lawns and vales which lay beyond this, the winding course of the river, and the slopes which rose on its farther side, were parts of this extensive scene. These objects were at any time fitted to inspire rapture. Now my delight was enhanced by the contrast which this lightsome and serene element bore to the glooms from which I had lately emerged. My station, also, was higher, and the limits of my view, consequently more ample than any which I had hitherto enjoyed.

I advanced to the outer verge of the hill, which I found to overlook a steep, no less inaccessible, and a glen equally profound. I changed frequently my station in order to diversify the scenery. At length it became necessary to inquire by what means I should return. I traversed the edge of the hill, but on every side it was equally steep and always too lofty to permit me to leap from it. As I kept along the verge, I perceived that it tended in a circular direction, and brought me back, at last, to the spot from which I had set out. From this inspection, it seemed as if return was impossible by any other way than that through the cavern.

I now turned my attention to the interior space. If you imagine a cylindrical mass, with a cavity dug in the centre, whose edge conforms to the exterior edge; and, if you place in this cavity another cylinder, higher than that which surrounds it, but so small as to leave between its sides and those of the cavity, an hollow space, you will gain as distinct an image of this hill as words can convey. The summit of the inner rock was rugged and covered with trees of unequal growth. To reach this summit would not render my return easier; but its greater elevation would extend my view, and perhaps furnish a spot from which the whole horizon was conspicuous.

As I had traversed the outer, I now explored the inner edge of this hill. At length I reached a spot where the chasm, separating the two rocks, was narrower than at any other part. At first view, it seemed as if it were possible to leap over it, but a nearer examination shewed me that the passage was impracticable. So far as my eye could estimate it, the breadth was thirty or forty feet. I could scarcely venture to look beneath. The height was dizzy, and the walls, which approached each other at top, receded at the bottom, so as to form the resemblance of an immense hall, lighted from a rift, which some convulsion of nature had made in the roof. Where I stood there ascended a perpetual mist, occasioned by a torrent that dashed along the rugged pavement below.

From these objects I willingly turned my eye upon those before and above me, on the opposite ascent. A stream, rushing from above, fell into a cavity, which its own force seemed gradually to have made. The noise and the motion equally attracted my attention. There was a desolate and solitary grandeur in the scene, enhanced by the circumstances in which it was beheld, and by the perils through which I had recently passed, that had never before been witnessed by me.

A sort of sanctity and awe environed it, owing to the consciousness of absolute and utter loneliness. It was probable that human feet had never before gained this recess, that human eyes had never been fixed upon these gushing waters. The aboriginal inhabitants had no motives to lead them into caves like this, and ponder on the verge of such a precipice. Their successors were still less likely to have wandered hither. Since the birth of this continent, I was probably the first who had deviated thus remotely from the customary paths of men.

While musing upon these ideas, my eye was fixed upon the foaming current. At length, I looked upon the rocks which confined and embarrassed its course. I admired their phantastic shapes, and endless irregularities. Passing from one to the other of these, my attention lighted, at length, as if by some magical transition, on . . . an human countenance!

My surprise was so abrupt, and my sensations so tumultuous that I forgot for a moment the perilous nature of my situation. I loosened my hold of a pine branch, which had been hitherto one of my supports, and almost started from my seat. Had my station been, in a slight

103

degree nearer the brink than it was, I should have fallen headlong into the abyss.

To meet an human creature, even on that side of the chasm which I occupied, would have been wholly adverse to my expectation. My station was accessible by no other road than that through which I had passed, and no motives were imaginable by which others could be prompted to explore this road. But he whom I now beheld, was seated where it seemed impossible for human efforts to have placed him. . . .

But this affected me but little in comparison with other incidents. Not only the countenance was human, but in spite of shaggy and tangled locks, and an air of melancholy wildness, I speedily recognized the features of the fugitive Clithero.

One glance was not sufficient to make me acquainted with this scene. I had come hither partly in pursuit of this man, but some casual appendage of his person, something which should indicate his past rather than his present existence, was all that I hoped to find. That he should be found alive in this desert; that he should have gained this summit, access to which was apparently impossible, were scarcely within the boundaries of belief.

His scanty and coarse garb, had been nearly rent away by brambles and thorns, his arms, bosom and cheek were overgrown and half-concealed by hair. There was somewhat in his attitude and looks denoting more than anarchy of thoughts and passions. His rueful, ghastly, and immoveable eyes, testified not only that his mind was ravaged by despair, but that he was pinched with famine.

These proofs of his misery thrilled to my inmost heart. Horror and shuddering invaded me as I stood gazing upon him, and, for a time, I was without the power of deliberating on the measures which it was my duty to adopt for his relief. The first suggestion was, by calling, to inform him of my presence. I knew not what counsel or comfort to offer. By what words to bespeak his attention, or by what topics to molify his direful passions I knew not. Though so near, the gulf by which we were separated was impassable. All that I could do was to speak.

My surprise and my horror were still strong enough to give a shrill and piercing tone to my voice. The chasm and the rocks loudened and reverberated my accents while I exclaimed . . . *Man! Clithero!*

My summons was effectual. He shook off his trance in a moment. He had been stretched upon his back, with his eyes fixed upon a craggy projecture above, as if he were in momentary expectation of its fall, and crushing him to atoms. Now he started on his feet. He was conscious of the voice, but not of the quarter whence it came. He was looking anxiously around when I again spoke . . . Look hither: It is I who called.

He looked. Astonishment was now mingled with every other dreadful meaning in his visage. He clasped his hands together and bent forward, as if to satisfy himself that his summoner was real. At the next moment he drew back, placed his hands upon his breast, and fixed his eyes on the ground.

This pause was not likely to be broken but by me. I was preparing again to speak. To be more distinctly heard, I advanced closer to the brink. During this action, my eye was necessarily withdrawn from him. Having gained a somewhat nearer station, I looked again, but . . . he was gone!

The seat which he so lately occupied was empty. I was not forewarned of his disappearance, or directed to the course of his flight by any rustling among leaves. These indeed would have been overpowered by the noise of the cataract. The place where he sat was the bottom of a cavity, one side of which terminated in the verge of the abyss, but the other sides were perpendicular or over-hanging. Surely he had not leaped into this gulf, and yet that he had so speedily scaled the steep was impossible.

I looked into the gulf, but the depth and the gloom allowed me to see nothing with distinctness. His cries or groans could not be overheard amidst the uproar of the

105

waters. His fall must have instantly destroyed him, and that he had fallen was the only conclusion I could draw.

My sensations on this incident cannot be easily described. The image of this man's despair, and of the sudden catastrophe to which my inauspicious interference had led, filled me with compunction and terror. Some of my fears were relieved by the new conjecture, that, behind the rock on which he had lain, there might be some aperture or pit into which he had descended, or in which he might be concealed.

I derived consolation from this conjecture. Not only the evil which I dreaded might not have happened, but some alleviation of his misery was possible. Could I arrest his footsteps and win his attention, I might be able to insinuate the lessons of fortitude; but if words were impotent, and arguments were nugatory, yet to set by him in silence, to moisten his hand with tears, to sigh in unison, to offer him the spectacle of sympathy, the solace of believing that his demerits were not estimated by so rigid a standard by others as by himself, that one at least among his fellow men regarded him with love and pity, could not fail to be of benign influence.

These thoughts inspired me with new zeal. To effect my purpose it was requisite to reach the opposite steep. I was now convinced that this was not an impracticable undertaking, since Clithero had already performed it. I once more made the circuit of the hill. Every side was steep and of enormous height, and the gulf was no where so narrow as at this spot. I therefore returned hither, and once more pondered on the means of passing this tremendous chasm in safety.

Casting my eyes upward, I noted the tree at the root of which I was standing. I compared the breadth of the gulf with the length of the trunk of this tree, and it appeared very suitable for a bridge. Happily it grew obliquely, and, if felled by an axe, would probably fall of itself, in such a manner as to be suspended across the chasm. The stock was thick enough to afford me footing, and would enable me to reach the opposite declivity without danger or delay.

A more careful examination of the spot, the scite of the tree, its dimensions and the direction of its growth convinced me fully of the practicability of this expedient, and I determined to carry it into immediate execution. For this end I must hasten home, procure an axe, and return with all expedition hither. I took my former way, once more entered the subterranean avenue, and slowly re-emerged into day. Before I reached home, the evening was at hand, and my tired limbs and jaded spirits obliged me to defer my undertaking till the morrow.

Though my limbs were at rest, my thoughts were active through the night. I carefully reviewed the situation of this hill, and was unable to conjecture by what means Clithero could place himself upon it. Unless he occasionally returned to the habitable grounds, it was impossible for him to escape perishing by famine. He might intend to destroy himself by this means, and my first efforts were to be employed to overcome this fatal resolution. To persuade him to leave his desolate haunts might be a laborious and tedious task; meanwhile all my benevolent intentions would be frustrated by his want of sustenance. It was proper, therefore, to carry bread with me, and to place it before him. The sight of food, the urgencies of hunger, and my vehement intreaties might prevail on him to eat, though no expostulation might suffice to make him seek food at a distance.

CHAPTER XI

NEXT morning I stored a small bag with meat and bread, and throwing an axe on my shoulder, set out, without informing any one of my intentions, for the hill. My passage was rendered more difficult by these incumbrances, but my perseverance surmounted every impediment, and I gained, in a few hours, the foot of the tree, whose trunk was to serve me for a bridge. In this journey I saw no traces of the fugitive.

A new survey of the tree confirmed my former conclusions, and I began my work with diligence. My strokes were repeated by a thousand echoes, and I paused at first somewhat startled by reverberations, which made it appear as if not one, but a score of axes, were employed at the same time on both sides of the gulf.

Quickly the tree fell, and exactly in the manner which I expected and desired. The wide-spread limbs occupied and choked up the channel of the torrent, and compelled it to seek a new outlet and multiplied its murmurs. I dared not trust myself to cross it in an upright posture, but clung, with hands and feet, to its rugged bark. Having reached the opposite cliff I proceeded to examine the spot where Clithero had disappeared. My fondest hopes were realised, for a considerable cavity appeared, which, on a former day, had been concealed from my distant view by the rock.

It was obvious to conclude that this was his present habitation, or that an avenue, conducting hither and terminating in the unexplored sides of this pit, was that by which he had come hither, and by which he had retired. I could not hesitate long to slide into the pit. I found an entrance through which I fearlessly penetrated. I was prepared to encounter obstacles and perils similar to those which I have already described, but was rescued from them by ascending, in a few minutes, into a kind of passage, open above, but walled by a continued rock on both sides. The sides of this passage conformed with the utmost exactness to each other. Nature, at some former period, had occasioned the solid mass to dispart at this place, and had thus afforded access to the summit of the hill. Loose stones and ragged points formed the flooring of this passage, which rapidly and circuitously ascended.

I was now within a few yards of the surface of the rock. The passage opened into a kind of chamber or pit, the sides of which were not difficult to climb. I rejoiced at the prospect of this termination of my journey. Here I paused, and throwing my weary limbs on the ground, began to examine the objects around me, and to meditate on the steps that were next to be taken.

My first glance lighted on the very being of whom I was in search. Stretched upon a bed of moss, at the distance of a few feet from my station, I beheld Clithero. He had not been roused by my approach, though my footsteps were perpetually stumbling and sliding. This reflection gave birth to the fear that he was dead. A nearer inspection dispelled my apprehensions, and shewed me that he was merely buried in profound slumber. Those vigils must indeed have been long which were at last succeeded by a sleep so oblivious.

This meeting was, in the highest degree, propitious. It not only assured me of his existence, but proved that his miseries were capable to be suspended. His slumber enabled me to pause, to ruminate on the manner by which his understanding might be most successfully addressed; to collect and arrange the topics fitted to rectify his gloomy and disastrous perceptions.

Thou knowest that I am qualified for such tasks neither

by my education nor my genius. The headlong and ferocious energies of this man could not be repelled or diverted into better paths by efforts so undisciplined as mine. A despair so stormy and impetuous would drown my feeble accents. How should I attempt to reason with him? How should I outroot prepossessions so inveterate; the fruits of his earliest education, fostered and matured by the observation and experience of his whole life? How should I convince him that since the death of Wiatte was not intended, the deed was without crime; that, if it had been deliberately concerted, it was still a virtue, since his own life could, by no other means, be preserved; that when he pointed a dagger at the bosom of his mistress he was actuated, not by avarice, or ambition, or revenge, or malice? He desired to confer on her the highest and the only benefit of which he believed her capable. He sought to rescue her from tormenting regrets and lingering agonies.

These positions were sufficiently just to my own view, but I was not called upon to reduce them to practice. I had not to struggle with the consciousness of having been rescued by some miraculous contingency, from embruing my hands in the blood of her whom I adored; of having drawn upon myself suspicions of ingratitude and murder too deep to be ever effaced; of having bereft myself of love, and honour, and friends, and spotless reputation; of having doomed myself to infamy and detestation, to hopeless exile, penury, and servile toil. These were the evils which his malignant destiny had made the unalterable portion of Clithero, and how should my imperfect eloquence annihilate these evils? Every man, not himself the victim of irretreivable disasters, perceives the folly of ruminating on the past, and of fostering a grief which cannot reverse or recall the decrees of an immutable necessity; but every man who suffers is unavoidably shackled by the errors which he censures in his neighbour, and his efforts to relieve himself are as fruitless as those with which he attempted the relief of others.

No topic, therefore, could be properly employed by me on the present occasion. All that I could do was to offer him food, and, by pathetic supplications, to prevail on him to eat. Famine, however obstinate, would scarcely refrain when bread was placed within sight and reach. When made to swerve from his resolution in one instance, it would be less difficult to conquer it a second time. The magic of sympathy, the perseverance of benevolence, though silent, might work a gradual and secret revolution, and better thoughts might insensibly displace those desperate suggestions which now governed him.

Having revolved these ideas, I placed the food which I had brought at his right hand, and, seating myself at his feet, attentively surveyed his countenance. The emotions, which were visible during wakefulness, had vanished during this cessation of remembrance and remorse, or were faintly discernible. They served to dignify and solemnize his features, and to embellish those immutable lines which betokened the spirit of his better days. Lineaments were now observed which could never co-exist with folly, or associate with obdurate guilt.

I had no inclination to awaken him. This respite was too sweet to be needlessly abridged. I determined to await the operation of nature, and to prolong, by silence and by keeping interruption at a distance, this salutary period of forgetfulness. This interval permitted new ideas to succeed in my mind.

Clithero believed his solitude to be unapproachable. What new expedients to escape inquiry and intrusion might not my presence suggest! Might he not vanish, as he had done on the former day, and afford me no time to assail his constancy and tempt his hunger? If, however, I withdrew during his sleep, he would awake without disturbance, and be unconscious for a time, that his secrecy had been violated. He would quickly perceive the victuals and would need no foreign inducements to eat. A provision, so unexpected and extraordinary, might suggest new thoughts, and be construed into a kind of heavenly condemnation of his purpose. He would not readily suspect the motives or person of his visitant, would take no precaution against the repetition of my visit, and, at the same time, our interview would not be attended with so much surpise. The more I revolved these reflections, the greater force they acquired. At length, I determined to withdraw, and, leaving the food where it could scarcely fail of attracting his notice, I returned by the way that I had come. I had scarcely reached home, when a messenger from Inglefield arrived, requesting me to spend the succeeding night at his house, as some engagement had occurred to draw him to the city.

I readily complied with this request. It was not necessary, however, to be early in my visit. I deferred going till the evening was far advanced. My way led under the branches of the elm which recent events had rendered so memorable. Hence my reflections reverted to the circumstances which had lately occurred in connection with this tree.

I paused, for some time, under its shade. I marked the spot where Clithero had been discovered digging. It shewed marks of being unsettled, but the sod which had formerly covered it and which had lately been removed, was now carefully replaced. This had not been done by him on that occasion in which I was a witness of his behaviour. The earth was then hastily removed and as hastily thrown again into the hole from which it had been taken.

Some curiosity was naturally excited by this appearance. Either some other person, or Clithero, on a subsequent occasion, had been here. I was now likewise led to reflect on the possible motives that prompted the maniac to turn up this earth. There is always some significance in the actions of a sleeper. Somewhat was, perhaps, buried in this spot, connected with the history of Mrs. Lorimer or of Clarice. Was it not possible to ascertain the truth in this respect?

There was but one method. By carefully uncovering

this hole, and digging as deep as Clithero had already dug, it would quickly appear whether any thing was hidden. To do this publickly by day-light was evidently indiscreet. Besides, a moment's delay was superfluous. The night had now fallen, and before it was past this new undertaking might be finished. An interview was, if possible, to be gained with Clithero on the morrow, and for this interview the discoveries made on this spot might eminently qualify me. Influenced by these considerations, I resolved to dig. I was first, however, to converse an hour with the house-keeper, and then to withdraw to my chamber. When the family were all retired, and there was no fear of observation or interruption, I proposed to rise and hasten, with a proper implement, hither.

One chamber, in Inglefield's house, was usually reserved for visitants. In this chamber thy unfortunate brother died, and here it was that I was to sleep. The image of its last inhabitant could not fail of being called up, and of banishing repose; but the scheme which I had meditated was an additional incitement to watchfulness. Hither I repaired, at the due season, having previously furnished myself with candles, since I knew not what might occur to make a light necessary.

I did not go to bed, but either sat musing by a table or walked across the room. The bed before me was that on which my friend breathed his last. To rest my head upon the same pillow, to lie on that pallet which sustained his cold and motionless limbs, were provocations to remembrance and grief that I desired to shun. I endeavoured to fill my mind with more recent incidents, with the disasters of Clithero, my subterranean adventures, and the probable issue of the schemes which I now contemplated.

I recalled the conversation which had just ended with the house-keeper. Clithero had been our theme, but she had dealt chiefly in repetitions of what had formerly been related by her or by Inglefield. I inquired what this man had left behind, and found that it consisted of a square box, put together by himself with uncommon strength, but of rugged workmanship. She proceeded to mention that she had advised her brother, Mr. Inglefield, to break open this box and ascertain its contents, but this he did not think himself justified in doing. Clithero was guilty of no known crime, was responsible to no one for his actions, and might sometime return to claim his property. This box contained nothing with which others had a right to meddle. Somewhat might be found in it, throwing light upon his past or present situation, but curiosity was not to be gratified by these means. What Clithero thought proper to conceal, it was criminal for us to extort from him.

The house-keeper was by no means convinced by these arguments, and at length, obtained her brother's permission to try whether any of her own keys would unlock this chest. The keys were produced, but no lock nor key-hole were discoverable. The lid was fast, but by what means it was fastened, the most accurate inspection could not detect. Hence she was compelled to lay aside her project. This chest had always stood in the chamber which I now occupied.

These incidents were now remembered, and I felt disposed to profit by this opportunity of examining this box. It stood in a corner, and was easily distinguished by its form. I lifted it and found its weight by no means extraordinary. Its structure was remarkable. It consisted of six sides, square and of similar dimensions. These were joined, not by mortice and tennon; not by nails, not by hinges, but the junction was accurate. The means by which they were made to cohere were invisible.

Appearances on every side were uniform, nor were there any marks by which the lid was distinguishable from its other surfaces.

During his residence with Inglefield, many specimens of mechanical ingenuity were given by his servant. This was the workmanship of his own hands. I looked at it, for some time, till the desire insensibly arose of opening and examining its contents.

114

I had no more right to do this than the Inglefields; perhaps indeed this curiosity was more absurd, and the gratification more culpable in me than in them. I was acquainted with the history of Clithero's past life, and with his present condition. Respecting these, I had no new intelligence to gain, and no doubts to solve. What excuse could I make to the proprietor, should he ever reappear to claim his own, or to Inglefield for breaking open a receptacle which all the maxims of society combine to render sacred?

But could not my end be gained without violence? The means of opening might present themselves on a patient scrutiny. The lid might be raised and shut down again without any tokens of my act; its contents might be examined, and all things restored to their former condition in a few minutes.

I intended not a theft. I intended to benefit myself without inflicting injury on others. Nay, might not the discoveries I should make, throw light upon the conduct of this extraordinary man, which his own narrative had withheld? Was there reason to confide implicitly on the tale which I had heard?

In spite of the testimony of my own feelings, the miseries of Clithero appeared in some degree, phantastic and groundless. A thousand conceivable motives might induce him to pervert or conceal the truth. If he were thoroughly known, his character might assume a new appearance, and what is now so difficult to reconcile to common maxims, might prove perfectly consistent with them. I desire to restore him to peace, but a thorough knowledge of his actions is necessary, both to shew that he is worthy of compassion, and to suggest the best means of extirpating his errors. It was possible that this box contained the means of this knowledge.

There were likewise other motives which, as they possessed some influence, however small, deserve to be mentioned. Thou knowest that I also am a mechanist. I had constructed a writing desk and cabinet, in which I had endeavoured to combine the properties of secrecy, security, and strength, in the highest possible degree. I looked upon this therefore with the eye of an artist, and was solicitous to know the principles on which it was formed. I determined to examine, and if possible to open it.

CHAPTER XII

I SURVEYED it with the utmost attention. All its
parts appeared equally solid and smooth. It could not
be doubted that one of its sides served the purpose of
a lid, and was possible to be raised. Mere strength could
not be applied to raise it, because there was no projecture
which might be firmly held by the hand, and by which
force could be exerted. Some spring, therefore, secretly
existed which might forever elude the senses, but on
which the hand, by being moved over it, in all directions,
might accidentally light.

This process was effectual. A touch, casually applied at
an angle, drove back a bolt, and a spring, at the same
time, was set in action, by which the lid was raised above
half an inch. No event could be supposed more fortuitous
than this. An hundred hands might have sought in vain
for this spring. The spot in which a certain degree of
pressure was sufficient to produce this effect, was of all,
the last likely to attract notice or awaken suspicion.

I opened the trunk with eagerness. The space within
was divided into numerous compartments, none of which
contained any thing of moment. Tools of different and
curious constructions, and remnants of minute machin-
ery, were all that offered themselves to my notice.

My expectations being thus frustrated, I proceeded to
restore things to their former state. I attempted to close
the lid; but the spring which had raised it refused to bend.

No measure that I could adopt, enabled me to place the lid in the same situation in which I had found it. In my efforts to press down the lid, which were augmented in proportion to the resistance that I met with, the spring was broken. This obstacle being removed, the lid resumed its proper place; but no means, within the reach of my ingenuity to discover, enabled me to push forward the bolt, and thus to restore the fastening.

I now perceived that Clithero had provided not only against the opening of his cabinet, but likewise against the possibility of concealing that it had been opened. This discovery threw me into some confusion. I had been tempted thus far, by the belief that my action was without witnesses, and might be forever concealed. This opinion was now confuted. If Clithero should ever reclaim his property, he would not fail to detect the violence of which I had been guilty. Inglefield would disapprove in another what he had not permitted to himself, and the unauthorized and clandestine manner in which I had behaved, would aggravate, in his eyes, the heinousness of my offence.

But now there was no remedy. All that remained was to hinder suspicion from lighting on the innocent, and to confess, to my friend, the offence which I had committed. Meanwhile my first project was resumed, and, the family being now wrapt in profound sleep, I left my chamber, and proceeded to the elm. The moon was extremely brilliant, but I hoped that this unfrequented road and unseasonable hour would hinder me from being observed. My chamber was above the kitchen, with which it communicated by a small stair-case, and the building to which it belonged was connected with the dwelling by a gallery. I extinguished the light, and left it in the kitchen, intending to relight it, by the embers that still glowed on the hearth, on my return.

I began to remove the sod, and cast out the earth, with little confidence in the success of my project. The issue of my examination of the box humbled and disheartened

me. For some time I found nothing that tended to invigo-
rate my hopes. I determined, however, to descend, as
long as the unsettled condition of the earth shewed me
that some one had preceded me. Small masses of stone
were occasionally met with, which served only to perplex
me with groundless expectations. At length my spade
struck upon something which emitted a very different
sound. I quickly drew it forth, and found it to be wood.
Its regular form, and the crevices which were faintly discernible, persuaded me that it was human workmanship,
and that there was a cavity within. The place in which it
was found, easily suggested some connection between this
and the destiny of Clithero. Covering up the hole with
speed, I hastened with my prize to the house. The door,
by which the kitchen was entered, was not to be seen from
the road. It opened on a field, the farther limit of which
was a ledge of rocks, which formed, on this side, the
boundary of Inglefield's estate and the westernmost barrier of Norwalk.

As I turned the angle of the house, and came in view of
this door, methought I saw a figure issue from it. I was
startled at this incident, and, stopping, crouched close to
the wall, that I might not be discovered. As soon as the
figure passed beyond the verge of the shade, it was easily
distinguished to be that of Clithero! He crossed the field
with a rapid pace, and quickly passed beyond the reach of
my eye.

This appearance was mysterious. For what end he
should visit this habitation, could not be guessed. Was the
contingency to be lamented, in consequence of which an
interview had been avoided? Would it have compelled me
to explain the broken condition of his trunk? I knew not
whether to rejoice at having avoided this interview, or to
deplore it.

These thoughts did not divert me from examining the
nature of the prize which I had gained. I relighted my
candle and hied once more to the chamber. The first
object, which, on entering it, attracted my attention, was

119

the cabinet broken into twenty fragments, on the hearth. I had left it on a low table, at a distant corner of the room.

No conclusion could be formed, but that Clithero had been here, had discovered the violence which had been committed on his property, and, in the first transport of his indignation, had shattered it to pieces. I shuddered on reflecting how near I had been to being detected by him in the very act, and by how small an interval I had escaped that resentment, which, in that case, would have probably been wreaked upon me.

My attention was withdrawn, at length, from this object, and fixed upon the contents of the box which I had dug up. This was equally inaccessible with the other. I had not the same motives for caution and forbearance. I was somewhat desperate, as the consequences of my indiscretion could not be aggravated, and my curiosity was more impetuous, with regard to the smaller than to the larger cabinet. I placed it on the ground and crushed it to pieces with my heel.

Something was within. I brought it to the light, and, after loosing numerous folds, at length drew forth a volume. No object, in the circle of nature, was more adapted than this, to rouse up all my faculties. My feelings were anew excited on observing that it was a manuscript. I bolted the door, and, drawing near the light, opened and began to read.

A few pages was sufficient to explain the nature of the work. Clithero had mentioned that his lady had composed a vindication of her conduct towards her brother, when her intercession in his favour was solicited and refused. This performance had never been published, but had been read by many, and was preserved by her friends as a precious monument of her genius and her virtue. This manuscript was now before me.

That Clithero should preserve this manuscript, amidst the wreck of his hopes and fortunes, was apparently conformable to his temper. That, having formed the resolution to die, he should seek to hide this volume from the

120

profane curiosity of survivors, was a natural proceeding. To bury it rather than to burn, or disperse it into fragments, would be suggested by the wish to conceal, without committing what his heated fancy would regard as sacrilege. To bury it beneath the elm, was dictated by no fortuitous or inexplicable caprice. This event could scarcely fail of exercising some influence on the perturbations of his sleep, and thus, in addition to other causes, might his hovering near this trunk, and throwing up this earth, in the intervals of slumber, be accounted for. Clithero, indeed, had not mentioned this proceeding in the course of his narrative; but that would have contravened the end for which he had provided a grave for this book.

I read this copious tale with unspeakable eagerness. It essentially agreed with that which had been told by Clithero. By drawing forth events into all their circumstances, more distinct impressions were produced on the mind, and proofs of fortitude and equanimity were here given, to which I had hitherto known no parallel. No wonder that a soul like Clithero's, pervaded by these proofs of inimitable excellence, and thrillingly alive to the passion of virtuous fame, and the value of that existence which he had destroyed, should be overborne by horror at the view of the past.

The instability of life and happiness was forcibly illustrated, as well as the perniciousness of error. Exempt as this lady was from almost every defect, she was indebted for her ruin to absurd opinions of the sacredness of consanguinity, to her anxiety for the preservation of a ruffian, because that ruffian was her brother. The spirit of Clithero was enlightened and erect, but he weakly suffered the dictates of eternal justice to be swallowed up by gratitude. The dread of unjust upbraiding hurried him to murder and to suicide, and the imputation of imaginary guilt, impelled him to the perpetration of genuine and enormous crimes.

The perusal of this volume ended not but with the

121

night. Contrary to my hopes, the next day was stormy and wet. This did not deter me from visiting the mountain. Slippery paths and muddy torrents were no obstacles to the purposes which I had adopted. I wrapt myself, and a bag of provisions, in a cloak of painted canvass and speeded to the dwelling of Clithero.

I passed through the cave and reached the bridge which my own ingenuity had formed. At that moment, torrents of rain poured from above, and stronger blasts thundered amidst these desolate recesses and profound chasms. Instead of lamenting the prevalence of this tempest, I now began to regard it with pleasure. It conferred new forms of sublimity and grandeur on this scene.

As I crept with hands and feet, along my imperfect bridge, a sudden gust had nearly whirled me into the frightful abyss below. To preserve myself, I was oblidged to loose my hold of my burthen and it fell into the gulf. This incident disconcerted and distressed me. As soon as I had effected my dangerous passage, I screened myself behind a cliff, and gave myself up to reflection.

The purpose of this arduous journey was defeated, by the loss of the provisions I had brought. I despaired of winning the attention of the fugitive to supplications, or arguments tending to smother remorse, or revive his fortitude. The scope of my efforts was to consist in vanquishing his aversion to food; but these efforts would now be useless, since I had no power to supply his cravings.

This deficiency, however, was easily supplied. I had only to return home and supply myself anew. No time was to be lost in doing this; but I was willing to remain under this shelter, till the fury of the tempest had subsided. Besides, I was not certain that Clithero had again retreated hither. It was requisite to explore the summit of this hill, and ascertain whether it had any inhabitant. I might likewise discover what had been the success of my former experiment, and whether the food, which had been left here on the former day, was consumed or neglected.

While occupied with these reflections, my eyes were fixed upon the opposite steeps. The tops of the trees, waving to and fro, in the wildest commotion, and their trunks, occasionally bending to the blast, which, in these lofty regions, blew with a violence unknown in the tracts below, exhibited an awful spectacle. At length, my attention was attracted by the trunk which lay across the gulf, and which I had converted into a bridge. I perceived that it had already somewhat swerved from its original position, that every blast broke or loosened some of the fibres by which its root was connected with the opposite bank, and that, if the storm did not speedily abate, there was imminent danger of its being torn from the rock and precipitated into the chasm. Thus my retreat would be cut off, and the evils, from which I was endeavouring to rescue another, would be experienced by myself.

I did not just then reflect that Clithero had found access to this hill by other means, and that the avenue by which he came, would be equally commodious to me. I believed my destiny to hang upon the expedition with which I should re-cross this gulf. The moments that were spent in these deliberations were critical, and I shuddered to observe that the trunk was held in its place by one or two fibres which were already stretched almost to breaking.

To pass along the trunk, rendered slippery by the wet, and unsteadfast by the wind, was eminently dangerous. To maintain my hold, in passing, in defiance of the whirlwind, required the most vigorous exertions. For this end it was necessary to discommode myself of my cloak, and of the volume, which I carried in the pocket of my cloak. I believed there was no reason to dread their being destroyed or purloined, if left, for a few hours or a day, in this recess. If laid beside a stone, under shelter of this cliff, they would, no doubt, remain unmolested till the disappearance of the storm should permit me to revisit this spot in the afternoon or on the morrow.

Just as I had disposed of these incumbrances, and had risen from my seat, my attention was again called to the opposite steep, by the most unwelcome object that, at this time, could possibly occur. Something was perceived moving among the bushes and rocks, which, for a time, I hoped was no more than a racoon or oppossum; but which presently appeared to be a panther. His grey coat, extended claws, fiery eyes, and a cry which he at that moment uttered, and which, by its resemblance to the human voice, is peculiarly terrific, denoted him to be the most ferocious and untamable of that detested race*.

The industry of our hunters has nearly banished animals of prey from these precincts. The fastnesses of Norwalk, however, could not but afford refuge to some of them. Of late I had met them so rarely, that my fears were seldom alive, and I trod, without caution, the ruggedest and most solitary haunts. Still, however, I had seldom been unfurnished in my rambles with the means of defence.

My temper never delighted in carnage and blood. I found no pleasure in plunging into bogs, wading through rivulets, and penetrating thickets, for the sake of dispatching wood-cocks and squirrels. To watch their gambols and flittings, and invite them to my hand, was my darling amusement when loitering among the woods and the rocks. It was much otherwise, however, with regard to rattlesnakes and panthers. These I thought it no breach of duty to exterminate wherever they could be found. These judicious and sanguinary spoilers were equally the enemies of man and of the harmless race that sported in the trees, and many of their skins are still preserved by me as trophies of my juvenile prowess.

As hunting was never my trade or my sport, I never loaded myself with fowling-piece or rifle. Assiduous exercise had made me master of a weapon of much easier carriage, and, within a moderate distance, more destructive and unerring. This was the tom-hawk. With this I

*The grey Cougar. This animal has all the essential characteristics of a tyger. Though somewhat inferior in size and strength, these are such as to make him equally formidable to man.

have often severed an oak branch and cut the sinews of a cat-o'mountain, at the distance of sixty feet.

The unfrequency with which I had lately encountered this foe, and the incumbrance of provision, made me neglect, on this occasion, to bring with me my usual arms. The beast that was now before me, when stimulated by hunger, was accustomed to assail whatever could provide him with a banquet of blood. He would set upon the man and the deer with equal and irresistible ferocity. His sagacity was equal to his strength, and he seemed able to discover when his antagonist was armed and prepared for defence.

My past experience enabled me to estimate the full extent of my danger. He sat on the brow of the steep, eyeing the bridge, and apparently deliberating whether he should cross it. It was probable that he had scented my footsteps thus far, and should he pass over, his vigilance could scarcely fail of detecting my assylum. The pit into which Clithero had sunk from my view was at some distance. To reach it was the first impulse of my fear, but this could not be done without exciting the observation and pursuit of this enemy. I deeply regretted the untoward chance that had led me, when I first came over, to a different shelter.

Should he retain his present station, my danger was scarcely lessened. To pass over in the face of a famished tyger was only to rush upon my fate. The falling of the trunk, which had lately been so anxiously deprecated, was now, with no less solicitude, desired. Every new gust, I hoped, would tear asunder its remaining bands, and, by cutting off all communication between the opposite steeps, place me in security.

My hopes, however, were destined to be frustrated. The fibres of the prostrate tree, were obstinately tenacious of their hold, and presently the animal scrambled down the rock and proceeded to cross it.

Of all kinds of death, that which now menaced me was the most abhorred. To die by disease, or by the hand of a

125

fellow-creature, was propitious and lenient in comparison with being rent to pieces by the fangs of this savage. To perish, in this obscure retreat, by means so impervious to the anxious curiosity of my friends, to lose my portion of existence by so untoward and ignoble a destiny, was insupportable. I bitterly deplored my rashness in coming hither unprovided for an encounter like this.

The evil of my present circumstances consisted chiefly in suspense. My death was unavoidable, but my imagination had leisure to torment itself by anticipations. One foot of the savage was slowly and cautiously moved after the other. He struck his claws so deeply into the bark that they were with difficulty withdrawn. At length he leaped upon the ground. We were now separated by an interval of scarcely eight feet. To leave the spot where I crouched, was impossible. Behind and beside me, the cliff rose perpendicularly, and before me was this grim and terrific visage. I shrunk still closer to the ground and closed my eyes.

From this pause of horror I was roused by the noise occasioned by a second spring of the animal. He leaped into the pit, in which I had so deeply regretted that I had not taken refuge, and disappeared. My rescue was so sudden, and so much beyond my belief or my hope, that I doubted, for a moment, whether my senses did not deceive me. This opportunity of escape was not to be neglected. I left my place, and scrambled over the trunk with a precipitation which had liked to have proved fatal. The tree groaned and shook under me, the wind blew with unexampled violence, and I had scarcely reached the opposite steep when the roots were severed from the rock and the whole fell thundering to the bottom of the chasm.

My trepidations were not speedily quieted. I looked back with wonder on my hair-breadth escape, and on that singular concurrence of events, which had placed me, in so short a period, in absolute security. Had the trunk fallen a moment earlier, I should have been imprisoned on the hill or thrown headlong. Had its fall been delayed another moment I should have been pursued; for the beast now issued from his den, and testified his surprise and disappointment by tokens the sight of which made my blood run cold.

He saw me, and hastened to the verge of the chasm. He squatted on his hind-legs and assumed the attitude of one preparing to leap. My consternation was excited afresh by these appearances. It seemed at first as if the rift was too wide for any power of muscles to carry him in safety over; but I knew the unparalleled agility of this animal, and that his experience had made him a better judge of the practicability of this exploit than I was.

Still there was hope that he would relinquish this design as desperate. This hope was quickly at an end. He sprung, and his fore-legs touched the verge of the rock on which I stood. In spite of vehement exertions, however, the surface was too smooth and too hard to allow him to make good his hold. He fell, and a piercing cry, uttered below, shewed that nothing had obstructed his descent to the bottom.

Thus was I again rescued from death. Nothing but the pressure of famine could have prompted this savage to so audacious and hazardous an effort; but, by yeilding to this impulse, he had made my future visits to this spot exempt from peril. Clithero was, likewise, relieved from a danger that was imminent and unforeseen. Prowling over these grounds the panther could scarcely have failed to meet with this solitary fugitive.

Had the animal lived, my first duty would have been to have sought him out, and assailed him with my tomhawk; but no undertaking would have been more hazardous. Lurking in the grass, or in the branches of a tree, his eye might have descried my approach, he might leap upon me unperceived, and my weapon would be useless.

With an heart beating with unwonted rapidity, I once more descended the cliff, entered the cavern, and arrived at Huntly farm, drenched with rain, and exhausted by fatigue.

By night the storm was dispelled; but my exhausted strength would not allow me to return to the mountain. At the customary hour I retired to my chamber. I incessantly ruminated on the adventures of the last day, and inquired into the conduct which I was next to pursue.

The bridge being destroyed, my customary access was cut off. There was no possibility of restoring this bridge. My strength would not suffice to drag a fallen tree from a distance, and there was none whose position would abridge or supersede that labour. Some other expedient must, therefore, be discovered to pass this chasm.

I reviewed the circumstances of my subterranean journey. The cavern was imperfectly explored. Its branches might be numerous. That which I had hitherto pursued, terminated in an opening at a considerable distance from the bottom. Other branches might exist, some of which might lead to the foot of the precipice, and thence a communication might be found with the summit of the interior hill.

The danger of wandering into dark and untried paths, and the commodiousness of that road which had at first been taken, were sufficient reasons for having hitherto suspended my examination of the different branches of this labyrinth. Now my customary road was no longer practicable, and another was to be carefully explored. For this end, on my next journey to the mountain, I determined to take with me a lamp, and unravel this darksome maze: This project I resolved to execute the next day.

I now recollected what, if it had more seasonably occurred, would have taught me caution. Some months before this a farmer, living in the skirts of Norwalk, discovered two marauders in his field, whom he imagined to be a male and female panther. They had destroyed some sheep, and had been hunted by the farmer, with long and fruitless diligence. Sheep had likewise been destroyed in different quarters; but the owners had fixed the imputation of the crime upon dogs, many of whom had atoned for their supposed offences by their death. He who had mentioned his discovery of panthers, received little credit from his neighbours; because a long time had elapsed since these animals were supposed to have been exiled from this district, and because no other person had seen them. The truth of this seemed now to be confirmed by the testimony of my own senses; but, if the rumour were true, there still existed another of these animals, who might harbour in the obscurities of this desert, and against whom it was necessary to employ some precaution. Henceforth I resolved never to traverse the wilderness unfurnished with my tom-hawk.

These images, mingled with those which the contemplation of futurity suggested, floated, for a time, in my brain; but at length gave place to sleep.

CHAPTER XIII

SINCE my return home, my mind had been fully occupied by schemes and reflections relative to Clithero. The project suggested by thee, and to which I had determined to devote my leisure, was forgotten, or remembered for a moment and at wide intervals. What, however, was nearly banished from my waking thoughts, occurred, in an incongruous and half-seen form, to my dreams. During my sleep, the image of Waldegrave flitted before me. Methought the sentiment that impelled him to visit me, was not affection or complacency, but inquietude and anger. Some service or duty remained to be performed by me, which I had culpably neglected: to inspirit my zeal, to awaken my remembrance, and incite me to the performance of this duty, did this glimmering messenger, this half indignant apparition, come.

I commonly awake soon enough to mark the youngest dawn of the morning. Now, in consequence perhaps of my perturbed sleep, I opened my eyes before the stars had lost any of their lustre. This circumstance produced some surprise, until the images that lately hovered in my fancy, were recalled, and furnished somewhat like a solution of the problem. Connected with the image of my dead friend, was that of his sister. The discourse that took place at our last interview; the scheme of transcribing, for thy use, all the letters which, during his short but busy life, I

130

received from him; the nature of this correspondence, and the opportunity which this employment would afford me of contemplating these ample and precious monuments of the intellectual existence and moral pre-eminence of my friend, occurred to my thoughts.

The resolution to prosecute the task was revived. The obligation of benevolence, with regard to Clithero, was not discharged. This, neither duty nor curiosity would permit to be overlooked or delayed; but why should my whole attention and activity be devoted to this man? The hours which were spent at home and in my chamber, could not be more usefully employed than in making my intended copy.

In a few hours after sun-rise I purposed to resume my way to the mountain. Could this interval be appropriated to a better purpose than in counting over my friend's letters, setting them apart from my own, and preparing them for that transcription from which I expected so high and yet so mournful a gratification?

This purpose, by no violent union, was blended with the recollection of my dream. This recollection infused some degree of wavering and dejection into my mind. In transcribing these letters I should violate pathetic and solemn injunctions frequently repeated by the writer. Was there some connection between this purpose and the incidents of my vision? Was the latter sent to enforce the interdictions which had been formerly imposed?

Thou art not fully acquainted with the intellectual history of thy brother. Some information on that head will be necessary to explain the nature of that reluctance which I now feel to comply with thy request, and which had formerly so much excited thy surprise.

Waldegrave, like other men, early devoted to meditation and books, had adopted, at different periods, different systems of opinion, on topics connected with religion and morals. His earliest creeds, tended to efface the impressions of his education; to deify necessity and universalize matter; to destroy the popular distinctions

131

between soul and body, and to dissolve the supposed connection between the moral condition of man, anterior and
subsequent to death.

This creed he adopted with all the fulness of conviction,
and propagated with the utmost zeal. Soon after our
friendship commenced, fortune placed us at a distance
from each other, and no intercourse was allowed but by
the pen. Our letters, however, were punctual and copious. Those of Waldegrave were too frequently devoted to
the defence of his favourite tenets.

Thou art acquainted with the revolution that afterwards took place in his mind. Placed within the sphere of
religious influence, and listening daily to the reasonings
and exhortations of Mr. S——, whose benign temper and
blameless deportment was a visible and constant lesson,
he insensibly resumed the faith which he had relinquished, and became the vehement opponent of all that
he had formerly defended. The chief object of his labours,
in this new state of his mind, was to counteract the effect
of his former reasonings on my opinions.

At this time, other changes took place in his situation,
in consequence of which we were once more permitted to
reside under the same roof. The intercourse now ceased
to be by letter, and the subtle and laborious argumenta-
tions which he had formerly produced against religion,
and which were contained in a permanent form, were
combatted in transient conversation. He was not only
eager to subvert those opinions, which he had contributed
to instil into me, but was anxious that the letters and
manuscripts, which had been employed in their support,
should be destroyed. He did not fear wholly or chiefly on
my own account. He believed that the influence of former
reasonings on my faith would be sufficiently eradicated
by the new; but he dreaded lest these manuscripts might
fall into other hands, and thus produce mischiefs which it
would not be in his power to repair. With regard to me,
the poison had been followed by its antidote; but with
respect to others, these letters would communicate the
poison when the antidote could not be administered.

I would not consent to this sacrifice. I did not entirely abjure the creed which had, with great copiousness and eloquence, been defended in these letters. Beside, mixed up with abstract reasonings, were numberless passages which elucidated the character and history of my friend. These were too precious to be consigned to oblivion, and to take them out of their present connection and arrangement, would be to mutilate and deform them.

His intreaties and remonstrances were earnest and frequent, but always ineffectual. He had too much purity of motives to be angry at my stubbornness, but his sense of the mischievous tendency of these letters, was so great, that my intractability cost him many a pang.

He was now gone, and I had not only determined to preserve these monuments, but had consented to copy them for the use of another: for the use of one whose present and eternal welfare had been the chief object of his cares and efforts. Thou, like others of thy sex, art unaccustomed to metaphysical refinements. Thy religion is the growth of sensibility and not of argument. Thou art not fortified and prepossessed against the subtleties, with which the being and attributes of the deity have been assailed. Would it be just to expose thee to pollution and depravity from this source? To make thy brother the instrument of thy apostacy, the author of thy fall? That brother, whose latter days were so ardently devoted to cherishing the spirit of devotion in thy heart?

These ideas now occurred with more force than formerly. I had promised, not without reluctance, to give thee the entire copy of his letters; but I now receded from this promise. I resolved merely to select for thy perusal such as were narrative or descriptive. This could not be done with too much expedition. It was still dark, but my sleep was at an end, and, by a common apparatus, that lay beside my bed, I could instantly produce a light.

The light was produced, and I proceeded to the cabinet where all my papers and books are deposited. This was my own contrivance and workmanship, undertaken by the advice of Sarsefield, who took infinite pains to foster

133

that mechanical genius, which displayed itself so early and so forcibly in thy friend. The key belonging to this, was, like the cabinet itself, of singular structure. For greater safety, it was constantly placed in a closet, which was likewise locked.

The key was found as usual, and the cabinet opened. The letters were bound together in a compact form, lodged in a parchment case, and placed in a secret drawer. This drawer would not have been detected by common eyes, and it opened by the motion of a spring, of whose existence none but the maker was conscious. This drawer I had opened before I went to sleep and the letters were then safe.

Thou canst not imagine my confusion and astonishment, when, on opening the drawer, I perceived that the pacquet was gone. I looked with more attention, and put my hand within it, but the space was empty. Whither had it gone, and by whom was it purloined? I was not conscious of having taken it away, yet no hands but mine could have done it. On the last evening I had doubtless removed it to some other corner, but had forgotten it. I tasked my understanding and my memory. I could not conceive the possibility of any motives inducing me to alter my arrangements in this respect, and was unable to recollect that I had made this change.

What remained? This invaluable relique had disappeared. Every thought and every effort must be devoted to the single purpose of regaining it. As yet I did not despair. Until I had opened and ransacked every part of the cabinet in vain, I did not admit the belief that I had lost it. Even then this persuasion was tumultuous and fluctuating. It had vanished to my senses, but these senses were abused and depraved. To have passed, of its own accord, through the pores of this wood, was impossible; but if it were gone, thus did it escape.

I was lost in horror and amazement. I explored every nook a second and a third time, but still it eluded my eye and my touch. I opened my closets and cases. I pryed every where, unfolded every article of cloathing, turned and scrutinized every instrument and tool, but nothing availed.

My thoughts were not speedily collected or calmed. I threw myself on the bed and resigned myself to musing. That my loss was irretreivable, was a supposition not to be endured. Yet ominous terrors haunted me. A whispering intimation that a relique which I valued more than life was torn forever away by some malignant and inscrutable destiny. The same power that had taken it from this receptacle, was able to waft it over the ocean or the mountains, and condemn me to a fruitless and eternal search.

But what was he that committed the theft? Thou only, of the beings who live, wast acquainted with the existence of these manuscripts. Thou art many miles distant, and art utterly a stranger to the mode or place of their concealment. Not only access to the cabinet, but access to the room, without my knowledge and permission, was impossible. Both were locked during this night. Not five hours had elapsed since the cabinet and drawer had been opened, and since the letters had been seen and touched, being in their ordinary position. During this interval, the thief had entered, and despoiled me of my treasure.

This event, so inexplicable and so dreadful, threw my soul into a kind of stupor or distraction, from which I was suddenly roused by a footstep, softly moving in the entry near my door. I started from my bed, as if I had gained a glimpse of the robber. Before I could run to the door, some one knocked. I did not think upon the propriety of answering the signal, but hastened with tremulous fingers and throbbing heart to open the door. My uncle, in his night-dress, and apparently just risen from his bed, stood before me!

He marked the eagerness and perturbation of my looks, and inquired into the cause. I did not answer his inquiries. His appearance in my chamber and in this guise, added to my surprise. My mind was full of the late discovery, and instantly conceived some connection between this unseasonable visit and my lost manuscript. I interrogated him in my turn as to the cause of his coming.

Why, said he, I came to ascertain whether it was you or not who amused himself so strangely at this time of night. What is the matter with you? Why are you up so early?

I told him that I had been roused by my dreams, and finding no inclination to court my slumber back again, I had risen, though earlier by some hours than the usual period of my rising.

Buy why did you go up stairs? You might easily imagine that the sound of your steps would alarm those below, who would be puzzled to guess who it was that had thought proper to amuse himself in this manner.

Up stairs? I have not left my room this night. It is not ten minutes since I awoke, and my door has not since been opened.

Indeed! That is strange. Nay, it is impossible. It was your feet surely that I heard pacing so solemnly and indefatigably across the *long-room* for near an hour. I could not for my life conjecture, for a time, who it was, but finally concluded that it was you. There was still, however, some doubt, and I came hither to satisfy myself.

These tidings were adapted to raise all my emotions to a still higher pitch. I questioned him with eagerness as to the circumstances he had noticed. He said he had been roused by a sound, whose power of disturbing him arose, not from its loudness, but from its uncommonness. He distinctly heard some one pacing to and fro with bare feet, in the long room: This sound continued, with little intermission, for an hour. He then noticed a cessation of the walking, and a sound as if some one were lifting the lid of the large cedar chest, that stood in the corner of this room. The walking was not resumed, and all was silent. He listened for a quarter of an hour, and busied himself in conjecturing the cause of this disturbance. The most probable conclusion was, that the walker was his nephew, and his curiosity had led him to my chamber to ascertain the truth.

This dwelling has three stories. The two lower stories are divided into numerous apartments. The upper story constitutes a single room whose sides are the four walls of the house, and whose ceiling is the roof. This room is unoccupied, except by lumber, and imperfectly lighted by a small casement at one end. In this room, were footsteps heard by my uncle.

The stair-case leading to it terminated in a passage near my door. I snatched the candle, and desiring him to follow me, added, that I would ascertain the truth in a moment. He followed, but observed that the walking had ceased long enough for the person to escape.

I ascended to the room, and looked behind and among the tables, and chairs, and casks, which were confusedly scattered through it, but found nothing in the shape of man. The cedar chest, spoken of by Mr. Huntly, contained old books, and remnants of maps and charts, whose worthlessness unfitted them for accommodation elsewhere. The lid was without hinges or lock. I examined this repository, but there was nothing which attracted my attention.

The way between the kitchen door, and the door of the long-room, had no impediments. Both were usually unfastened but the motives by which any stranger to the dwelling, or indeed any one within it, could be prompted to chuse this place and hour, for an employment of this kind, were wholly incomprehensible.

When the family rose, inquiries were made but no satisfaction was obtained. The family consisted only of four persons, my uncle, my two sisters, and myself. I mentioned to them the loss I had sustained, but their conjectures were no less unsatisfactory on this than on the former incident.

There was no end to my restless meditations. Waldegrave was the only being, beside myself, acquainted with the secrets of my cabinet. During his life these manuscripts had been the objects of perpetual solicitude; to gain possession, to destroy, or secrete them, was the strongest of his wishes. Had he retained his sensibility on the approach of death, no doubt he would have renewed, with irresistable solemnity, his injunctions to destroy them.

Now, however, they had vanished. There were no materials of conjecture; no probabilities to be weighed, or suspicions to revolve. Human artifice or power was unequal to this exploit. Means less than preternatural would not furnish a conveyance for this treasure.

It was otherwise with regard to this unseasonable walker. His inducements indeed were beyond my power to conceive, but to enter these doors and ascend these stairs, demanded not the faculties of any being more than human.

This intrusion, and the pillage of my cabinet were contemporary events. Was there no more connection between them than that which results from time? Was not the purloiner of my treasure and the wanderer the same person? I could not reconcile the former incident with the attributes of man, and yet a secret faith, not to be outrooted or suspended, swayed me, and compelled me to imagine that the detection of this visitant, would unveil the thief.

These thoughts were pregnant with dejection and reverie. Clithero, during the day, was forgotten. On the succeeding night, my intentions, with regard to this man, returned. I derived some slender consolation from reflecting, that time, in its long lapse and ceaseless revolutions, might dissipate the gloom that environed me. Meanwhile I struggled to dismiss the images connected with my loss and to think only of Clithero.

My impatience was as strong as ever to obtain another interview with this man. I longed with vehemence for the return of day. I believed that every moment added to his sufferings, intellectual and physical, and confided in the efficacy of my presence to alleviate or suspend them. The provisions I had left would be speedily consumed, and the abstinence of three days was sufficient to undermine the vital energies. I, some times, hesitated whether I ought not instantly to depart. It was night indeed, but the late storm had purified the air, and the radiance of a full moon was universal and dazling.

From this attempt I was deterred by reflecting that my own frame needed the repairs of sleep. Toil and watchfulness, if prolonged another day, would deeply injure a constitution by no means distinguished for its force. I must, therefore, compel, if it were possible, some hours of repose. I prepared to retire to bed, when a new incident occurred to divert my attention for a time from these designs.

CHAPTER XIV

WHILE sitting alone by the parlour fire, marking the effects of moon-light, I noted one on horseback coming towards the gate. At first sight, methought his shape and guise were not wholly new to me; but all that I could discern was merely a resemblance to some one whom I had before seen. Presently he stopped, and, looking towards the house, made inquiries of a passenger who chanced to be near. Being apparently satisfied with the answers he received, he rode with a quick pace, into the court and alighted at the door. I started from my seat, and, going forth, waited with some impatience to hear his purpose explained.

He accosted me with the formality of a stranger, and asked if a young man, by name Edgar Huntly, resided here. Being answered in the affirmative, and being requested to come in, he entered, and seated himself, without hesitation, by the fire. Some doubt and anxiety were visible in his looks. He seemed desirous of information upon some topic, and yet betrayed terror lest the answers he might receive should subvert some hope, or confirm some foreboding.

Meanwhile I scrutinized his features with much solicitude. A nearer and more deliberate view convinced me that the first impression was just; but still I was unable to call up his name or the circumstances of our former meeting. The pause was at length ended by his saying, in a faltering voice:

My name is Weymouth. I came hither to obtain information on a subject in which my happiness is deeply concerned.

At the mention of his name, I started. It was a name too closely connected with the image of thy brother, not to call up affecting and vivid recollections. Weymouth thou knowest, was thy brother's friend. It is three years since this man left America, during which time no tidings had been heard of him, at least, by thy brother. He had now returned, and was probably unacquainted with the fate of his friend.

After an anxious pause, he continued. . . . Since my arrival I have heard of an event which has, on many accounts, given me the deepest sorrow. I loved Waldegrave, and know not any person in the world whose life was dearer to me than his. There were considerations, however, which made it more precious to me than the life of one whose merits might be greater. With his life, my own existence and property were, I have reason to think, inseparably united.

On my return to my country, after a long absence, I made immediate inquiries after him. I was informed of his untimely death. I had questions, of infinite moment to my happiness, to decide with regard to the state and disposition of his property. I sought out those of his friends who had maintained with him the most frequent and confidential intercourse, but they could not afford me any satisfaction. At length, I was informed that a young man of your name, and living in this district, had enjoyed more of his affection and society than any other, had regulated the property which he left behind, and was best qualified to afford the intelligence which I sought. You, it seems, are this person, and of you I must make inquiries to which I conjure you to return sincere and explicit answers.

That, said I, I shall find no difficulty in doing. Whatever questions you shall think proper to ask, I will answer with readiness and truth.

What kind of property and to what amount was your friend possessed of at his death?

It was money, and consisted of deposits at the bank of North America. The amount was little short of eight thousand dollars.

On whom has this property devolved?

His sister was his only kindred, and she is now in possession of it.

Did he leave any will by which he directed the disposition of his property? While thus speaking, Weymouth fixed his eyes upon my countenance, and seemed anxious to pierce into my inmost soul. I was somewhat surprised at his questions, but much more at the manner in which they were put. I answered him, however, without delay. . . . He left no will, nor was any paper discovered, by which we could guess at his intentions. No doubt, indeed, had he made a will his sister would have been placed precisely in the same condition in which she now is. He was not only bound to her by the strongest ties of kindred, but by affection and gratitude.

Weymouth now withdrew his eyes from my face, and sunk into a mournful reverie. He sighed often and deeply. This deportment and the strain of his inquiries excited much surprise. His interest in the fate of Waldegrave ought to have made the information he had received, a source of satisfaction rather than of regret. The property which Waldegrave left was much greater than his mode of life, and his own professions had given us reason to expect, but it was no more than sufficient to insure to thee an adequate subsistence. It ascertained the happiness of those who were dearest to Waldegrave, and placed them forever beyond the reach of that poverty which had hitherto beset them. I made no attempt to interrupt the silence, but prepared to answer any new interrogatory. At length, Weymouth resumed:

Waldegrave was a fortunate man, to amass so considerable a sum in so short a time. I remember, when we parted, he was poor. He used to lament that his scrupulous integrity precluded him from all the common roads to wealth. He did not contemn riches, but he set the highest value upon competence; and imagined that he was doomed forever to poverty. His religious duty compelled him to seek his livelihood by teaching a school of blacks. The labour was disproportioned to his feeble constitution, and the profit was greatly disproportioned to the labour. It scarcely supplied the necessities of nature, and was reduced sometimes even below that standard by his frequent indisposition. I rejoice to find that his scruples had somewhat relaxed their force, and that he had betaken himself to some more profitable occupation. Pray, what was his new way of business?

Nay, said I, his scruples continued as rigid, in this respect, as ever. He was teacher of the Negro free-school when he died.

Indeed! How then came he to amass so much money? Could he blend any more lucrative pursuit with his duty as a school-master?

So it seems.

What was his pursuit?

That question, I believe, none of his friends are qualified to answer. I thought myself acquainted with the most secret transactions of his life, but this had been carefully concealed from me. I was not only unapprised of any other employment of his time, but had not the slightest suspicion of his possessing any property beside his clothes and books. Ransacking his papers, with a different view, I lighted on his bank-book, in which was a regular receipt for seven thousand five hundred dollars. By what means he acquired this money, and even the acquisition of it, till his death put us in possession of his papers, was wholly unknown to us.

Possibly he might have held it in trust for another. In this case some memorandums or letters would be found explaining this affair.

True. This supposition could not fail to occur, in consequence of which the most diligent search was made

143

among his papers, but no shred or scrap was to be found which countenanced our conjecture.

You may reasonably be surprised, and perhaps offended, said Weymouth, at these inquiries; but it is time to explain my motives for making them. Three years ago I was, like Waldegrave, indigent, and earned my bread by daily labour. During seven years service in a public office, I saved, from the expences of subsistence, a few hundred dollars. I determined to strike into a new path, and, with this sum, to lay the foundation of better fortune. I turned it into a bulky commodity, freighted and loaded a small vessel, and went with it to Barcelona in Spain. I was not unsuccessful in my projects, and, changing my abode to England, France and Germany, according as my interest required, I became finally possessed of sufficient for the supply of all my wants. I then resolved to return to my native country, and, laying out my money in land, to spend the rest of my days in the luxury and quiet of an opulent farmer. For this end I invested the greatest part of my property in a cargo of wine from Madeira. The remainder I turned into a bill of exchange for seven thousand five hundred dollars. I had maintained a friendly correspondence with Waldegrave during my absence. There was no one with whom I had lived on terms of so much intimacy, and had boundless confidence in his integrity. To him therefore I determined to transmit this bill, requesting him to take the money into safe keeping until my return. In this manner I endeavoured to provide against the accidents that might befall my person or my cargo in crossing the ocean.

It was my fate to encounter the worst of these disasters. We were overtaken by a storm, my vessel was driven ashore on the coast of Portugal, my cargo was utterly lost, and the greater part of the crew and passengers were drowned. I was rescued from the same fate by some fishermen. In consequence of the hardships to which I had been exposed, having laboured for several days at the pumps, and spent the greater part of a winter night,

144

hanging from the rigging of the ship, and perpetually beaten by the waves, I contracted a severe disease, which bereaved me of the use of my limbs. The fishermen who rescued me, carried me to their huts, and there I remained three weeks helpless and miserable.

That part of the coast on which I was thrown, was, in the highest degree, sterile and rude. Its few inhabitants subsisted precariously on the produce of the ocean. Their dwellings were of mud, low, filthy, dark, and comfortless. Their fuel was the stalks of shrubs, sparingly scattered over a sandy desert. Their poverty scarcely allowed them salt and black bread with their fish, which was obtained in unequal and sometimes insufficient quantities, and which they ate with all its impurities and half cooked.

My former habits as well as my present indisposition required very different treatment from what the ignorance and penury of these people obliged them to bestow. I lay upon the moist earth, imperfectly sheltered from the sky, and with neither raiment or fire to keep me warm. My hosts had little attention or compassion to spare to the wants of others. They could not remove me to a more hospitable district, and here, without doubt, I should have perished had not a monk chanced to visit their hovels. He belonged to a convent of St. Jago, some leagues farther from the shore, who used to send one of its members annually to inspect the religious concerns of those outcasts. Happily this was the period of their visitations.

My abode in Spain had made me somewhat conversant with its language. The dialect of this monk did not so much differ from Castilian, but that, with the assistance of Latin, we were able to converse. The jargon of the fishermen was unintelligible, and they had vainly endeavoured to keep up my spirits by informing me of this expected visit.

This monk was touched with compassion at my calamity, and speedily provided the means of my removal to his convent. Here I was charitably entertained, and the aid of a physician was procured for me. He was but poorly skilled in his profession, and rather confirmed than alleviated my disease. The Portuguese of his trade, especially in remoter districts, are little more than dealers in talismans and nostrums. For a long time I was unable to leave my pallet, and had no prospect before me but that of consuming my days in the gloom of this cloister.

All the members of this convent, but he who had been my first benefactor, and whose name was Chaledro, were bigotted and sordid. Their chief motive for treating me with kindness, was the hope of obtaining a convert from heresy. They spared no pains to subdue my errors, and were willing to prolong my imprisonment, in the hope of finally gaining their end. Had my fate been governed by those, I should have been immured in this convent, and compelled, either to adopt their fanatical creed or to put an end to my own life, in order to escape their well meant persecutions. Chaledro, however, though no less sincere in his faith and urgent in his intreaties, yet finding me invincible, exerted his influence to obtain my liberty.

After many delays, and strenuous exertions of my friend, they consented to remove me to Oporto. The journey was to be performed in an open cart over a mountainous country, in the heats of summer. The monks endeavoured to dissuade me from the enterprize, for my own sake, it being scarcely possible that one in my feeble state, should survive a journey like this; but I despaired of improving my condition by other means. I preferred death to the imprisonment of a Portuguese monastery, and knew that I could hope for no alleviation of my disease, but from the skill of Scottish or French physicians, whom I expected to meet with in that city. I adhered to my purpose with so much vehemence and obstinacy, that they finally yielded to my wishes.

My road lay through the wildest and most rugged districts. It did not exceed ninety miles, but seven days were consumed on the way. The motion of the vehicle racked me with the keenest pangs, and my attendants concluded that every stage would be my last. They had been selected without due regard to their characters. They were knavish and inhuman, and omitted nothing, but actual violence, to hasten my death. They purposely retarded the journey, and protracted to seven, what might have been readily performed in four days. They neglected to execute the orders which they had received, respecting my lodging and provisions, and from them, as well as from the peasants, who were sure to be informed that I was an heretic, I suffered every species of insult and injury. My constitution, as well as my frame, possessed a fund of strength of which I had no previous conception. In spite of hardship and exposure and abstinence, I, at last, arrived at Oporto.

Instead of being carried, agreeably to Chaledro's direction, to a convent of St. Jago, I was left, late in the evening, in the porch of a common hospital. My attendants, having laid me on the pavement and loaded me with imprecations, left me to obtain admission by my own efforts. I passed the live-long night in this spot, and in the morning was received into the house, in a state which left it uncertain whether I was alive or dead.

After recovering my sensibility, I made various efforts to procure a visit from some English merchant. This was no easy undertaking for one in my deplorable condition. I was too weak to articulate my words distinctly, and these words were rendered by my foreign accent, scarcely intelligible. The likelihood of my speedy death made the people about me more indifferent to my wants and petitions.

I will not dwell upon my repeated disappointments, but content myself with mentioning that I gained the attention of a French gentleman, whose curiosity brought him to view the hospital. Through him, I obtained a visit from an English merchant, and finally gained the notice of a person, who formerly resided in America, and of whom I had imperfect knowledge. By their kindness I was removed from the hospital to a private house. A Scottish surgeon was summoned to my assistance, and in seven months, I was restored to my present state of health.

At Oporto, I embarked, in an American ship, for New-York. I was destitute of all property, and relied, for the payment of the debts which I was obliged to contract, as well as for my future subsistence, on my remittance to Waldegrave. I hastened to Philadelphia, and was soon informed that my friend was dead. His death had taken place a long time since my remittance to him, hence this disaster was a subject of regret chiefly on his own account. I entertained no doubt but that my property had been secured, and that either some testamentary directions, or some papers had been left behind respecting this affair.

I sought out those who were formerly our mutual acquaintance, I found that they were wholly strangers to his affairs. They could merely relate some particulars of his singular death, and point out the lodgings which he formerly occupied. Hither I forthwith repaired, and discovered that he lived in this house with his sister, disconnected with its other inhabitants. They described his mode of life in terms that shewed them to be very imperfectly acquainted with it. It was easy indeed to infer, from their aspect and manners, that little sympathy or union could have subsisted between them and their co-tenants, and this inference was confirmed by their insinuations, the growth of prejudice and envy. They told me that Waldegrave's sister had gone to live in the country, but whither or for how long, she had not condescended to inform them, and they did not care to ask. She was a topping dame whose notions were much too high for her station. Who was more nice than wise, and yet was one who could stoop, when it most became her to stand upright. It was no business of theirs, but they could not but mention their suspicions that she had good reasons for leaving the city, and for concealing the place of her retreat. Some things were hard to be disguised. They spoke for themselves, and the only way to hinder disagreeable discoveries, was to keep out of sight.

I was wholly a stranger to Waldegrave's sister. I knew merely that he had such a relation. There was nothing therefore to outbalance this unfavourable report, but the apparent malignity and grossness of those who gave it. It was not, however, her character about which I was solicitous, but merely the place where she might be found, and the suitable inquiries respecting her deceased brother, be answered. On this head, these people professed utter ignorance and were either unable or unwilling to direct me to any person in the city who knew more than themselves. After much discourse they, at length, let fall an intimation that if any one knew her place of retreat, it was probably a country lad, by name Huntly, who lived near the *Forks* of Delaware. After Waldegrave's death, this lad had paid his sister a visit, and seemed to be admitted on a very confidential footing. She left the house, for the last time, in his company, and he, therefore, was most likely to know what had become of her.

The name of Huntly was not totally unknown to me. I myself was born and brought up in the neighbouring township of Chetasco. I had some knowledge of your family, and your name used often to be mentioned by Waldegrave, as that of one who, at a maturer age, would prove himself useful to his country. I determined therefore to apply to you for what information you could give. I designed to visit my father who lives in Chetasco and relieve him from that disquiet which his ignorance of my fate could not fail to have inspired, and both these ends could be thus, at the same time, accomplished.

Before I left the city, I thought it proper to apply to the merchant on whom my bill had been drawn. If this bill had been presented and paid, he had doubtless preserved some record of it, and hence a clue might be afforded, though every other expedient should fail. My usual ill fortune pursued me upon this occasion, for the merchant had lately become insolvent, and, to avoid the rage of his creditors, had fled, without leaving any vestige of this or similar transactions behind him. He had, some years since, been an adventurer from Holland, and was suspected to have returned thither.

149

CHAPTER XV

I CAME hither with an heart desponding of success. Adversity had weakened my faith in the promises of the future, and I was prepared to receive just such tidings as you have communicated. Unacquainted with the secret motives of Waldegrave and his sister, it is impossible for me to weigh the probabilities of their rectitude. I have only my own assertion to produce in support of my claim. All other evidence, all vouchers and papers, which might attest my veracity, or sanction my claim in a court of law, are buried in the ocean. The bill was transmitted just before my departure from Madeira, and the letters by which it was accompanied, informed Waldegrave of my design to follow it immediately. Hence he did not, it is probable, acknowledge the receipt of my letters. The vessels in which they were sent, arrived in due season. I was assured that all letters were duly deposited in the post-office, where, at present, mine are not to be found.

You assure me that nothing has been found among his papers, hinting at any pecuniary transaction between him and me. Some correspondence passed between us previous to that event. Have no letters, with my signature, been found? Are you qualified, by your knowledge of his papers, to answer me explicitly? Is it not possible for some letters to have been mislaid?

I am qualified, said I, to answer your inquiries beyond

any other person in the world. Waldegrave maintained only general intercourse with the rest of mankind. With me his correspondence was copious, and his confidence, as I imagined, without bounds. His books and papers were contained in a single chest, at his lodgings, the keys of which he had about him when he died. These keys I carried to his sister, and was authorized by her to open and examine the contents of this chest. This was done with the utmost care. These papers are now in my possession. Among them no paper, of the tenor you mention, was found, and no letter with your signature. Neither Mary Waldegrave nor I are capable of disguising the truth or committing an injustice. The moment she receives conviction of your right she will restore this money to you. The moment I imbibe this conviction, I will exert all my influence, and it is not small, to induce her to restore it. Permit me, however, to question you in your turn. Who was the merchant on whom your bill was drawn, what was the date of it, and when did the bill and its counterparts arrive?

I do not exactly remember the date of the bills. They were made out, however, six days before I myself embarked which happened on the tenth of August 1784. They were sent by three vessels, one of which was bound to Charleston and the others to New-York. The last arrived within two days of each other, and about the middle of November in the same year. The name of the payer was Monteith.

After a pause of recollection, I answered, I will not hesitate to apprise you of every thing which may throw light upon this transaction, and whether favourable or otherwise to your claim. I have told you among my friend's papers your name is not to be found. I must likewise repeat that the possession of this money by Waldegrave was wholly unknown to us till his death. We are likewise unacquainted with any means by which he could get possession of so large a sum in his own right. He spent no more than his scanty stipend as a teacher, though

151

this stipend was insufficient to supply his wants. This Bank-receipt is dated in December 1784, a fortnight, perhaps, after the date that you have mentioned. You will perceive how much this coincidence, which could scarcely have taken place by chance, is favourable to your claim.

Mary Waldegrave resides, at present, at Abingdon. She will rejoice, as I do, to see one who, as her brother's friend, is entitled to her affection. Doubt not but that she will listen with impartiality and candour to all that you can urge in defence of your title to this money. Her decision will not be precipitate, but it will be generous and just, and founded on such reasons that, even if it be adverse to your wishes, you will be compelled to approve it.

I can entertain no doubt, he answered, as to the equity of my claim. The coincidences you mention are sufficient to convince me, that this sum was received upon my bill, but this conviction must necessarily be confined to myself. No one but I can be conscious to the truth of my own story. The evidence on which I build my faith, in this case, is that of my own memory and senses; but this evidence cannot make itself conspicuous to you. You have nothing but my bare assertion, in addition to some probabilities flowing from the conduct of Waldegrave. What facts may exist to corroborate my claim, which you have forgotten, or which you may think proper to conceal, I cannot judge. I know not what is passing in the secret of your hearts; I am unacquainted with the character of this lady and with yours. I have nothing on which to build surmises and suspicions of your integrity, and nothing to generate unusual confidence. The frailty of your virtue and the strength of your temptations I know not. However she decides in this case, and whatever opinion I shall form as to the reasonableness of her decision, it will not become me either to upbraid her, or to nourish discontentment and repinings.

I know that my claim has no legal support: that, if this money be resigned to me, it will be the impulse of spontaneous justice, and not the coercion of law to which I am indebted for it. Since, therefore, the justice of my claim is to be measured not by law, but by simple equity, I will candidly acknowledge that, as yet it is uncertain whether I ought to receive, even should Miss Waldegrave be willing to give it. I know my own necessities and schemes, and in what degree this money would be subservient to these; but I know not the views and wants of others, and cannot estimate the usefulness of this money to them. However I decide upon your conduct in withholding or retaining it, I shall make suitable allowance for my imperfect knowledge of your motives and wants, as well as for your unavoidable ignorance of mine.

I have related my sufferings from shipwreck and poverty, not to bias your judgment or engage your pity, but merely because the impulse to relate them chanced to awake; because my heart is softened by the remembrance of Waldegrave, who has been my only friend, and by the sight of one whom he loved.

I told you that my father lived in Chetasco. He is now aged, and I am his only child. I should have rejoiced in being able to relieve his grey hairs from labour to which his failing strength cannot be equal. This was one of my inducements in coming to America. Another was, to prepare the way for a woman whom I married in Europe and who is now awaiting intelligence from me in London. Her poverty is not less than my own, and by marrying against the wishes of her kindred, she has bereaved herself of all support but that of her husband. Whether I shall be able to rescue her from indigence, whether I shall alleviate the poverty of my father, or increase it by burthening his scanty funds by my own maintenance as well as his, the future alone can determine.

I confess that my stock of patience and hope has never been large, and that my misfortunes have nearly exhausted it. The flower of my years has been consumed in struggling with adversity, and my constitution has received a shock, from sickness and mistreatment in Portugal, which I cannot expect long to survive. . . . But I make you sad (he continued.) I have said all that I meant to say in this interview. I am impatient to see my father, and night has already come. I have some miles yet to ride to his cottage and over a rough road. I will shortly visit you again, and talk to you at greater leisure on these and other topics. At present I leave you.

I was unwilling to part so abruptly with this guest, and intreated him to prolong his visit, but he would not be prevailed upon. Repeating his promise of shortly seeing me again, he mounted his horse and disappeared. I looked after him with affecting and complex emotions. I reviewed the incidents of this unexpected and extraordinary interview, as if it had existed in a dream. An hour had passed, and this stranger had alighted among us as from the clouds, to draw the veil from those obscurities which had bewildered us so long, to make visible a new train of disastrous consequences flowing from the untimely death of thy brother, and to blast that scheme of happiness on which thou and I had so fondly meditated.

But what wilt thou think of this new born claim? The story, hadst thou observed the features and guize of the relater, would have won thy implicit credit. His countenance exhibited deep traces of the afflictions he had endured and the fortitude which he had exercised. He was sallow and emaciated, but his countenance was full of seriousness and dignity. A sort of ruggedness of brow, the token of great mental exertion and varied experience, argued a premature old age.

What a mournful tale! Is such the lot of those who wander from their rustic homes in search of fortune? Our countrymen are prone to enterprize, and are scattered over every sea and every land in pursuit of that wealth which will not screen them from disease and infirmity, which is missed much oftener than found, and which, when gained, by no means compensates them for the hardships and vicissitudes endured in the pursuit.

But what if the truth of these pretentions be admitted?

154

The money must be restored to its right owner. I know that whatever inconveniences may follow the deed, thou wilt not hesitate to act justly. Affluence and dignity, however valuable, may be purchased too dear. Honesty will not take away its keenness from the winter-blast, its ignominy and unwholesomeness from servile labour, or strip of its charms the life of elegance and leisure; but these, unaccompanied with self-reproach, are less deplorable than wealth and honour, the possession of which is marred by our own disapprobation.

I know the bitterness of this sacrifice. I know the impatience with which your poverty has formerly been borne, how much your early education is at war with that degradation and obscurity to which your youth has been condemned. How earnestly your wishes panted after a state, which might exempt you from dependence upon daily labour and on the caprices of others, and might secure to you leisure to cultivate and indulge your love of knowledge and your social and beneficent affections.

Your motive for desiring a change of fortune has been greatly enforced since we have become known to each other. Thou hast honoured me with thy affection, but that union, on which we rely for happiness, could not take place while both of us were poor. My habits, indeed, have made labour and rustic obscurity less painful than they would prove to my friend, but my present condition is wholly inconsistent with marriage. As long as my exertions are insufficient to maintain us both, it would be unjustifiable to burthen you with new cares and duties. Of this you are more thoroughly convinced than I am. The love of independence and ease, and impatience of drudgery are woven into your constitution. Perhaps they are carried to an erroneous extreme, and derogate from that uncommon excellence by which your character is, in other respects, distinguished, but they cannot be removed.

This obstacle was unexpectedly removed by the death of your brother. However justly to be deplored was this catastrophe, yet like every other event, some of its consequences were good. By giving you possession of the means of independence and leisure, by enabling us to complete a contract which poverty alone had thus long delayed, this event has been, at the same time, the most disastrous and propitious which could have happened.

Why thy brother should have concealed from us the possession of this money; why, with such copious means of indulgence and leisure, he should still pursue his irksome trade, and live in so penurious a manner, has been a topic of endless and unsatisfactory conjecture between us. It was not difficult to suppose that this money was held in trust for another, but in that case it was unavoidable that some document or memorandum, or at least some claimant would appear. Much time has since elapsed, and you have thought yourself at length justified in appropriating this money to your own use.

Our flattering prospects are now shut in. You must return to your original poverty, and once more depend for precarious subsistence on your needle. You cannot restore the whole, for unavoidable expenses and the change of your mode of living, has consumed some part of it. For so much you must consider yourself as Weymouth's debtor.

Repine not, my friend, at this unlooked-for reverse. Think upon the merits and misfortunes of your brother's friend, think upon his aged father whom we shall enable him to rescue from poverty; think upon his desolate wife, whose merits are, probably, at least equal to your own, and whose helplessness is likely to be greater. I am not insensible to the evils which have returned upon us with augmented force, after having, for a moment, taken their flight. I know the precariousness of my condition and that of my sisters, that our subsistence hangs upon the life of an old man. My uncle's death will transfer this property to his son, who is a stranger and an enemy to us, and the first act of whose authority will unquestionably be to turn us forth from these doors. Marriage with thee was anticipated with joyous emotions, not merely on my own

156

account or on thine, but likewise for the sake of those beloved girls, to whom that event would enable me to furnish an asylum.

But wedlock is now more distant than ever. My heart bleeds to think of the sufferings which my beloved Mary is again fated to endure, but regrets are only aggravations of calamity. They are pernicious, and it is our duty to shake them off.

I can entertain no doubts as to the equity of Weymouth's claim. So many coincidences could not have happened by chance. The non-appearance of any letters or papers connected with it is indeed a mysterious circumstance, but why should Waldegrave be studious of preserving these? They were useless paper, and might, without impropriety, be cast away or made to serve any temporary purpose. Perhaps, indeed, they still lurk in some unsuspected corner. To wish that time may explain this mystery in a different manner, and so as to permit our retention of this money, is, perhaps, the dictate of selfishness. The transfer to Weymouth will not be productive of less benefit to him and to his family, than we should derive from the use of it.

These considerations, however, will be weighed when we meet. Meanwhile I will return to my narrative.

CHAPTER XVI

HERE, my friend, thou must permit me to pause. The following incidents are of a kind to which the most ardent invention has never conceived a parallel. Fortune, in her most wayward mood, could scarcely be suspected of an influence like this. The scene was pregnant with astonishment and horror. I cannot, even now, recall it without reviving the dismay and confusion which I then experienced.

Possibly, the period will arrive when I shall look back without agony on the perils I have undergone. That period is still distant. Solitude and sleep are now no more than the signals to summon up a tribe of ugly phantoms. Famine, and blindness, and death, and savage enemies, never fail to be conjured up by the silence and darkness of the night. I cannot dissipate them by any efforts of reason. My cowardice requires the perpetual consolation of light. My heart droops when I mark the decline of the sun, and I never sleep but with a candle burning at my pillow. If, by any chance, I should awake and find myself immersed in darkness, I know not what act of desperation I might be suddenly impelled to commit.

I have delayed this narrative, longer than my duty to my friend enjoined. Now that I am able to hold a pen, I will hasten to terminate that uncertainty with regard to my fate, in which my silence has involved thee. I will recall that series of unheard of and disastrous vicissitudes which has constituted the latest portion of my life.

158

I am not certain, however, that I shall relate them in an intelligible manner. One image runs into another, sensations succeed in so rapid a train, that I fear, I shall be unable to distribute and express them with sufficient perspicuity. As I look back, my heart is sore and aches within my bosom. I am conscious to a kind of complex sentiment of distress and forlornness that cannot be perfectly pourtrayed by words; but I must do as well as I can. In the utmost vigour of my faculties, no eloquence that I possess would do justice to the tale. Now in my languishing and feeble state, I shall furnish thee with little more than a glimpse of the truth. With these glimpses, transient and faint as they are, thou must be satisfied.

I have said that I slept. My memory assures me of this: It informs of the previous circumstances of my laying aside my clothes, of placing the light upon a chair within reach of my pillow, of throwing myself upon the bed, and of gazing on the rays of the moon reflected on the wall, and almost obscured by those of the candle. I remember my occasional relapses into fits of incoherent fancies, the harbingers of sleep: I remember, as it were, the instant when my thoughts ceased to flow, and my senses were arrested by the leaden wand of forgetfulness.

My return to sensation and to consciousness took place in no such tranquil scene. I emerged from oblivion by degrees so slow and so faint, that their succession cannot be marked. When enabled at length to attend to the information which my senses afforded, I was conscious, for a time, of nothing but existence. It was unaccompanied with lassitude or pain, but I felt disinclined to stretch my limbs, or raise my eye-lids. My thoughts were wildering and mazy, and though consciousness were present, it was disconnected with the loco-motive or voluntary power.

From this state a transition was speedily effected. I perceived that my posture was supine, and that I lay upon my back. I attempted to open my eyes. The weight that oppressed them was too great for a slight exertion to remove. The exertion which I made cost me a pang more acute than any which I ever experienced. My eyes, how-

159

ever, were opened; but the darkness that environed me was as intense as before.

I attempted to rise, but my limbs were cold, and my joints had almost lost their flexibility. My efforts were repeated, and at length I attained a sitting posture. I was now sensible of pain in my shoulders and back. I was universally in that state to which the frame is reduced by blows of a club, mercilessly and endlessly repeated; my temples throbbed and my face was covered with clamy and cold drops, but that which threw me into deepest consternation was, my inability to see. I turned my head to different quarters, I stretched my eye-lids, and exerted every visual energy, but in vain. I was wrapt in the murkiest and most impenetrable gloom.

The first effort of reflection was to suggest the belief that I was blind; that disease is known to assail us in a moment and without previous warning. This surely was the misfortune that had now befallen me. Some ray, however fleeting and uncertain, could not fail to be discerned, if the power of vision were not utterly extinguished. In what circumstances could I possibly be placed, from which every particle of light should, by other means, be excluded?

This led my thoughts into a new train. I endeavoured to recall the past, but the past was too much in contradiction to the present, and my intellect was too much shattered by external violence, to allow me accurately to review it.

Since my sight availed nothing to the knowledge of my condition, I betook myself to other instruments. The element which I breathed was stagnant and cold. The spot where I lay was rugged and hard. I was neither naked nor clothed. A shirt and trossers composed my dress, and the shoes and stockings, which always accompanied these, were now wanting. What could I infer from this scanty garb, this chilling atmosphere, this stony bed?

I had awakened as from sleep. What was my condition when I fell asleep? Surely it was different from the

160

present. Then I inhabited a lightsome chamber, and was stretched upon a down bed. Now I was supine upon a rugged surface and immersed in palpable obscurity. Then I was in perfect health; now my frame was covered with bruises and every joint was racked with pain. What dungeon or den had received me, and by whose command was I transported hither?

After various efforts I stood upon my feet. At first I tottered and staggered. I stretched out my hands on all sides but met only with vacuity. I advanced forward. At the third step my foot moved something which lay upon the ground. I stooped and took it up, and found, on examination, that it was an Indian tom-hawk. This incident afforded me no hint from which I might conjecture my state.

Proceeding irresolutely and slowly forward, my hands at length touched a wall. This, like the flooring, was of stone, and was rugged and impenetrable. I followed this wall. An advancing angle occurred at a short distance, which was followed by similar angles. I continued to explore this clue, till the suspicion occurred that I was merely going round the walls of a vast and irregular apartment.

The utter darkness disabled me from comparing directions and distances. This discovery, therefore, was not made on a sudden and was still entangled with some doubt. My blood recovered some warmth, and my muscles some elasticity, but in proportion as my sensibility returned my pains augmented. Overpowered by my fears and my agonies I desisted from my fruitless search, and sat down, supporting my back against the wall.

My excruciating sensations for a time occupied my attention. These, in combination with other causes, gradually produced a species of delirium. I existed as it were in a wakeful dream. With nothing to correct my erroneous perceptions, the images of the past occurred in capricious combinations, and vivid hues. Methought I was the victim of some tyrant who had thrust me into a dungeon of his fortress, and left me no power to determine whether he intended I should perish with famine, or linger out a long life in hopeless imprisonment: Whether the day was shut out by insuperable walls, or the darkness that surrounded me, was owing to the night and to the smallness of those cranies through which day-light was to be admitted, I conjectured in vain.

Sometimes I imagined myself buried alive. Methought I had fallen into seeming death and my friends had consigned me to the tomb, from which a resurrection was impossible. That in such a case, my limbs would have been confined to a coffin, and my coffin to a grave, and that I should instantly have been suffocated, did not occur to destroy my supposition: Neither did this supposition overwhelm me with terror or prompt my efforts at deliverance. My state was full of tumult and confusion, and my attention was incessantly divided between my painful sensations and my feverish dreams.

There is no standard by which time can be measured, but the succession of our thoughts, and the changes that take place in the external world. From the latter I was totally excluded. The former made the lapse of some hours appear like the tediousness of weeks and months. At length, a new sensation, recalled my rambling meditations, and gave substance to my fears. I now felt the cravings of hunger, and perceived that unless my deliverance were speedily effected, I must suffer a tedious and lingering death.

I once more tasked my understanding and my senses, to discover the nature of my present situation and the means of escape. I listened to catch some sound. I heard an unequal and varying echo, sometimes near and sometimes distant, sometimes dying away and sometimes swelling into loudness. It was unlike any thing I had before heard, but it was evident that it arose from wind sweeping through spacious halls and winding passages. These tokens were incompatible with the result of the examination I had made. If my hands were true I was immured between walls, through which there was no avenue.

I now exerted my voice, and cried as loud as my wasted strength would admit. Its echoes were sent back to me in broken and confused sounds and from above. This effort was casual, but some part of that uncertainty in which I was involved, was instantly dispelled by it. In passing through the cavern on the former day, I have mentioned the verge of the pit at which I arrived. To acquaint me as far as was possible, with the dimensions of the place, I had hallooed with all my force, knowing that sound is reflected according to the distance and relative positions of the substances from which it is repelled.

The effect produced by my voice on this occasion resembled, with remarkable exactness, the effect which was then produced. Was I then shut up in the same cavern? Had I reached the brink of the same precipice and been thrown headlong into that vacuity? Whence else could arise the bruises which I had received, but from my fall? Yet all remembrance of my journey hither was lost. I had determined to explore this cave on the ensuing day, but my memory informed me not that this intention had been carried into effect. Still it was only possible to conclude that I had come hither on my intended expedition and had been thrown by another, or had, by some ill chance, fallen into the pit.

This opinion was conformable to what I had already observed. The pavement and walls were rugged like those of the footing and sides of the cave through which I had formerly passed.

But if this were true, what was the abhorred catastrophe to which I was now reserved? The sides of this pit were inaccessible: human footsteps would never wander into these recesses. My friends were unapprised of my forlorn state. Here I should continue till wasted by famine. In this grave should I linger out a few days, in unspeakable agonies, and then perish forever.

The inroads of hunger were already experienced, and

this knowledge of the desperateness of my calamity, urged me to phrenzy. I had none but capricious and unseen fate to condemn. The author of my distress and the means he had taken to decoy me hither, were incomprehensible. Surely my senses were fettered or depraved by some spell. I was still asleep, and this was merely a tormenting vision, or madness had seized me, and the darkness that environed and the hunger that afflicted me, existed only in my own distempered imagination.

The consolation of these doubts could not last long. Every hour added to the proofs that my perceptions were real. My hunger speedily became ferocious. I tore the linen of my shirt between my teeth and swallowed the fragments. I felt a strong propensity to bite the flesh from my arm. My heart overflowed with cruelty, and I pondered on the delight I should experience in rending some living animal to pieces, and drinking its blood and grinding its quivering fibres between my teeth.

This agony had already passed beyond the limits of endurance. I saw that time, instead of bringing respite or relief, would only aggravate my wants, and that my only remaining hope was to die before I should be assaulted by the last extremes of famine. I now recollected that a tomhawk was at hand, and rejoiced in the possession of an instrument by which I could so effectually terminate my sufferings.

I took it in my hand, moved its edge over my fingers, and reflected on the force that was required to make it reach my heart. I investigated the spot where it should enter, and strove to fortify myself with resolution to repeat the stroke a second or third time, if the first should prove insufficient. I was sensible that I might fail to inflict a mortal wound, but delighted to consider that the blood which would be made to flow, would finally release me, and that meanwhile my pains would be alleviated by swallowing this blood.

You will not wonder that I felt some reluctance to employ so fatal though indispensable a remedy. I once more ruminated on the possibility of rescuing myself by other means. I now reflected that the upper termination of the wall could not be at an immeasurable distance from the pavement. I had fallen from an height, but if that height had been considerable, instead of being merely bruised, should I not have been dashed into pieces?

Gleams of hope burst anew upon my soul. Was it not possible, I asked, to reach the top of this pit? The sides were rugged and uneven. Would not their projectures and abruptnesses serve me as steps by which I might ascend in safety? This expedient was to be tried without delay. Shortly my strength would fail and my doom would be irrevocably sealed.

I will not enumerate my laborious efforts, my alternations of despondency and confidence, the eager and unwearied scrutiny with which I examined the surface, the attempts which I made, and the failures which, for a time, succeeded each other. An hundred times, when I had ascended some feet from the bottom, I was compelled to relinquish my undertaking by the *untenable* smoothness of the spaces which remained to be gone over. An hundred times I threw myself, exhausted by fatigue and my pains, on the ground. The consciousness was gradually restored that till I had attempted every part of the wall, it was absurd to despair, and I again drew my tottering limbs and aching joints to that part of the wall which had not been surveyed.

At length, as I stretched my hand upward, I found somewhat that seemed like a recession in the wall. It was possible that this was the top of the cavity, and this might be the avenue to liberty. My heart leaped with joy, and I proceeded to climb the wall. No undertaking could be conceived more arduous than this. The space between this verge and the floor was nearly smooth. The verge was higher from the bottom than my head. The only means of ascending that were offered me were by my hands, with which I could draw myself upward so as, at length, to maintain my hold with my feet.

My efforts were indefatigable, and at length I placed myself on the verge; when this was accomplished my strength was nearly gone. Had I not found space enough beyond this brink to stretch myself at length, I should unavoidably have fallen backward into the pit, and all my pains had served no other end than to deepen my despair and hasten my destruction.

What impediments and perils remained to be encountered I could not judge. I was now inclined to forbode the worst. The interval of repose which was necessary to be taken, in order to recruit my strength, would accelerate the ravages of famine, and leave me without the power to proceed.

In this state, I once more consoled myself that an instrument of death was at hand. I had drawn up with me the tom-hawk, being sensible that should this impediment be overcome others might remain that would prove insuperable. Before I employed it, however, I cast my eyes wildly and languidly around. The darkness was no less intense than in the pit below, and yet two objects were distinctly seen.

They resembled a fixed and obscure flame. They were motionless. Though lustrous themselves they created no illumination around them. This circumstance, added to others, which reminded me of similar objects, noted on former occasions, immediately explained the nature of what I beheld. These were the eyes of a panther.

Thus had I struggled to obtain a post where a savage was lurking, and waited only till my efforts should place me within reach of his fangs. The first impulse was to arm myself against this enemy. The desperateness of my condition was, for a moment, forgotten. The weapon which was so lately lifted against my own bosom, was now raised to defend my life against the assault of another.

There, was no time for deliberation and delay. In a moment he might spring from his station and tear me to pieces. My utmost speed might not enable me to reach him where he sat, but merely to encounter his assault. I did not reflect how far my strength was adequate to save me. All the force that remained was mustered up and exerted in a throw.

No one knows the powers that are latent in his constitution. Called forth by imminent dangers, our efforts frequently exceed our most sanguine belief. Though tottering on the verge of dissolution, and apparently unable to crawl from this spot, a force was exerted in this throw, probably greater than I had ever before exerted. It was resistless and unerring. I aimed at the middle space between these glowing orbs. It penetrated the scull and the animal fell, struggling and shrieking, on the ground.

My ears quickly informed me when his pangs were at an end. His cries and his convulsions lasted for a moment and then ceased. The effect of his voice, in these subterranean abodes, was unspeakably rueful.

The abruptness of this incident, and the preternatural exertion of my strength, left me in a state of languor and sinking from which slowly and with difficulty I recovered. The first suggestion that occurred was to feed upon the carcass of this animal. My hunger had arrived at that pitch where all fastidiousness and scruples are at an end. I crept to the spot. . . . I will not shock you by relating the extremes to which dire necessity had driven me. I review this scene with loathing and horror. Now that it is past I look back upon it as on some hideous dream. The whole appears to be some freak of insanity. No alternative was offered, and hunger was capable to be appeased, even by a banquet so detestable.

If this appetite has sometimes subdued the sentiments of nature, and compelled the mother to feed upon the flesh of her offspring, it will not excite amazement that I did not turn from the yet warm blood and reeking fibres of a brute.

One evil was now removed, only to give place to another. The first sensations of fullness had scarcely been felt when my stomach was seized by pangs whose acuteness exceeded all that I ever before experienced. I bitterly lamented my inordinate avidity. The excruciations of famine were better than the agonies which this abhorred meal had produced. Death was now impending with no less proximity and certainty, though in a different form. Death was a sweet relief for my present miseries, and I vehemently longed for its arrival. I stretched myself on the ground. I threw myself into every posture that promised some alleviation of this evil. I rolled along the pavement of the cavern, wholly inattentive to the dangers that environed me. That I did not fall into the pit, whence I had just emerged, must be ascribed to some miraculous chance.

How long my miseries endured, it is not possible to tell. I cannot even form a plausible conjecture. Judging by the lingering train of my sensations, I should conjecture that some days elapsed in this deplorable condition, but nature could not have so long sustained a conflict like this.

Gradually my pains subsided and I fell into a deep sleep. I was visited by dreams of a thousand hues. They led me to flowing streams and plenteous banquets, which, though placed within my view, some power forbade me to approach. From this sleep I recovered to the fruition of solitude and darkness, but my frame was in a state less feeble than before. That which I had eaten had produced temporary distress, but on the whole had been of use. If this food had not been provided for me I should scarcely have avoided death. I had reason therefore to congratulate myself on the danger that had lately occurred.

I had acted without foresight, and yet no wisdom could have prescribed more salutary measures. The panther was slain, not from a view to the relief of my hunger, but from the self-preserving and involuntary impulse. Had I fore-known the pangs to which my ravenous and bloody meal would give birth, I should have carefully abstained, and yet these pangs were a useful effort of nature to subdue and convert to nourishment the matter I had swallowed.

I was now assailed by the torments of thirst. My invention and my courage were anew bent to obviate this pressing evil. I reflected that there was some recess from this cavern, even from the spot where I now stood. Before, I was doubtful whether in this direction from this pit any avenue could be found, but since the panther had come hither there was reason to suppose the existence of some such avenue.

I now likewise attended to a sound, which, from its invariable tenour, denoted somewhat different from the whistling of a gale. It seemed like the murmur of a running stream. I now prepared to go forward, and endeavoured to move along in that direction in which this sound apparently came.

On either side and above my head, there was nothing but vacuity. My steps were to be guided by the pavement, which, though unequal and rugged, appeared, on the whole, to ascend. My safety required that I should employ both hands and feet in exploring my way.

I went on thus for a considerable period. The murmur, instead of becoming more distinct, gradually died away. My progress was arrested by fatigue, and I began once more to despond. My exertions, produced a perspiration, which, while it augmented my thirst, happily supplied me with imperfect means of appeasing it.

This expedient would, perhaps, have been accidentally suggested, but my ingenuity was assisted by remembering the history of certain English prisoners in Bengal, whom their merciless enemy imprisoned in a small room, and some of whom preserved themselves alive merely by swallowing the moisture that flowed from their bodies. This experiment I now performed with no less success.

This was slender and transitory consolation. I knew that, wandering at random, I might never reach the outlet of this cavern, or might be disabled, by hunger and fatigue, from going farther than the outlet. The cravings which had lately been satiated, would speedily return, and my negligence had cut me off from the resource which had recently been furnished. I thought not till now that a second meal might be indispensable.

To return upon my footsteps to the spot where the dead

animal lay was an heartless project. I might thus be placing myself at an hopeless distance from liberty. Besides my track could not be retraced. I had frequently deviated from a straight direction for the sake of avoiding impediments. All of which I was sensible was, that I was travelling up a irregular acclivity. I hoped sometime to reach the summit, but had no reason for adhering to one line of ascent in preference to another.

To remain where I was, was manifestly absurd. Whether I mounted or descended, a change of place was most likely to benefit me. I resolved to vary my direction, and, instead of ascending, keep along the side of what I accounted an hill. I had gone some hundred feet when the murmur, before described, once more saluted my ear.

This sound, being imagined to proceed from a running stream, could not but light up joy in the heart of one nearly perishing with thirst. I proceeded with new courage. The sound approached no nearer nor became more distinct, but as long as it died not away, I was satisfied to listen and to hope.

I was eagerly observant if any the least glimmering of light, should visit this recess. At length, on the right hand a gleam, infinitely faint, caught my attention. It was wavering and unequal. I directed my steps towards it. It became more vivid, and permanent. It was of that kind, however, which proceeded from a fire, kindled with dry sticks, and not from the sun. I now heard the crackling of flames.

This sound made me pause, or at least to proceed with circumspection. At length the scene opened, and I found myself at the entrance of a cave. I quickly reached a station where I saw a fire burning. At first no other object was noted, but it was easy to infer that the fire was kindled by men, and that they who kindled it could be at no great distance.

CHAPTER XVII

THUS was I delivered from my prison and restored to the enjoyment of the air and the light. Perhaps the chance was almost miraculous that led me to this opening. In any other direction, I might have involved myself in an inextricable maze, and rendered my destruction sure: but what now remained to place me in absolute security? Beyond the fire I could see nothing; but since the smoke rolled rapidly away, it was plain that on the opposite side the cavern was open to the air.

I went forward, but my eyes were fixed upon the fire; presently, in consequence of changing my station, I perceived several feet, and the skirts of blankets. I was somewhat startled at these appearances. The legs were naked, and scored into uncouth figures. The *mocassins* which lay beside them, and which were adorned in a grotesque manner, in addition to other incidents, immediately suggested the suspicion that they were Indians. No spectacle was more adapted than this to excite wonder and alarm. Had some mysterious power snatched me from the earth, and cast me, in a moment, into the heart of the wilderness? Was I still in the vicinity of my paternal habitation, or was I thousands of miles distant?

Were these the permanent inhabitants of this region, or were they wanderers and robbers? While in the heart of the mountain I had entertained a vague belief that I was still within the precincts of Norwalk. This opinion was shaken for a moment by the objects which I now beheld, but it insensibly returned; yet, how was this opinion to be reconciled to appearances so strange and uncouth, and what measure did a due regard to my safety enjoin me to take?

I now gained a view of four brawny and terrific figures, stretched upon the ground. They lay parallel to each other, on their left sides; in consequence of which their faces were turned from me. Between each was an interval where lay a musquet. Their right hands seemed placed upon the stocks of their guns, as if to seize them on the first moment of alarm.

The aperture through which these objects were seen, was at the back of the cave, and some feet from the ground. It was merely large enough to suffer an human body to pass. It was involved in profound darkness, and there was no danger of being suspected or discovered as long as I maintained silence, and kept out of view.

It was easily imagined that these guests would make but a short sojourn in this spot. There was reason to suppose that it was now night, and that after a short repose, they would start up and resume their journey. It was my first design to remain shrouded in this covert till their departure, and I prepared to endure imprisonment and thirst somewhat longer.

Meanwhile my thoughts were busy in accounting for this spectacle. I need not tell thee that Norwalk is the termination of a sterile and narrow tract, which begins in the Indian country. It forms a sort of rugged and rocky vein, and continues upwards of fifty miles. It is crossed in a few places by narrow and intricate paths, by which a communication is maintained between the farms and settlements on the opposite sides of the ridge.

During former Indian wars, this rude surface was sometimes traversed by the Red-men, and they made, by means of it, frequent and destructive inroads into the heart of the English settlements. During the last war, notwithstanding the progress of population, and the mul-

172

tiplied perils of such an expedition, a band of them had once penetrated into Norwalk, and lingered long enough to pillage and murder some of the neighbouring inhabitants.

I have reason to remember that event. My father's house was placed on the verge of this solitude. Eight of these assassins assailed it at the dead of night. My parents and an infant child were murdered in their beds; the house was pillaged, and then burnt to the ground. Happily, myself and my two sisters were abroad upon a visit. The preceding day had been fixed for our return to our father's house, but a storm occurred, which made it dangerous to cross the river, and by obliging us to defer our journey, rescued us from captivity or death.

Most men are haunted by some species of terror or antipathy, which they are, for the most part, able to trace to some incident which befel them in their early years. You will not be surprized that the fate of my parents, and the sight of the body of one of this savage band, who, in the pursuit that was made after them, was overtaken and killed, should produce lasting and terrific images in my fancy. I never looked upon, or called up the image of a savage without shuddering.

I knew that, at this time, some hostilities had been committed on the frontier; that a long course of injuries and encroachments had lately exasperated the Indian tribes; that an implacable and exterminating war was generally expected. We imagined ourselves at an inaccessible distance from the danger, but I could not but remember that this persuasion was formerly as strong as at present, and that an expedition, which had once succeeded, might possibly be attempted again. Here was every token of enmity and bloodshed. Each prostrate figure was furnished with a rifled musquet, and a leathern bag tied round his waist, which was, probably, stored with powder and ball.

From these reflections, the sense of my own danger was revived and enforced, but I likewise ruminated on the evils which might impend over others. I should, no doubt, be safe by remaining in this nook; but might not some means be pursued to warn others of their danger? Should they leave this spot, without notice of their approach being given to the fearless and pacific tenants of the neighbouring district, they might commit, in a few hours, the most horrid and irreparable devastation.

The alarm could only be diffused in one way. Could I not escape, unperceived, and without alarming the sleepers, from this cavern? The slumber of an Indian is broken by the slightest noise; but if all noise be precluded, it is commonly profound. It was possible, I conceived, to leave my present post, to descend into the cave, and issue forth without the smallest signal. Their supine posture assured me that they were asleep. Sleep usually comes at their bidding, and if, perchance, they should be wakeful at an unseasonable moment, they always sit upon their haunches, and, leaning their elbows on their knees, consume the tedious hours in smoking. My peril would be great. Accidents which I could not foresee, and over which I had no command, might occur to awaken some one at the moment I was passing the fire. Should I pass in safety, I might issue forth into a wilderness, of which I had no knowledge, where I might wander till I perished with famine, or where my footsteps might be noted and pursued, and overtaken by these implacable foes. These perils were enormous and imminent; but I likewise considered that I might be at no great distance from the habitations of men, and, that my escape might rescue them from the most dreadful calamities, I determined to make this dangerous experiment without delay.

I came nearer to the aperture, and had, consequently, a larger view of this recess. To my unspeakable dismay, I now caught a glimpse of one, seated at the fire. His back was turned towards me so that I could distinctly survey his gigantic form and fantastic ornaments.

My project was frustrated. This one was probably commissioned to watch and to awaken his companions when a due portion of sleep had been taken. That he would not be unfaithful or remiss in the performance of the part assigned to him was easily predicted. To pass him without exciting his notice, and the entrance could not otherwise be reached, was impossible. Once more I shrunk back and revolved with hopelessness and anguish, the necessity to which I was reduced.

This interval of dreary foreboding did not last long. Some motion in him that was seated by the fire attracted my notice. I looked, and beheld him rise from his place and go forth from the cavern. This unexpected incident led my thoughts into a new channel. Could not some advantage be taken of his absence? Could not this opportunity be seized for making my escape? He had left his gun and hatchet on the ground. It was likely, therefore, that he had not gone far, and would speedily return. Might not these weapons be seized, and some provision be thus made against the danger of meeting him without, or of being pursued?

Before a resolution could be formed, a new sound saluted my ear. It was a deep groan, succeeded by sobs that seemed struggling for utterance, but were vehemently counteracted by the sufferer. This low and bitter lamentation apparently proceeded from some one within the cave. It could not be from one of this swarthy band. It must then proceed from a captive, whom they had reserved for torment or servitude, and who had seized the opportunity afforded by the absence of him that watched, to give vent to his despair.

I again thrust my head forward, and beheld, lying on the ground, apart from the rest, and bound hand and foot, a young girl. Her dress was the coarse russet garb of the country, and bespoke her to be some farmer's daughter. Her features denoted the last degree of fear and anguish, and she moved her limbs in such a manner as shewed that the ligatures by which she was confined, produced, by their tightness, the utmost degree of pain.

My wishes were now bent not only to preserve myself, and to frustrate the future attempts of these savages, but likewise to relieve this miserable victim. This could only be done by escaping from the cavern and returning with seasonable aid. The sobs of the girl were likely to rouse the sleepers. My appearance before her would prompt her to testify her surprise by some exclamation or shriek. What could hence be predicted but that the band would start on their feet, and level their unerring pieces at my head!

I know not why I was insensible to these dangers. My thirst was rendered by these delays intolerable. It took from me, in some degree, the power of deliberation. The murmers which had drawn me hither continued still to be heard. Some torrent or cascade could not be far distant from the entrance of the cavern, and it seemed as if one draught of clear water was a luxury cheaply purchased by death itself. This, in addition to considerations more disinterested, and which I have already mentioned, impelled me forward.

The girl's cheek rested on the hard rock, and her eyes were dim with tears. As they were turned towards me, however, I hoped that my movements would be noticed by her gradually and without abruptness. This expectation was fulfilled. I had not advanced many steps before she discovered me. This moment was critical beyond all others in the course of my existence. My life was suspended, as it were, by a spider's thread. All rested on the effect which this discovery should make upon this feeble victim.

I was watchful of the first movement of her eye, which should indicate a consciousness of my presence. I laboured, by gestures and looks, to deter her from betraying her emotion. My attention was, at the same time, fixed upon the sleepers, and an anxious glance was cast towards the quarter whence the watchful savage might appear.

I stooped and seized the musquet and hatchet. The space beyond the fire was, as I expected, open to the air. I issued forth with trembling steps. The sensations inspired by the dangers which environed me, added to my recent horrors, and the influence of the moon, which had now gained the zenith, and whose lustre dazzled my long benighted senses, cannot be adequately described.

For a minute I was unable to distinguish objects. This confusion was speedily corrected, and I found myself on the verge of a steep. Craggy eminences arose on all sides. On the left hand was a space that offered some footing, and hither I turned. A torrent was below me, and this path appeared to lead to it. It quickly appeared in sight, and all foreign cares were, for a time, suspended.

This water fell from the upper regions of the hill, upon a flat projecture which was continued on either side, and on part of which I was now standing. The path was bounded on the left by an inaccessible wall, and on the right terminated at the distance of two or three feet from the wall, in a precipice. The water was eight or ten paces distant, and no impediment seemed likely to rise between us. I rushed forward with speed.

My progress was quickly checked. Close to the falling water, seated on the edge, his back supported by the rock, and his legs hanging over the precipice, I now beheld the savage who left the cave before me. The noise of the cascade and the improbability of interruption, at least from this quarter, had made him inattentive to my motions.

I paused. Along this verge lay the only road by which I could reach the water, and by which I could escape. The passage was completely occupied by this antagonist. To advance towards him, or to remain where I was, would produce the same effect. I should, in either case, be detected. He was unarmed; but his outcries would instantly summon his companions to his aid. I could not hope to overpower him, and pass him in defiance of his opposition. But if this were effected, pursuit would be instantly commenced. I was unacquainted with the way. The way was unquestionably difficult. My strength was nearly annihilated: I should be overtaken in a moment, or their deficiency in speed would be supplied by the accuracy of their aim. Their bullets, at least, would reach me.

There was one method of removing this impediment.

The piece which I held in my hand was cocked. There could be no doubt that it was loaded. A precaution of this kind would never be omitted by a warrior of this hue. At a greater distance than this, I should not fear to reach the mark. Should I not discharge it, and, at the same moment, rush forward to secure the road which my adversary's death would open to me?

Perhaps you will conceive a purpose like this to have argued a sanguinary and murderous disposition. Let it be remembered, however, that I entertained no doubts about the hostile designs of these men. This was sufficiently indicated by their arms, their guise, and the captive who attended them. Let the fate of my parents be, likewise, remembered. I was not certain but that these very men were the assassins of my family, and were those who had reduced me and my sisters to the condition of orphans and dependants. No words can describe the torments of my thirst. Relief to these torments, and safety to my life, were within view. How could I hesitate?

Yet I did hesitate. My aversion to bloodshed was not to be subdued but by the direst necessity. I knew, indeed, that the discharge of a musket would only alarm the enemies which remained behind; but I had another and a better weapon in my grasp. I could rive the head of my adversary, and cast him headlong, without any noise which should be heard, into the cavern.

Still I was willing to withdraw, to re-enter the cave, and take shelter in the darksome recesses from which I had emerged. Here I might remain, unsuspected, till these detested guests should depart. The hazards attending my re-entrance were to be boldly encountered, and the torments of unsatisfied thirst were to be patiently endured, rather than imbrue my hands in the blood of my fellow men. But this expedient would be ineffectual if my retreat should be observed by this savage. Of that I was bound to be incontestibly assured. I retreated, therefore, but kept my eye fixed at the same time upon the enemy.

Some ill fate decreed that I should not retreat unobserved. Scarcely had I withdrawn three paces when he started from his seat, and turning towards me, walked with a quick pace. The shadow of the rock, and the improbability of meeting an enemy here, concealed me for a moment from his observation. I stood still. The slightest motion would have attracted his notice. At present, the narrow space engaged all his vigilance. Cautious footsteps, and attention to the path, were indispensable to his safety. The respite was momentary, and I employed it in my own defence.

How otherwise could I act? The danger that impended aimed at nothing less than my life. To take the life of another was the only method of averting it. The means were in my hand, and they were used. In an extremity like this, my muscles would have acted almost in defiance of my will.

The stroke was quick as lightning, and the wound mortal and deep. He had not time to descry the author of his fate; but, sinking on the path, expired without a groan. The hatchet buried itself in his breast, and rolled with him to the bottom of the precipice.

Never before had I taken the life of an human creature. On this head, I had, indeed, entertained somewhat of religious scruples. These scruples did not forbid me to defend myself, but they made me cautious and reluctant to decide. Though they could not withhold my hand, when urged by a necessity like this, they were sufficient to make me look back upon the deed with remorse and dismay.

I did not escape all compunction in the present instance, but the tumult of my feelings was quickly allayed. To quench my thirst was a consideration by which all others were supplanted. I approached the torrent, and not only drank copiously, but laved my head, neck, and arms, in this delicious element.

CHAPTER XVIII

NEVER was any delight worthy of comparison with the raptures which I then experienced. Life, that was rapidly ebbing, appeared to return upon me with redoubled violence. My languors, my excruciating heat, vanished in a moment, and I felt prepared to undergo the labours of Hercules. Having fully supplied the demands of nature in this respect, I returned to reflection on the circumstances of my situation. The path winding round the hill was now free from all impediments. What remained but to precipitate my flight? I might speedily place myself beyond all danger. I might gain some hospitable shelter, where my fatigues might be repaired by repose, and my wounds be cured. I might likewise impart to my protectors seasonable information of the enemies who meditated their destruction.

I thought upon the condition of the hapless girl whom I had left in the power of the savages. Was it impossible to rescue her? Might I not relieve her from her bonds, and make her the companion of my flight? The exploit was perilous but not impracticable. There was something dastardly and ignominious in withdrawing from the danger, and leaving an helpless being exposed to it. A single minute might suffice to snatch her from death or captivity. The parents might deserve that I should hazard or even sacrifice my life, in the cause of their child.

After some fluctuation, I determined to return to the

cavern, and attempt the rescue of the girl. The success of this project depended on the continuance of their sleep. It was proper to approach with wariness, and to heed the smallest token which might bespeak their condition. I crept along the path, bending my ear forward to catch any sound that might arise. I heard nothing but the half-stifled sobs of the girl.

I entered with the slowest and most anxious circumspection. Every thing was found in its pristine state. The girl noticed my entrance with a mixture of terror and joy. My gestures and looks enjoined upon her silence. I stooped down, and taking another hatchet, cut assunder the deer-skin thongs by which her wrists and ancles were tied. I then made signs for her to rise and follow me. She willingly complied with my directions; but her benumbed joints and lacerated sinews, refused to support her. There was no time to be lost; I therefore, lifted her in my arms, and, feeble and tottering as I was, proceeded with this burthen, along the perilous steep, and over a most rugged path.

I hoped that some exertion would enable her to retrieve the use of her limbs. I set her, therefore, on her feet, exhorting her to walk as well as she was able, and promising her my occasional assistance. The poor girl was not deficient in zeal, and presently moved along with light and quick steps. We speedily reached the bottom of the hill.

No fancy can conceive a scene more wild and desolate than that which now presented itself. The soil was nearly covered with sharp fragments of stone. Between these sprung brambles and creeping vines, whose twigs, crossing and intertwining with each other, added to the roughnesses below, made the passage infinitely toilsome. Scattered over this space were single cedars with their ragged spines and wreaths of moss, and copses of dwarf oaks, which were only new emblems of sterility.

I was wholly unacquainted with the scene before me. No marks of habitation or culture, no traces of the foot-

181

steps of men, were discernible. I scarcely knew in what region of the globe I was placed. I had come hither by means so inexplicable, as to leave it equally in doubt, whether I was separated from my paternal abode by a river or an ocean.

I made inquiries of my companion, but she was unable to talk coherently. She answered my questions with weeping, and sobs, and intreaties, to fly from the scene of her distress. I collected from her, at length, that her father's house had been attacked on the preceding evening, and all the family but herself destroyed. Since this disaster she had walked very fast and a great way, but knew not how far or in what direction.

In a wilderness like this, my only hope was to light upon obscure paths, made by cattle. Meanwhile I endeavoured to adhere to one line, and to burst through the vexatious obstacles which encumbered our way. The ground was concealed by the bushes, and we were perplexed and fatigued by a continual succession of hollows and prominences. At one moment we were nearly thrown headlong into a pit. At another we struck our feet against the angles of stones. The branches of the oak rebounded in our faces or entangled our legs, and the unseen thorns inflicted on us a thousand wounds.

I was obliged, in these arduous circumstances, to support not only myself but my companion. Her strength was overpowered by her evening journey, and the terror of being overtaken, incessantly harrassed her.

Sometimes we lighted upon tracks which afforded us an easier footing, and inspired us with courage to proceed. These, for a time, terminated at a brook or in a bog, and we were once more compelled to go forward at random. One of these tracks insensibly became more beaten, and, at length, exhibited the traces of wheels. To this I adhered, confident that it would finally conduct us to a dwelling.

On either side, the undergrowth of shrubs and brambles continued as before. Sometimes small spaces were observed, which had lately been cleared by fire. At length a vacant space of larger dimensions than had hitherto occurred, presented itself to my view. It was a field of some acres, that had, apparently, been upturned by the hoe. At the corner of this field was a small house.

My heart leaped with joy at this sight. I hastened toward it, in the hope that my uncertainties, and toils, and dangers, were now drawing to a close. This dwelling was suited to the poverty and desolation which surrounded it. It consisted of a few unhewn logs laid upon each other, to the height of eight or ten feet, including a quadrangular space of similar dimensions, and covered by thatch. There was no window, light being sufficiently admitted into the crevices between the logs. These had formerly been loosely plastered with clay, but air and rain had crumbled and washed the greater part of this rude cement away. Somewhat like a chimney, built of half-burnt bricks, was perceived at one corner. The door was fastened by a leathern thong, tied to a peg.

All within was silence and darkness. I knocked at the door and called, but no one moved or answered. The tenant, whoever he was, was absent. His leave could not be obtained, and I, therefore, entered without it. The autumn had made some progress, and the air was frosty and sharp. My mind and muscles had been, of late, so strenuously occupied, that the cold had not been felt. The cessation of exercise, however, quickly restored my sensibility in this respect, but the unhappy girl complained of being half frozen.

Fire, therefore, was the first object of my search. Happily, some embers were found upon the hearth, together with potatoe stalks and dry chips. Of these, with much difficulty, I kindled a fire, by which some warmth was imparted to our shivering limbs. The light enabled me, as I sat upon the ground, to survey the interior of this mansion.

Three saplins, stripped of their branches, and bound together at their ends by twigs, formed a kind of bedstead, which was raised from the ground by four stones. Ropes stretched across these, and covered by a blanket, constituted the bed. A board, of which one end rested on the bedstead, and the other was thrust between the logs that composed the wall, sustained the stale fragments of a rye-loaf, and a cedar bucket kept entire by withs instead of hoops. In the bucket was a little water, full of droppings from the roof, drowned insects and sand; a basket or two neatly made, and an hoe, with a stake thrust into it by way of handle, made up all the furniture that was visible.

Next to cold, hunger was the most urgent necessity by which we were now pressed. This was no time to give ear to scruples. We, therefore, unceremoniously divided the bread and the water between us. I had now leisure to bestow some regards upon the future.

These remnants of fire and food convinced me that this dwelling was usually inhabited, and that it had lately been deserted. Some engagement had probably carried the tenant abroad. His absence might be terminated in a few minutes, or might endure through the night. On his return, I questioned not my power to appease any indignation he might feel at the liberties which I had taken. I was willing to suppose him one who would readily afford us all the information and succour that we needed.

If he should not return till sunrise, I meant to resume my journey. By the comfortable meal we had made, and the repose of a few hours, we should be considerably invigorated and refreshed, and the road would lead us to some more hospitable tenement.

My thoughts were too tumultuous, and my situation too precarious, to allow me to sleep. The girl, on the contrary, soon sunk into a sweet oblivion of all her cares. She laid herself, by my advice, upon the bed, and left me to ruminate without interruption.

I was not wholly free from the apprehension of danger. What influence his boisterous and solitary life might have upon the temper of the being who inhabited this hut, I could not predict. How soon the Indians might awake, and what path they would pursue, I was equally unable to guess. It was by no means impossible that they might tread upon my footsteps, and knock, in a few minutes, at the door of this cottage. It behoved me to make all the preparation in my power against untoward incidents.

I had not parted with the gun which I had first seized in the cavern, nor with the hatchet which I had afterwards used to cut the bands of the girl. These were, at once, my trophies and my means of defence, which it had been rash and absurd to have relinquished. My present reliance was placed upon these.

I now, for the first time, examined the prize that I had made. Other considerations had prevented me till now, from examining the structure of the piece, but I could not but observe that it had two barrels, and was lighter and smaller than an ordinary musquet. The light of the fire now enabled me to inspect it with more accuracy.

Scarcely had I fixed my eyes upon the stock, when I perceived marks that were familiar to my apprehension. Shape, ornaments, and cyphers, were evidently the same with those of a piece which I had frequently handled. The marks were of a kind which could not be mistaken. This piece was mine; and when I left my uncle's house, it was deposited, as I believed, in the closet of my chamber.

Thou wilt easily conceive the inference which this circumstance suggested. My hairs rose and my teeth chattered with horror. My whole frame was petrified, and I paced to and fro, hurried from the chimney to the door, and from the door to the chimney, with the misguided fury of a maniac.

I needed no proof of my calamity more incontestible than this. My uncle and my sisters had been murdered; the dwelling had been pillaged, and this had been a part of the plunder. Defenceless and asleep, they were assailed by these inexorable enemies, and I, who ought to have been their protector and champion, was removed to an immeasurable distance, and was disabled, by some accursed chance, from affording them the succour which they needed.

For a time, I doubted whether I had not witnessed and shared this catastrophe. I had no memory of the circumstances that preceded my awaking in the pit. Had not the cause of my being cast into this abyss some connection with the ruin of my family? Had I not been dragged hither by these savages, and reduced, by their malice, to that breathless and insensible condition? Was I born to a malignant destiny never tired of persecuting? Thus had my parents and their infant offspring perished, and thus completed was the fate of all those to whom my affections cleaved, and whom the first disaster had spared.

Hitherto the death of the savage, whom I had dispatched with my hatchet, had not been remembered without some remorse. Now my emotions were totally changed: I was somewhat comforted in thinking that thus much of necessary vengeance had been executed. New and more vehement regrets were excited by reflecting on the forbearance I had practised when so much was in my power. All the miscreants had been at my mercy, and a bloody retribution might, with safety and ease, have been inflicted on their prostrate bodies.

It was now too late. What of consolation or of hope remained to me? To return to my ancient dwelling, now polluted with blood, or perhaps, nothing but a smoking ruin, was abhorred. Life, connected with remembrances of my misfortunes was detestable. I was no longer anxious for flight. No change of the scene but that which terminated all consciousness, could I endure to think of.

Amidst these gloomy meditations the idea was suddenly suggested of returning, with the utmost expedition, to the cavern. It was possible that the assassins were still asleep. He who was appointed to watch and to make, in due season, the signal for resuming their march, was forever silent. Without this signal it was not unlikely that they would sleep till dawn of day. But if they should be roused, they might be overtaken or met, and by choosing a proper station, two victims might at least fall. The ultimate event to myself would surely be fatal; but my own death was an object of desire rather than of dread. To die thus speedily, and after some atonement was made for those who had already been slain, was sweet.

The way to the mountain was difficult and tedious, but the ridge was distinctly seen from the door of the cottage, and I trusted that auspicious chance would lead me to that part of it where my prey was to be found. I snatched up the gun and tom-hawk in a transport of eagerness. On examining the former, I found that both barrels were deeply loaded.

This piece was of extraordinary workmanship. It was the legacy of an English officer, who died in Bengal, to Sarsefield. It was constructed for the purposes not of sport but of war. The artist had made it a congeries of tubes and springs, by which every purpose of protection and offence was effectually served. A dagger's blade was attached to it, capable of being fixed at the end, and of answering the destructive purpose of a bayonet. On his departure from Solebury, my friend left it, as a pledge of his affection, in my possession. Hitherto I had chiefly employed it in shooting at a mark, in order to improve my sight; now was I to profit by the gift in a different way.

Thus armed, I prepared to sally forth on my adventurous expedition. Sober views might have speedily succeeded to the present tempest of my passions. I might have gradually discovered the romantic and criminal temerity of my project, the folly of revenge, and the duty of preserving my life for the benefit of mankind. I might have suspected the propriety of my conclusion, and have admitted some doubts as to the catastrophe which I imagined to have befallen my uncle and sisters. I might, at least, have consented to ascertain their condition with my own eyes; and for this end have returned to the cottage, and have patiently waited till the morning light should permit me to resume my journey.

This conduct was precluded by a new incident. Before I opened the door I looked through a crevice of the wall, and perceived three human figures at the farther end of the field. They approached the house. Though indistinctly seen, something in their port persuaded me that these were the Indians from whom I had lately parted. I was startled but not dismayed. My thirst of vengeance was still powerful, and I believed that the moment of its gratification was hastening. In a short time they would arrive and enter the house. In what manner should they be received?

I studied not my own security. It was the scope of my wishes to kill the whole number of my foes; but that being done, I was indifferent to the consequences. I desired not to live to relate or to exult in the deed.

To go forth was perilous and useless. All that remained was to sit upon the ground opposite the door, and fire at each as he entered. In the hasty survey I had taken of this apartment, one object had been overlooked, or imperfectly noticed. Close to the chimney was an aperture, formed by a cavity partly in the wall and in the ground. It was the entrance of an oven, which resembled, on the outside, a mound of earth, and which was filled with dry stalks of potatoes and other rubbish.

Into this it was possible to thrust my body. A sort of screen might be formed of the brush-wood, and more deliberate and effectual execution be done upon the enemy. I weighed not the disadvantages of this scheme, but precipitately threw myself into this cavity. I discovered, in an instant, that it was totally unfit for my purpose, but it was too late to repair my miscarriage.

This wall of the hovel was placed near the verge of a sand-bank. The oven was erected on the very brink. This bank being of a loose and mutable soil, could not sustain my weight. It sunk, and I sunk along with it. The height of the bank was three or four feet, so that, though disconcerted and embarrassed, I received no injury. I still grasped my gun, and resumed my feet in a moment.

What was now to be done? The bank screened me from the view of the savages. The thicket was hard by, and if I were eager to escape, the way was obvious and sure. But though single, though enfeebled by toil, by abstinence and by disease, and though so much exceeded in numbers and strength, by my foes, I was determined to await and provoke the contest.

In addition to the desperate impulse of passion, I was swayed by thoughts of the danger which beset the sleeping girl, and from which my flight would leave her without protection. How strange is the destiny that governs mankind! The consequence of shrouding myself in this cavity had not been foreseen. It was an expedient which courage, and not cowardice suggested; and yet it was the only expedient by which flight had been rendered practicable. To have issued from the door would only have been to confront, and not to elude the danger.

The first impulse prompted me to re-enter the cottage by this avenue, but this could not be done with certainty and expedition. What then remained? While I deliberated, the men approached, and, after a moment's hesitation, entered the house, the door being partly open.

The fire on the hearth enabled them to survey the room. One of them uttered a sudden exclamation of surprize. This was easily interpreted. They had noticed the girl who had lately been their captive lying asleep on the blanket. Their astonishment at finding her here, and in this condition, may be easily conceived.

I now reflected that I might place myself, without being observed, near the entrance, at an angle of the building, and shoot at each as he successively came forth. I perceived that the bank conformed to two sides of the house, and that I might gain a view of the front and of the entrance, without exposing myself to observation.

I lost no time in gaining this station. The bank was as high as my breast. It was easy, therefore, to crouch beneath it, to bring my eye close to the verge, and, laying my gun upon the top of it among the grass, with its muzzles pointed to the door, patiently to wait their forth-coming.

My eye and my ear were equally attentive to what was passing. A low and muttering conversation was maintained in the house. Presently I heard an heavy stroke descend. I shuddered, and my blood ran cold at the sound. I entertained no doubt but that it was the stroke of an hatchet on the head or breast of the helpless sleeper.

It was followed by a loud shriek. The continuance of these shrieks proved that the stroke had not been instantly fatal. I waited to hear it repeated, but the sounds that now arose were like those produced by dragging somewhat along the ground. The shrieks, meanwhile, were incessant and piteous. My heart faltered, and I saw that mighty efforts must be made to preserve my joints and my nerves stedfast. All depended on the strenuous exertions and the fortunate dexterity of a moment.

One now approached the door, and came forth, dragging the girl, whom he held by the hair, after him. What hindered me from shooting at his first appearance, I know not. This had been my previous resolution. My hand touched the trigger, and as he moved, the piece was levelled at his right ear. Perhaps the momentous consequences of my failure, made me wait till his ceasing to move might render my aim more sure.

Having dragged the girl, still piteously shrieking, to the distance of ten feet from the house, he threw her from him with violence. She fell upon the ground, and observing him level his piece at her breast, renewed her supplications in a still more piercing tone. Little did the forlorn wretch think that her deliverance was certain and near. I rebuked myself for having thus long delayed. I fired, and my enemy sunk upon the ground without a struggle.

Thus far had success attended me in this unequal contest. The next shot would leave me nearly powerless. If that, however, proved as unerring as the first, the chances of defeat were lessened. The savages within, knowing the intentions of their associate with regard to the captive girl, would probably mistake the report which they heard for that of his piece. Their mistake, however, would speedily give place to doubts, and they would rush forth to ascertain the truth. It behoved me to provide a similar reception for him that next appeared.

It was as I expected. Scarcely was my eye again fixed upon the entrance, when a tawny and terrific visage was stretched fearfully forth. It was the signal of his fate. His glances cast wildly and swiftly round, lighted upon me, and on the fatal instrument which was pointed at his forehead. His muscles were at once exerted to withdraw his head, and to vociferate a warning to his fellow, but his movement was too slow. The ball entered above his ear: He tumbled headlong to the ground, bereaved of sensation, though not of life, and had power only to struggle and mutter.

CHAPTER XIX

THINK not that I relate these things with exultation or tranquility. All my education and the habits of my life tended to unfit me for a contest and a scene like this. But I was not governed by the soul which usually regulates my conduct. I had imbibed from the unparalleled events which had lately happened a spirit vengeful, unrelenting, and ferocious.

There was now an interval for flight. Throwing my weapons away, I might gain the thicket in a moment. I had no ammunition, nor would time be afforded me to reload my piece. My antagonist would render my poniard and my speed of no use to me. Should he miss me as I fled, the girl would remain to expiate, by her agonies and death, the fate of his companions.

These thoughts passed through my mind in a shorter time than is demanded to express them. They yielded to an expedient suggested by the sight of the gun that had been raised to destroy the girl, and which now lay upon the ground. I am not large of bone, but am not deficient in agility and strength. All that remained to me of these qualities was now exerted; and dropping my own piece, I leaped upon the bank, and flew to seize my prize.

It was not till I snatched it from the ground, that the propriety of regaining my former post, rushed upon my apprehension. He that was still posted in the hovel would mark me through the seams of the wall, and render my

destruction sure. I once more ran towards the bank, with
the intention to throw myself below it. All this was performed in an instant; but my vigilant foe was aware of his
advantage, and fired through an opening between the
logs. The bullet grazed my cheek, and produced a
benumbing sensation that made me instantly fall to the
earth. Though bereaved of strength, and fraught with the
belief that I had received a mortal wound, my caution was
not remitted. I loosened not my grasp of the gun, and the
posture into which I accidentally fell enabled me to keep
an eye upon the house and an hand upon the trigger.
Perceiving my condition, the savage rushed from his covert in order to complete his work; but at three steps from
the threshold, he received my bullet in his breast. The
uplifted tom-hawk fell from his hand, and, uttering a loud
shriek, he fell upon the body of his companion. His cries
struck upon my heart, and I wished that his better fortune
had cast this evil from him upon me.

Thus I have told thee a bloody and disastrous tale.
When thou reflectest on the mildness of my habits, my
antipathy to scenes of violence and bloodshed, my unacquaintance with the use of fire-arms, and the motives of a
soldier, thou wilt scarcely allow credit to my story. That
one rushing into these dangers, unfurnished with stratagems or weapons, disheartened and enfeebled by hardships and pain, should subdue four antagonists, trained
from their infancy to the artifices and exertions of Indian
warfare, will seem the vision of fancy, rather than the
lesson of truth.

I lifted my head from the ground and pondered upon
this scene. The magnitude of this exploit made me question its reality. By attending to my own sensations, I
discovered that I had received no wound, or at least, none
of which there was reason to complain. The blood flowed
plentifully from my cheek, but the injury was superficial.
It was otherwise with my antagonists. The last that had
fallen now ceased to groan. Their huge limbs, inured to

combat and *war-worn*, were useless to their own defence, and to the injury of others.

The destruction that I witnessed was vast. Three beings, full of energy and heroism, endowed with minds strenuous and lofty, poured out their lives before me. I was the instrument of their destruction. This scene of carnage and blood was laid by me. To this havock and horror was I led by such rapid footsteps!

My anguish was mingled with astonishment. In spite of the force and uniformity with which my senses were impressed by external objects, the transition I had undergone was so wild and inexplicable; all that I had performed; all that I had witnessed since my egress from the pit, were so contradictory to precedent events, that I still clung to the belief that my thoughts were confused by delirium. From these reveries I was at length recalled by the groans of the girl, who lay near me on the ground.

I went to her and endeavoured to console her. I found that while lying in the bed, she had received a blow upon the side, which was still productive of acute pain. She was unable to rise or to walk, and it was plain that one or more of her ribs had been fractured by the blow.

I knew not what means to devise for our mutual relief. It was possible that the nearest dwelling was many leagues distant. I knew not in what direction to go in order to find it, and my strength would not suffice to carry my wounded companion thither in my arms. There was no expedient but to remain in this field of blood till the morning.

I had scarcely formed this resolution before the report of a musquet was heard at a small distance. At the same moment, I distinctly heard the whistling of a bullet near me. I now remembered that of the five Indians whom I saw in the cavern, I was acquainted with the destiny only of four. The fifth might be still alive, and fortune might reserve for him the task of avenging his companions. His steps might now be tending hither in search of them.

The musquet belonging to him who was shot upon the threshold, was still charged It was discreet to make all the provision in my power against danger. I possessed myself of this gun, and seating myself on the ground, looked carefully on all sides, to descry the approach of the enemy. I listened with breathless eagerness.

Presently voices were heard. They ascended from that part of the thicket from which my view was intercepted by the cottage. These voices had something in them that bespoke them to belong to friends and countrymen. As yet I was unable to distinguish words.

Presently my eye was attracted to one quarter, by a sound as of feet trampling down bushes. Several heads were seen moving in succession, and at length, the whole person was conspicuous. One after another leaped over a kind of mound which bordered the field, and made towards the spot where I sat. This band was composed of ten or twelve persons, with each a gun upon his shoulder. Their guise, the moment it was perceived, dissipated all my apprehensions.

They came within the distance of a few paces before they discovered me. One stopped, and bespeaking the attention of his followers, called to know who was there? I answered that I was a friend, who intreated their assistance. I shall not paint their astonishment when, on coming nearer, they beheld me surrounded by the arms and dead bodies of my enemies.

I sat upon the ground, supporting my head with my left hand, and resting on my knee the stock of an heavy musquet. My countenance was wan and haggard, my neck and bosom were died in blood, and my limbs, almost stripped by the brambles of their slender covering, were lacerated by a thousand wounds. Three savages, two of whom were steeped in gore, lay at a small distance, with the traces of recent life on their visages. Hard by was the girl, venting her anguish in the deepest groans, and intreating relief from the new comers.

One of the company, on approaching the girl, betrayed the utmost perturbation. "Good God!" he cried, "is this a dream? Can it be you? Speak!"

"Ah, my father! my father!" answered she, "it is I indeed."

The company, attracted by this dialogue, crowded round the girl, whom her father, clasping in his arms, lifted from the ground, and pressed, in a transport of joy to his breast. This delight was succeeded by solicitude respecting her condition. She could only answer his inquiries by complaining that her side was bruised to pieces. How came you here? . . . Who hurt you? . . . Where did the Indians carry you? were questions to which she could make no reply but by sobs and plaints.

My own calamities were forgotten in contemplating the fondness and compassion of the man for his child. I derived new joy from reflecting that I had not abandoned her, and that she owed her preservation to my efforts. The inquiries which the girl was unable to answer, were now put to me. Every one interrogated who I was, whence I had come, and what had given rise to this bloody contest?

I was not willing to expatiate on my story. The spirit which had hitherto sustained me, began now to subside. My strength ebbed away with my blood. Tremors, lassitude, and deadly cold, invaded me, and I fainted on the ground.

Such is the capricious constitution of the human mind. While dangers were at hand, while my life was to be preserved only by zeal, and vigilance, and courage, I was not wanting to myself. Had my perils continued or even multiplied, no doubt my energies would have kept equal pace with them, but the moment that I was encompassed by protectors, and placed in security, I grew powerless and faint. My weakness was proportioned to the duration and intensity of my previous efforts, and the swoon into which I now sunk, was no doubt, mistaken by the spectators, for death.

On recovering from this swoon, my sensations were not unlike those which I had experienced on awaking in the pit. For a moment a mistiness involved every object, and I was able to distinguish nothing. My sight, by rapid degrees, was restored, my painful dizziness was banished, and I surveyed the scene before me with anxiety and wonder.

I found myself stretched upon the ground. I perceived the cottage and the neighbouring thicket, illuminated by a declining moon. My head rested upon something, which, on turning to examine, I found to be one of the slain Indians. The other two remained upon the earth at a small distance, and in the attitudes in which they had fallen. Their arms, the wounded girl, and the troop who were near me when I fainted, were gone.

My head had reposed upon the breast of him whom I had shot in this part of his body. The blood had ceased to ooze from the wound, but my dishevelled locks were matted and steeped in that gore which had overflowed and choked up the orifice. I started from this detestable pillow, and regained my feet.

I did not suddenly recall what had lately passed, or comprehend the nature of my situation. At length, however, late events were recollected.

That I should be abandoned in this forlorn state by these men, seemed to argue a degree of cowardice or cruelty, of which I should have thought them incapable. Presently, however, I reflected that appearances might have easily misled them into a belief of my death: on this supposition, to have carried me away, or to have stayed beside me, would be useless. Other enemies might be abroad, or their families, now that their fears were somewhat tranquilized, might require their presence and protection.

I went into the cottage. The fire still burned, and afforded me a genial warmth. I sat before it and began to ruminate on the state to which I was reduced, and on the measures I should next pursue. Day-light could not be very distant. Should I remain in this hovel till the morning, or immediately resume my journey? I was feeble, indeed, but by remaining here should I not increase my feebleness? The sooner I should gain some human habitation the better; whereas watchfulness and hunger would render me, at each minute, less able to proceed than on the former.

This spot might be visited on the next day; but this was involved in uncertainty. The visitants, should any come, would come merely to examine and bury the dead, and bring with them neither the clothing nor the food which my necessities demanded. The road was sufficiently discernible, and would, unavoidably, conduct me to some dwelling. I determined, therefore, to set out without delay. Even in this state I was not unmindful that my safety might require the precaution of being armed. Besides the fusil, which had been given me by Sarsefield, and which I had so unexpectedly recovered, had lost none of its value in my eyes. I hoped that it had escaped the search of the troop who had been here, and still lay below the bank, in the spot where I had dropped it.

In this hope I was not deceived. It was found. I possessed myself of the powder and shot belonging to one of the savages, and loaded it. Thus equipped for defence, I regained the road, and proceeded, with alacrity, on my way. For the wound in my cheek, nature had provided a styptic, but the soreness was extreme, and I thought of no remedy but water, with which I might wash away the blood. My thirst likewise incommoded me, and I looked with eagerness for the traces of a spring. In a soil like that of the wilderness around me, nothing was less to be expected than to light upon water. In this respect, however, my destiny was propitious. I quickly perceived water in the ruts. It trickled hither from the thicket on one side, and, pursuing it among the bushes, I reached the bubbling source. Though scanty and brackish, it afforded me unspeakable refreshment.

Thou wilt think, perhaps, that my perils were now at

an end; that the blood I had already shed was sufficient for my safety. I fervently hoped that no new exigence would occur, compelling me to use the arms that I bore in my own defence. I formed a sort of resolution to shun the contest with a new enemy, almost at the expense of my own life. I was satiated and gorged with slaughter, and thought upon a new act of destruction with abhorrence and loathing.

But though I dreaded to encounter a new enemy, I was sensible that an enemy might possibly be at hand. I had moved forward with caution, and my sight and hearing were attentive to the slightest tokens. Other troops, besides that which I encountered, might be hovering near, and of that troop, I remembered that one at least had survived.

The gratification which this spring had afforded me was so great, that I was in no haste to depart. I lay upon a rock, which chanced to be shaded by a tree behind me. From this post I could overlook the road to some distance, and, at the same time, be shaded from the observation of others.

My eye was now caught by movements which appeared like those of a beast. In different circumstances, I should have instantly supposed it to be a wolf, or panther, or bear. Now my suspicions were alive on a different account, and my startled fancy figured to itself nothing but an human adversary.

A thicket was on either side of the road. That opposite to my station was discontinued at a small distance by the cultivated field. The road continued along this field, bounded by the thicket on the one side, and the open space on the other. To this space the being who was now descried was cautiously approaching.

He moved upon all fours, and presently came near enough to be distinguished. His disfigured limbs, pendants from his ears and nose, and his shorn locks, were indubitable indications of a savage. Occasionally he reared himself above the bushes, and scanned, with suspi-

199

cious vigilance, the cottage and the space surrounding it. Then he stooped, and crept along as before.

I was at no loss to interpret these appearances. This was my surviving enemy. He was unacquainted with the fate of his associates, and was now approaching the theatre of carnage, to ascertain their fate.

Once more was the advantage afforded me. From this spot might unerring aim be taken, and the last of this hostile troop be made to share the fate of the rest. Should I fire or suffer him to pass in safety?

My abhorrence of bloodshed was not abated. But I had not foreseen this occurrence. My success hitherto had seemed to depend upon a combination of fortunate incidents, which could not be expected again to take place; but now was I invested with the same power. The mark was near; nothing obstructed or delayed; I incurred no danger, and the event was certain.

Why should he be suffered to live? He came hither to murder and despoil my friends; this work he has, no doubt, performed. Nay, has he not borne his part in the destruction of my uncle and my sisters? He will live only to pursue the same sanguinary trade; to drink the blood and exult in the laments of his unhappy foes, and of my own brethren. Fate has reserved him for a bloody and violent death. For how long a time soever it may be deferred, it is thus that his career will inevitably terminate.

Should he be spared, he will still roam in the wilderness, and I may again be fated to encounter him. Then our mutual situation may be widely different, and the advantage I now possess may be his.

While hastily revolving these thoughts I was thoroughly aware that one event might take place which would render all deliberation useless. Should he spy me where I lay, my fluctuations must end. My safety would indispensably require me to shoot. This persuasion made me keep a stedfast eye upon his motions, and be prepared to anticipate his assault.

It now most seasonably occurred to me that one essential duty remained to be performed. One operation, without which fire arms are useless, had been unaccountably omitted. My piece was uncocked. I did not reflect that in moving the spring, a sound would necessarily be produced, sufficient to alarm him. But I knew that the chances of escaping his notice, should I be perfectly mute and still, were extremely slender, and that, in such a case, his movements would be quicker than the light; it behoved me, therefore, to repair my omission.

The sound struck him with alarm. He turned and darted at me an inquiring glance. I saw that forbearance was no longer in my power; but my heart sunk while I complied with what may surely be deemed an indispensable necessity. This faltering, perhaps it was, that made me swerve somewhat from the fatal line. He was disabled by the wound, but not killed.

He lost all power of resistance, and was, therefore, no longer to be dreaded. He rolled upon the ground, uttering doleful shrieks, and throwing his limbs into those contorsions which bespeak the keenest agonies to which ill-fated man is subject. Horror, and compassion, and remorse, were mingled into one sentiment, and took possession of my heart. To shut out this spectacle, I withdrew from the spot, but I stopped before I had moved beyond hearing of his cries.

The impulse that drove me from the scene was pusillanimous and cowardly. The past, however deplorable, could not be recalled; but could not I afford some relief to this wretch? Could not I, at least, bring his pangs to a speedy close? Thus he might continue, writhing and calling upon death for hours. Why should his miseries by uselessly prolonged?

There was but one way to end them. To kill him outright, was the dictate of compassion and of duty. I hastily returned, and once more levelled my piece at his head. It was a loathsome obligation, and was performed with unconquerable reluctance. Thus to assault and to mangle

201

the body of an enemy, already prostrate and powerless, was an act worthy of abhorrence; yet it was, in this case, prescribed by pity.

My faltering hand rendered this second bullet ineffectual. One expedient, still more detestable, remained. Having gone thus far, it would have been inhuman to stop short. His heart might easily be pierced by the bayonet, and his struggles would cease.

This task of cruel lenity was at length finished. I dropped the weapon and threw myself on the ground, overpowered by the horrors of this scene. Such are the deeds which perverse nature compels thousands of rational beings to perform and to witness! Such is the spectacle, endlessly prolonged and diversified, which is exhibited in every field of battle; of which, habit and example, the temptations of gain, and the illusions of honour, will make us, not reluctant or indifferent, but zealous and delighted actors and beholders!

Thus, by a series of events impossible to be computed or foreseen, was the destruction of a band, selected from their fellows for an arduous enterprise, distinguished by prowess and skill, and equally armed against surprize and force, completed by the hand of a boy, uninured to hostility, unprovided with arms, precipitate and timerous! I have noted men who seemed born for no end but by their achievements to belie experience, and baffle foresight, and outstrip belief. Would to God that I had not deserved to be numbered among these! But what power was it that called me from the sleep of death, just in time to escape the merciless knife of this enemy? Had my swoon continued till he had reached the spot, he would have effectuated my death by new wounds and torn away the skin from my brows. Such are the subtile threads on which hangs the fate of man and of the universe!

While engaged in these reflections, I perceived that the moon-light had began to fade before that of the sun. A dusky and reddish hue spread itself over the east. Cheered by this appearance, I once more resumed my feet and the road. I left the savage where he lay, but made prize of his tom-hawk. I had left my own in the cavern; and this weapon added little to my burthen. Prompted by some freak of fancy, I stuck his musquet in the ground, and left it standing upright in the middle of the road.

CHAPTER XX

I MOVED forward with as quick a pace as my feeble limbs would permit. I did not allow myself to meditate. The great object of my wishes was a dwelling where food and repose might be procured. I looked earnestly forward, and on each side, in search of some token of human residence; but the spots of cultivation, the *well-pole*, the *worm-fence*, and the hay-rick, were no where to be seen. I did not even meet with a wild hog, or a bewildered cow. The path was narrow, and on either side was a trackless wilderness. On the right and left were the waving lines of mountainous ridges which had no peculiarity enabling me to ascertain whether I had ever before seen them.

At length I noticed that the tracks of wheels had disappeared from the path that I was treading; that it became more narrow, and exhibited fewer marks of being frequented. These appearances were discouraging. I now suspected that I had taken a wrong direction, and instead of approaching, was receding from the habitation of men.

It was wisest, however, to proceed. The road could not but have some origin as well as end. Some hours passed away in this uncertainty. The sun rose, and by noon-day I seemed to be farther than ever from the end of my toils. The path was more obscure, and the wilderness more rugged. Thirst more incommoded me than hunger, but relief was seasonably afforded by the brooks that flowed across the path.

Coming to one of these, and having slaked my thirst, I sat down upon the bank, to reflect on my situation. The circuity of the path had frequently been noticed, and I began to suspect that though I had travelled long, I had not moved far from the spot where I had commenced my pilgrimage.

Turning my eyes on all sides, I noticed a sort of pool, formed by the rivulet, at a few paces distant from the road. In approaching and inspecting it, I observed the footsteps of cattle, who had retired by a path that seemed much beaten; I likewise noticed a cedar bucket, broken and old, lying on the margin. These tokens revived my drooping spirits, and I betook myself to this new track. It was intricate; but, at length, led up a steep, the summit of which was of better soil than that of which the flats consisted. A clover field, and several apple-trees, sure attendants of man, were now discovered. From this space I entered a corn-field, and at length, to my inexpressible joy, caught a glimpse of an house.

This dwelling was far different from that I had lately left. It was as small and as low, but its walls consisted of boards. A window of four panes admitted the light, and a chimney of brick, well burnt, and neatly arranged, peeped over the roof. As I approached I heard the voice of children, and the hum of a spinning-wheel.

I cannot make thee conceive the delight which was afforded me by all these tokens. I now found myself, indeed, among beings like myself, and from whom hospitable entertainment might be confidently expected. I compassed the house, and made my appearance at the door.

A good woman, busy at her wheel, with two children playing on the ground before her, were the objects that now presented themselves. The uncouthness of my garb, my wild and weather-worn appearance, my fusil and

tom-hawk, could not but startle them. The woman stopt
her wheel, and gazed as if a spectre had started into view.

I was somewhat aware of these consequences, and
endeavoured to elude them, by assuming an air of suppli-
cation and humility. I told her that I was a traveller, who
had unfortunately lost his way, and had rambled in this
wild till nearly famished for want. I intreated her to give
me some food; any thing however scanty or coarse, would
be acceptable.

After some pause she desired me, though not without
some marks of fear, to walk in. She placed before me
some brown bread and milk. She eyed me while I eagerly
devoured this morsel. It was, indeed, more delicious than
any I had ever tasted. At length she broke silence, and
expressed her astonishment and commiseration at my
seemingly forlorn state, adding, that perhaps I was the
man whom the men were looking after who had been
there some hours before.

My curiosity was roused by this intimation. In answer
to my interrogations, she said, that three persons had
lately stopped, to inquire if her husband had not met,
within the last three days, a person of whom their description seemed pretty much to suit my person and dress. He
was tall, slender, wore nothing but shirt and trowsers, and
was wounded on the cheek.

What, I asked, did they state the rank or condition of
the person to be?

He lived in Solebury. He was supposed to have rambled in the mountains, and to have lost his way, or to have
met with some mischance. It was three days since he had
disappeared, but had been seen, by some one, the last
night, at Deb's hut.

What and where was Deb's hut?

It was a hut in the wilderness, occupied by an old
Indian woman, known among her neighbours by the
name of Old Deb. Some people called her Queen Mab.
Her dwelling was eight *long* miles from this house.

A thousand questions were precluded, and a thousand

doubts solved by this information. *Queen Mab* were sounds familiar to my ears; for they originated with myself.

This woman originally belonged to the tribe of Delawares or Lennilennapee. All these districts were once comprised within the dominions of that nation. About thirty years ago, in consequence of perpetual encroachments of the English colonists, they abandoned their ancient seats and retired to the banks of the Wabash and Muskingum.

This emigration was concerted in a general council of the tribe, and obtained the concurrence of all but one female. Her birth, talents, and age, gave her much consideration and authority among her countrymen; and all her zeal and eloquence were exerted to induce them to lay aside their scheme. In this, however, she could not succeed. Finding them refractory, she declared her resolution to remain behind, and maintain possession of the land which her countrymen should impiously abandon.

The village inhabited by this clan was built upon ground which now constitutes my uncle's barn yard and orchard. On the departure of her countrymen, this female burnt the empty wigwams and retired into the fastnesses of Norwalk. She selected a spot suitable for an Indian dwelling and a small plantation of maize, and in which she was seldom liable to interruption and intrusion.

Her only companions were three dogs, of the Indian or wolf species. These animals differed in nothing from their kinsmen of the forest, but in their attachment and obedience to their mistress. She governed them with absolute sway: they were her servants and protectors, and attended her person or guarded her threshold, agreeably to her directions. She fed them with corn and they supplied her and themselves with meat, by hunting squirrels, racoons, and rabbits.

To the rest of mankind they were aliens or enemies. They never left the desert but in company with their mistress, and when she entered a farm-house, waited her return at a distance. They would suffer none to approach them, but attacked no one who did not imprudently crave their acquaintance, or who kept at a respectful distance from their wigwam. That sacred asylum they would not suffer to be violated, and no stranger could enter it but at the imminent hazard of his life, unless accompanied and protected by their dame.

The chief employment of this woman, when at home, besides plucking the weeds from among her corn; bruising the grain between two stones, and setting her snares, for rabbits and apossums, was to talk. Though in solitude, her tongue was never at rest but when she was asleep; but her conversation was merely addressed to her dogs. Her voice was sharp and shrill, and her gesticulations were vehement and grotesque. An hearer would naturally imagine that she was scolding; but, in truth, she was merely giving them directions. Having no other object of contemplation or subject of discourse, she always found, in their postures and looks, occasion for praise, or blame, or command. The readiness with which they understood, and the docility with which they obeyed her movements and words, were truly wonderful.

If a stranger chanced to wander near her hut, and overhear her jargon, incessant as it was, and shrill, he might speculate in vain on the reason of these sounds. If he waited in expectation of hearing some reply, he waited in vain. The strain, always voluble and sharp, was never intermitted for a moment, and would continue for hours at a time.

She seldom left the hut but to visit the neighbouring inhabitants, and demand from them food and cloathing, or whatever her necessities required. These were exacted as her due: to have her wants supplied was her prerogative, and to withhold what she claimed was rebellion. She conceived that by remaining behind her countrymen she succeeded to the government, and retained the possession of all this region. The English were aliens and sojourners, who occupied the land merely by her connivance and permission, and whom she allowed to remain on no terms but those of supplying her wants.

Being a woman aged and harmless, her demands being limited to that of which she really stood in need, and which her own industry could not procure, her pretensions were a subject of mirth and good humour, and her injunctions obeyed with seeming deference and gravity. To me she early became an object of curiosity and speculation. I delighted to observe her habits and humour her prejudices. She frequently came to my uncle's house, and I sometimes visited her; insensibly she seemed to contract an affection for me, and regarded me with more complacency and condescension than any other received.

She always disdained to speak English, and custom had rendered her intelligible to most in her native language, with regard to a few simple questions. I had taken some pains to study her jargon, and could make out to discourse with her on the few ideas which she possessed. This circumstance, likewise, wonderfully prepossessed her in my favour.

The name by which she was formerly known was Deb; but her pretensions to royalty, the wildness of her aspect and garb, her shrivelled and diminutive form, a constitution that seemed to defy the ravages of time and the influence of the elements; her age, which some did not scruple to affirm exceeded an hundred years, her romantic solitude and mountainous haunts suggested to my fancy the appellation of *Queen Mab*. There appeared to me some rude analogy between this personage and her whom the poets of old-time have delighted to celebrate: thou perhaps wilt discover nothing but incongruities between them, but, be that as it may, Old Deb and Queen Mab soon came into indiscriminate and general use.

She dwelt in Norwalk upwards of twenty years. She was not forgotten by her countrymen, and generally received from her brothers and sons an autumnal visit; but no solicitations or entreaties could prevail on her to return with them. Two years ago, some suspicion or disgust induced her to forsake her ancient habitation, and to seek a new one. Happily she found a more convenient habitation twenty miles to the westward, and in a spot abundantly sterile and rude.

This dwelling was of logs, and had been erected by a Scottish emigrant, who not being rich enough to purchase land, and entertaining a passion for solitude and independence, cleared a field in the unappropriated wilderness, and subsisted on its produce. After some time he disappeared. Various conjectures were formed as to the cause of his absence. None of them were satisfactory; but that which obtained most credit was, that he had been murdered by the Indians, who, about the same period, paid their annual visit to the *Queen*. This conjecture acquired some force, by observing that the old woman shortly after took possession of his hut, his implements of tillage, and his corn-field.

She was not molested in her new abode, and her life passed in the same quiet tenour as before. Her periodical rambles, her regal claims, her guardian wolfs, and her uncouth volubility, were equally remarkable, but her circuits were new. Her distance made her visit to Solebury more rarely, and had prevented me from ever extending my pedestrian excursions to her present abode.

These recollections were now suddenly called up by the information of my hostess. The hut where I had sought shelter and relief was, it seems, the residence of Queen Mab. Some fortunate occurrence had called her away during my visit. Had she and her dogs been at home, I should have been set upon by these ferocious centinels, and, before their dame could have interfered, have been, together with my helpless companion, mangled or killed. These animals never barked. I should have entered unaware of my danger, and my fate could scarcely have been averted by my fusil.

Her absence at this unseasonable hour was mysterious. It was now the time of year when her countrymen were accustomed to renew their visit. Was there a league between her and the plunderers whom I had encountered?

But who were they by whom my footsteps were so industriously traced? Those whom I had seen at Deb's hut were strangers to me, but the wound upon my face was known only to them. To this circumstance was now added my place of residence and name. I supposed them impressed with the belief that I was dead; but this mistake must have speedily been rectified. Revisiting the spot, finding me gone, and obtaining some intelligence of my former condition, they had instituted a search after me.

But what tidings were these? I was supposed to have been bewildered in the mountains, and three days were said to have passed since my disappearance. Twelve hours had scarcely elapsed since I emerged from the cavern. Had two days and an half been consumed in my subterranean prison?

These reflections were quickly supplanted by others. I now gained a sufficient acquaintance with the region that was spread around me. I was in the midst of a vale, included between ridges that gradually approached each other, and when joined, were broken up into hollows and steeps, and spreading themselves over a circular space, assumed the appellation of Norwalk. This vale gradually widened as it tended to the westward, and was, in this place ten or twelve miles in breadth. My devious footsteps had brought me to the foot of the southern barrier. The outer basis of this was laved by the river, but, as it tended eastward, the mountain and river receded from each other, and one of the cultivable districts lying between them was Solebury, my natal *township*. Hither it was now my duty to return with the utmost expedition.

There were two ways before me. One lay along the interior base of the hill, over a sterile and trackless space, and exposed to the encounter of savages, some of whom might possibly be lurking here. The other was the well frequented road, on the outside and along the river, and which was to be gained by passing over this hill. The practicability of the passage was to be ascertained by inquiries made to my hostess. She pointed out a path that led to the rocky summit and down to the river's brink. The path was not easy to be kept in view or to be trodden, but it was undoubtedly to be preferred to any other.

A route, somewhat circuitous, would terminate in the river road. Thenceforward the way to Solebury was level and direct; but the whole space which I had to traverse was not less than thirty miles. In six hours it would be night, and, to perform the journey in that time would demand the agile boundings of a leopard and the indefatigable sinews of an elk.

My frame was in miserable plight. My strength had been assailed by anguish, and fear, and watchfulness; by toil, and abstinence, and wounds. Still, however, some remnant was left; would it not enable me to reach my home by night-fall? I had delighted, from my childhood, in feats of agility and perseverance. In roving through the maze of thickets and precipices, I had put my energies both moral and physical, frequently to the test. Greater achievements than this had been performed, and I disdained to be out-done in perspicacity by the lynx, in his sure-footed instinct by the roe, or in patience under hardship, and contention with fatigue, by the Mohawk. I have ever aspired to transcend the rest of animals in all that is common to the rational and brute, as well as in all by which they are distinguished from each other.

CHAPTER XXI

I LIKEWISE burned with impatience to know the
condition of my family, to dissipate at once their
tormenting doubts and my own, with regard to our
mutual safety. The evil that I feared had befallen them
was too enormous to allow me to repose in suspense, and
my restlessness and ominous forebodings would be more
intolerable than any hardship or toils to which I could
possibly be subjected during this journey.

I was much refreshed and invigorated by the food that I
had taken, and by the rest of an hour. With this stock of
recruited force I determined to scale the hill. After receiving minute directions, and returning many thanks for my
hospitable entertainment, I set out.

The path was indeed intricate, and deliberate attention
was obliged to be exerted in order to preserve it. Hence
my progress was slower than I wished. The first impulse
was to fix my eye upon the summit, and to leap from crag
to crag till I reached it, but this my experience had taught
me was impracticable. It was only by winding through
gullies, and coasting precipices and bestriding chasms,
that I could hope finally to gain the top, and I was assured
that by one way only was it possible to accomplish even
this.

An hour was spent in struggling with impediments,
and I seemed to have gained no way. Hence a doubt was
suggested whether I had not missed the true road. In this

doubt I was confirmed by the difficulties which now grew up before me. The brooks, the angles and the hollows, which my hostess had described, were not to be seen. Instead of these, deeper dells, more headlong torrents and wider gaping rifts were incessantly encountered.

To return was as hopeles as to proceed. I consoled myself with thinking that the survey which my informant had made of the hill-side, might prove inaccurate, and that in spite of her predictions, the heights might be reached by other means than by those pointed out by her. I will not enumerate my toilsome expedients, my frequent disappointments and my desperate exertions. Suffice it to say that I gained the upper space, not till the sun had dipped beneath the horizon.

My satisfaction at accomplishing thus much was not small, and I hied, with renovated spirits, to the opposite brow. This proved to be a steep that could not be descended. The river flowed at its foot. The opposite bank was five hundred yards distant, and was equally towering and steep as that on which I stood. Appearances were adapted to persuade you that these rocks had formerly joined, but by some mighty effort of nature, had been severed, that the stream might find way through the chasm. The channel, however, was encumbered with asperities over which the river fretted and foamed with thundering impetuosity.

I pondered for a while on these stupendous scenes. They ravished my attention from considerations that related to myself; but this interval was short, and I began to measure the descent, in order to ascertain the practicability of treading it. My survey terminated in bitter disappointment. I turned my eye successively eastward and westward. Solebury lay in the former direction, and thither I desired to go. I kept along the verge in this direction, till I reached an impassable rift. Beyond this I saw that the steep grew lower, but it was impossible to proceed farther. Higher up the descent might be practicable, and though more distant from Solebury, it was better to reach the road, even at that distance, than never to reach it.

Changing my course, therefore, I explored the spaces above. The night was rapidly advancing, the grey clouds gathered in the south-east, and a chilling blast, the usual attendant of a night in October, began to whistle among the pigmy cedars that scantily grew upon these heights. My progress would quickly be arrested by darkness, and it behoved me to provide some place of shelter and repose. No recess, better than an hollow in the rock, presented itself to my anxious scrutiny.

Meanwhile I would not dismiss the hope of reaching the road, which I saw some hundred feet below, winding along the edge of the river, before daylight should utterly fail. Speedily these hopes derived new vigour from meeting a ledge that irregularly declined from the brow of the hill. It was wide enough to allow of cautious footing. On a similar stratum, or ledge, projecting still further from the body of the hill, and close to the surface of the river, was the road. This stratum ascended from the level of the stream, while that on which I trod rapidly descended. I hoped that they would speedily be blended, or at least approach so near as to allow me to leap from one to the other without enormous hazard.

This fond expectation was frustrated. Presently I perceived that the ledge below began to descend, while that above began to tend upward, and was quickly terminated by the uppermost surface of the cliff. Here it was needful to pause. I looked over the brink and considered whether I might not leap from my present station, without endangering my limbs. The road into which I should fall was a rocky pavement far from being smooth. The descent could not be less than forty or fifty feet. Such an attempt was, to the last degree, hazardous, but was it not better to risque my life by leaping from this eminence, than to remain and perish on the top of this inhospitable mountain? The toils which I had endured, in reaching this height appeared to my panic-struck fancy, less easy to be borne again than death.

I know not but that I should have finally resolved to leap, had not different views been suggested by observing that the outer edge of the road was, in like manner, the brow of a steep which terminated in the river. The surface of the road, was twelve or fifteen feet above the level of the stream, which, in this spot was still and smooth. Hence I inferred that the water was not of inconsiderable depth. To fall upon rocky points was, indeed, dangerous, but to plunge into water of sufficient depth, even from an height greater than that at which I now stood, especially to one to whom habit had rendered water almost as congenial an element as air, was scarcely attended with inconvenience. This expedient was easy and safe. Twenty yards from this spot, the channel was shallow, and to gain the road from the stream, was no difficult exploit.

Some disadvantages, however, attended this scheme. The water was smooth, but this might arise from some other cause than its depth. My gun, likewise, must be left behind me, and that was a loss to which I felt invincible repugnance. To let it fall upon the road, would put it in my power to retrieve the possession, but it was likely to be irreparably injured by the fall.

While musing upon this expedient, and weighing injuries with benefits, the night closed upon me. I now considered that should I emerge in safety from the stream, I should have many miles to travel before I could reach an house. My clothes meanwhile would be loaded with wet. I should be heart-pierced by the icy blast that now blew, and my wounds and bruises would be chafed into insupportable pain.

I reasoned likewise on the folly of impatience and the necessity of repose. By thus long continuance in one posture, my sinews began to stiffen, and my reluctance to make new exertions to encrease. My brows were heavy,

216

and I felt an irresistible propensity to sleep. I concluded to seek some shelter, and resign myself, my painful recollections, and my mournful presages to sweet forgetfulness. For this end, I once more ascended to the surface of the cliff. I dragged my weary feet forward, till I found somewhat that promised me the shelter that I sought.

A cluster of cedars appeared, whose branches overarched a space that might be called a bower. It was a slight cavity, whose flooring was composed of loose stones and a few faded leaves blown from a distance, and finding a temporary lodgement here. On one side was a rock, forming a wall rugged and projecting above. At the bottom of the rock was a rift, some-what resembling a coffin in shape, and not much larger in dimensions. This rift terminated on the opposite side of the rock, in an opening that was too small for the body of a man to pass. The distance between each entrance was twice the length of a man.

This bower was open to the South-east whence the gale now blew. It therefore imperfectly afforded the shelter of which I stood in need; but it was the best that the place and the time afforded. To stop the smaller entrance of the cavity with a stone, and to heap before the other, branches lopped from the trees with my hatchet, might somewhat contribute to my comfort.

This was done, and thrusting myself into this recess, as far as I was able, I prepared for repose. It might have been reasonably suspected to be the den of rattle-snakes or panthers; but my late contention with superior dangers and more formidable enemies made me reckless of these, but another inconvenience remained. In spite of my precautions, my motionless posture and slender covering exposed me so much to the cold that I could not sleep.

The air appeared to have suddenly assumed the temperature of mid-winter. In a short time, my extremities were benumbed, and my limbs shivered and ached as if I had been seized by an ague. My bed likewise was dank and uneven, and the posture I was obliged to assume, unnatural and painful. It was evident that my purpose could not be answered by remaining here.

I, therefore, crept forth, and began to reflect upon the possibility of continuing my journey. Motion was the only thing that could keep me from freezing, and my frame was in that state which allowed me to take no repose in the absence of warmth; since warmth were indispensible. It now occurred to me to ask whether it were not possible to kindle a fire.

Sticks and leaves were at hand. My hatchet and a pebble would enable me to extract a spark. From this, by suitable care and perseverance, I might finally procure sufficient fire to give me comfort and ease, and even enable me to sleep. This boon was delicious and I felt as if I were unable to support a longer deprivation of it.

I proceeded to execute this scheme. I took the dryest leaves, and endeavoured to use them as tinder, but the driest leaves were moistened by the dews. They were only to be found in the hollows, in some of which were pools of water and others were dank. I was not speedily discouraged, but my repeated attempts failed, and I was finally compelled to relinquish this expedient.

All that now remained was to wander forth and keep myself in motion till the morning. The night was likely to prove tempestuous and long. The gale seemed freighted with ice, and acted upon my body like the points of a thousand needles. There was no remedy, and I mustered my patience to endure it.

I returned again, to the brow of the hill. I ranged along it till I reached a place where the descent was perpendicular, and, in consequence of affording no sustenance to trees or bushes, was nearly smooth and bare. There was no road to be seen, and this circumstance, added to the sounds which the ripling current produced, afforded me some knowledge of my situation.

The ledge, along which the road was conducted, disappeared near this spot. The opposite sides of the chasm through which flowed the river, approached nearer to each other, in the form of jutting promontories. I now stood upon the verge of that on the northern side. The water flowed at the foot, but, for the space of ten or twelve feet from the rock, was so shallow as to permit the traveller and his horse to wade through it, and thus to regain the road which the receding precipice had allowed to be continued on the farther side.

I knew the nature and dimensions of this ford. I knew that, at a few yards from the rock, the channel was of great depth. To leap into it, in this place, was a less dangerous exploit, than at the spot where I had formerly been tempted to leap. There I was unacquainted with the depth, but here I knew it to be considerable. Still there was some ground of hesitation and fear. My present station was loftier, and how deeply I might sink into this gulf, how far the fall and the concussion would bereave me of my presence of mind, I could not determine. This hesitation vanished, and placing my tom-hawk and fusil upon the ground, I prepared to leap.

This purpose was suspended, in the moment of its execution, by a faint sound, heard from the quarter whence I had come. It was the warning of men, but had nothing in common with those which I had been accustomed to hear. It was not the howling of a wolf or the yelling of a panther. These had often been overheard by night during my last year's excursion to the lakes. My fears whispered that this was the vociferation of a savage.

I was unacquainted with the number of the enemies who had adventured into this district. Whether those whom I had encountered at *Deb's hut* were of that band whom I had met with in the cavern, was merely a topic of conjecture. There might be an half-score of troops, equally numerous, spread over the wilderness, and the signal I had just heard might betoken the approach of one of these. Yet by what means they should gain this nook, and what prey they expected to discover, were not easily conceived.

The sounds, somewhat diversified, nearer and rising from different quarters, were again heard. My doubts and apprehensions were increased. What expedient to adopt for my own safety, was a subject of rapid meditation. Whether to remain stretched upon the ground or to rise and go forward. Was it likely the enemy would coast along the edge of the steep? Would they ramble hither to look upon the ample scene which spread on all sides around the base of this rocky pinnacle? In that case, how should I conduct myself? My arms were ready for use. Could I not elude the necessity of shedding more blood? Could I not anticipate their assault by casting myself without delay into the stream?

The sense of danger demanded more attention to be paid to external objects than to the motives by which my future conduct should be influenced. My post was on a circular projecture, in some degree, detached from the body of the hill, the brow of which continued in a streight line, uninterrupted by this projecture, which was somewhat higher than the continued summit of the ridge. This line ran at the distance of a few paces from my post. Objects moving along this line could merely be perceived to move, in the present obscurity.

My scrutiny was entirely directed to this quarter. Presently the treading of many feet was heard, and several figures were discovered, following each other in that streight and regular succession which is peculiar to the Indians. They kept along the brow of the hill joining the promontory. I distinctly marked seven figures in succession.

My resolution was formed. Should any one cast his eye hither, suspect, or discover an enemy, and rush towards me, I determined to start upon my feet, fire on my foe as he advanced, throw my piece on the ground, and then leap into the river.

Happily, they passed unobservant and in silence. I remained, in the same posture, for several minutes. At length, just as my alarms began to subside, the halloos,

220

before heard, arose, and from the same quarter as before. This convinced me that my perils were not at an end. This now appeared to be merely the vanguard, and would speedily be followed by others, against whom the same caution was necessary to be taken.

My eye, anxiously bent the only way by which any one could approach, now discerned a figure, which was indubitably that of a man armed; none other appeared in company, but doubtless others were near. He approached, stood still, and appeared to gaze stedfastly at the spot where I lay.

The optics of a *Lennilennapee* I knew to be far keener than my own. A log or a couched fawn would never be mistaken for a man, nor a man for a couched fawn or a log. Not only a human being would be instantly detected, but a decision be unerringly made whether it were friend or foe. That my prostrate body was the object on which the attention of this vigilant and stedfast gazer was fixed, could not be doubted. Yet, since he continued an inactive gazer, there was ground for a possibility to stand upon, that I was not recognized. My fate, therefore, was still in suspense.

This interval was momentary. I marked a movement, which my fears instantly interpreted to be that of leveling a gun at my head. This action was sufficiently comformable to my prognostics. Supposing me to be detected, there was no need for him to change his post. Aim might too fatally be taken, and his prey be secured, from the distance at which he now stood.

These images glanced upon my thought, and put an end to my suspense. A single effort placed me on my feet. I fired with precipitation that precluded the certainty of hitting my mark, dropped my piece upon the ground, and leaped from this tremendous height into the river. I reached the surface, and sunk in a moment to the bottom.

Plunging endlong into the water, the impetus created by my fall from such an height, would be slowly resisted by this denser element. Had the depth been less, its resistance would not perhaps have hindered me from being mortally injured against the rocky bottom. Had the depth been greater, time enough would not have been allowed me to regain the surface. Had I fallen on my side, I should have been bereaved of life or sensibility by the shock which my frame would have received. As it was, my fate was suspended on a thread. To have lost my presence of mind, to have forborne to counteract my sinking, for an instant, after I had reached the water, would have made all exertions to regain the air, fruitless. To so fortunate a concurrence of events, was thy friend indebted for his safety!

Yet I only emerged from the gulf to encounter new perils. Scarcely had I raised my head above the surface, and inhaled the vital breath, when twenty shots were aimed at me from the precipice above. A shower of bullets fell upon the water. Some of them did not fall further than two inches from my head. I had not been aware of this new danger, and now that it assailed me continued gasping the air, and floundering at random. The means of eluding it did not readily occur. My case seemed desperate and all caution was dismissed.

This state of discomfiting surprise quickly disappeared. I made myself acquainted, at a glance, with the position of surrounding objects. I conceived that the opposite bank of the river would afford me most security, and thither I tended with all the expedition in my power.

Meanwhile, my safety depended on eluding the bullets that continued incessantly to strike the water at an arm's length from my body. For this end I plunged beneath the surface, and only rose to inhale fresh air. Presently the firing ceased, the flashes that lately illuminated the bank disappeared, and a certain bustle and murmur of confused voices gave place to solitude and silence.

CHAPTER XXII

I REACHED without difficulty the opposite bank, but the steep was inaccessible. I swam along the edge in hopes of meeting with some projection or recess where I might, at least, rest my weary limbs, and if it were necessary to recross the river, to lay in a stock of recruited spirits and strength for that purpose. I trusted that the water would speedily become shoal, or that the steep would afford rest to my feet. In both these hopes I was disappointed.

There is no one to whom I would yield the superiority in swimming, but my strength, like that of other human beings, had its limits. My previous fatigues had been enormous, and my clothes, heavy with moisture, greatly incumbered and retarded my movements. I had proposed to free myself from this imprisonment, but I foresaw the inconveniences of wandering over this scene in absolute nakedness, and was willing therefore, at whatever hazard, to retain them. I continued to struggle with the current and to search for the means of scaling the steeps. My search was fruitless, and I began to meditate the recrossing of the river.

Surely my fate has never been paralleled! Where was this series of hardships and perils to end? No sooner was one calamity eluded, than I was beset by another. I had emerged from abhorred darkness in the heart of the earth, only to endure the extremities of famine and encounter

223

the fangs of a wild beast. From these I was delivered only to be thrown into the midst of savages, to wage an endless and hopeless war with adepts in killing; with appetites that longed to feast upon my bowels and to quaff my heart's-blood. From these likewise was I rescued, but merely to perish in the gulfs of the river, to welter on unvisited shores or to be washed far away from curiosity or pity.

Formerly water was not only my field of sport but my sofa and my bed. I could float for hours on the surface, enjoying its delicious cool, almost without the expense of the slightest motion. It was an element as fitted for repose as for exercise, but now the buoyant spirit seemed to have flown. My muscles were shrunk, the air and water were equally congealed, and my most vehement exertions were requisite to sustain me on the surface.

At first I had moved along with my wonted celerity and ease, but quickly my forces were exhausted. My pantings and efforts were augmented and I saw that to cross the river again was impracticable. I must continue, therefore, to search out some accessible spot in the bank along which I was swimming.

Each moment diminished my stock of strength, and it behoved me to make good my footing before another minute should escape. I continued to swim, to survey the bank, and to make ineffectual attempts to grasp the rock. The shrubs which grew upon it would not uphold me, and the fragments which, for a moment, inspired me with hope, crumbled away as soon as they were touched.

At length, I noticed a pine, which was rooted in a crevice near the water. The trunk, or any part of the root, was beyond my reach, but I trusted that I could catch hold of the branch which hung lowest, and that, when caught, it would assist me in gaining the trunk, and thus deliver me from the death which could not be otherwise averted.

The attempt was arduous. Had it been made when I first reached the bank, no difficulty had attended it, but now, to throw myself some feet above the surface could scarcely be expected from one whose utmost efforts seemed to be demanded to keep him from sinking. Yet this exploit, arduous as it was, was attempted and accomplished. Happily the twigs were strong enough to sustain my weight till I caught at other branches and finally placed myself upon the trunk.

This danger was now past, but I admitted the conviction that others, no less formidable remained to be encountered and that my ultimate destiny was death. I looked upward. New efforts might enable me to gain the summit of this steep, but, perhaps, I should thus be placed merely in the situation from which I had just been delivered. It was of little moment whether the scene of my imprisonment was a dungeon not to be broken, or a summit from which descent was impossible.

The river, indeed, severed me from a road which was level and safe, but my recent dangers were remembered only to make me shudder at the thought of incurring them a second time, by attempting to cross it. I blush at the recollection of this cowardice. It was little akin to the spirit which I had recently displayed. It was, indeed, an alien to my bosom, and was quickly supplanted by intrepidity and perseverance.

I proceeded to mount the hill. From root to root, and from branch to branch, lay my journey. It was finished, and I sat down upon the highest brow to meditate on future trials. No road lay along this side of the river. It was rugged and sterile, and farms were sparingly dispersed over it. To reach one of these was now the object of my wishes. I had not lost the desire of reaching Solebury before morning, but my wet clothes and the coldness of the night seemed to have bereaved me of the power.

I traversed this summit, keeping the river on my right hand. Happily, its declinations and ascents were by no means difficult, and I was cheered in the midst of my vexations, by observing that every mile brought me nearer to my uncle's dwelling. Meanwhile I anxiously looked for some tokens of an habitation. These at length presented themselves. A wild heath, whistled over by October blasts, meagrely adorned with the dry stalks of scented shrubs and the bald heads of the sapless mullen, was succeeded by a fenced field and a corn-stack. The dwelling to which these belonged was eagerly sought.

I was not surprised that all voices were still and all lights extinguished, for this was the hour of repose. Having reached a piazza before the house, I paused. Whether, at this drousy time, to knock for admission, to alarm the peaceful tenants and take from them the rest which their daily toils and their rural innocence had made so sweet, or to retire to what shelter an hay-stack or barn could afford, was the theme of my deliberations.

Meanwhile I looked up at the house. It was the model of cleanliness and comfort. It was built of wood; but the materials had undergone the plane, as well as the axe and the saw. It was painted white, and the windows not only had sashes, but these sashes were supplied, contrary to custom, with glass. In most cases, the aperture where glass should be is stuffed with an old hat or a petticoat. The door had not only all its parts entire, but was embellished with mouldings and a pediment. I gathered from these tokens that this was the abode not only of rural competence and innocence, but of some beings, raised by education and fortune, above the intellectual mediocrity of clowns.

Methought I could claim consanguinity with such beings. Not to share their charity and kindness would be inflicting as well as receiving injury. The trouble of affording shelter, and warmth, and wholesome diet to a wretch destitute as I was, would be eagerly sought by them.

Still I was unwilling to disturb them. I bethought myself that their kitchen might be entered, and all that my necessities required be obtained without interrupting their slumber. I needed nothing but the warmth which their kitchen hearth would afford. Stretched upon the bricks, I might dry my clothes, and perhaps enjoy some unmolested sleep. In spite of presages of ill and the horrid remembrances of what I had performed and endured, I believed that nature would afford a short respite to my cares.

I went to the door of what appeared to be a kitchen. The door was wide open. This circumstance portended evil. Though it be not customary to lock or to bolt, it is still less usual to have entrances unclosed. I entered with suspicious steps, and saw enough to confirm my apprehensions. Several pieces of wood half burned, lay in the midst of the floor. They appeared to have been removed hither from the chimney, doubtless with a view to set fire to the whole building.

The fire had made some progress on the floor, but had been seasonably extinguished by pails-full of water, thrown upon it. The floor was still deluged with wet, the pail not emptied of all its contents stood upon the hearth. The earthen vessels and plates whose proper place was the dresser, were scattered in fragments in all parts of the room. I looked around me for some one to explain this scene, but no one appeared.

The last spark of fire was put out, so that had my curiosity been idle, my purpose could not be accomplished. To retire from this scene, neither curiosity nor benevolence would permit. That some mortal injury had been intended was apparent. What greater mischief had befallen, or whether greater might not, by my interposition, be averted, could only be ascertained by penetrating further into the house. I opened a door on one side which led to the main body of the building and entered to a bed-chamber. I stood at the entrance and knocked, but no one answered my signals.

The sky was not totally clouded, so that some light pervaded the room. I saw that a bed stood in the corner, but whether occupied or not, its curtains hindered me from judging. I stood in suspense a few minutes, when a motion in the bed shewed me that some one was there. I knocked again but withdrew to the outside of the door. This roused the sleeper, who, half-groaning and puffing the air through his nostrils, grumbled out in the hoarsest voice that I ever heard, and in a tone of surly impatience . . . Who is there?

I hesitated for an answer, but the voice instantly continued in the manner of one half-asleep and enraged at being disturbed . . . Is't you Peg? Damn ye, stay away, now; I tell ye stay away, or, by God I will cut your throat . . . I will. . . . He continued to mutter and swear, but without coherence or distinctness.

These were the accents of drunkenness, and denoted a wild and ruffian life. They were little in unison with the external appearances of the mansion, and blasted all the hopes I had formed of meeting under this roof with gentleness and hospitality. To talk with this being, to attempt to reason him into humanity and soberness, was useless. I was at a loss in what manner to address him, or whether it was proper to maintain any parley. Meanwhile, my silence was supplied by the suggestions of his own distempered fancy. Ay, said he, ye will, will ye? well come on, let's see who's the better at the oak-stick. If I part with ye, before I have bared your bones . . . I'll teach ye to be always dipping in my dish, ye devil's dam! ye!

So saying, he tumbled out of bed. At the first step, he struck his head against the bed-post, but setting himself upright, he staggered towards the spot where I stood. Some new obstacle occurred. He stumbled and fell at his length upon the floor.

To encounter or expostulate with a man in this state was plainly absurd. I turned and issued forth, with an aching heart, into the court before the house. The miseries which a debauched husband or father inflicts upon all whom their evil destiny allies to him were pictured by my fancy, and wrung from me tears of anguish. These images, however, quickly yielded to reflections on my own state. No expedient now remained, but to seek the barn, and find a covering and a bed of straw.

I had scarcely set foot within the barn-yard when I heard a sound as of the crying of an infant. It appeared to issue from the barn. I approached softly and listened at the door. The cries of the babe continued, but were accompanied by intreaties of a nurse or a mother to be quiet. These intreaties were mingled with heart-breaking sobs and exclamations of . . . Ah! me, my babe! Canst thou not sleep and afford thy unhappy mother some peace? Thou art cold, and I have not sufficient warmth to cherish thee! What will become of us? Thy deluded father cares not if we both perish.

A glimpse of the true nature of the scene seemed to be imparted by these words. I now likewise recollected incidents that afforded additional light. Somewhere on this bank of the river, there formerly resided one by name Selby. He was an aged person, who united science and taste to the simple and laborious habits of an husband-man. He had a son who resided several years in Europe, but on the death of his father, returned home, accompanied by a wife. He had succeeded to the occupation of the farm, but rumour had whispered many tales to the disadvantage of his morals. His wife was affirmed to be of delicate and polished manners, and much unlike her companion.

It now occurred to me that this was the dwelling of the Selbys, and I seemed to have gained some insight into the discord and domestic miseries by which the unhappy lady suffered. This was no time to waste my sympathy on others. I could benefit her nothing. Selby had probably returned from a carousal, with all his malignant passions raised into phrensy by intoxication. He had driven his desolate wife from her bed and house, and to shun outrage and violence she had fled, with her helpless infant, to the barn. To appease his fury, to console her, to suggest a remedy for this distress, was not in my power. To have sought an interview would be merely to excite her terrors and alarm her delicacy, without contributing to alleviate her calamity. Here then was no asylum for me. A place of rest must be sought at some neighbouring habitation. It was probable that one would be found at no great distance; the path that led from the spot where I stood, through a gate into a meadow, might conduct me to the nearest dwelling, and this path I immediately resolved to explore.

I was anxious to open the gate without noise, but I could not succeed. Some creaking of its hinges, was unavoidably produced, which I feared would be overheard by the lady and multiply her apprehensions and perplexities. This inconvenience was irremediable. I therefore closed the gate and pursued the foot way before me with the utmost expedition. I had not gained the further end of the meadow when I lighted on something which lay across the path, and which, on being closely inspected, appeared to be an human body. It was the corse of a girl, mangled by an hatchet. Her head gory and deprived of its locks, easily explained the kind of enemies by whom she had been assailed. Here was proof that this quiet and remote habitation had been visited, in their destructive progress by the Indians. The girl had been slain by them, and her scalp, according to their savage custom, had been torn away to be preserved as a trophy.

The fire which had been kindled on the kitchen floor was now remembered, and corroborated the inferences which were drawn from this spectacle. And yet that the mischief had been thus limited, that the besotted wretch who lay helpless on his bed, and careless of impending danger, and that the mother and her infant should escape, excited some degree of surprise. Could the savages have been interrupted in their work, and obliged to leave their vengeance unfinished?

Their visit had been recent. Many hours had not elapsed since they prowled about these grounds. Had they wholly disappeared and meant they not to return? To what new danger might I be exposed in remaining thus guideless and destitute of all defence?

In consequence of these reflections, I proceeded with more caution. I looked with suspicious glances, before and on either side of me. I now approached the fence which, on this side, bounded the meadow. Something was discerned or imagined, stretched close to the fence, on the ground, and filling up the path-way. My apprehensions of a lurking enemy, had been previously awakened, and my fancy instantly figured to itself an armed man, lying on the ground and waiting to assail the unsuspecting passenger.

At first I was prompted to fly, but a second thought shewed me that I had already approached near enough to be endangered. Notwithstanding my pause, the form was motionless. The possibility of being misled in my conjectures was easily supposed. What I saw might be a log or it might be another victim to savage ferocity. This tract was that which my safety required me to pursue. To turn aside or go back would be merely to bewilder myself anew.

Urged by these motives, I went nearer, and at last was close enough to perceive that the figure was human. He lay upon his face; near his right hand was a musquet, unclenched. This circumstance, his death-like attitude and the garb and ornaments of an Indian, made me readily suspect the nature and cause of this catastrophe. Here the invaders had been encountered and repulsed, and one at least of their number had been left upon the field.

I was weary of contemplating these rueful objects. Custom, likewise, even in so short a period, had inured me to spectacles of horror. I was grown callous and immoveable. I staid not to ponder on the scene, but snatching the musquet, which was now without an owner, and which might be indispensable to my defence, I hastened into the wood. On this side the meadow was skirted by a forest, but a beaten road led into it, and might therefore be attempted without danger.

CHAPTER XXIII

THE road was intricate and long. It seemed designed to pervade the forest in every possible direction. I frequently noticed cut wood, piled in heaps upon either side, and rejoiced in these tokens that the residence of men was near. At length I reached a second fence, which proved to be the boundary of a road still more frequented. I pursued this, and presently beheld, before me, the river and its opposite barriers.

This object afforded me some knowledge of my situation. There was a ford over which travellers used to pass, and in which the road that I was now pursuing terminated. The stream was rapid and tumultuous, but in this place it did not rise higher than the shoulders. On the opposite side was an highway, passable by horses and men, though not carriages, and which led into the midst of Solebury. Should I not rush into the stream, and still aim at reaching my uncle's house before morning? Why should I delay?

Thirty hours of incessant watchfulness and toil, of enormous efforts and perils, preceded and accompanied by abstinence and wounds, were enough to annihilate the strength and courage of ordinary men. In the course of them, I had frequently believed myself to have reached the verge beyond which my force would not carry me, but experience as frequently demonstrated my error. Though many miles were yet to be traversed, though my clothes were once more to be drenched and loaded with moisture, though every hour seemed to add somewhat to the keenness of the blast: yet how should I know, but by trial, whether my stock of energy was not sufficient for this last exploit?

My resolution to proceed was nearly formed, when the figure of a man moving slowly across the road, at some distance before me, was observed. Hard by this ford lived a man by name Bisset, of whom I had slight knowledge. He tended his two hundred acres with a plodding and money-doating spirit, while his son overlooked a Gristmill, on the river. He was a creature of gain, coarse and harmless. The man whom I saw before me might be he, or some one belonging to his family. Being armed for defence, I less scrupled a meeting with any thing in the shape of man. I therefore called. The figure stopped and answered me, without surliness or anger. The voice was unlike that of Bisset, but this person's information I believed would be of some service.

Coming up to him, he proved to be a clown, belonging to Bisset's habitation. His panic and surprise on seeing me made him aghast. In my present garb I should not have easily been recognized by my nearest kinsman, and much less easily by one who had seldom met me.

It may be easily conceived that my thoughts, when allowed to wander from the objects before me, were tormented with forebodings and inquietudes on account of the ills which I had so much reason to believe had befallen my family. I had no doubt that some evil had happened, but the full extent of it was still uncertain. I desired and dreaded to discover the truth, and was unable to interrogate this person in a direct manner. I could deal only in circuities and hints. I shuddered while I waited for an answer to my inquiries.

Had not Indians, I asked, been lately seen in this neighbourhood? Were they not suspected of hostile designs? Had they not already committed some mischief? Some passenger, perhaps, had been attacked; or fire had

233

been set to some house? On which side of the river had their steps been observed, or any devastation been committed? Above the ford or below it? At what distance from the river?

When his attention could be withdrawn from my person and bestowed upon my questions, he answered that some alarm had indeed been spread about Indians, and that parties from Solebury and Chetasko were out in pursuit of them, that many persons had been killed by them, and that one house in Solebury had been rifled and burnt on the night before the last.

These tidings were a dreadful confirmation of my fears. There scarcely remained a doubt: but still my expiring hope prompted me to inquire to whom did the house belong?

He answered that he had not heard the name of the owner. He was a stranger to the people on the other side of the river.

Were any of the inhabitants murdered?

Yes. All that were at home except a girl whom they carried off. Some said that the girl had been retaken.

What was the name? Was it Huntly?

Huntly? Yes. No. He did not know. He had forgotten.

I fixed my eyes upon the ground. An interval of gloomy meditation succeeded. All was lost, all for whose sake I desired to live, had perished by the hands of these assassins. That dear home, the scene of my sportive childhood, of my studies, labours and recreations, was ravaged by fire and the sword: was reduced to a frightful ruin.

Not only all that embellished and endeared existence was destroyed, but the means of subsistence itself. Thou knowest that my sisters and I were dependants on the bounty of our uncle. His death would make way for the succession of his son, a man fraught with envy and malignity: who always testified a mortal hatred to us, merely because we enjoyed the protection of his father. The ground which furnished me with bread was now become the property of one, who, if he could have done it with security, would gladly have mingled poison with my food.

All that my imagination or my heart regarded as of value had likewise perished. Whatever my chamber, my closets, my cabinets contained, my furniture, my books, the records of my own skill, the monuments of their existence whom I loved, my very cloathing, were involved in indiscriminate and irretreivable destruction. Why should I survive this calamity?

But did not he say that one had escaped? The only females in the family were my sisters. One of these had been reserved for a fate worse than death; to gratify the innate and insatiable cruelty of savages by suffering all the torments their invention can suggest, or to linger out years of dreary bondage and unintermitted hardship in the bosom of the wilderness. To restore her to liberty; to cherish this last survivor of my unfortunate race was a sufficient motive to life and to activity.

But soft! Had not rumour whispered that the captive was retaken? Oh! who was her angel of deliverance? Where did she now abide? Weeping over the untimely fall of her protector and her friend? Lamenting and upbraiding the absence of her brother? Why should I not haste to find her? To mingle my tears with hers, to assure her of my safety and expiate the involuntary crime of my desertion, by devoting all futurity to the task of her consolation and improvement?

The path was open and direct. My new motives, would have trampled upon every impediment and made me reckless of all dangers and all toils. I broke from my reverie, and without taking leave or expressing gratitude to my informant, I ran with frantic expedition towards the river, and plunging into it gained the opposite side in a moment.

I was sufficiently acquainted with the road. Some twelve or fifteen miles remained to be traversed. I did not fear that my strength would fail in the performance of my journey. It was not my uncle's habitation to which I directed my steps. Inglefield was my friend. If my sister had existence, or was snatched from captivity, it was here that an asylum had been afforded to her, and here was I to seek the knowledge of my destiny. For this reason having reached a spot where the road divided into two branches, one of which led to Inglefield's and the other to Huntly's, I struck into the former.

Scarcely had I passed the angle when I noticed a building, on the right hand, at some distance from the road. In the present state of my thoughts, it would not have attracted my attention, had not a light gleamed from an upper window, and told me that all within were not at rest.

I was acquainted with the owner of this mansion. He merited esteem and confidence, and could not fail to be acquainted with recent events. From him I should obtain all the information that I needed, and I should be delivered from some part of the agonies of my suspense. I should reach his door in a few minutes, and the window-light was a proof that my entrance at this hour would not disturb the family, some of whom were stirring.

Through a gate, I entered an avenue of tall oaks, that led to the house. I could not but reflect on the effect which my appearance would produce upon the family. The sleek locks, neat apparel, pacific guise, sobriety and gentleness of aspect by which I was customarily distinguished, would in vain be sought in the apparition which would now present itself before them. My legs, neck and bosom were bare, and their native hue were exchanged for the livid marks of bruises and scarrifications. An horrid scar upon my cheek, and my uncombed locks; hollow eyes, made ghastly by abstinence and cold, and the ruthless passions of which my mind had been the theatre, added to the musquet which I carried in my hand, would prepossess them with the notion of a maniac or ruffian.

Some inconveniences might hence arise, which however could not be avoided. I must trust to the speed with which my voice and my words should disclose my true character and rectify their mistake.

I now reached the principal door of the house. It was open, and I unceremoniously entered. In the midst of the room stood a German stove, well heated. To thaw my half frozen limbs was my first care. Meanwhile, I gazed around me, and marked the appearances of things.

Two lighted candles stood upon the table. Beside them were cyder-bottles and pipes of tobacco. The furniture and room was in that state which denoted it to have been lately filled with drinkers and smokers, yet neither voice, nor visage, nor motion were any where observable. I listened but neither above nor below, within or without, could any tokens of an human being be perceived.

This vacancy and silence must have been lately preceded by noise and concourse and bustle. The contrast was mysterious and ambiguous. No adequate cause of so quick and absolute a transition occurred to me. Having gained some warmth and lingered some ten or twenty minutes in this uncertainty, I determined to explore the other apartments of the building. I knew not what might betide in my absence, or what I might encounter in my search to justify precaution, and, therefore, kept the gun in my hand. I snatched a candle from the table and proceeded into two other apartments on the first floor and the kitchen. Neither was inhabited, though chairs and tables were arranged in their usual order, and no traces of violence or hurry were apparent.

Having gained the foot of the stair-case, I knocked, but my knocking was wholly disregarded. A light had appeared in an upper chamber. It was not, indeed, in one of those apartments which the family permanently occupied, but in that which, according to rural custom, was reserved for guests; but it indubitably betokened the presence of some being by whom my doubts might be solved. These doubts were too tormenting to allow of scruples and delay. —I mounted the stairs.

At each chamber door I knocked, but I knocked in

vain. I tried to open, but found them to be locked. I at length reached the entrance of that in which a light had been discovered. Here, it was certain, that some one would be found; but here, as well as elsewhere, my knocking was unnoticed.

To enter this chamber was audacious, but no other expedient was afforded me to determine whether the house had any inhabitants. I, therefore, entered, though with caution and reluctance. No one was within, but there were sufficient traces of some person who had lately been here. On the table stood a travelling escrutoire, open, with pens and ink-stand. A chair was placed before it, and a candle on the right hand. This apparatus was rarely seen in this country. Some traveller it seemed occupied this room, though the rest of the mansion was deserted. The pilgrim, as these appearances testified, was of no vulgar order, and belonged not to the class of periodical and every-day guests.

It now occurred to me that the occupant of this apartment could not be far off, and that some danger and embarrassment could not fail to accrue from being found, thus accoutred and garbed, in a place sacred to the study and repose of another. It was proper, therefore, to withdraw, and either to resume my journey, or wait for the stranger's return, whom perhaps some temporary engagement had called away, in the lower and public room. The former now appeared to be the best expedient, as the return of this unknown person was uncertain, as well as his power to communicate the information which I wanted.

Had paper, as well as the implements of writing, lain upon the desk, perhaps my lawless curiosity would not have scrupled to have pryed into it. On the first glance nothing of that kind appeared, but now, as I turned towards the door, somewhat, lying beside the desk, on the side opposite the candle, caught my attention. The impulse was instantaneous and mechanical, that made me leap to the spot, and lay my hand upon it. Till I felt it between my fingers, till I brought it near my eyes and read frequently the inscriptions that appeared upon it, I was doubtful whether my senses had deceived me.

Few, perhaps, among mankind have undergone vicissitudes of peril and wonder equal to mine. The miracles of poetry, the transitions of enchantment, are beggarly and mean compared with those which I had experienced: Passage into new forms, overleaping the bars of time and space, reversal of the laws of inanimate and intelligent existence had been mine to perform and to witness.

No event had been more fertile of sorrow and perplexity than the loss of thy brother's letters. They went by means invisible, and disappeared at a moment when foresight would have least predicted their disappearance. They now placed themselves before me, in a manner equally abrupt, in a place and by means, no less contrary to expectation. The papers which I now seized were those letters. The parchment cover, the string that tied, and the wax that sealed them, appeared not to have been opened or violated.

The power that removed them from my cabinet, and dropped them in this house, a house which I rarely visited, which I had not entered during the last year, with whose inhabitants I maintained no cordial intercourse, and to whom my occupations and amusements, my joys and my sorrows, were unknown, was no object even of conjecture. But they were not possessed by any of the family. Some stranger was here, by whom they had been stolen, or into whose possession, they had, by some incomprehensible chance, fallen.

That stranger was near. He had left this apartment for a moment. He would speedily return. To go hence, might possibly occasion me to miss him. Here then I would wait, till he should grant me an interview. The papers were mine, and were recovered. I would never part with them. But to know by whose force or by whose stratagems I had been bereaved of them thus long, was now the supreme passion of my soul. I seated myself near a table and anxiously awaited for an interview, on which I was irresistably persuaded to believe that much of my happiness depended.

Meanwhile, I could not but connect this incident with the destruction of my family. The loss of these papers had excited transports of grief, and yet, to have lost them thus, was perhaps the sole expedient, by which their final preservation could be rendered possible. Had they remained in my cabinet, they could not have escaped the destiny which overtook the house and its furniture. Savages are not accustomed to leave their exterminating work unfinished. The house which they have plundered, they are careful to level with the ground. This not only their revenge, but their caution prescribes. Fire may originate by accident as well as by design, and the traces of pillage and murder are totally obliterated by the flames.

These thoughts were interrupted by the shutting of a door below, and by footsteps ascending the stairs. My heart throbbed at the sound. My seat became uneasy and I started on my feet. I even advanced half way to the entrance of the room. My eyes were intensely fixed upon the door. My impatience would have made me guess at the person of this visitant by measuring his shadow, if his shadow were first seen; but this was precluded by the position of the light. It was only when the figure entered, and the whole person was seen, that my curiosity was gratified. He who stood before me was the parent and fosterer of my mind, the companion and instructor of my youth, from whom I had been parted for years; from whom I believed myself to be forever separated; — *Sarsefield* himself!

CHAPTER XXIV

MY deportment, at an interview so much desired and so wholly unforeseen, was that of a maniac. The petrifying influence of surprise, yielded to the impetuosities of passion. I held him in my arms: I wept upon his bosom, I sobbed with emotion which, had it not found passage at my eyes, would have burst my heart-strings. Thus I who had escaped the deaths that had previously assailed me in so many forms, should have been reserved to solemnize a scene like this by . . . *dying for joy!*

The sterner passions and habitual austerities of my companion, exempted him from pouring out this testimony of his feelings. His feelings were indeed more allied to astonishment and incredulity than mine had been. My person was not instantly recognized. He shrunk from my embrace, as if I were an apparition or impostor. He quickly disengaged himself from my arms, and withdrawing a few paces, gazed upon me as on one whom he had never before seen.

These repulses were ascribed to the loss of his affection. I was not mindful of the hideous guise in which I stood before him, and by which he might justly be misled to imagine me a ruffian or a lunatic. My tears flowed now on a new account, and I articulated in a broken and faint voice — My master! my friend! Have you forgotten? have you ceased to love me?

The sound of my voice made him start and exclaim —

241

Am I alive? am I awake? Speak again I beseech you, and convince me that I am not dreaming or delirious.

Can you need any proof, I answered, that it is Edgar Huntly, your pupil, your child that speaks to you?

He now withdrew his eyes from me and fixed them on the floor. After a pause he resumed, in emphatic accents. Well, I have lived to this age in unbelief. To credit or trust in miraculous agency was foreign to my nature, but now I am no longer sceptical. Call me to any bar, and exact from me an oath that you have twice been dead and twice recalled to life; that you move about invisibly, and change your place by the force, not of muscles, but of thought, and I will give it.

How came you hither? Did you penetrate the wall? Did you rise through the floor?

Yet surely 'tis an error. You could not be he whom twenty witnesses affirmed to have beheld a lifeless and mangled corpse upon the ground, whom my own eyes saw in that condition.

In seeking the spot once more to provide you a grave, you had vanished. Again I met you. You plunged into a rapid stream, from an height from which it was impossible to fall and to live: yet, as if to set the limits of nature at defiance; to sport with human penetration, you rose upon the surface: You floated; you swam: Thirty bullets were aimed at your head, by marks-men celebrated for the exactness of their sight. I myself was of the number, and I never missed what I desired to hit.

My predictions were confirmed by the event. You ceased to struggle; you sunk to rise no more, and yet after these accumulated deaths, you light upon this floor: so far distant from the scene of your catastrophe; over spaces only to be passed, in so short a time as has since elapsed, by those who have wings.

My eyes, my ears bear testimony to your existence now, as they formerly convinced me of your death — What am I to think; What proofs am I to credit? — There he stopped.

Every accent of this speech added to the confusion of my thoughts. The allusions that my friend had made were not unintelligible. I gained a glimpse of the complicated errors by which we had been mutually deceived. I had fainted on the area before Deb's hut. I was found by Sarsefield in this condition, and imagined to be dead.

The man whom I had seen upon the promontory was not an Indian. He belonged to a numerous band of pursuers, whom my hostile and precipitate deportment caused to suspect me for an enemy. They that fired from the steep were friends. The interposition that screened me from so many bullets, was indeed miraculous. No wonder that my voluntary sinking, in order to elude their shots, was mistaken for death, and that, having accomplished the destruction of this foe, they resumed their pursuit of others. But how was Sarsefield apprized that it was I who plunged into the river? No subsequent event was possible to impart to him the incredible truth.

A pause of mutual silence ensued. At length, Sarsefield renewed his expressions of amazement at this interview, and besought me to explain why I had disappeared by night from my Uncle's house, and by what series of unheard of events this interview was brought about. Was it indeed Huntly whom he examined and mourned over at the threshold of Deb's hut? Whom he had sought in every thicket and cave in the ample circuit of Norwalk and Chetasco? Whom he had seen perish in the current of the Delaware?

Instead of noticing his questions, my soul was harrowed with anxiety respecting the fate of my uncle and sisters. Sarsefield could communicate the tidings which would decide on my future lot, and set my portion in happiness or misery. Yet I had not breath to speak my inquiries. Hope tottered, and I felt as if a single word would be sufficient for its utter subversion. At length, I articulated the name of my Uncle.

The single word sufficiently imparted my fears, and these fears needed no verbal confirmation. At that dear

243

name, my companion's features were overspread by sorrow — Your Uncle, said he, is dead.

Dead? Merciful Heaven! And my sisters too? Both?

Your Sisters are alive and well.

Nay, resumed I, in faultering accents, jest not with my feelings. Be not cruel in your pity. Tell me the truth.

I have said the truth. They are well, at Mr. Inglefield's.

My wishes were eager to assent to the truth of these tidings. The better part of me was then safe: but how did they escape the fate that overtook my uncle? How did they evade the destroying hatchet and the midnight conflagration? These doubts were imparted in a tumultuous and obscure manner to my friend. He no sooner fully comprehended them, than he looked at me, with some inquietude and surprise.

Huntly, said he, are you mad — What has filled you with these hideous prepossessions? Much havoc has indeed been committed in Chetasco and the wilderness; and a log hut has been burnt by design or by accident in Solebury, but that is all. Your house has not been assailed by either fire-brand or tom-hawk. Every thing is safe and in its ancient order. The master indeed is gone, but the old man fell a victim to his own temerity and hardihood. It is thirty years since he retired with three wounds, from the field of Braddock; but time, in no degree, abated his adventurous and military spirit. On the first alarm, he summoned his neighbours, and led them in pursuit of the invaders. Alas! he was the first to attack them, and the only one who fell in the contest.

These words were uttered in a manner that left me no room to doubt of their truth. My uncle had already been lamented, and the discovery of the nature of his death, so contrary to my forebodings, and of the safety of my girls, made the state of my mind partake more of exultation and joy, than of grief or regret.

But how was I deceived? Had not my fusil been found in the hands of an enemy? Whence could he have plundered it but from my own chamber? It hung against the wall of a closet; from which no stranger could have taken it except by violence. My perplexities and doubts were not at an end, but those which constituted my chief torment were removed. I listened to my friend's intreaties to tell him the cause of my elopement, and the incidents that terminated in the present interview.

I began with relating my return to consciousness in the bottom of the pit; my efforts to free myself from this abhorred prison; the acts of horror to which I was impelled by famine, and their excruciating consequences; my gaining the outlet of the cavern, the desperate expedient by which I removed the impediment to my escape, and the deliverance of the captive girl; the contest I maintained before Deb's hut; my subsequent wanderings; the banquet which hospitality afforded me; my journey to the river-bank; my meditations on the means of reaching the road; my motives for hazarding my life, by plunging into the stream; and my subsequent perils and fears till I reached the threshold of this habitation.

Thus, continued I, I have complied with your request. I have told all that I, myself, know. What were the incidents between my sinking to rest at my Uncle's, and my awaking in the chambers of the hill; by which means and by whose contrivance, preternatural or human, this transition was effected, I am unable to explain; I cannot even guess.

What has eluded my sagacity may not be beyond the reach of another. Your own reflections on my tale, or some facts that have fallen under your notice, may enable you to furnish a solution. But, meanwhile, how am I to account for your appearance on this spot? This meeting was unexpected and abrupt to you, but it has not been less so to me. Of all mankind, Sarsefield was the farthest from my thoughts, when I saw these tokens of a traveller and a stranger.

You were imperfectly acquainted with my wanderings. You saw me on the ground before Deb's hut. You saw me plunge into the river. You endeavoured to destroy me while swimming; and you knew, before my narrative was heard, that Huntly was the object of your enmity. What was the motive of your search in the desert, and how were you apprized of my condition? These things are not less wonderful than any of those which I have already related.

During my tale the features of Sarsefield betokened the deepest attention. His eye strayed not a moment from my face. All my perils and forebodings, were fresh in my remembrance, they had scarcely gone by; their skirts, so to speak, were still visible. No wonder that my eloquence was vivid and pathetic, that I pourtrayed the past as if it were the present scene; and that not my tongue only, but every muscle and limb, spoke.

When I had finished my relation, Sarsefield sunk into thoughtfulness. From this, after a time, he recovered and said: Your tale, Huntly, is true, yet, did I not see you before me, were I not acquainted with the artlessness and rectitude of your character, and, above all, had not my own experience, during the last three days, confirmed every incident, I should question its truth. You have amply gratified my curiosity, and deserve that your own, should be gratified as fully. Listen to me.

Much has happened since we parted, which shall not be now mentioned. I promised to inform you of my welfare by letter, and did not fail to write, but whether my letters were received, or any were written by you in return, or if written were ever transmitted, I cannot tell; none were ever received.

Some days since, I arrived, in company with a lady who is my wife, in America. You have never been forgotten by me. I knew your situation to be little in agreement with your wishes, and one of the benefits which fortune has lately conferred upon me, is the power of snatching you from a life of labour and obscurity; whose goods, scanty as they are, were transient and precarious; and affording you the suitable leisure and means of intellectual gratification and improvement.

Your silence made me entertain some doubts concerning your welfare, and even your existence. To solve these doubts, I hastened to Solebury; some delays upon the road, hindered me from accomplishing my journey by day-light. It was night before I entered the Norwalk path, but my ancient rambles with you made me familiar with it, and I was not affraid of being obstructed or bewildered.

Just as I gained the southern outlet, I spied a passenger on foot, coming towards me with a quick pace. The incident was of no moment, and yet the time of night, the seeming expedition of the walker, recollection of the mazes and obstacles which he was going to encounter, and a vague conjecture that, perhaps, he was unacquainted with the difficulties that awaited him, made me eye him with attention as he passed.

He came near, and I thought I recognized a friend in this traveller. The form, the gesture, the stature bore a powerful resemblance to those of Edgar Huntly. This resemblance was so strong, that I stopped, and after he had gone by, called him by your name. That no notice was taken of my call proved that the person was mistaken, but even though it were another, that he should not even hesitate or turn at a summons which he could not but perceive to be addressed, though erroneously, to him, was the source of some surprize. I did not repeat my call, but proceeded on my way.

All had retired to repose in your uncle's dwelling. I did not scruple to rouse them, and was received with affectionate and joyous greetings. That you allowed your uncle to rise before you, was a new topic of reflection. To my inquiries concerning you, answers were made that accorded with my wishes. I was told that you were in good health and were then abed. That you had not heard and risen at my knocking, was mentioned with surprise, but your uncle accounted for your indolence by saying that during the last week you had fatigued yourself by rambling night and day, in search of some maniac, or visionary who was supposed to have retreated into Norwalk.

I insisted upon awakening you myself. I anticipated the effect of this sudden and unlooked for meeting, with some emotions of pride as well as of pleasure. To find, in opening your eyes, your old preceptor standing by your bedside and gazing in your face, would place you, I conceived, in an affecting situation.

Your chamber door was open, but your bed was empty. Your uncle and sisters were made acquainted with this circumstance. Their surprise gave way to conjectures that your restless and romantic spirit, had tempted you from your repose, that you had rambled abroad on some phantastic errand, and would probably return before the dawn. I willingly acquiesced in this opinion, and my feelings being too thoroughly aroused to allow me to sleep, I took possession of your chamber, and patiently awaited your return.

The morning returned but Huntly made not his appearance. Your uncle became somewhat uneasy at this unseasonable absence. Much speculation and inquiry, as to the possible reasons of your flight was made. In my survey of your chamber, I noted that only part of your cloathing remained beside your bed. Coat, hat, stockings and shoes lay upon the spot where they had probably been thrown when you had disrobed yourself, but the pantaloons, which according to Mr. Huntly's report, completed your dress, were no where to be found. That you should go forth on so cold a night so slenderly appareled, was almost incredible. Your reason or your senses had deserted you, before so rash an action could be meditated.

I now remembered the person I had met in Norwalk. His resemblance to your figure, his garb, which wanted hat, coat, stockings and shoes, and your absence from your bed at that hour, were remarkable coincidences: but why did you disregard my call? Your name, uttered by a voice that could not be unknown, was surely sufficient to arrest your steps.

Each hour added to the impatience of your friends; to

their recollections and conjectures, I listened with a view
to extract from them some solution of this mystery. At
length, a story was alluded to, of some one who, on the
preceding night, had been heard walking in the long
room; to this was added, the tale of your anxieties and
wonders occasioned by the loss of certain manuscripts.

While ruminating upon these incidents, and endeavouring to extract from this intelligence a clue, explanatory
of your present situation, a single word, casually dropped
by your uncle, instantly illuminated my. darkness and
dispelled my doubts. — After all, said the old man, ten to
one, but Edgar himself was the man whom we heard
walking, but the lad was asleep, and knew not what he
was about.

Surely said I, this inference is just. His manuscripts
could not be removed by any hands but his own, since the
rest of mankind were unacquainted not only with the
place of their concealment, but with their existence. None
but a man, insane or asleep, would wander forth so
slightly dressed, and none but a sleeper would have disregarded my calls. This conclusion was generally adopted,
but it gave birth in my mind, to infinite inquietudes. You
had roved into Norwalk, a scene of inequalities, of prominences and pits, among which, thus destitute of the guidance of your senses, you could scarcely fail to be
destroyed, or at least, irretreivably bewildered. I painted
to myself the dangers to which you were subjected. Your
careless feet would bear you into some whirlpool or to the
edge of some precipice, some internal revolution or out-
ward shock would recall you to consciousness at some
perilous moment. Surprise and fear would disable you
from taking seasonable or suitable precautions, and your
destruction be made sure.

The lapse of every new hour, without bringing tidings
of your state, enhanced these fears. At length, the propriety of searching for you occurred. Mr. Huntly and I
determined to set out upon this pursuit, as well as to
commission others. A plan was laid by which every acces-

sible part of Norwalk, the wilderness beyond the flats of Solebury, and the valey of Chetasco, should be traversed and explored.

Scarcely had we equipped ourselves for this expedition, when a messenger arrived, who brought the disastrous news of Indians being seen within these precincts, and on the last night a farmer was shot in his fields, a dwelling in Chetasco was burnt to the ground, and its inhabitants murdered or made captives. Rumour and inquiry had been busy, and a plausible conjecture had been formed, as to the course and number of the enemies. They were said to be divided into bands, and to amount in the whole to thirty or forty warriors. This messenger had come to warn us of danger which might impend, and to summon us to join in the pursuit and extirpation of these detestable foes.

Your uncle, whose alacrity and vigour age had not abated, eagerly engaged in this scheme. I was not averse to contribute my efforts to an end like this. The road which we had previously designed to take, in search of my fugitive pupil, was the same by which we must trace or intercept the retreat of the savages. Thus two purposes, equally momentous, would be answered by the same means.

Mr. Huntly armed himself with your fusil; Inglefield supplied me with a gun; during our absence the dwelling was closed and locked, and your sisters placed under the protection of Inglefield, whose age and pacific sentiments unfitted him for arduous and sanguinary enterprises. A troop of rustics was collected, half of whom remained to traverse Solebury and the other, whom Mr. Huntly and I accompanied, hastened to Chetasco.

CHAPTER XXV

IT was noon day before we reached the theatre of action. Fear and revenge combined to make the people of Chetasco diligent and zealous in their own defence. The havock already committed had been mournful. To prevent a repetition of the same calamities, they resolved to hunt out the hostile footsteps and exact a merciless retribution.

It was likely that the enemy, on the approach of day, had withdrawn from the valley and concealed themselves in the thickets, between the parrallel ridges of the mountain. This space, which, according to the object with which it is compared is either a vale or the top of an hill, was obscure and desolate. It was undoubtedly the avenue by which the robbers had issued forth, and by which they would escape to the Ohio. Here they might still remain, intending to emerge from their concealment on the next night, and perpetrate new horrors.

A certain distribution was made of our number, so as to move in all directions at the same time. I will not dwell upon particulars. It will suffice to say that keen eyes and indefatigable feet, brought us at last to the presence of the largest number of these marauders. Seven of them were slain by the edge of a brook, where they sat wholly unconscious of the danger which hung over them. Five escaped, and one of these secured his retreat by wresting your fusil from your uncle, and shooting him dead. Before our companion could be rescued or revenged, the assassin, with the remnant of the troop, disappeared, and bore away with him the fusil as a trophy of his victory.

This disaster was deplored not only on account of that life which had thus been sacrificed, but because a sagacious guide and intrepid leader was lost. His acquaintance with the habits of the Indians, and his experience in their wars made him trace their footsteps with more certainty than any of his associates.

The pursuit was still continued, and parties were so stationed that the escape of the enemy was difficult, if not impossible. Our search was unremitted, but during twelve or fourteen hours, unsuccessful. Queen Mab did not elude all suspicion. Her hut was visited by different parties, but the old woman and her dogs had disappeared.

Meanwhile your situation was not forgotten. Every one was charged to explore your footsteps as well as those of the savages, but this search was no less unsuccessful than the former. None had heard of you or seen you.

This continued till midnight. Three of us, made a pause at a brook, and intended to repair our fatigues by a respite of a few hours, but scarcely had we stretched ourselves on the ground when we were alarmed by a shot which seemed to have been fired at a short distance. We started on our feet and consulted with each other on the measures to be taken. A second, a third and a fourth shot, from the same quarter, excited our attention anew. Mab's hut was known to stand at the distance and in the direction of this sound, and thither we resolved to repair.

This was done with speed but with the utmost circumspection. We shortly gained the road that leads near this hut and at length gained a view of the building. Many persons were discovered, in a sort of bustling inactivity, before the hut. They were easily distinguished to be friends, and were therefore approached without scruple.

The objects that presented themselves to a nearer view were five bodies stretched upon the ground. Three of them were savages. The fourth was a girl, who though alive seemed to have received a mortal wound. The fifth, breathless and mangled and his features almost concealed by the blood that overspread his face, was Edgar; the fugitive for whom I had made such anxious search.

About the same hour on the last night I had met you hastening into Norwalk. Now were you, lying in the midst of savages, at the distance of thirty miles from your home, and in a spot, which it was impossible for you to have reached unless by an immense circuit over rocks and thickets. That you had found a rift at the basis of the hill, and thus permeated its solidities, and thus precluded so tedious and circuitous a journey as must otherwise have been made, was not to be imagined.

But whence arose this scene? It was obvious to conclude that my associates had surprised their enemies in this house, and exacted from them the forfeit of their crimes, but how you should have been confounded with their foes, or whence came the wounded girl was a subject of astonishment.

You will judge how much this surprise was augmented when I was informed that the party whom we found had been attracted hither by the same signals, by which we had been alarmed. That on reaching this spot you had been discovered, alive, seated on the ground and still sustaining the gun with which you had apparently completed the destruction of so many adversaries. In a moment after their arrival you sunk down and expired.

This scene was attended with inexplicable circumstances. The musquet which lay beside you appeared to have belonged to one of the savages. The wound by which each had died was single. Of the four shots we had distinguished at a distance, three of them were therefore fatal to the Indians and the fourth was doubtless that by which you had fallen, yet three musquets only were discoverable.

The arms were collected, and the girl carried to the nearest house in the arms of her father. Her situation was deemed capable of remedy, and the sorrow and wonder

253

which I felt at your untimely and extraordinary fate, did not hinder me from endeavouring to restore the health of this unfortunate victim. I reflected likewise that some light might be thrown upon transactions so mysterious, by the information which might be collected from her story. Numberless questions and hints were necessary to extract from her a consistent or intelligible tale. She had been dragged, it seems, for miles, at the heels of her conquerors, who at length, stopped in a cavern for the sake of some repose; all slept but one, who sat and watched. Something called him away, and, at the same moment, you appeared at the bottom of the cave half naked and without arms. You instantly supplied the last deficiency, by seizing the gun and tom-hawk of him who had gone forth, and who had negligently left his weapons behind. Then stepping over the bodies of the sleepers, you rushed out of the cavern.

She then mentioned your unexpected return, her deliverance and flight, and arrival at Deb's hut. You watched upon the hearth and she fell asleep upon the blanket. From this sleep she was aroused by violent and cruel blows. She looked up: — you were gone and the bed on which she lay was surrounded by the men from whom she had so lately escaped. One dragged her out of the hut and levelled his gun at her breast. At the moment when he touched the trigger, a shot came from an unknown quarter, and he fell at her feet. Of subsequent events she had an incoherent recollection. The Indians were successively slain, and you came to her, and interrogated and consoled her.

In your journey to the hut you were armed. This in some degree accounted for appearances, but where were your arms? Three musquets only were discovered and these undoubtedly belonged to your enemies.

I now had leisure to reflect upon your destiny. I had arrived soon enough on this shore merely to witness the catastrophe of two beings whom I most loved. Both were overtaken by the same fate, nearly at the same hour. The same hand had possibly accomplished the destruction of uncle and nephew.

Now, however, I began to entertain an hope that your state might not be irretreivable. You had walked and spoken after the firing had ceased, and your enemies had ceased to contend with you. A wound had, no doubt, been previously received. I had hastily inferred that the wound was mortal, and that life could not be recalled. Occupied with attention to the wailings of the girl, and full of sorrow and perplexity I had admitted an opinion which would have never been adopted in different circumstances. My acquaintance with wounds would have taught me to regard sunken muscles, lividness and cessation of the pulse as mere indications of a swoon, and not as tokens of death.

Perhaps my error was not irreparable. By hastening to the hut, I might ascertain your condition and at least transport your remains to some dwelling and finally secure to you the decencies of burial.

Of twelve savages, discovered on the preceding day, ten were now killed. Two, at least remained, after whom the pursuit was still zealously maintained. Attention to the wounded girl, had withdrawn me from the party, and I had now leisure to return to the scene of these disasters. The sun had risen, and, accompanied by two others, I repaired thither.

A sharp turn in the road, at the entrance of the field, set before us a starting spectacle. An Indian, mangled by repeated wounds of bayonet and bullet, was discovered. His musquet was stuck in the ground, by way of beacon attracting our attention to the spot. Over this space I had gone a few hours before, and nothing like this was then seen. The parties abroad, had hied away to a distant quarter. Some invisible power seemed to be enlisted in our defence and to preclude the necessity of our arms.

We proceeded to the hut. The savages were there, but Edgar had risen and flown! Nothing now seemed to be incredible. You had slain three foes, and the weapon with which the victory had been achieved, had vanished. You had risen from the dead, had assailed one of the surviving enemies, had employed bullet and dagger in his destruction, with both of which you could only be supplied by supernatural means, and had disappeared. If any inhabitant of Chetasco had done this, we should have heard of it.

But what remained? You were still alive. Your strength was sufficient to bear you from this spot. Why were you still invisible and to what dangers might you not be exposed, before you could disinvolve yourself from the mazes of this wilderness?

Once more I procured indefatigable search to be made after you. It was continued till the approach of evening and was fruitless. Inquiries were twice made at the house where you were supplied with food and intelligence. On the second call I was astonished and delighted by the tidings received from the good woman. Your person and demeanour and arms were described, and mention made of your resolution to cross the southern ridge, and traverse the Solebury road with the utmost expedition.

The greater part of my inquietudes were now removed. You were able to eat and to travel, and there was little doubt that a meeting would take place between us on the next morning. Meanwhile, I determined to concur with those who pursued the remainder of the enemy. I followed you, in the path that you were said to have taken, and quickly joined a numerous party who were searching for those who, on the last night, had attacked a plantation that lies near this, and destroyed the inhabitants.

I need not dwell upon our doublings and circuities. The enemy was traced to the house of Selby. They had entered, they had put fire on the floor, but were compelled to relinquish their prey. Of what number they consisted could not be ascertained, but one, lingering behind his fellows, was shot, at the entrance of the wood, and on the spot where you chanced to light upon him.

Selby's house was empty, and before the fire had made any progress we extinguished it. The drunken wretch whom you encountered, had probably returned from his nocturnal debauch, after we had left the spot.

The flying enemy was pursued with fresh diligence. They were found, by various tokens, to have crossed the river, and to have ascended the mountain. We trod closely on their heels. When we arrived at the promontory, described by you, the fatigues of the night and day rendered me unqualified to proceed. I determined that this should be the bound of my excursions. I was anxious to obtain an interview with you, and unless I paused here, should not be able to gain Inglefield's as early in the morning as I wished. Two others concurred with me in this resolution and prepared to return to this house which had been deserted by its tenants till the danger was past and which had been selected as the place of rendezvous.

At this moment, dejected and weary, I approached the ledge which severed the head-land from the mountain. I marked the appearance of some one stretched upon the ground where you lay. No domestic animal would wander hither and place himself upon this spot. There was something likewise in the appearance of the object that bespoke it to be man, but if it were man, it was, incontrovertibly, a savage and a foe. I determined therefore to rouse you by a bullet.

My decision was perhaps absurd. I ought to have gained more certainty before I hazarded your destruction. Be that as it will, a moment's lingering on your part would have probably been fatal. You started on your feet, and fired. See the hole which your random shot made through my sleeve! This surely was a day destined to be signalized by hair-breadth escapes.

Your action seemed incontestably to confirm my prognostics. Every one hurried to the spot and was eager to destroy an enemy. No one hesitated to believe that some of the shots aimed at you, had reached their mark, and that you had sunk to rise no more.

The gun which was fired and thrown down was taken and examined. It had been my companion in many a toilsome expedition. It had rescued me and my friends from a thousand deaths. In order to recognize it, I needed only to touch and handle it. I instantly discovered that I held in my hand the fusil which I had left with you on parting, with which your uncle had equipped himself, and which had been ravished from him by a savage. What was I hence to infer respecting the person of the last possessor?

My inquiries respecting you of the woman whose milk and bread you had eaten, were minute. You entered, she said, with an hatchet and gun in your hand. While you ate, the gun was laid upon the table. She sat near, and the piece became the object of inquisitive attention. The stock and barrels were described by her in such terms as left no doubt that this was the *Fusil*.

A comparison of incidents enabled me to trace the manner in which you came into possession of this instrument. One of those whom you found in the cavern was the assassin of your uncle. According to the girl's report, on issuing from your hiding place, you seized a gun that was unoccupied, and this gun chanced to be your own.

Its two barrels was probably the cause of your success in that unequal contest at Mab's hut. On recovering from *deliquium*, you found it where it had been dropped by you, out of sight and unsuspected by the party that had afterwards arrived. In your passage to the river had it once more fallen into hostile hands, or, had you missed the way, wandered to this promontory, and mistaken a troop of friends for a band of Indian marauders?

Either supposition was dreadful. The latter was the most plausible. No motives were conceivable by which one of the fugitives could be induced to post himself here, in this conspicuous station: whereas, the road which led you to the summit of the hill, to that spot where descent to the river road was practicable, could not be found but by those who were accustomed to traverse it. The directions which you had exacted from your hostess, proved your previous unacquaintance with these tracts.

I acquiesced in this opinion with an heavy and desponding heart. Fate had led us into a maze, which could only terminate in the destruction of one or of the other. By the breadth of an hair, had I escaped death from your hand. The same fortune had not befriended you. After my tedious search, I had lighted on you, forlorn, bewildered, perishing with cold and hunger. Instead of recognizing and affording you relief, I compelled you to leap into the river, from a perilous height, and had desisted from my persecution only when I had bereaved you of life, and plunged you to the bottom of the gulf.

My motives in coming to America were numerous and mixed. Among these was the parental affection with which you had inspired me. I came with fortune and a better gift than fortune in my hand. I intended to bestow both upon you, not only to give you competence, but one who would endear to you that competence, who would enhance, by participating, every gratification.

My schemes were now at an end. You were gone, beyond the reach of my benevolence and justice. I had robbed your two sisters of a friend and guardian. It was some consolation to think that it was in my power to stand, with regard to them, in your place, that I could snatch them from the poverty, dependence and humiliation, to which your death and that of your uncle had reduced them.

I was now doubly weary of the enterprise in which I was engaged, and returned, with speed, to this rendezvouz. My companions have gone to know the state of the family who resided under this roof and left me to beguile the tedious moments in whatever manner I pleased.

I have omitted mentioning one incident that happened between the detection of your flight and our expedition to

Chetasco. Having formed a plausible conjecture as to him who walked in the Long-room, it was obvious to conclude that he who purloined your manuscripts and the walker were the same personage. It was likewise easily inferred that the letters were secreted in the Cedar Chest or in some other part of the room. Instances similar to this have heretofore occurred. Men have employed anxious months in search of that which, in a freak of Noctambulation, was hidden by their own hands.

A search was immediately commenced, and your letters were found, carefully concealed between the rafters and shingles of the roof, in a spot, where, if suspicion had not been previously excited, they would have remained till the vernal rains and the summer heats, had insensibly destroyed them. This pacquet I carried with me, knowing the value which you set upon them, and there being no receptacle equally safe, but your own cabinet, which was locked.

Having, as I said, reached this house, and being left alone, I bethought me of the treasure I possessed. I was unacquainted with the reasons for which these papers were so precious. They probably had some momentous and intimate connection with your own history. As such they could not be of little value to me, and this moment of inoccupation and regrets, was as suitable as any other to the task of perusing them. I drew them forth, therefore, and laid them on the table in this chamber.

The rest is known to you. During a momentary absence you entered. Surely no interview of ancient friends ever took place in so unexpected and abrupt a manner. You were dead. I mourned for you, as one whom I loved, and whom fate had snatched forever from my sight. Now, in a blissful hour, you had risen, and my happiness in thus embracing you, is tenfold greater than would have been experienced, if no uncertainties and perils had protracted our meeting.

CHAPTER XXVI

HERE ended the tale of Sarsefield. Humiliation and joy were mingled in my heart. The events that preceded my awakening in the cave were now luminous and plain. What explication was more obvious? What but this solution ought to have been suggested by the conduct I had witnessed in Clithero?

Clithero! Was not this the man whom Clithero had robbed of his friend? Was not this the lover of Mrs. Lorimer, the object of the persecutions of Wiatte? Was it not now given me to investigate the truth of that stupendous tale? To dissipate the doubts which obstinately clung to my imagination respecting it?

But soft! Had not Sarsefield said that he was married? Was Mrs. Lorimer so speedily forgotten by him, or was the narrative of Clithero the web of imposture or the raving of insanity?

These new ideas banished all personal considerations from my mind. I looked eagerly into the face of my friend, and exclaimed in a dubious accent—How say you? Married? When? To whom?

Yes, Huntly, I am wedded to the most excellent of women. To her am I indebted for happiness and wealth and dignity and honour. To her do I owe the power of being the benefactor and protector of you and your sisters. She longs to embrace you as a son. To become truly her son, will depend upon your own choice and that of one, who was the companion of our voyage.

Heavens! cried I, in a transport of exultation and astonishment. Of whom do you speak? Of the mother of Clarice? The sister of Wiatte? The sister of the ruffian who laid snares for her life? Who pursued you and the unhappy Clithero, with the bitterest animosity?

My friend started at these sounds as if the earth had yawned at his feet. His countenance was equally signifi-cant of terror and rage. As soon as he regained the power of utterance, he spoke — Clithero! Curses light upon thy lips for having uttered that detested name! Thousands of miles have I flown to shun the hearing of it. Is the mad-man here? Have you set eyes upon him? Does he yet crawl upon the face of the earth? Unhappy? Unparal-leled, unheard of, thankless miscreant! Has he told his execrable falsehoods here? Has he dared to utter names so sacred as those of Euphemia Lorimer and Clarice?

He has: He has told a tale, that had all the appearances of truth —

Out upon the villain! The truth! Truth would prove him to be unnatural; develish; a thing for which no lan-guage has yet provided a name! He has called himself unhappy? No doubt, a victim to injustice! Overtaken by unmerited calamity! Say! Has he fooled thee with such tales?

No. His tale was a catalogue of crimes and miseries of which he was the author and sufferer. You know not his motives, his horrors: —

His deeds were monstrous and infernal. His motives were sordid and flagitious. To display all their ugliness and infamy was not his province. No: He did not tell you that he stole at midnight to the chamber of his mistress: a woman who astonished the world by her loftiness and magnanimity; by indefatigable beneficence and unswerv-ing equity; who had lavished on this wretch, whom she snatched from the dirt, all the goods of fortune; all the

benefits of education; all the treasures of love; every provocation to gratitude; every stimulant to justice.

He did not tell you that in recompense for every benefit, he stole upon her sleep and aimed a dagger at her
breast. There was no room for flight or ambiguity or
prevarication. She whom he meant to murder stood near,
saw the lifted weapon, and heard him confess and glory in
his purposes.

No wonder that the shock bereft her, for a time, of life.
The interval was seized by the ruffian to effect his escape.
The rebukes of justice, were shunned by a wretch conscious of his inexpiable guilt. These things he has hidden
from you, and has supplied their place by a tale specious
as false.

No. Among the number of his crimes, hypocrisy is not
to be numbered. These things are already known to me:
he spared himself too little in the narrative. The excellencies of his lady; her claims to gratitude and veneration,
were urged beyond their true bounds. His attempts upon
her life, were related. It is true that he desired and
endeavoured to destroy her.

How? Has he told you this?

He has told me all. Alas! the criminal intention has
been amply expiated—

What mean you? Whence and how came he hither?
Where is he now? I will not occupy the same land, the
same world with him. Have this woman and her daughter
lighted on the shore haunted by this infernal and implacable enemy?

Alas! It is doubtful whether he exists. If he lives, he is
no longer to be feared; but he lives not. Famine and
remorse have utterly consumed him.

Famine? Remorse? You talk in riddles.

He has immured himself in the desert. He has abjured
the intercourse of mankind. He has shut himself in caverns where famine must inevitably expedite that death for
which he longs as the only solace of his woes. To no

263

imagination are his offences blacker and more odious than to his own. I had hopes of rescuing him from this fate, but my own infirmities and errors have afforded me sufficient occupation.

Sarsefield renewed his imprecations on the memory of that unfortunate man: and his inquiries as to the circumstances that led him into this remote district. His inquiries were not to be answered by one in my present condition — My languors and fatigues had now gained a pitch that was insupportable. The wound in my face had been chafed, and inflamed by the cold water and the bleak air; and the pain attending it, would no longer suffer my attention to stray. I sunk upon the floor, and intreated him to afford me the respite of a few hours repose.

He was sensible of the deplorableness of my condition, and chid himself for the negligence of which he had already been guilty. He lifted me to the bed, and deliberated on the mode he should pursue for my relief. Some molifying application to my wound, was immediately necessary; but in our present lonely condition, it was not at hand. It could only be procured from a distance. It was proper therefore to hasten to the nearest inhabited dwelling, which belonged to one, by name Walton, and supply himself with such medicines as could be found.

Meanwhile there was no danger of molestation and intrusion. There was reason to expect the speedy return of those who had gone in pursuit of the savages. This was their place of rendezvous, and hither they appointed to re-assemble before the morrow's dawn. The distance of the neighbouring farm was small, and Sarsefield promised to be expeditious. He left me to myself and my own ruminations.

Harrassed by fatigue and pain, I had yet power to ruminate on that series of unparalleled events, that had lately happened. I wept, but my tears flowed from a double source; from sorrow, on account of the untimely fate of my uncle, and from joy, that my sisters were preserved, that Sarsefield had returned and was not unhappy.

I reflected on the untoward destiny of Clithero. Part of his calamity consisted in the consciousness of having killed his patronness; but it now appeared, though by some infatuation, I had not previously suspected, that the first impulse of sorrow in the lady, had been weakened by reflection and by time. That the prejudice persuading her that her life and that of her brother were to endure and to terminate together, was conquered by experience or by argument. She had come, in company with Sarsefield and Clarice to America. What influence might these events have upon the gloomy meditations of Clithero? Was it possible to bring them together; to win the maniac from his solitude, wrest from him his fatal purposes, and restore him to communion with the beings whose imagined indignation is the torment of his life?

These musings were interrupted by a sound from below which were easily interpreted into tokens of the return of those with whom Sarsefield had parted at the promontory; voices were confused and busy but not turbulent. They entered the lower room and the motion of chairs and tables shewed that they were preparing to rest themselves after their toils.

Few of them were unacquainted with me, since they probably were residents in this district. No inconvenience, therefore, would follow from an interview, though, on their part, wholly unexpected. Besides, Sarsefield would speedily return and none of the present visitants would be likely to withdraw to this apartment.

Meanwhile I lay upon the bed, with my face turned towards the door, and languidly gazing at the ceiling and walls. Just then a musquet was discharged in the room below. The shock affected me mechanically and the first impulse of surprise, made me almost start upon my feet.

The sound was followed by confusion and bustle. Some rushed forth and called on each other to run different ways, and the words "That is he" — "Stop him" were spoken in a tone of eagerness, and rage. My weakness and pain were for a moment forgotten, and my whole attention was bent to discover the meaning of this hubbub. The musquet which I had brought with me to this chamber, lay across the bed. Unknowing of the consequences of this affray, with regard to myself, I was prompted by a kind of self-preserving instinct, to lay hold of the gun, and prepare to repell any attack that might be made upon me.

A few moments elapsed when I thought I heard light footsteps in the entry leading to this room. I had no time to construe these signals, but watching fearfully the entrance, I grasped my weapon with new force, and raised it so as to be ready at the moment of my danger. I did not watch long. A figure cautiously thrust itself forward. The first glance was sufficient to inform me that this intruder was an Indian, and, of consequence, an enemy. He was unarmed. Looking eagerly on all sides, he at last spied me as I lay. My appearance threw him into consternation, and after the fluctuation of an instant, he darted to the window, threw up the sash, and leaped out upon the ground.

His flight might have been easily arrested by my shot, but surprize, added to my habitual antipathy to bloodshed, unless in cases of absolute necessity, made me hesitate. He was gone, and I was left to mark the progress of the drama. The silence was presently broken by firing at a distance. Three shots, in quick succession, were followed by the deepest pause.

That the party, recently arrived, had brought with them one or more captives, and that by some sudden effort, the prisoners had attempted to escape, was the only supposition that I could form. By what motives either of them could be induced to seek concealment in my chamber, could not be imagined.

I now heard a single step on the threshold below. Some one entered the common room. He traversed the floor during a few minutes, and then, ascending the stair-case, he entered my chamber. It was Sarsefield. Trouble and dismay were strongly written on his countenance. He seemed totally unconscious of my presence, his eyes were

266

fixed upon the floor, and as he continued to move across the room, he heaved forth deep sighs.

This deportment was mournful and mysterious. It was little in unison with those appearances which he wore at our parting, and must have been suggested by some event that had since happened. My curiosity impelled me to recall him from his reverie. I rose and seizing him by the arm, looked at him with an air of inquisitive anxiety. It was needless to speak.

He noticed my movement, and turning towards me, spoke in a tone of some resentment—Why did you deceive me? Did you not say Clithero was dead?

I said so because it was my belief. Know you any thing to the contrary? Heaven grant that he is still alive, and that our mutual efforts may restore him to peace.

Heaven grant, replied my friend, with a vehemence that bordered upon fury, Heaven grant that he may live thousands of years, and know not, in their long course, a moment's respite from remorse and from anguish; but this prayer is fruitless. He is not dead, but death hovers over him. Should he live, he will live only to defy justice and perpetrate new horrors. My skill might perhaps save him, but a finger shall not be moved to avert his fate.

Little did I think, that the wretch whom my friends rescued from the power of the savages, and brought wounded and expiring hither was Clithero. They sent for me in haste to afford him surgical assistance. I found him stretched upon the floor below, deserted, helpless and bleeding. The moment I beheld him, he was recognized. The last of evils was to look upon the face of this assassin, but that evil is past, and shall never be endured again.

Rise and come with me. Accommodation is prepared for you at Walcot's. Let us leave this house, and the moment you are able to perform a journey, abandon forever this district.

I could not readily consent to this proposal. Clithero had been delivered from captivity but was dying for want of that aid which Sarsefield was able to afford. Was it not inhuman to desert him in this extremity? What offence had he committed that deserved such implacable vengeance? Nothing I had heard from Sarsefield was in contradiction to his own story. His deed, imperfectly observed, would appear to be atrocious and detestable, but the view of all its antecedent and accompanying events and motives, would surely place it in the list not of crimes, but of misfortunes.

But what is that guilt which no penitence can expiate? Had not Clithero's remorse been more than adequate to crimes far more deadly and enormous than this? This, however, was no time to argue with the passions of Sarsefield. Nothing but a repetition of Clithero's tale, could vanquish his prepossessions and mollify his rage, but this repetition was impossible to be given by me, till a moment of safety and composure.

These thoughts made me linger, but hindered me from attempting to change the determination of my friend. He renewed his importunities for me to fly with him. He dragged me by the arm, and wavering and reluctant I followed where he chose to lead. He crossed the common-room, with hurried steps and eyes averted from a figure, which instantly fastened my attention.

It was, indeed, Clithero, whom I now beheld, supine, polluted with blood, his eyes closed and apparently insensible. This object was gazed at with emotions that rooted me to the spot. Sarsefield, perceiving me determined to remain where I was, rushed out of the house, and disappeared.

CHAPTER XXVII

I HUNG over the unhappy wretch whose emaciated form and rueful features, sufficiently bespoke that savage hands had only completed that destruction which his miseries had begun. He was mangled by the tom-hawk in a shocking manner, and there was little hope that human skill could save his life.

I was sensible of nothing but compassion. I acted without design, when seating myself on the floor I raised his head and placed it on my knees. This movement awakened his attention, and opening his eyes he fixed them on my countenance. They testified neither insensibility, nor horror nor distraction. A faint emotion of surprise gave way to an appearance of tranquillity — Having perceived these tokens of a state less hopeless than I at first imagined, I spoke to him: — My friend! How do you feel? Can any thing be done for you?

He answered me, in a tone more firm and with more coherence of ideas than previous appearances had taught me to expect. No, said he, thy kindness good youth, can avail me nothing. The end of my existence here is at hand. May my guilt be expiated by the miseries that I have suffered, and my good deeds only attend me to the presence of my divine judge.

I am waiting, not with trembling or dismay, for this close of my sorrows. I breathed but one prayer, and that prayer has been answered. I asked for an interview with thee, young man, but feeling as I now feel, this interview, so much desired, was beyond my hope. Now thou art come, in due season, to hear the last words that I shall need to utter.

I wanted to assure thee that thy efforts for my benefit were not useless. They have saved me from murdering myself, a guilt more inexpiable than any which it was in my power to commit.

I retired to the innermost recess of Norwalk, and gained the summit of an hill, by subterranean paths. This hill I knew to be on all sides inaccessible to human footsteps, and the subterranean passages was closed up by stones. Here I believed my solitude exempt from interruption and my death, in consequence of famine, sure.

This persuasion was not taken away by your appearance on the opposite steep. The chasm which severed us I knew to be impassable. I withdrew from your sight.

Some time after, awakening from a long sleep, I found victuals beside me. He that brought it was invisible. For a time, I doubted whether some messenger of heaven had not interposed for my salvation. How other than by supernatural means, my retreat should be explored, I was unable to conceive. The summit was encompassed by dizzy and profound gulfs, and the subterranean passages was still closed.

This opinion, though corrected by subsequent reflection, tended to change the course of my desperate thoughts. My hunger, thus importunately urged, would not abstain, and I ate of the food that was provided. Henceforth I determined to live, to resume the path of obscurity and labour, which I had relinquished, and wait till my God should summon me to retribution. To anticipate his call, is only to redouble our guilt.

I designed not to return to Inglefield's service, but to chuse some other and remoter district. Meanwhile, I had left in his possession, a treasure, which my determination to die, had rendered of no value, but which, my change of resolution, restored. Inclosed in a box at Inglefield's, were the memoirs of Euphemia Lorimer, by which in all my vicissitudes, I had been hitherto accompanied, and from which I consented to part only because I had refused to live. My existence was now to be prolonged and this manuscript was once more to constitute the torment and the solace of my being.

I hastened to Inglefield's by night. There was no need to warn him of my purpose. I desired that my fate should be an eternal secret to my ancient master and his neighbours. The apartment, containing my box was well known, and easily accessible.

The box was found but broken and rifled of its treasure. My transports of astonishment, and indignation and grief yielded to the resumption of my fatal purpose. I hastened back to the hill, and determined anew to perish.

This mood continued to the evening of the ensuing day. Wandering over rocks and pits, I discovered the manuscript, lying under a jutting precipice. The chance that brought it hither was not less propitious and miraculous than that by which I had been supplied with food. It produced a similar effect upon my feelings, and, while in possession of this manuscript I was reconciled to the means of life. I left the mountain, and traversing the wilderness, stopped in Chetasco. That kind of employment which I sought was instantly procured; but my new vocation was scarcely assumed when a band of savages invaded our security.

Rambling in the desert, by moonlight, I encountered these foes. They rushed upon me, and after numerous wounds which, for the present, neither killed nor disabled me, they compelled me to keep pace with them in their retreat. Some hours have passed since the troop was overtaken, and my liberty redeemed. Hardships, and repeated wounds, inflicted at the moment when the invaders were surprised and slain, have brought me to my present condition. I rejoice that my course is about to terminate.

Here the speaker was interrupted by the tumultuous

271

entrance of the party, by whom he had been brought hither. Their astonishment at seeing me, sustaining the head of the dying man, may be easily conceived. Their surprise was more strongly excited by the disappearance of the captive whom they had left in this apartment, bound hand and foot. It now appeared that of the savage troop who had adventured thus far in search of pillage and blood, all had been destroyed but two, who, had been led hither as prisoners. On their entrance into this house, one of the party had been sent to Walcot's to summon Sarsefield to the aid of the wounded man, while others had gone in search of chords to secure the arms and legs of the captives, who had hitherto been manacled imperfectly.

The chords were brought and one of them was bound, but the other, before the same operation was begun upon him, broke, by a sudden effort, the feeble ligatures by which he was at present constrained, and seizing a musquet that lay near him, fired on his enemies, and then rushed out of doors. All eagerly engaged in the pursuit. The savage was fleet as a deer and finally eluded his pursuers.

While their attention was thus engaged abroad, he that remained found means to extricate his wrists and ancles from his bonds and betaking himself to the stairs, escaped, as I before described, through the window of the room which I had occupied. They pestered me with their curiosity and wonder, for I was known to all of them; but waving the discussion of my own concerns I intreated their assistance to carry Clithero to the chamber and the bed which I had just deserted.

I now in spite of pain, fatigue and watchfulness, set out to go to Walton's. Sarsefield was ready to receive me at the door, and the kindness and compassion of the family were active in my behalf. I was conducted to a chamber and provided with suitable attendance and remedies.

I was not unmindful of the more deplorable condition

of Clithero. I incessantly meditated on the means for his relief. His case stood in need of all the vigilance and skill of a physician, and Sarsefield was the only one of that profession whose aid could be seasonably administered. Sarsefield therefore must be persuaded to bestow this aid.

There was but one mode of conquering his abhorrence of this man. To prepossess my friend with the belief of the innocence of Clithero, or to soothe him into pity by a picture of remorse and suffering. This could best be done, and in the manner most conformable to truth, by a simple recital of the incidents that had befallen, and by repeating the confession which had been extorted from Clithero.

I requested all but my friend to leave my chamber, and then, soliciting a patient hearing, began the narrative of Waldegrave's death; of the detection of Clithero beneath the shade of the elm; of the suspicions which were thence produced; and of the forest interview to which these suspicions gave birth; I then repeated, without variation or addition, the tale which was then told. I likewise mentioned my subsequent transactions in Norwalk so far as they illustrated the destiny of Clithero.

During this recital, I fixed my eyes upon the countenance of Sarsefield, and watched every emotion as it rose or declined. With the progress of my tale, his indignation and his fury grew less, and at length gave place to horror and compassion.

His seat became uneasy, his pulse throbbed with new vehemence. When I came to the motives which prompted the unhappy man to visit the chamber of his mistress, he started from his seat, and sometimes strode across the floor in a troubled mood, and sometimes stood before me, with his breath almost suspended in the eagerness of his attention. When I mentioned the lifted dagger, the shriek from behind, and the apparition that interposed, he shuddered and drew back as if a dagger had been aimed at his breast.

When the tale was done, some time elapsed in mutual

and profound silence. My friend's thoughts were involved in a mournful and indefinable reverie. From this he at length recovered and spoke.

It is true. A tale like this could never be the fruit of invention or be invented to deceive. He has done himself injustice. His character was spotless and fair: All his moral properties seemed to have resolved themselves into gratitude, fidelity and honour.

We parted at the door, late in the evening, as he mentioned, and he guessed truly that subsequent reflection had induced me to return and to disclose the truth to Mrs. Lorimer. Clarice relieved by the sudden death of her friend, and unexpectedly by all, arrived at the same hour.

These tidings, astonished, afflicted, and delighted the lady. Her brother's death had been long believed by all but herself. To find her doubts verified, and his existence ascertained was the dearest consolation that he ever could bestow. She was afflicted at the proofs that had been noted of the continuance of his depravity, but she dreaded no danger to herself from his malignity or vengeance.

The ignorance and prepossessions of this woman were remarkable. On this subject only she was perverse, headlong, obstinate. Her anxiety to benefit this arch-ruffian occupied her whole thoughts and allowed her no time to reflect upon the reasonings or remonstrances of others. She could not be prevailed on to deny herself to his visits, and I parted from her in the utmost perplexity.

A messenger came to me at mid-night intreating my immediate presence. Some disaster had happened, but of what kind the messenger was unable to tell. My fears easily conjured up the image of Wiatte. Terror scarcely allowed me to breathe. When I entered the house of Mrs. Lorimer, I was conducted to her chamber. She lay upon the bed in a state of stupefaction, that rose from some mental cause. Clarice sat by her, wringing her hands and pouring forth her tears without intermission. Neither could explain to me the nature of the scene. I made inquiries of the servants and attendants. They merely said that the family as usual had retired to rest, but their lady's bell rung with great violence, and called them in haste, to her chamber, where they found her in a swoon upon the floor and the young lady in the utmost affright and perturbation.

Suitable means being used Mrs. Lorimer had, at length, recovered, but was still nearly insensible. I went to Clithero's apartments but he was not to be found, and the domestics informed me that since he had gone with me, he had not returned. The doors between this chamber and the court were open; hence that some dreadful interview had taken place, perhaps with Wiatte, was an unavoidable conjecture. He had withdrawn, however, without committing any personal injury.

I need not mention my reflections upon this scene. All was tormenting doubt and suspence till the morning arrived, and tidings were received that Wiatte had been killed in the streets: This event was antecedent to that which had occasioned Mrs. Lorimer's distress and alarm. I now remembered that fatal prepossession by which the lady was governed, and her frantic belief that her death and that of her brother were to fall out at the same time. Could some witness of his death, have brought her tidings of it: Had he penetrated, unexpected and unlicensed to her chamber, and were these the effects produced by the intelligence?

Presently I knew that not only Wiatte was dead, but that Clithero had killed him. Clithero had not been known to return and was no where to be found. He then was the bearer of these tidings, for none but he could have found access or egress without disturbing the servants.

These doubts were at length at an end. In a broken and confused manner, and after the lapse of some days the monstrous and portentous truth was disclosed. After our interview, the lady and her daughter had retired to the same chamber; the former had withdrawn to her closet and the latter to bed. Some one's entrance alarmed the lady, and coming forth after a moment's pause, the spectacle which Clithero has too faithfully described, presented itself.

What could I think? A life of uniform hypocrisy or a sudden loss of reason were the only suppositions to be formed. Clithero was the parent of fury and abhorrence in my heart. In either case I started at the name. I shuddered at the image of the apostate or the maniac.

What? Kill the brother whose existence was interwoven with that of his benefactress and his friend? Then hasten to her chamber, and attempt her life? Lift a dagger to destroy her who had been the author of his being and his happiness?

He that could meditate a deed like this was no longer man. An agent from Hell had mastered his faculties. He was become the engine of infernal malice against whom it was the duty of all mankind to rise up in arms and never to desist till, by shattering it to atoms, its power to injure was taken away.

All inquiries to discover the place of his retreat were vain. No wonder methought that he wrapt himself in the folds of impenetrable secrecy. Curbed, checked, baffled in the midst of his career, no wonder that he shrunk into obscurity, that he fled from justice and revenge, that he dared not meet the rebukes of that eye which, dissolving in tenderness or flashing with disdain, had ever been irresistable.

But how shall I describe the lady's condition? Clithero she had cherished from his infancy. He was the stay, the consolation, the pride of her life. His projected alliance with her daughter, made him still more dear. Her eloquence was never tired of expatiating on his purity and rectitude. No wonder that she delighted in this theme, for he was her own work. His virtues were the creatures of her bounty.

How hard to be endured was this sad reverse! She can be tranquil, but never more will she be happy. To promote her forgetfulness of him, I persuaded her to leave her country, which contained a thousand memorials of past calamity, and which was lapsing fast into civil broils. Clarice has accompanied us, and time may effect the happiness of others, by her means, though she can never remove the melancholy of her mother.

I have listened to your tale, not without compassion. What would you have me to do? To prolong his life, would be merely to protract his misery.

He can never be regarded with complacency by my wife. He can never be thought of without shuddering by Clarice. Common ills are not without a cure less than death, but here, all remedies are vain. Consciousness itself is the malady; the pest; of which he only is cured who ceases to think.

I could not but assent to this mournful conclusion; yet, though death was better to Clithero than life, could not some of his mistakes be rectified? Euphemia Lorimer, contrary to his belief, was still alive. He dreamed that she was dead, and a thousand evils were imagined to flow from that death. This death and its progeny of ills, haunted his fancy, and added keenness to his remorse. Was it not our duty to rectify this error?

Sarsefield reluctantly assented to the truth of my arguments on this head. He consented to return, and afford the dying man, the consolation of knowing that the being whom he adored as a benefactor and parent, had not been deprived of existence, though bereft of peace by his act.

During Sarsefield's absence my mind was busy in revolving the incidents that had just occurred. I ruminated the last words of Clithero. There was somewhat in his narrative that was obscure and contradictory. He had left the manuscript which he so much and so justly prized, in his cabinet. He entered the chamber in my absence, and found the cabinet unfastened and the manuscript gone. It was I by whom the cabinet was opened, but the manuscript supposed to be contained in it, was buried in the earth beneath the elm. How should Clithero be unacquainted with its situation, since none but Clithero could have dug for it this grave?

This mystery vanished when I reflected on the history of my own manuscript. Clithero had buried his treasure with his own hands as mine had been secreted by myself, but both acts had been performed during sleep. The deed was neither prompted by the will, nor noticed by the senses of him, by whom it was done. Disastrous and humiliating is the state of man! By his own hands, is constructed the mass of misery and error in which his steps are forever involved.

Thus it was with thy friend. Hurried on by phantoms too indistinct to be now recalled, I wandered from my chamber to the desert. I plunged into some unvisited cavern, and easily proceeded till I reached the edge of a pit. There my step was deceived, and I tumbled headlong from the precipice. The fall bereaved me of sense, and I continued breathless and motionless during the remainder of the night and the ensuing day.

How little cognizance have men over the actions and motives of each other! How total is our blindness with regard to our own performances! Who would have sought me in the bowels of this mountain? Ages might have passed away, before my bones would be discovered in this tomb, by some traveller whom curiosity had prompted to explore it.

I was roused from these reflections by Sarsefield's return. Inquiring into Clithero's condition, he answered that the unhappy man was insensible, but that notwithstanding numerous and dreadful gashes, in different parts of his body, it was possible that by submitting to the necessary treatment, he might recover.

Encouraged by this information, I endeavoured to awaken the zeal and compassion of my friend in Clithero's behalf. He recoiled with involuntary shuddering from any task which would confine him to the presence of this man. Time and reflection he said, might introduce different sentiments and feelings, but at present he could not but regard this person as a maniac, whose disease was irremediable, and whose existence could not be protracted, but to his own misery and the misery of others.

Finding him irreconcilably averse to any scheme, connected with the welfare of Clithero, I began to think that his assistance as a surgeon was by no means necessary. He had declared that the sufferer needed nothing more than common treatment, and to this the skill of a score of aged women in this district, furnished with simples culled from the forest, and pointed out, of old time, by Indian *Leeches* was no less adequate than that of Sarsefield. These women were ready and officious in their charity, and none of them were prepossessed against the sufferer by a knowledge of his genuine story.

Sarsefield, meanwhile, was impatient for my removal to Inglefield's habitation, and that venerable friend was no less impatient to receive me. My hurts were superficial, and my strength sufficiently repaired by a night's repose. Next day, I went thither, leaving Clithero to the care of his immediate neighbours.

Sarsefield's engagements compelled him to prosecute his journey into Virginia, from which he had somewhat deviated, in order to visit Solebury. He proposed to return in less than a month and then to take me in his company to New-York. He has treated me with paternal tenderness, and insists upon the privilege of consulting for my interest, as if he were my real father. Meanwhile, these views have been disclosed to Inglefield, and it is with him that I am to remain, with my sisters, until his return.

My reflections have been various and tumultuous. They have been busy in relation to you, to Weymouth, and especially to Clithero. The latter polluted with gore and weakened by abstinence, fatigue and the loss of blood, appeared in my eyes, to be in a much more dangerous condition than the event proved him to be. I was punctually informed of the progress of his cure, and proposed in a few days to visit him. The duty of explaining the truth, respecting the present condition of Mrs. Lorimer, had devolved upon me. By imparting this intelligence, I hoped to work the most auspicious revolutions in his feelings, and prepared therefore, with alacrity, for an interview.

In this hope I was destined to be disappointed. On the morning on which I intended to visit him, a messenger arrived from the house in which he was entertained, and informed us that the family on entering the sick man's apartment, had found it deserted. It appeared that Clithero, had, during the night, risen from his bed, and gone secretly forth. No traces of his flight have since been discovered.

But, O! my friend! The death of Waldegrave, thy brother, is at length divested of uncertainty and mystery. Hitherto, I had been able to form no conjecture respecting it, but the solution was found shortly after this time.

Queen Mab, three days after my adventure, was seized in her hut on suspicion of having aided and counselled her countrymen, in their late depredations. She was not to be awed or intimidated by the treatment she received, but readily confessed and gloried in the mischief she had done; and accounted for it by enumerating the injuries which she had received from her neighbours.

These injuries consisted in contemptuous or neglectful treatment, and in the rejection of groundless and absurd claims. The people of Chetasco were less obsequious to her humours than those of Solebury, her ancient neighbourhood, and her imagination brooded for a long time, over nothing but schemes of revenge. She became sullen, irascible and spent more of her time in solitude than ever.

A troop of her countrymen at length visited her hut. Their intentions being hostile, they concealed from the inhabitants their presence in this quarter of the country. Some motives induced them to withdraw and postpone, for the present, the violence which they meditated. One of them, however, more sanguinary and audacious than the rest would not depart, without some gratification of his vengeance. He left his associates and penetrated by night into Solebury, resolving to attack the first human being whom he should meet. It was the fate of thy unhappy brother to encounter this ruffian, whose sagacity made him forbear to tear away the usual trophy from the dead, least he should afford grounds for suspicion as to the authors of the evil.

Satisfied with this exploit he rejoined his companions, and after an interval of three weeks returned with a more numerous party, to execute a more extensive project of destruction. They were councelled and guided, in all their movements, by Queen Mab, who now explained these particulars, and boldly defied her oppressors. Her usual obstinacy and infatuation induced her to remain in her ancient dwelling and prepare to meet the consequences.

This disclosure awakened anew all the regrets and anguish which flowed from that disaster. It has been pro-ductive, however, of some benefit. Suspicions and doubts, by which my soul was harrassed, and which were injurious to the innocent are now at an end. It is likewise some imperfect consolation to reflect that the assassin has himself been killed and probably by my own hand. The shedder of blood no longer lives to pursue his vocation, and justice is satisfied.

Thus have I fulfilled my promise to compose a minute relation of my sufferings. I remembered my duty to thee, and as soon as I was able to hold a pen, employed it to inform thee of my welfare. I could not at that time enter into particulars, but reserved a more copious narrative till a period of more health and leisure.

On looking back I am surprised at the length to which my story has run. I thought that a few days would suffice to complete it, but one page has insensibly been added to another till I have consumed weeks and filled volumes. Here I will draw to a close; I will send you what I have written, and discuss with you in conversation, my other immediate concerns, and my schemes for the future. As soon as I have seen Sarsefield, I will visit you.

Farewell.

E.H.

Solebury, November, 10.

LETTER I

TO MR. SARSEFIELD
Philadelphia.

I CAME hither but ten minutes ago, and write this letter in the bar of the Stagehouse. I wish not to lose a moment in informing you of what has happened. I cannot do justice to my own feelings when I reflect upon the rashness of which I have been guilty.

I will give you the particulars to-morrow. At present, I shall only say that Clithero is alive, is apprised of your wife's arrival and abode in New-York, and has set out, with mysterious intentions to visit her.

May heaven avert the consequences of such a design. May you be enabled by some means to prevent their meeting. If you cannot prevent it — but I must not reason on such an event, nor lengthen out this letter.

E.H.

LETTER II

TO THE SAME

I WILL now relate the particulars which I yesterday promised to send you. You heard through your niece of my arrival at Inglefield's in Solebury: My inquiries, you may readily suppose, would turn upon the fate of my friend's servant, Clithero, whose last disappearance was so strange and abrupt, and of whom since that time, I had heard nothing. You are indifferent to his fate and are anxious only that his existence and misfortunes may be speedily forgotten. I confess that it is somewhat otherwise with me. I pity him: I wish to relieve him, and cannot admit the belief that his misery is without a cure. I want to find him out. I want to know his condition, and if possible to afford him comfort, and inspire him with courage and hope.

Inglefield replied to my questions. O yes! He has appeared. The strange being is again upon the stage. Shortly after he left his sick bed, I heard from Philip Beddington, of Chetasco, that Deb's hut had found a new tenant. At first, I imagined that the Scotsman who built it had returned, but making closer inquiries, I found that the new tenant was my servant. I had no inclination to visit him myself, but frequently inquired respecting him of those, who lived or past that way, and find that he still lives there.

But how, said I. What is his mode of subsistance? The

winter has been no time for cultivation, and he found, I presume, nothing in the ground.

Deb's hut, replied my friend, is his lodging and his place of retirement, but food and cloathing he procures by labouring on a neighbouring farm. This farm is next to that of Beddington, who consequently knows something of his present situation. I find little or no difference in his present deportment, and those appearances which he assumed, while living with me, except that he retires every night to his hut, and holds as little intercourse as possible with the rest of mankind. He dines at his employer's table, but his supper, which is nothing but rye-bread, he carries home with him, and at all those times when disengaged from employment, he secludes himself in his hut, or wanders nobody knows whither.

This was the substance of Inglefield's intelligence. I gleaned from it some satisfaction. It proved the condition of Clithero to be less deplorable and desperate than I had previously imagined. His fatal and gloomy thoughts seemed to have somewhat yielded to tranquillity.

In the course of my reflections, however, I could not but perceive, that his condition, though eligible when compared with what it once was, was likewise disastrous and humiliating, compared with his youthful hopes and his actual merits. For such an one to mope away his life in this unsocial and savage state, was deeply to be deplored. It was my duty, if possible, to prevail on him to relinquish his scheme. And what would be requisite, for that end, but to inform him of the truth?

The source of his dejection was the groundless belief that he had occasioned the death of his benefactress. It was this alone that could justly produce remorse or grief. It was a distempered imagination both in him and in me, that had given birth to this opinion, since the terms of his narrative, impartially considered, were far from implying that catastrophe. To him, however, the evidence which he possessed was incontestable. No deductions from probability could overthrow his belief. This could only be effected by similar and counter evidence. To apprize him that she was now alive, in possession of some degree of happiness, the wife of Sarsefield, and an actual resident on this shore, would dissipate the sanguinary apparition that haunted him; cure his diseased intellects, and restore him to those vocations for which his talents, and that rank in society for which his education had qualified him. Influenced by these thoughts, I determined to visit his retreat. Being obliged to leave Solebury the next day, I resolved to set out the same afternoon, and stopping in Chetasco, for the night, seek his habitation at the hour when he had probably retired to it.

This was done. I arrived at Beddington's, at night-fall. My inquiries respecting Clithero obtained for me the same intelligence from him, which I had received from Inglefield. Deb's hut was three miles from this habitation, and thither, when the evening had somewhat advanced, I repaired. This was the spot which had witnessed so many perils during the last year, and my emotions, on approaching it, were awful. With palpitating heart and quick steps I traversed the road, skirted on each side by thickets, and the area before the house. The dwelling was by no means in so ruinous a state as when I last visited it. The crannies between the logs had been filled up, and the light within was perceivable only at a crevice in the door.

Looking through this crevice I perceived a fire in the chimney, but the object of my visit was no where to be seen. I knocked and requested admission, but no answer was made. At length I lifted the latch and entered. Nobody was there.

It was obvious to suppose that Clithero had gone abroad for a short time, and would speedily return, or perhaps some engagement had detained him at his labour, later than usual. I therefore seated myself on some straw near the fire, which, with a woollen rug, appeared to constitute his only bed. The rude bedstead which I

formerly met with, was gone. The slender furniture, likewise, which had then engaged my attention, had disappeared. There was nothing capable of human use, but a
heap of faggots in the corner, which seemed intended for
fuel. How slender is the accommodation which nature has
provided for man, and how scanty is the portion which
our physical necessities require.

While ruminating upon this scene, and comparing past
events with the objects before me, the dull whistling of the
gale without gave place to the sound of footsteps. Presently the door opened, and Clithero entered the apartment. His aspect and guise were not essentially different
from those which he wore when an inhabitant of Solebury.

To find his hearth occupied by another, appeared to
create the deepest surprise. He looked at me without any
tokens of remembrance! His features assumed a more
austere expression, and after scowling on my person for a
moment, he withdrew his eyes, and placing in a corner, a
bundle which he bore in his hand, he turned and seemed
preparing to withdraw.

I was anxiously attentive to his demeanor, and as soon
as I perceived his purpose to depart, leaped on my feet to
prevent it. I took his hand, and affectionately pressing it,
said, do you not know me? Have you so soon forgotten
me who is truly your friend?

He looked at me with some attention, but again withdrew his eyes, and placed himself in silence on the seat
which I had left. I seated myself near him, and a pause of
mutual silence ensued.

My mind was full of the purpose that brought me
hither, but I knew not in what manner to communicate
my purpose. Several times I opened my lips to speak, but
my perplexity continued, and suitable words refused to
suggest themselves. At length, I said, in a confused tone:

I came hither with a view to benefit a man, with whose
misfortunes his own lips have made me acquainted, and
who has awakened in my breast the deepest sympathy. I

know the cause and extent of his dejection. I know the event which has given birth to horror and remorse in his heart. He believes that, by his means, his patroness and benefactress has found an untimely death.

These words produced a visible shock in my companion, which evinced that I had at least engaged his attention. I proceeded:

This unhappy lady was cursed with a wicked and unnatural brother. She conceived a disproportionate affection for this brother, and erroneously imagined that her fate was blended with his; that their lives would necessarily terminate at the same period, and that therefore, whoever was the contriver of his death, was likewise, by a fatal and invincible necessity, the author of her own.

Clithero was her servant, but was raised by her bounty, to the station of her son and the rank of her friend. Clithero, in self-defence took away the life of that unnatural brother, and, in that deed, falsely but cogently believed, that he had perpetrated the destruction of his benefactress.

To ascertain the truth, he sought her presence. She was found, the tidings of her brother's death were communicated, and she sunk breathless at his feet.

At these words Clithero started from the ground, and cast upon me looks of furious indignation — And come you hither, he muttered, for this end; to recount my offences, and drive me again to despair?

No, answered I, with quickness, I come to out-root a fatal, but powerful illusion. I come to assure you that the woman, with whose destruction you charge yourself, is *not dead.*

These words, uttered with the most emphatical solemnity, merely produced looks in which contempt was mingled with anger. He continued silent.

I perceive, resumed I, that my words are disregarded. Would to Heaven I were able to conquer your incredulity, could shew you not only the truth, but the probability of my tale. Can you not confide in me; that Euphemia Lorimer is now alive, is happy, is the wife of Sarsefield; that her brother is forgotten and his murderer regarded without enmity or vengeance?

He looked at me with a strange expression of contempt—Come, said he, at length, make out thy assertion to be true. Fall on thy knees and invoke the thunder of heaven to light on thy head if thy words be false. Swear that Euphemia Lorimer is alive; happy; forgetful of Wiatte and compassionate of me. Swear that thou hast seen her; talked with her; received from her own lips the confession of her pity for him who aimed a dagger at her bosom. Swear that she is Sarsefield's wife.

I put my hands together, and lifting my eyes to heaven, exclaimed: I comply with your conditions; I call the omniscient God to witness that Euphemia Lorimer is alive; that I have seen her with these eyes; have talked with her; have inhabited the same house for months.

These asseverations were listened to with shuddering. He laid not aside, however, an air of incredulity and contempt. Perhaps, said he, thou canst point out the place of her abode. Canst guide me to the city, the street, the very door of her habitation?

I can. She rises at this moment in the city of New-York; in Broadway; in an house contiguous to the ——.

'Tis well, exclaimed my companion, in a tone, loud, abrupt, and in the utmost degree, vehement. 'Tis well. Rash and infatuated youth. Thou hast ratified, beyond appeal or forgiveness, thy own doom. Thou hast once more let loose my steps, and sent me on a fearful journey. Thou hast furnished the means of detecting thy imposture. I will fly to the spot which thou describest. I will ascertain thy falsehood with my own eyes. If she be alive then am I reserved for the performance of a new crime. My evil destiny will have it so. If she be dead, I shall make *thee* expiate.

So saying, he darted through the door, and was gone in a moment, beyond my sight and my reach. I ran to the road, looked on every side, and called; but my calls were repeated in vain. He had fled with the swiftness of a deer.

My own embarrassment, confusion and terror were inexpressible. His last words were incoherent. They denoted the tumult and vehemence of phrenzy. They intimated his resolution to seek the presence of your wife. I had furnished a clue, which could not fail to conduct him to her presence. What might not be dreaded from the interview? Clithero is a maniac. This truth cannot be concealed. Your wife can with difficulty preserve her tranquillity, when his image occurs to her remembrance. What must it be when he starts up before her in his neglected and ferocious guise, and armed with purposes, perhaps as terrible as those, which had formerly led him to her secret chamber, and her bed side?

His meaning was obscurely conveyed. He talked of a deed, for the performance of which, his malignant fate had reserved him; which was to ensue their meeting, and which was to afford disastrous testimony of the infatuation which had led me hither.

Heaven grant that some means may suggest themselves to you of intercepting his approach. Yet I know not what means can be conceived. Some miraculous chance may befriend you; yet this is scarcely to be hoped. It is a visionary and fantastic base on which to rest our security.

I cannot forget that my unfortunate temerity has created this evil. Yet who could foresee this consequence of my intelligence? I imagined, that Clithero was merely a victim of erroneous gratitude, a slave of the errors of his education, and the prejudices of his rank, that his understanding was deluded by phantoms in the mask of virtue and duty, and not as you have strenuously maintained, utterly subverted.

I shall not escape your censure, but I shall, likewise, gain your compassion. I have erred, not through sinister or malignant intentions, but from the impulse of misguided, indeed, but powerful benevolence.

E.H.

LETTER III

New-York.

Edgar,

A FTER the fatigues of the day, I returned home. As I entered, my wife was breaking the seal of a letter, but, on seeing me, she forbore and presented the letter to me.

I saw, said she, by the superscription of this letter, who the writer was. So agreeably to your wishes, I proceeded to open it, but you have come just time enough to save me the trouble.

This letter was from you. It contained information relative to Clithero. See how imminent a chance it was that saved my wife from a knowledge of its contents. It required all my efforts to hide my perturbation from her, and excuse myself from shewing her the letter.

I know better than you the character of Clithero, and the consequences of a meeting between him and my wife. You may be sure that I would exert myself to prevent a meeting.

The method for me to pursue was extremely obvious. Clithero is a madman whose liberty is dangerous, and who requires to be fettered and imprisoned as the most atrocious criminal.

I hastened to the chief Magistrate, who is my friend, and by proper representations, obtained from him authority to seize Clithero wherever I should meet with him, and effectually debar him from the perpetration of new mischiefs.

291

New-York does not afford a place of confinement for lunatics, as suitable to his case, as Pennsylvania. I was desirous of placing him as far as possible from the place of my wife's residence. Fortunately there was a packet for Philadelphia, on the point of setting out on her voyage. This vessel I engaged to wait a day or two, for the purpose of conveying him to the Pennsylvania hospital. Meanwhile, proper persons were stationed at Powles-hook, and at the quays where the various stageboats from Jersey arrive.

These precautions were effectual. Not many hours after the receipt of your intelligence, this unfortunate man applied for a passage at Elizabeth-town, was seized the moment he set his foot on shore, and was forthwith conveyed to the packet, which immediately set sail.

I designed that all these proceedings should be concealed from the women, but unfortunately neglected to take suitable measures for hindering the letter which you gave me reason to expect on the ensuing day, from coming into their hands. It was delivered to my wife in my absence and opened immediately by her.

You know what is, at present, her personal condition. You know what strong reasons I had to prevent any danger or alarm from approaching her. Terror could not assume a shape, more ghastly than this. The effects have been what might have been easily predicted. Her own life has been imminently endangered and an untimely birth, has blasted my fondest hope. Her infant, with whose future existence so many pleasures were entwined, *is dead*.

I assure you Edgar, my philosophy has not found itself lightsome and active under this burthen. I find it hard to forbear commenting on your rashness in no very mild terms. You acted in direct opposition to my council, and to the plainest dictates of propriety. Be more circumspect and more obsequious for the future.

You knew the liberty that would be taken of opening my letters; you knew of my absence from home, during the greatest part of the day, and the likelihood therefore that your letters would fall into my wife's hands before they came into mine. These considerations should have prompted you to send them under cover to Whitworth or Harvey, with directions to give them immediately to *me*.

Some of these events happened in my absence, for I determined to accompany the packet myself and see the madman safely delivered to the care of the hospital.

I will not torture your sensibility by recounting the incidents of his arrest and detention. You will imagine that his strong, but perverted reason exclaimed loudly against the injustice of his treatment. It was easy for him to outreason his antagonist, and nothing but force could subdue his opposition. On me devolved the province of his jailor and his tyrant; a province which required an heart more steeled by spectacles of suffering and the exercise of cruelty, than mine had been.

Scarcely had we passed *The Narrows,* when the lunatic, being suffered to walk the deck, as no apprehensions were entertained of his escape in such circumstances, threw himself overboard, with a seeming intention to gain the shore. The boat was immediately manned, the fugitive was pursued, but at the moment, when his flight was overtaken, he forced himself beneath the surface, and was seen no more.

With the life of this wretch, let our regrets and our forebodings terminate. He has saved himself from evils, for which no time would have provided a remedy, from lingering for years in the noisome dungeon of an hospital. Having no reason to continue my voyage, I put myself on board a coasting sloop, and regained this city in a few hours. I persuade myself that my wife's indisposition will be temporary. It was impossible to hide from her the death of Clithero, and its circumstances. May this be the last arrow in the quiver of adversity! Farewell.

END

HISTORICAL ESSAY

I

With *Edgar Huntly*, we find Brown at the apogee of his career as published novelist returning to the subject of psychic imbalance with which he had embarked on it less than a year earlier in *Wieland*. In between had come the two novels (*Ormond* and *Arthur Mervyn*) treating embattled innocence exposed to the pressure of urban sophisticates and a raging pestilence. Often prone to double back onto old territory, Brown essentially did a rewrite for *Huntly* of ideas that had gone into his first novel — through a fortunate misfortune not published in that original, presumably cruder form of "Sky-Walk." On his return, though, he seems to have been quite up to handling the energies that crowded a mind prone to gothicize the inner world by projecting it into nature. We get nocturnal journeys through a landscape of tortuous pathways, craggy eminences, caverns within them, and cavities within the caverns; and these mazy pursuits are recapitulated with the pursuer himself pursued, twice rising from the dead, and compelled — against his better feelings — also to deliver death, though abashed at "the deeds which perverse nature compels . . . rational beings to perform . . ." (p. 202).[1]

Given to writing by immersion, Brown spoke of his consciousness of a "double mental existence" — the imaginative/creative and the social — and regarding the former, he observed, "When I am sufficiently excited to

[1] All quotations are from the text of the present edition.

295

write, all my ideas flow naturally and irresistibly through the medium of sympathies which steep them in shade. . . ."[2] If his perception of writing from the dark side of the psyche seems predictable enough, that accompanying sense of "otherness" is suggestive of an inclination less frequently recognized, but one closely connected with Brown's becoming the first in a roster of American novelists to make pervasive use of the motif of the double — a factor to be explored later on, for doubleness acts as a key structural agent in *Edgar Huntly*. The idea had after all acquired much public fascination, and notoriety, in the late eighteenth century, from — among various sources — Mesmer's experiments in "animal magnetism," which attracted a host of amateur expositors and adherents of mind science, including, e.g., Lafayette, Dupont de Nemours, and William Temple Franklin. And somnambulism, of course, was then, as now, understood to be a hypnotic condition in which the subject lives a second existence wholly dissociated from his primary self; indeed, in Huntly's case there is the compound duplication of his sympathetically reenacting Edny's state. At any rate — to proceed with the genetic parallel — in the writing of fiction, Brown felt himself submerged in a quite other, unexpressed world of his own making. While at work on a "new novel" and "making his pen fly before him," he was visited by John Davis, the British author-traveler, who had likewise been published by Hocquet Caritat. Davis gives us a cameo of Brown locked in "a dismal room in a dismal street" and somewhat impatient of Davis' query as to whether he might not be more propitiously quartered for such work with "a view of nature" — to which the abrupt response is: "Sir . . . good pens, thick paper, and ink well diluted, would facilitate my composition more than the prospect of the broadest expanse of water, or mountains rising above the clouds."[3]

[2] John Bernard, *Retrospections of America, 1797–1811* (New York: Harper & Brothers, 1887), p. 252.

[3] *Travels of Four Years and a Half in the United States of America During*

A typical product of this kind of mood, the intensities of Huntly and Edny seem to come at us from a sort of closeted obsession; and absorption in composition goes together with the fact that *Huntly* was also written during a time of rising expectations for Brown. In the opening sentence of his preface to *Huntly*, "To The Public," which was used as well for the subscription advertisement in the *Philadelphia Gazette and Universal Daily Advertiser* (10 August 1799), he sounds like an author who feels himself launched: "The flattering reception that has been given, by the public, to Arthur Mervyn, has prompted the writer to solicit a continuance of the same favour . . ." (p. 3). Discounting the promotionalism, this is still fairly upbeat for Brown and reflects a certain behind-the-scenes excitement about prospects — in spite of prior disappointment — which we rarely see elsewhere. A good deal less exciting, to be sure, is what little has been available to us of how and when Brown went about the writing of *Edgar Huntly*, though we do have some interesting clues.

The tone and content of Brown's letter to his brother

1798, 1799, 1800, 1801, and 1802, ed. A. J. Morrison (London, 1803, rpt. New York: Henry Holt and Co., 1909), pp. 163-164. In keeping with these sentiments, it is of more than marginal importance that, however much Brown may have been praised for the realism of his American setting in *Edgar Huntly*, his descriptive passages actually tend to be rather synthetic, possibly because of his stated detachment while writing, but mainly because of the effect they were meant to sustain. As he put it in *Jane Talbot*: "The mere arrangement of inanimate objects, wood, grass, and rock, is nothing. It owes its power of bewitching us to the memory, the fancy and the heart" (*Jane Talbot, A Novel* [Philadelphia: John Conrad & Co., 1801], pp. 318-319). This is not inconsistent, by the way, with Brown's editorial note citing "the exactness of the *local* descriptions" in *Huntly*, for there he was making the conventional plea that readers first accept the truthfulness of his incidents, whatever else they might make of them (*Monthly Magazine*, 1 [April, 1799], 21; see p. 493). Concerning the largely symbolic and psychological tendencies of description in the novel, see Kenneth Bernard, "Charles Brockden Brown and the Sublime," *The Personalist*, 45 (April, 1964), 235-249, and George Toles, "Charting the Hidden Landscape: *Edgar Huntly*," *Early American Literature*, 16 (Fall, 1981), 133-153.

James of 15 February 1799 inquiring about publication of *Mervyn* suggest that to this point he probably had not yet done anything substantial with *Huntly.* "The last fortnight," he remarks, "has been whiled away in desultory reading." His main interest for the moment centers on "the projected magazine" (his *Monthly Magazine*), but since he does mention "plying the quill" as part of his "customary series of . . . employments," a *start* on his next novel is not wholly to be ruled out, though while he makes reference to the first three, none is made to *Huntly* or its subject. Certainly, there is incentive to do another novel, as this is where Brown notes, "I find to be the writer of Wieland and Ormond is a greater recommendation than I ever imagined it would be."[4] The unexpected prestige obviously gives him encouragement; he *is* being *read*, and talked about. Nonetheless, throughout the composition of *Huntly* Brown was singularly incommunicative about it — at least as far as the extant record goes.

Dunlap stated that *Huntly* "rapidly" followed *Arthur Mervyn* and attributed the "defects" of both to "haste in composition" (*Life*, II, 30, 39-40) — a comment more legitimately reserved for *Ormond.* Let us assume then that work on *Huntly* is silently begun some time after mid-February. Brown continues in New York while writing *Huntly*, mainly to stay on top of his first venture in magazining, which is to be published by Thomas and James Swords, the printers of *Alcuin* and *Wieland.* Evidently, that is economically more important to Brown than being in Philadelphia, where *Huntly* is to be published by Maxwell, who has just done *Arthur Mervyn, First Part*, and where the partially printed "Sky-Walk" also remains — which is why the borrowing Brown makes from it is retrieved by "memory" (*Life*, I, 259). Also, his brother James has seen *Mervyn* through the press satisfactorily enough for Brown to feel he could be depended on to do the same for another book if it came to that. In a letter of 3 April 1799, his

[4]William Dunlap, *The Life of Charles Brockden Brown* . . . (Philadelphia: James P. Parke, 1815), II, 98-99. Hereafter *Life*.

friend Samuel Miller refers to Brown's preoccupation with the *Monthly Magazine* and his continued residence in New York. Brown had to have been at work on *Edgar Huntly* during this time, but he still seems not to have been talking about it. Miller writes: "The principal Editor of the A. M. Mag. [*The Monthly Magazine and American Review*, here mistitled the *American Monthly Magazine*] is a Mr Charles B. Brown lately of Phil. . . . There is a *society* [or] *club* of about ten gentlemen who meet once a week, to consult about the Mag. and concert plans to make up its contents, and to promote its interests" (ALS, Yale).

The "Fragment" of *Edgar Huntly* (roughly Chapters 17 through 20), which picks up the first set of Indian encounters on Huntly's emergence from the cave, was published in the first issue of the *Monthly Magazine*, the April 1799 number (not out till May). There are several pieces of information to be inferred from the "Fragment." Among the more obvious of them is the idea that the novel would likely have been written to at least Chapter 20 by April (leaving seven more to go, plus the three concluding letters); and while this supposes sequential composition, it seems a fair enough assumption in the absence of evidence for a contrary method, here or elsewhere, and on the common-sense basis that Brown would not seem to have had the time to write by episodes and later rearrange a work having the complication of a *Huntly*. (A major internal argument for continuity of composition is that one can see Brown clearly anticipating himself in plotting, preparing the way for what is to follow pretty much as he goes along.[5]) In any case, though the "Fragment" would

[5]For example, when Huntly declares the Indians would ordinarily have "no motives" to lead them into a cave like Clithero's (p. 103) that pre-establishes his belief in its safety and the unexpectedness of his actually discovering Indians at the cave mouth. With regard to his between-the-eyes strike in the panther episode, one recalls that word had already been given about his skill with the tomahawk (had he not cut the sinews of a catamount at sixty feet? — p. 125). Also, the mention of a *pair* of panthers — male and female — after the first plunges to its death (p. 128), prepares us for an encounter with a second. And

put Brown about two-thirds of the way through the novel, this doesn't mean he could not have been further along even than that. In fact, his saying in the introductory remark to the "Fragment" that "these memoirs will shortly be published" suggests there was rather little more to do on them. Certainly, he had to have been close enough to the end for this extract to stand as an advertisement from which the published book could benefit.

Another kind of evidence furnished by the "Fragment" has to do with revision. The changes observable between the texts of the "Fragment" and published book are of a sort that mainly result in clarifications, greater concreteness, minor stylistic improvements, and the like.[6] These are typical of the kinds of alteration Brown might make in transcribing his manuscript for printer's copy—a matter he took some pains with, as explained in connection with the composition of "Sky-Walk" (*Life*, I, 107). Thus, if we have *Huntly* brought to completion in late April or early May and allow time for Brown to go back over it to make changes in preparing the final transcription that is to be submitted to Maxwell, he should have the novel ready for

---

prior to Huntly's dive from the cliff into the Delaware, Brown tells us that water was a "congenial . . . element" for him (p. 216).

[6]Occasionally, one does find a change made for the sake of propriety; in the "Fragment," whereas Brown has the girl hostage laying "her head upon [Huntly's] knees," in the book "She laid herself, by [his] advice, upon the bed" (*MM*, 1 [April, 1799], 29; see p. 184). But the most extensive single revision better represents Brown's immediate concern, which was not with structure or meaning, but with tidying up his description and providing more specific detail. It has to do with Deb's hut, in which Huntly and the girl find temporary refuge. Instead of just alluding to a cedar bucket with brackish water, a loaf of stale rye bread, and an axe, spade, and hoe as comprising some of the contents of the house, Brown more carefully particularizes, as follows: the cedar bucket is "kept entire by withs instead of hoops. In the bucket was a little water, full of droppings from the roof, drowned insects and sand; a basket or two neatly made, and an hoe, with a stake thrust into it by way of handle, made up all the furniture . . ." (p. 184).

the press by about mid-May. And, we do in fact have evidence that *Huntly* may indeed have been finished about then. It comes in a letter from Brown's friend William Johnson to their mutual friend James Kent, dated 29 May 1799, in which Johnson writes: "Mr. B. has been absent, for the fortnight past, on a visit to Philadelphia."[7] So Brown left New York around the middle of May for Philadelphia; and we may assume that one thing which would be significant enough to take him away from New York for that length of time, when he had a monthly magazine to be filled, edited, and proofed to satisfy subscribers (who, having gotten their first issue late, were assured of future punctuality), would be the need to deliver the manuscript of *Huntly* to Maxwell and to discuss terms of publication. His business being concluded, Brown is back in New York in June planning an excursion to Connecticut and saying: "I expected to write but little during my absence from New York; little more at least than letters" (*Life*, II, 47). Obviously, *Huntly* is off his hands, and he feels free to enjoy a little "indolence." He leaves on a Friday morning. (The first Friday in June, 1799, incidentally, was the 6th.) And in the July number of his *Monthly Magazine*, Brown has the announcement: "A new ROMANCE, written by the author of Mervyn, Wieland, Ormond, &c. and entitled 'Edgar Huntley [*sic*], or the Sleep-Walker,' is now printing in Philadelphia" (*MM*, 1 [July, 1799], 316). That Brown should have allowed *Huntly* to be misspelled in print and forget the correct form of his subtitle (*Memoirs of a Sleep-Walker*) was unfortunately not atypical. The book was advertised in the *Philadelphia Gazette and Universal Daily Advertiser* on 30 July and thereafter twelve times through 15 August 1799, as "In the Press," with Volume I to be published "in a few Days," and the entire work to be "contained in 3 volumes."

[7]Daniel Edwards Kennedy, "Charles Brockden Brown: His Life and Works," p. 1072. Kennedy's unpublished MS biography is in the Kent State Brown Collection. It is referred to hereafter as Kennedy.

Publication of Brown's preface in the *Gazette* subscription notice of 10 August gives us a fix on the approximate date before which the printing of Volume I had very likely been consummated, for the preliminary gathering would have been done last. Since it looks as if the volumes were being printed seriatim, and Maxwell's rate of production may have run to about two months per volume (as a longside estimate, based on his performance with the first volume), it might be that he barely got Volume III out before year's end.[8] Since there was likely some spillover—at least as far as sales are concerned—that may explain why a number of copies of Volume III bear an 1800 title leaf.[9]

In a letter to his brother James of 26 July 1799, Brown seems to have anticipated problems as well with the probable reception of *Edgar Huntly*: "I am afraid that M. has projected the printing of Huntley [*sic*] on too large a scale though, perhaps, he is best qualified to judge" (*Life*, II, 97). While he had had somewhat the same feeling about *Arthur Mervyn* ("I shall not be at all surprised if M. obtains fewer subscribers than he expected . . ." [*Life*, II, 98]), Brown seems to have had higher hopes for *Edgar Huntly*; but it would appear that once the book was finished and he knew what he had, uncertainty arose about its being the kind that could win the "favor" he wanted.[10] Yet there is something to be said for the fact that *Huntly* was the

[8]There was good reason for Maxwell to seek subscription sales (the notice ran intermittently through August in the *Gazette*), since each of the first two volumes would provide cash-flow for the next, and that method would enable Maxwell to get a better idea of his market for the book and determine the number of copies to be printed and bound for sale.

[9]Although the *printing* of III might have been concluded before January, it may have been felt that copies bound for sale thereafter should be given the new date. This, to be sure, is but one possibility. For a fuller treatment of the matter, see "Textual Essay," pp. 412–413.

[10]Interestingly, the opening piece in the first number of the *Monthly Magazine*, purportedly written by a plain-spoken reader ("Candidus")—but which has a decidedly Brownian ring to it—deals

only one of his novels that would be reissued in America during Brown's lifetime, as Conrad was optimistic enough to buy the remaindered sheets from Maxwell and have them bound with a new title page in 1801. That Brown would so peremptorily decide to renounce the type of "out-of-nature" subject treated in *Edgar Huntly* (*Life*, II, 100) is actually part of the general ambivalence created by his desires to both please himself and gain a following. (Brown accepted his brother James's criticism of the "gloominess" of *Huntly* on the basis it was "doubtless" the verdict of "most readers," because he was clearly worried about the "salelibilty [*sic*] of [his] works," ibid.[11]) From its inception in "Sky-Walk," it would seem that the material of *Edgar Huntly* was to be rooted in a not always harmonious dualism. This is further reflected internally in the age-old romantic theme of the doubleness of human existence (already noted), as we both comprehend it and fail to — which Edgar Huntly prototypically exemplifies, joining a notable gallery of like characters in western fiction, seen in works like Poe's "William Wilson," Twain's *Pudd'nhead Wilson*, Dostoevsky's *The Double*, James's "The Jolly Corner," Wilde's *The Picture of Dorian Gray*, Stevenson's *Dr. Jekyll and Mr. Hyde*, Conrad's "The Secret Sharer," Hesse's *Steppenwolf*, and Ellison's *Invisible Man*.

II

And whence came *Edgar Huntly*? For *Wieland* there had been the Yates murders, for *Ormond* and *Arthur Mervyn* the

with the near impossibility of satisfying the public at large. The "fictions" he selects, for example, "will be condemned as soaring too high or sinking too low," and, among other things, "as exhibiting impossible events or contradictory characters" (p. 2).

[11]Brown had more than once sworn off the gloominess mode, vowing — as in a letter to his friend Joseph Bringhurst — that he was "determined . . . no longer to be the slave of useless Melancholy" (undated shorthand letter transcribed by Daniel Edwards Kennedy, photocopy in Kent State Brown Collection). But that was before he thought it would cost him in the marketplace.

yellow fever epidemic of 1793. For *Edgar Huntly* there was "Sky-Walk," which meant the rugged hinterland just outside the Capital, and somnambulism — or a joining of the physical and psychological frontiers. Two weeks after an "Extract" from "Sky-Walk" had been published in James Watters' *Weekly Magazine*, a query was received about the title. In response, it was explained (probably by Brown himself) that "Sky-Walk" represented "a popular corruption of 'Ski Wakkee,' or *Big Spring*, the name given by the Lenni Lenaffee, or Delaware Indians, to the district where the principal scenes of this novel are transacted" (*WM*, 1 [7 April 1798], 318).[12] It began then with the river, the region, with former Indian territory, the idea,

[12]Not alone does Brown seem to have been the actual respondent, but there is a good possibility that he promotionally fabricated the inquiring correspondent as well, since the latter is said to be a certain "A. Z.," and these were the initials Brown affixed to two of his works published in the *Weekly Magazine*, where author identification was uniformly avoided: "A Series of Original Letters" and "A Lesson on Sensibility" (1 [21 April 1798], 364; 2 [19 May 1798], 76). Kennedy makes a fairly good case for crediting Brown with another *Weekly Magazine* piece signed "A. Z." (pp. 1042–1045A), this being a series of twenty-two "Queries" on scientific, philosophic, and psychological matters, several having to do with, respectively, sleep, somnambulism, and ventriloquism (2 [23 June 1798], 232–233).

Because he was unable to turn up anything resembling "Ski Wakkee" in two major reference works (John Heckewelder's *Names Which the Lenni Lennapi or Delaware Indians Gave to the Rivers, Streams and Localities* . . . [1872] and Daniel Garrison Brinton's *Lênapé-English Dictionary* [1888]), Kennedy inferred that they were Brown's private invention. Warfel, on the other hand, located a source for "Ski Wakkee" in the Algonquian language where, however, this had the meaning of "fresh or new earth or ground." (*The Rhapsodist and Other Uncollected Writings by Charles Brockden Brown* [New York: Scholars' Facsimiles & Reprints], p. ix). There is no need to ask where Brown may have gotten his definition. But Kennedy's thought that "walk" associates with the infamous "Walking Purchase Treaty," whereby the Indians were defrauded of some 1,200 square miles of land (p. 1146B), is independently worthy of consideration. (Under the original treaty of 1683 negotiated by William Penn, the area agreed to was the distance a man could walk in about a day, or the forty miles that Penn actually walked in a day and a half. When the treaty was presumably, of a national and virgin subject; and that was the conception which would remain uppermost for Brown in commending *Edgar Huntly* to the public: it was his "purpose" to show how America could furnish "themes to the moral painter . . . new springs of action, and new motives to curiosity . . . [that] should differ essentially from those which exist in Europe" (p. 3). But before inquiring into the local inspiration, we should look at what there is to be said about "Sky-Walk" itself and what it foretells about *Huntly*.

Knowledge of a tie between "Sky-Walk" and *Edgar Huntly* originates with notations by William Dunlap and Elihu Hubbard Smith, chief among the in-group to whom the unpublished novel was circulated. In a biographical sketch of Brown written many years after the *Life*, Dunlap casts the early work somewhat in the role of progenitor, saying *Huntly* "partook largely of his first composition of the same kind . . . 'Sky-walk' [*sic*]."[13] Though he remembered "Sky-Walk" to have been "commenced without definite plan or object" (ibid., pp. 2-3)—which really seems to have been the case—Dunlap had previously reported that at the time when he first gained "some account" of the novel, Brown had it explicitly "founded on Somnambulism," the mechanism of plot apparently.[14] The fact that Smith's corroborating note was made after a reading of only the introduction and first four chapters tells us its "basis" in "*Somnambulism*" was established from the beginning—an attention-getter to be sure, but, artistically, one which set the tone of the "extraordinary," as

renegotiated in 1737, professional walkers—more like runners—were hired and they covered over half again as much territory.) Norwalk, as far as one can tell, falls well within the region of the "Walking Purchase," and, of course, territoriality had been the root cause of Indian hostility in *Huntly*.

[13]"Charles Brockden Brown," *National Portrait Gallery of Distinguished Americans*, ed. James Herring and James B. Longacre (New York: Hermon Bancroft, 1836), III, 5.

[14]*Diary of William Dunlap* (New York: New York Historical Society, 1930), I, 240-241.

Smith termed it.[15] Strangely enough, however, no one makes any mention of conflict with Indians, the second major subject-matter of *Huntly*, which is at least as provocative as sleep-walking. Instead, we are informed that "Sky-Walk," like *Huntly*, had simply been environed in "the wild district of Norwalk" (Dunlap, *Life*, I, 259). Obviously, there was more to "Sky-Walk"; and, in relation to *Huntly*, evidently less — less, that is, than he was yet to produce.

The point is, since Brown had every reason to mention Indian participation in elucidating his title and a perfect excuse to do so besides as a means of exciting curiosity but used the occasion to give no more than the locale of his novel (if anything, a demystification), one has reason to assume that, in spite of publisher Watters' advertisement describing "Sky-Walk" as an "AMERICAN TALE," hostile Indians probably were not part of its Americanness, but rather became a subsequent addition to Brown's initial plan. Interestingly, from what Brown divulges about the composition of his first "Romance" (which almost *has* to be "Sky-Walk" — see n. 18), it sounds very much as if he found himself drawn into a single, continuous subject and did not deviate from it: while he had started with "no definitive conceptions of [his] design" (the situation alluded to by Dunlap), once his material began to jell, he "continued to view [his] scheme in the same light in which it had at first presented itself" (Dunlap, *Life*, I, 107). Everything would appear to indicate the "scheme" was somnamublism — and that alone.[16] As will be seen, nothing in the "Extract" remotely hints at an Indian presence; this in contrast to the *Huntly* chapters selected for preview, which, omitting even the pit and panther, focus exclusively on the first, longest, and most

[15] *The Diary of Elihu Hubbard Smith*, ed. James E. Cronin (Philadelphia: American Philosophical Society, 1973), p. 438.

[16] Note that Dunlap observes, "Edgar Huntley, [*sic*] *unites* to events, founded on somnambulism, 'incidents of Indian hostility . . .'" (italics added; *Life*, II, 30).

spectacular, of the Indian episodes. Thus, if omission of a reference to Indian activity signifies more than inadvertence on *everybody's* part — as it seems to — its implications about what Brown did in moving from "Sky-Walk" to *Edgar Huntly* are considerable, suggesting, to begin with, a critical leap from the wild landscape to its wild inhabitants as an available increment in complication — and terror — for helpless somnambulists. Certainly, ready access was to be had to an entire repertoire of narratives on Indian captivity and warfare, the standard images of which had abounded in popular literature from the late seventeenth century on.[17] Why Brown chose only belatedly to draw upon it for a native American novel, we cannot know. But essentially he lacked worthy precedents, and, inasmuch as he spent some time finding his way into "Sky-Walk," he had to have gone through a period of uncertainty regarding his direction, though, to judge by *Wieland*, there would have been little hesitancy about the uses of sensation, even in a maiden effort, had he decided on a special instance of it.

On the other hand, once Brown is of mind to treat Indians, he talks about them — up-front. He could not have been more emphatic about his reasons for introducing Indians, citing their "depiction" in *Huntly* as acutely

[17]For background on the Indian in American fiction around Brown's time and before see Fred Lewis Pattee, *The First Century of American Literature, 1770–1870* (1935; rpt. New York: Cooper Square Publishers, 1966), pp. 346–352; Alexander Cowie, *The Rise of the American Novel* (New York: American Book Co., 1948), pp. 30–37; Roy Harvey Pearce, *The Savages in America*, rev. ed. (Baltimore: The Johns Hopkins Univ. Press, 1965), pp. 196–199; Henri Petter, *The Early American Novel* (Columbus: Ohio State Univ. Press, 1971), pp. 371–376. Pattee saw Brown as "the first to introduce Indians into prose fiction" and to try to treat them with "realism," p. 351. The most exhaustive study of the subject from its beginnings is to be found in Richard R. Slotkin, *Regeneration Through Violence: The Mythology of the American Frontier, 1600–1860* (Middletown, Conn.: Wesleyan Univ. Press, 1973). Other works on the subject are given in section VI of this essay, where the entire matter of Brown's use of the Indian is discussed.

relevant to his purpose and a proper substitute for the paraphernalia of Gothic romance: "The incidents of Indian hostility, and the perils of the western wilderness, are far more suitable [than conventional Gothicism]; and, for a native of America to overlook these, would admit of no apology." He sees himself taking a new departure, "engaging the sympathy of the reader, by means hitherto unemployed by preceding authors" ("To the Public," p. 3). Having tried spontaneous combustion, mass murder, revolutionary radicalism, attempted rape, and yellow fever epidemics without notable success, Brown may have turned to warring Indians in one final bid for public approval, as well as credibility with publishers, for which — had he only known — he would be about a generation too early.

Several additional items shed light on the status of "Sky-Walk" and its relationship to *Huntly*. One is a set of questions about plot and character by Dunlap and another the *Weekly Magazine* "Extract." Meager as they are, these yield just about the only clues we have as to the real content of "Sky-Walk" — pieces of it, anyway. A glance at them in a moment.

Dunlap received the manuscript of "Sky-Walk" in mid-April 1798, about three weeks after it had been completed.[18] It came to him with the "continuation" of *Alcuin*,

---

[18]The dating here is based on Smith's memo of 27 March that he had a letter from Brown declaring "his first novel is complete," followed by a note three days later of his receiving Brown's "proposals for his Novel — 'Sky-Walk'" (*Diary*, pp. 433–434). The "proposals" most likely had to do with Brown's announcement in the *Weekly Magazine* for 17 March that subscriptions would "in a short time" be solicited for "Sky-Walk" (p. 202).

In the introductory paragraph to the "Extract" appearing in the next issue of the *Weekly Magazine*, 24 March, the work is said to be "ready to be offered to public patronage" (p. 228). Watters' standing advertisement must have brought in custom, for his notice of 28 July has "Sky-Walk" advertised as "NOW IN THE PRESS!" In spite of such fixed dates, confusion remains over when "Sky-Walk" may actually have been completed. Partially, this is due to ambiguity over when it was begun. In a letter of 16 September 1797, the ever accomboth of which he shared with Smith (*Diary*, p. 438). The two of them, along with William Johnson, immediately began reading the novel at a steady pace, large portions of it aloud to one another, Mrs. Dunlap and friends, and they were through it in four days. It seems little short of

modating Smith tells Brown he is eager to see, and will gladly give him a critique of, the "precious Romance" Brown said he was working on along with the "continuation" of *Alcuin* (*Diary*, p. 364), Parts I and II of which Smith had received on 7 August (ibid., p. 342). Brown had long since shown himself deaf to entreaties, or obscure in responding to them. Smith, for example, had complained to Dunlap in late July 1797 "as usual, it is difficult to learn from [Charles's letter] what he is about" (ibid., p. 338). And it was no different with the unnamed novel. Hence, though we are in no better position than Smith was to know whether the "precious Romance" might have been "Sky-Walk," it seems a reasonable supposition that "Sky-Walk" *was* the "Romance" which Brown mentioned in his journal as the one he began after completing the third and fourth parts of *Alcuin* and finished on "the last day of December" 1797 (Dunlap, *Life*, I, 107–109). The gap between that date and March 1798 is quite easily explained: the romance having been "first written in an hasty and inaccurate way," Brown felt "as much time" would be required to put it into respectable shape for submission to a publisher "as was necessary to the original composition" (ibid.). (If he completed *Alcuin* III and IV sometime in the fall of 1797 and did not get them to Dunlap till April when they arrived simultaneously with "Sky-Walk," it is quite possible that both — first works of their kind — had been given a similar rewrite in transcription.)

Two bits of supporting evidence for identifying "Sky-Walk" as the "Romance" undertaken after *Alcuin* III and IV are worth noting. First of all, Brown specifically called this work his "first novel," and we have no record of any other on hand, or contemplated (certainly none named) during the time in question. Also, since it is so mentioned in the past tense, the reference has to be to *the* novel known to have been his first. Secondly, the wording of his journal apologia that his Romance is not so good as he would like it to be (apprentice work next to *Caleb Williams*) directly echoes sentiments expressed in the *Weekly Magazine* announcement of "Sky-Walk." The apologia reads: "every new attempt will be better than the last, and . . . considered in the light of a prelude or first link, it may merit that praise to which it may possess no claim, considered as a last best creation" (Dunlap, *Life*, I, 107). And, as he has it in the *Weekly Magazine*: "Every new attempt will, of course, be more likely to succeed than the last" (1 [17 March 1798], 202).

the impossible that they could have finished a physically weighty manuscript written in a far from lucid hand, that was supposed to make 800 duodecimo pages in print (Watters had it so projected, in two volumes)[19] in so brief a time, some of it orally, by candlelight.[20] But however it was done, the fact that it somehow was would imply a narrative of more than ordinary interest (Smith and Dunlap each said as much, ibid.), even for eager readers of the long-awaited first novel by a friend they had been rather solicitous of. Smith, who overall took more time with "Sky-Walk" and was to read parts of it twice, said his "whole spirit was affected by it" the first time and that the second only increased his "admiration" (*Diary*, p. 439). Johnson, meanwhile, was so shaken by the book that he "retired to his bed in a throb & tumult of curiosity, interest, & admiration" (ibid.).[21] Smith's regard was such that on finishing *Wieland* he made the complimentary comparison of calling it in "no way inferior to 'Sky-Walk'" (*Diary*, p. 455). Dunlap alone had his doubts and it is these that

---

[19]This was stated in the advertisement printed on the back wrapper of the *Weekly Magazine* for 23 March 1798, and successively thereafter till the magazine suspended publication with the number of 25 August. (Watters had succumbed to yellow fever and died in the first week of September.) Smith's listing the manuscript of "Sky-Walk" among his readings for April 1798 as in "2 vols." (*Diary*, p. 442) may have been based on the advertisement, or at least on Brown's telling him about Watters' intention; however, considering the length, it is not impossible that Brown himself had divided it into two parts. He would make like divisions with *Alcuin* and *Arthur Mervyn*.

[20]Though Dunlap would speak of a reading *in* "Sky-Walk" (*Diary*, I, 248), Smith clearly read the whole of it (*Diary*, pp. 438–439).

[21]Possibly one can interpret this as a sign of Brown's method of writing, a reflection of his gift, as Paul Allen observed, for getting characters into "incredible and mysterious adventures" from which "extrication" is precarious; of his expending "so much energy of pathos that the reader in spite of his better judgment yields to momentary conviction," and soon finds himself pushed to "the brink of another catastrophe" (*The Life of Charles Brockden Brown*, ed. Charles E. Bennett [Delmar, N.Y.: Scholars' Facsimiles & Reprints, 1975], p. 389).

at last give us an inkling of what all the excitement was about. After "Sky-Walk" was read to its conclusion, Dunlap gave Brown "high credit," but nevertheless found himself "not satisfied." With his instinct for structure, playwright Dunlap wanted more consistency of characterization and greater plausibility in the motivation of action: "Is not Lorimer to [*sic*] much exalted—too fascinating? Why are we not satisfied as to the pistol of Avonedge? and how are we to account for the dagger, so oppertunely [*sic*] ready in the Chamber of Mrs [*sic*] Courtney?" (*Diary*, I, 249).

Sketchy as these complaints may be, they reveal not only a carry-over of episodes from "Sky-Walk" to *Huntly*, but also areas of apparent change in the transition. Plainly, the Mrs. Courtney character, who likewise appears in the "Extract," becomes Mrs. Lorimer, whereas Edny, it would seem, had formerly been called Lorimer.[22] One supposes that one meaning for Dunlap's remark about Lorimer is that in the original this guilt-ridden personage had occasionally fallen out of character by taking on some of the traits of high passion attributable to the more audacious type described in the announcement for "Sky-Walk"—a defect which, if it existed, certainly gets attended to in the rewrite. However, the somewhat too coincidental dagger in the patroness's bedroom obviously remains as initially given; and there is validity in Brown's keeping it that way. For it is psychologically quite appropriate to have a wrought-up and unwilling Edny going into Mrs. Lorimer's bedroom unarmed. Furthermore, the accidentally found dagger becomes a fitting provocation for him to go forward with a deed on sudden impulse, which a Hamlet-type brooder might otherwise have aborted. Avonedge is Arthur Wiatte. Dunlap's question apparently has to do with Brown's failure to explain how

---

[22]In the *Wieland* notebook, Brown had listed in one column the names Lorimer, Edny, Wyatte and Inglefield, without signifying their sex. Lorimer, cancelled, also appears on another list with Avonedge (*Wieland*, pp. 423, 440).

he came by the pistol. (Perhaps he was thinking in terms of stage props.) But, since there is little reason to doubt a shady figure like Wiatte *would* have one (Edny's suddenly drawing *his* pistol is a greater surprise), it is just possible that Dunlap was wondering why Wiatte's shot at close range (near the *ear*) was not good enough to kill Lorimer-Edny instead of just grazing his forehead. These being the only direct references Dunlap makes to the content of "Sky-Walk," the Edny-Lorimer-Wiatte triad must have played a more prominent role in "Sky-Walk" than they do in *Huntly*—where they take up but five of twenty-seven chapters. Reducing the story to Edny's retrospective narrative would better bring it into line with Brown's dominant subjects (the somnambulism and Indians) and prevent its competing with them. One other point. As Dunlap would be prone to comment on matters that were freshest in mind, and, as he did so after having just read the last part of a very long—and assumedly complicated—novel, there seems a good likelihood that Edny's confessional appeared somewhat near the end of "Sky-Walk," meaning that for purposes of suspense an explanation of his strange behavior may have been withheld for the major part of the novel. (Hence—if this be so—the curiosity that so strongly affected Smith and Johnson.) Brown's moving that material forward would again suggest he did not want us to remain fixated on Edny through the middle part of *Huntly*, and it would indicate something of how Brown may have decided to integrate him with the other things he had working in the novel.

If this illustrates probable modifications in the transfer of "Sky-Walk" material to *Huntly*, the "Extract," on the other hand, is important for disclosing the sort of conventionalized melodrama of good will abused that Brown started off with and then largely disposed of. Moreover, we see the inadequacy of his narrative to sustain the subtler aspects of misguided benevolence which functioned so well in *Huntly*. But mainly the "Extract" seems quite foreign to the stuff of *Huntly* in its blandness of tone—leaving aside the literally foreign setting for the moment — and it has none of the up-close tension of characters steadily haunted by psychological — to say nothing of physical — pressures, some of their own making.

The passage begins with our anonymous narrator, sounding much like Edny (and resembling him as well in Irish background, though he is evidently a step up in social class), determined to resist any further "obligations" beyond those already incurred through the benevolence of an extravagantly solicitous patroness, Mrs. Courtney. (That she would seize any opportunity for "extraordinary or eccentric obligation" suggests an idiosyncrasy quite absent in Mrs. Lorimer.) Events of the tale he is about to tell, however, put her in precisely the position to vastly increase his indebtedness, which he, similarly concerned for a friend facing ruination, finds it ironically impossible to deny. The Edny character says these circumstances "contributed to aggravate the remorse to which I was ultimately destined." This gives us our sole intimation — which can easily be missed — of ominous times down the road, that will eventuate in the disabling psychopathology of a Clithero Edny. As for the tale proper, it seems that the narrator is traveling on the continent in company with Ormond Courtney, his patroness's son. (This character may have played a larger role in "Sky-Walk" than the incidental one he has in *Huntly*, where his being disqualified as a suitor for Clarice creates the opening that will compound Edny's indebtedness.) While in Bordeaux, the narrator meets an old acquaintance from Dublin College, Annesley, a "guileless" youth of "considerable talents" and "industry," who is on the way toward making a prosperous merchant of himself. Having missed Annesley on the merchant's return to Ireland, the narrator later runs into him at the city prison, while on an errand for Mrs. Courtney. It turns out that a debtor for whom Annesley and his father had stood security had absconded, and the creditor, wanting quick payment, lured Annesley back to Ireland, where instant apprehen-

313

sion made his baggage easy prey for thieves who took his entire "fortune." The narrator's appeals to the vengeful creditor are unavailing, and when Mrs. Courtney finally compels him to reveal the reason for his dejection, which he had withheld, fearing it would "augment the burthen of obligation," her sympathy becomes profuse. Annesley's debts are paid and he is given an estate "on easy terms, by which he was placed in a situation little inferior to that which his fancy had sketched as the summit of his wishes" (*Weekly Magazine*, 1 [24 March 1798], 228–231). The only thing of any consequence that Brown could reclaim from this sort of tale is the irony that out of an immediate good would come the larger evil of Lorimer-Edny's having immeasurably increased an indebtedness he had been struggling — till then rather successfully — to contain.[23]

There are a number of riddles surrounding the "Extract" which, though not very significant in themselves, help to clarify a final hiatus in the connection of "Sky-Walk" to *Edgar Huntly*. Not only does place in the "Extract" bear no relationship to that given by the title (so laboriously explained beforehand), but also this sample of an "American Tale" is situated exclusively in Ireland and France, contradicting Brown's recommendation that as "the United States is a new and untrodden field" the native novelist should use "all that is genuine and peculiar in the scene before him" (*Weekly Magazine*, 1 [17 March 1798], 202). So far as one can tell, not one of the characters is American. Nor do these events convey the slightest

[23]This whole problem is, of course, played off against the more obvious contradiction of a legal system that punishes indebtedness by preventing the jailed debtor from ever being able to satisfy his creditor. Brown discusses the two-sidedness of debtor imprisonment — the inequities it both incurs and deters — in the final sketch of his "Man At Home" series, a work he had taken up about the time he was bringing "Sky-Walk" to a close (*Weekly Magazine* 1 [28 April 1798], 383–386). In *Huntly*, the issues of moral and psychological indebtedness loom much larger than the social ones. Also, Mrs. Lorimer, as patroness, has a more believable motivation than her predecessor, and is personally more complicated.

association with his intriguing subtitle, "The Man Unknown to Himself." Even harder to fathom is why Brown in his announcement of the "Extract" should have made such altitudinous statements about appealing to "those who are satisfied with nothing but . . . the exhibition of powerful motives, and a sort of audaciousness of character"—a kind of elite readership that would understand "the world is governed, not by the simpleton, but by the man of soaring passions and intellectual energy" (ibid.). Brown sounds as if he were introducing a work of *Sturm und Drang* heroics—in the manner, say, of a Schiller, Herder, Goethe, or Bürger, some of whom would occasionally be cited in the *Weekly Magazine*, and were quite well known to the Smith-Dunlap-Johnson-Brown coterie. To all of this the "Extract" is anticlimax. And the cause of it seems to be that Watters, rather than Brown, finally decided what would be extracted as a "specimen" of the new work.[24] To wit: if he is going to assume the risk of publishing "Sky-Walk," Watters wants to make sure nobody will be scared off. So he seizes upon a passage with the comforting parable that for the hardworking young merchant circumstantially undone by the world of defalcation, thievery, and grasping creditors, a saving benefactor is still to be found. The man of soaring passions, presumably lost to us in "Sky-Walk," reappears soon enough in Theodore Wieland and Ormond.

The fact is, once the manuscript of "Sky-Walk" left Brown's hand, he effectively lost all future control over it. It will be recalled that for about a year—from July 1798 to June 1799—Brown remained pretty much in New York, save for a convalescence at Dunlap's Amboy home in the fall and his brief trip to Philadelphia in May concerning *Huntly*. At the time of Watters' death in September 1798,

[24]Watters made no secret of this. Among other things, the "nature of its design" and "singularity of its title . . . have induced us," he wrote, "for the satisfaction of our readers, to solicit, from the author, the privilege of making an extract from his manuscript" (*Weekly Magazine* 1 [24 March 1798], 228).

the printing of "Sky-Walk," which—as indicated—had gone to press toward the end of July, was almost completed. Its having been advertised for sale on the back wrapper of the *Weekly Magazine* for 9 February 1799, when publication of the journal was resumed, suggests that Watters' executors may have briefly considered going through with the completion and sale of "Sky-Walk." However, inasmuch as the executors, we are told, "did not choose to finish it and would not or could not sell the sheets for such price, as Mr. Brown's friends thought proper to offer for them," the work was never to be recovered (Dunlap, *Life*, I, 259). The haggling finished it. (If his friends, who were on the spot, could not negotiate for the sheets, Brown was in no position to do so—least of all financially.) Clearly, he did not see "Sky-Walk" again, so that instead of browsing through an early work for a simple redaction of old material, he had to make an entirely fresh start with *Huntly*, reviving only such ideas as could be used in the new venture, which, in any case, had to be pretty much reconceived.

"Sky-Walk," however, had not been a total waste. It had served its purpose. After several years of inconclusive starts—each so buoyantly undertaken and fitfully abandoned—Brown in 1797 had yet to learn what it took to write a novel.[25] "Sky-Walk" launched him. Indeed, as his potentially longest novel and the one longest in composition, "Sky-Walk" ushered in the most intense period of sustained productivity in Brown's career as novelist; and the novel that abruptly ended it would go back to the lost beginnings and turn them into a finished whole that could pay its way as a work of literature. Even if "Sky-

[25]One counts at least three unfinished novels mentioned by Smith that Brown had on hand during 1796–1797, in addition to other projects (*Diary*, pp. 118–119, 231, 233, 290). As Smith characterized his writing activity at this time: "he starts an idea; pursues it a little way; new ones spring up; he runs a short distance after each; meantime the original one is likely to escape intirely" (ibid., p. 272).

Walk" had been saved, after *Huntly*, it would have been superfluous.

III

Sky-Walk, Norwalk, Sleep-Walk. *Edgar Huntly* would seem to have germinated from one controlling image: a walk in the wild of the unknown Self. By the time he put the novel together, Brown had enough material for two delusional characters — or, depending on how one treats the double, dual aspects of one. Blindness and burial — sleepwalking and the cave — are Brown's central metaphors for a subconscious state that betrays the true condition of the psyche: one seeks but withdraws from knowing. For Huntly, the walk is itself an act of unknowing — somnambulism aside. He has no idea of what it will mean "to tread, as closely as possible, in [Edny's] footsteps" (p. 18). Perilous as the going is, neither man can do other than persist. Perversity in the one abets it in the other. Himself driven by unreason, Edny tells Huntly, when pressed to open his past, "You, like others, are blind to the most momentous consequences of your own actions" (p. 36). Though Huntly will echo Edny's warning toward the end ("How total is our blindness with regard to our own performances!" [p. 278]) that doesn't materially effect any change in him. He is only commenting on the unaccountability of sleepwalking — more of which later.

The fact is, both men seem constitutionally unable to read what they do and their doubling at it suggests a potential for contrariety bordering on the universal. This happens not because they suffer from a lack of self-scrutiny, but rather from a hyperextension of that faculty. Huntly becomes so engrossed in pondering alternatives that he constantly reverses himself. One moment he feels remiss that his murdered friend goes unavenged and the next he is sobbing in sympathy with the supposed mur-

317

derer. Reluctant at first to confirm his suspicion, he fatigues himself with arguments for and against it, and overcomes the latter on the rationalization that curiosity, like knowledge, is "its own reward," even though the knowledge he seeks will "excite the most complex and fiery sentiment in [his] bosom" (p. 16) — which has him coming out about where he went in.

Trailing Edny, nonetheless, into "a maze, oblique, circuitous, upward and downward" (p. 23), typical, we are told, of "*Solebury*" (suddenly symbolic, though an actual place name), Edgar, as hunter of Waldegrave's murderer, peremptorily gets himself buried in the woods. In name and deed — even pun — the burial metaphor keeps reappearing throughout the quest, often in situations quite as obvious as this. On his second trip out after Edny, for instance, Huntly senses he is being diabolically led "into the deepest thickets, . . . the darkest cavities, . . . [to] the slippery and tremulous verge of the dizziest precipices" (ibid.). But the danger — and futility — seem only to increase his determination. In no other novel of Brown's, or, for that matter, of any American author before the great romantic triumvirate of Poe, Hawthorne and Melville, are physical phenomena so thoroughly interpenetrated by their psycho-symbolic counterparts.

But to go back to the pervasive theme of "The Man Unknown to Himself" — possibly Brown's most significant borrowing from "Sky-Walk" — this questing walker of his, a prime example of the unreliable narrator, is least knowing when he claims to be most so. Looking back as he readies himself for the ordeal of telling his tale, Huntly boasts, "What light has burst upon my ignorance of myself and of mankind!" (p. 6). Yet, the truth is, neither he, nor we, can be very sure of the knowledge he professes to have earned in his dark pilgrimage. Quite the reverse, it is ignorance that seems to predominate. To the very end, he least understands the man he most wants to help by understanding. Worse, he literally misunderstands Edny unto death, failing to perceive that a comfortless

318

soul can be more damaged by comforting than otherwise. Those instances in which actions by Huntly have pulled his suicidal quarry back from disaster become effective only accidentally. The food he left for Edny was mistakenly seen as a sign of divine intercession; and in the chance discovery of Mrs. Lorimer's manuscript left by Huntly on the jutting precipice Edny saw a similar manifestation of the miraculous (pp. 270–271). Well beyond the time he should have learned not to meddle with Edny's pathetic madness, Huntly compulsively insists he must "relieve him." He will not "admit the belief that [Edny's] misery is without a cure" (p. 284). Edny cannot help himself, and Huntly benevolently feels he should, unaware of the extent to which *he* cannot help *him*self. How little, after all, should it take to cure this lunatic: one need merely disclose the saving truth that Euphemia Lorimer lives. What an overpowering shock to Huntly's trust in the salutary powers of Reason, and in the whole eighteenth-century structure of the moral contagion of sensibility, is the response Edny gives: "Rash and infatuated youth. Thou hast ratified, beyond appeal or forgiveness, thy own doom." He thinks Huntly is telling him a story, but he will go to New York and look into it, leaving Huntly with the admonition: "If she be alive then am I reserved for the performance of a new crime. My evil destiny will have it so." Edny still has it in his head that he *must* kill her; that difficult is it for him to get untracked from the need for guilt. And should it turn out that he has been trifled with, Huntly beware ("If she be dead, I shall make *thee* expiate" [p. 289]). With his "impulse of . . . powerful benevolence" (p. 290), the incessantly well-meaning Huntly has bred nothing but intolerable grief. Although he is not alone in this regard — upon the arrival of Weymouth, for example, even Waldegrave's intended beneficence misfires — the curse primarily falls on him because he pushes it: while Edny will resign himself to unmerited despair, Huntly's immitigable altruism cannot accept the fact that it is defeating itself by not accepting defeat. So Edgar Huntly is Clithero's nemesis; he is his own and almost everyone else's too, and this does not yet take into account what happens among the Indians. Euphemia Lorimer is so traumatized at the prospect of seeing Edny again that she and Sarsefield lose their unborn child; Edny takes his life (for him *the* most "inexpiable" sin [p. 270]), and Huntly several times comes very close to losing his. So complete is the subversion of Huntly's world that he ironically pleads for Sarsefield's "compassion"—not thinking of what had already been accomplished by that route.

Is Edgar Huntly then to be taken as a well-meaning Arthur Mervyn run amuck, a blunderer senselessly committed to human caring, who will not go away?[26] Surely, this protagonist raises some rather disturbing questions about the possibilities of self-knowledge. It should not be overlooked perhaps that to some extent the apparent inversion of good and evil in *Edgar Huntly* invokes the modish Burkeyan notion of sublime terror, wherewith abhorrence becomes a property of exaltation and repulsion attracts. However, out of this very mix comes the inescapably destructive corollary that, with Huntly's fall, down come the prime suppositions of eighteenth-century meliorism; gone, in other words, is Shaftesbury's curative moral of the spontaneous virtues of the heart. One conclusion to be drawn from this wreckage is that Brown has written a story of the failure of more than goodwill; indeed, this novel gives us an account of the failed American somewhat ahead of his time.[27]

However one reads it, *Edgar Huntly* is indubitably a dark book. We must now pick up the inner current of this

---

[26]Mervyn unwittingly makes the self-damning admission that, failing of its effect, good will has its selfish reward: "Honest purposes, though they may not bestow happiness on others [i.e., Wallace], will, at least, secure it to him who fosters them" (*Arthur Mervyn, Second Part*, p. 270).

[27]See Sydney J. Krause, "*Edgar Huntly* and the American Nightmare," *Studies in the Novel*, 13 (Fall, 1981), 294–302.

darkness; for, as we have seen, Brown started out with what he conceived to be a certain enigma of human conduct, and it can tell us something of where the troubles of Self were assumed to have originated. Diagnosis begins with the fact that Brown was actually merging—or barely separating—the characters of Huntly and Edny. The name Edny is, after all, anagrammatically submerged in *Ed*gar Hu*nt*ly. Huntly may be the doctor sicker than his patient, but much of our difficulty in understanding him subsides once we see that his neurotic contradictions are symptomatic of autoscopy: he hallucinates his own being in Edny.

All the external manifestations are there, even before the subjective ones emerge; though, of course, the two coexist, and only from Huntly's consciousness is their presence masked. Plainly, something other than surface mystification attends his first sighting of the ghostly figure in the nocturnal "shade" of the great elm. In spite of Edny's rather hefty spading, we are told—unabashedly: "To a casual observer this appearance would have been unnoticed." No one but Huntly would see it? Edny is an "apparition," a phantom "being," with "the shape of a man" (p. 10). Instinctively drawn to him, Huntly would "hold his hand," for the figure has become an instant "object of compassion" (p. 11). But the figure does not see him, and on disappearing among rocks and bushes leaves Huntly "rooted to the spot," baffled (p. 12). Acting precisely like a vision of the second self, that capricious figure will have his own way.

Thus, shadowing what he recounts at the story level is the ulterior (one could say "clinical") tale of Huntly's dramatizing his state of mind, specifically in this case an engagement with his subconscious, and what it feels like to be so engaged. Throughout, he has the sense of being "suspended in astonishment" (p. 11). The trick in all this being—and it is a key explanation of Huntly's unknowing—that while the ego can look upon its self as object—a thing apart—it can be quite unaware (like Narcissus) that it is doing so. (The subconscious by its very nature cannot, of course, be consciously known.)[28]

The second time out, Edny appears to have material-ized out of thin air: "He seemed like one, whom an effort of will, without the exercise of locomotion, had trans-ported hither, or made visible" (pp. 17–18). That this specter, his kindred in sensitivity, should keep rising before him is suspicious to the observer, though for the wrong reasons. Each encounter is enveloped in a kind of haze—mental and environmental. Things seem to be happening as if called forth by psychic projection. By Huntly's own statement of his expectations, "the obscurity in which external objects were wrapped . . . did not draw my attention from the images of fancy" (p. 9). His fancy offers him the images he wants to see, but it gives him more than sight alone can perceive. Some characters do not know what it is they don't know; some do not know *that* they don't know. The first would be Edny, the second Huntly. In any case, Edny seems to be urged on Huntly in response to the demands of conscience (why has he not found Waldegrave's killer?); and yet, once found, so intense is Huntly's empathy for him that he must identify

---

[28]It is not simply a narrative convenience, by the way, that the somnambulating Edny happens to be in a hypnotic trance; rather the conditions under which Huntly, the watcher, follows him seem just short of hallucinative for him as well. If, as indicated, how he sees the world around him objectifies the world within, this type of medium is particularly conducive to self-revelation. As a whole, the structure is such that having produced only Huntly's vision of things, Brown has the reader situated in an inside position, where he can experience for himself the difficulty of distinguishing the true state of affairs—which parallels the sort of perplexity that occurs with regard to Clara Wieland.

In the analysis which follows, it goes without saying that for Edny to have the role of Huntly's double does not mean his extinction as a character. It is just that to view his mode of being as a reflection of Huntly's subconscious best explains the extravagance—indeed, morbidity—of Huntly's interest in him; why, in the face of other obligations, he finds he can "think only of Clithero" (p. 138).

with the very person on whom he pins the unconscionable crime.[29] Carefully examined, however, the idea that— insanely—he can simultaneously have it both ways, brings forth its own inherent rationale. In short, it goes to the crux of how the mechanism of the double operates. A textbook case history this one. For a juxtaposition of this kind exactly reenacts the guilt formation out of which a second self is created: his entire raison d'être is to bear the onus of self-loathing that the defensive ego wants to push off onto somebody else.[30]

[29]The extreme position on the meaning of this identification is that Edny exists only in Huntly's tormented subconscious, and Huntly himself is therefore the murderer. This scenario is ably argued by Kenneth Bernard, who, interestingly, points out that, with but a lone exception, each of Huntly's ten meetings with Edny are one-on-one. "*Edgar Huntly*: Charles Brockden Brown's Unsolved Murder," *Library Chronicle*, 33 (Winter, 1967), 30–53.

[30]The double has, of course, had a long history in western litera- ture, going back at least to Ovid and Attic Comedy; even Satan as double has come in for his share of attention. But the character-type has attracted an especially lively interest among twentieth-century critics—psychoanalytic, literary, and combinations of the two— literature being a perennial stalking ground for Freudian sleuthing, much of it of late very insightful.

The pioneering study of the double is Otto Rank's well-known essay "Der Doppelgänger," originally published in Freud's journal *Imago* in 1914, and subsequently expanded and incorporated in other works, last appearing as Chapter 2 of *Beyond Psychology* (Camden, N.J.: Haddon Craftsmen, Inc., 1941), pp. 62–101. Several of Rank's main points have to do with the phenomena of narcissism, projection, ego preservation, and disintegrative tendencies in the modern per- sonality. He works from the origin of the double in myth and folk superstition. A good recent translation is Harry Tucker's *The Double: A Psychoanalytic Study by Otto Rank* (Chapel Hill: Univ. of North Caro- lina Press, 1971). Out of the extensive secondary literature, I have found three other works particularly useful and have drawn on them in a general way, along with Rank, for my consideration of the double in *Edgar Huntly*. These are: Ralph Tymms, *Doubles in Literary Psychol- ogy* (Cambridge, England: Bowes & Bowes, 1949); Robert Rogers, *A Psychoanalytic Study of the Double in Literature* (Detroit: Wayne State Univ. Press, 1970); and C. F. Keppler, *The Literature of the Second Self* (Tuscon, Ariz.: Univ. of Arizona Press, 1972).

And whence the guilt? It is itself an outgrowth of overt doubling. For in his prior identification with Waldegrave, Huntly's "unutterable" sorrow springs from the horror that the paragon of "piety" and soul of "benevolence," for whom it was "impossible" to conceive the "existence of an enemy," (p. 7) should have been wantonly slain, the victim of a motiveless crime. Huntly clearly thinks well enough of himself—and his intentions with Edny bear him out—that since he sees in Waldegrave the model person he believes himself to be, he is also entitled to feel threatened by his friend's fate: there but for the grace of God. So one comes here at the etiological base of doubling itself: "primary narcissism," the primitive drive for "preservation against extinction" (to cite Freud on Rank[31]). Hence the paranoid guilt of Edny-Huntly, which is made all the more desperate by the facts: a) that the one double—in this case, Huntly's superego—has already expired, making restitution impossible, and b) that his supposed murderer shames Huntly by emotionally outdoing him in lamentation over responsibility for the monstrous act—an unhappy reminder to Huntly of his own multiple responsibility. He *could* have prevented Waldegrave from taking "his ill-omened journey" (p. 7); the fact

Donald Ringe touches on Edny's status as Huntly's double ("Charles Brockden Brown," *Major Writers of Early American Literature*, ed. Everett Emerson [Madison: Univ. of Wisconsin Press, 1972], p. 281). But the fullest and most convincing treatment of Brown's use of the double is that by Norman S. Grabo (*The Coincidental Art of Charles Brockden Brown* [Chapel Hill: Univ. of North Carolina Press, 1981], pp. 160–185, et passim.) He does not, however, get into an intensive analysis of the manifest doubling in *Huntly*.

Though Brown's novels were written during the high tide of German romantic fiction, so far as we can tell he had scant knowledge of those authors who would make significant contributions to the literature of the Doppelgänger: Goethe, Tieck, von Kleist, Baron de la Motte-Fouqué, E. T. A. Hoffmann, and Jean Paul Richter, with whom—Jean Paul, that is—the German term originated.

[31] *Collected Papers*, tr. under supervision of Joan Riviere, ed. Ernest Jones (New York: Basic Books, Inc., 1959), IV, 387.

that his death remains unavenged has become a nagging accusation of a breach of faith; and then there are those heterodox letters of Waldegrave's, which Huntly had promised Mary he would transcribe, against his better judgment, and worse yet against Waldegrave's "solemn injunctions" (p. 131)—for this reason had "the image of Waldegrave" visited him in his sleep expressing "inquietude and anger" (p. 130).

Edgar Huntly is permeated with dualities: coupling, twinning, doubling, and a variety of like correspondences. Some are consequential (as Mrs. Lorimer's feeling that her life is inscrutably linked to that of her evil twin brother, or the hiding by Huntly and Edny of sensitive manuscripts while sleepwalking); some are purely incidental (as, Edny's mistaking Clarice for Mrs. Lorimer, or his supplanting her son); and many lie somewhere in-between (as, Huntly's bedding down in the same room at Inglefield's where Waldegrave had died, or Sarsefield's being a father-figure for both Huntly and Edny). Others are simply to be taken at face value—as the two panthers, or Huntly's recapturing his musket from the Indians, using it against them, and then disposing of and recovering it a second time. This is not the place to catalogue all the instances of doubling large and small, nor is there enough to go on that might suggest some steady purpose for it on Brown's part; however, we do find him to have been somewhat obsessed with doubles,[32] and,

[32]To cite but a few instances: Carwin imitates the voices of others; Welbeck mimics the voice of the betrayer, Colvill; Ormond disguises himself as others, and he has a counterpart adventure-loving sister; Craig feigns a closely resembling brother; Stephen Calvert has a trouble-making twin mistaken for himself; Jane Talbot, like Mrs. Lorimer, has a satanic brother who has a strong claim on her feelings; Arthur Mervyn has two loves, and there are two versions of his character; Mervyn's father remarries a woman not much older than Arthur, with whom the young man was at one time presumed to have been intimate; Cambridge tells his niece Clara Wieland of a strange madness in the family whereby a grandfather believed that his own death would inevitably follow on that of his brother—etc., etc.

whether arrived at systematically or not, there is very much of a pattern to their recurrence in *Edgar Huntly*. Even without that, the cumulative weight of their multiple guises is not alone reinforcing for all, but they seem to be saying something important about Huntly's world, and how he takes it in. In any event, while the double invites all sorts of technical virtuosity, as Brown was aware,[33] our concern must be limited to the logic that underlies the main strand of doubling—specifically, how it takes the novel to its necessary conclusion. As will be seen, it becomes the implicit motivation that makes a compelling case of what might otherwise seem a strained dénouement of the Edny-Huntly entanglement.

First, there is the factor of psychomachy, a fundamental cause of one's experience of the double; the psyche is at war with itself, but it is conflict by virtue of sameness. It will be remembered that Huntly not only identifies with Edny's innermost feelings ("I am no stranger to your gnawing cares. To the deep and incurable despair that haunts you . . . ."), but his "generous sympathy" is so lavish as to seem contrary: ". . . I might see reason to embrace the assassin as my best friend" (pp. 32, 33, 32). He would embrace the hateful other self, who "inflicted the greatest possible injury" on him (p. 32), because emotionally he recognizes it *is* nonetheless himself, rejected. So completely does the otherness of self absorb him that

[33]For example, in Huntly's marveling at the assumedly prophetic death of Euphemia Lorimer following that of Wiatte, we catch a glimpse of Brown (momentarily off-guard) beguiled by the ironies his subject seems capable of generating. His tone is almost Jamesean: "By such circuitous, and yet infallible means, were the prediction of the lady and the vengeance of the brother accomplished! In how many cases may it be said . . . that the prediction was the cause of its own fulfilment? That the very act, which considerate observers, and even himself, for a time, imagined to have utterly precluded the execution of Wiatte's menaces, should be that inevitably leading to it? That the execution should be assigned to him, who, abounding in abhorrence, and in the act of self-defense, was the slayer of the menacer?" (pp. 92–93).

even though he has gratuitously forgiven Edny beforehand and should be done with him ("Remorse," of itself, is
"ample . . . expiation for all offences," p. 24), and even
though he learns Edny had no probable connection with
the Waldegrave murder, Huntly will always find a reason
to cling to the man: if he is a suicide his remains must be
given a decent burial, and if he lives the suicide must be
averted and he be restored to tranquility (pp. 94–95).
One moment Huntly is certain that Edny's "phrensy" is
"curable" by "reason" (p. 95), and the next he places himself in Edny's shoes and knows it is incurable. As he gen-
eralizes the situation, he interchanges himself with Edny
and makes both kin with all men:

> Every man, not himself the victim of irretreivable
> disasters [Huntly], perceives the folly of . . . fostering
> a grief which cannot reverse or recall the decrees of
> . . . necessity; but every man who suffers [Edny-
> Huntly-Everyman] is unavoidably shackled by the
> errors which he censures in his neighbour, and his
> efforts to relieve himself [Edny] are as fruitless as
> those with which he [Huntly] attempted the relief of
> others. (p. 110)

Temporarily, Huntly's insights find the universal in his
relationship to Edny, and the vanity of rehabilitation — for
both. But this is also an excuse for persisting, an admission of parallel irrationality, and a giving himself up to it.
All in the name of *salvation* — an assuaging motive to make
the alter ego self-destruct. It fits, for on hearing him out
regarding Wiatte and the near assault on Mrs. Lorimer,
Huntly decides that Edny's "conduct was dictated by a
motive allied to virtue" (p. 91); and his first response to
the story is that Edny could still have dispatched with
Waldegrave, by "an act . . . originated in a like spirit of
mistaken benevolence" (pp. 90–91). For the alter ego,
apology is automatic, but the identity factor — it's *me*, after
all — leaves one, in spite of the hoped for "magic of sympa-

327

thy" (p. 111), more conflicted than if it were wholly some-one else, and so suppressed resentment must have its outlet. Hence murder and suicide are close adjuncts of the doubling process. As Erich Stern pointed out in his review of Rank: "In order to escape [his] fear of death, the [subject] resorts to suicide which, however, he carries out on his double, because he loves and esteems his ego so very much."[34]

When Huntly pauses to take stock, after his set-to with panther-one, the voice of conscience becomes prelude to his somnambulating in the "long room." He reminds him-self that he has defaulted on his pledge to furnish Mary with a copy of her brother's letters; a cloud hangs over the enterprise in that he cannot be true to both in going through with it. Compounding the dilemma, his diver-sionary "obligation of benevolence" to Edny was likewise "not discharged." Thus, frustrated that his alibi doesn't work out either, he testily berates himself: "but why should my whole attention and activity be devoted to this man?" (p. 131). Unaccountability here is a pretense of the ego; obviously, the answer is implicit in his question. So at sunrise Huntly proposes to go back to the mountain. He must cure this Clithero Edny or kill him, admit only to the former, not mean the latter, and forge ahead with it anyway, Sarsefield's warning that "all remedies [for Edny] are vain" notwithstanding. As Sarsefield describes Edny's madness, we see that it applies equally to Huntly: "Con-sciousness itself is the malady; the pest; of which he only is cured who ceases to think" (p. 277).

If Edny's grip on Huntly is that of the alter ego, con-sider what it means for Huntly to say of him: "To no imagination are his offences blacker and more odious than to his own" (pp. 263–264). Heightened conscious-ness of his Self in another is the malady which brings this anxiety-persona so close to Huntly; and his self-

[34]Cited by Tucker in the introduction to his translation, p. xix. See Rank's account of the "slaying of the double," pp. 79–80.

abomination forces Huntly to concur that "death was better to Clithero than life" (p. 277). So something in Huntly
requires Edny's death, and he will blunder around long
enough (hoping to "rectify" his "mistakes") to get it done.
Only then can the story be ended; it is, in fact, prolonged
beyond its expected ending (the disclosure, at last, of who
really killed Waldegrave) because Edny cannot be left in
limbo — or, more accurately, because Huntly cannot let
him alone.

The concluding drama resumes its course when the two
somnambulists have emerged from the wilderness, the
look of mortality upon them. Parallel to the very end —
almost — each had been out there wandering among angry
Indians, had nearly been slain by them, and returned
physically half-dead (as if, indeed, back from the dead),
with the difference that Huntly also has a sense of rebirth
(p. 239), while Edny is genuinely "expiring" (p. 267).
Significantly, it is the hard-nosed Sarsefield (physician,
mentor, man of reason), with the "skill . . . [to] save him,"
who implacably maintains not "a finger shall . . . be
moved to avert his fate" (ibid.). He is the essential figure
at this point, just the man to be Huntly's accomplice — he
whom Huntly says, "has treated me with paternal tenderness, and insists upon the privilege of consulting for my
interest, as if he were my real father" (p. 279). Not even
after Huntly has corrected his misconceptions regarding
Edny is Sarsefield's attitude measurably softened. He still
refuses to give any medical care (recoils, in fact, "with
involuntary shuddering from any task which would confine him to the presence of this man," p. 278) and reiter-
ates his position that this maniac's "existence could not be
protracted, but to his own misery and the misery of others" (p. 279). If one wants Edny dead, who better to send
him to than Sarsefield?

Despite Huntly's protestations of innocent well-
meaning — which are authentic (he erred, as he says, "not
through sinister or malignant intentions, but from . . .
misguided . . . but powerful benevolence" [p. 290]) —

329

there is an unwholesome inevitability about the process that will not end until Edny has forced himself beneath the icy waters of the Narrows (p. 293). It is important to notice that he really does not will to die. When he goes overboard, he is making a break for freedom (his "seeming intention [is] to gain the shore"), but when he sees himself about to be overtaken by the rescue boat, the stark alternative of being thrown into a lunatic asylum by Sarsefield makes death instantly preferable.

It will be recalled that before Huntly walked back into his life, a fully recovered and functional Clithero Edny had been making it quite nicely on his own at Deb's hut; as a matter of fact, his former melancholia "seemed to have somewhat yielded to tranquillity" (p. 285). It is Huntly who deplores Edny's situation, Huntly who continues to insist "it was a distempered imagination both in him and me" that gave credence to "the groundless belief that he had occasioned the death of his benefactress" (ibid.). In short, the uncontrollable powers of identification have provoked Huntly's fateful intrusion. Clithero's indignant caveat ("come you hither . . . to recount my offences, and drive me again to despair?" p. 288) far from deterring Huntly, only quickens his resolve and makes it desperate. Identification had likewise prevented him from accepting the plain fact, of which Sarsefield had carefully apprised him, that Edny's "understanding" was not merely "deluded by phantoms in the mask of virtue and duty . . . [but was] utterly subverted" (p. 290). Resisting reality, Huntly, alas, was at the mercy of psychological necessity — a victim of his double-fixation. What will one not do for the suffering Self apart. That — given the push of a relentless sensibility — is what makes it all so sadly happen.

IV

Sleepwalking, a metaphor of both the duplication and loss of self, is the one spectacular manifestation of doubling deliberately skirted in the previous section, which because of its obviousness did not need to be explicated there per se. Each of the coordinates of the doubling process doubles himself, and there is little difficulty in tracing its consequences. (Actually, this has less bearing on the outcome of character relationships than those aspects just examined.) Rather, it makes more sense to try to determine what somnambulism meant to Brown for the purposes of his novel and to see how that works out in his use of it.

Brown's preoccupation with sleep disorders may have been occasioned by one of those pathological anomalies Smith kept sending his way (unless he was feeding an interest already aroused), for in November 1796, Smith obtained a copy of Benjamin Gooch's *Practical Treatise on Wounds and Other Chirurgical Subjects* (1767–1773) for the express purpose "of shewing Brown the History of the Sleepless Man of Madrid" (*Diary*, p. 267). Once something the least bit mysterious inhabited Brown's mind, it often took up residence for a while. Thus, toward the end of June 1798, with "Sky-Walk" well behind him and *Wieland* about three months in the works, he compiles a potpourri of bizarre "Queries,"[35] which range from differential calculus, planetary motions, and sun spots to the "variolous contagion" (smallpox), "intestinal motion," the utility of dead languages, and discouragement of the slave trade. But interspersed are questions as to whether his readers have witnessed "an instance of ventriloquism" or "the vagaries of a somnambulist." Surrounding these are questions as to whether "the mind [can] contemplate two ideas at the same time," and whether anyone has ever met two persons (presumably not twins) who are completely "undistinguishable from each other." The questions about sleep focus on what transpires on the other side of consciousness, our ambiguous mode of being there: "Is sleep the suspension of thought or only of memory?" (which

---

[35] *Weekly Magazine*, 2 (23 June 1798), 232–233. This is the piece mentioned in n.12, preceding.

intimates that we take on another form of existence); and "Is sleep a perfection or a defect in the human frame? — If the latter, is it curable?" (though universal, it is not unlike a diseased condition, an approximation of death even if considered ideal, a "perfection"). There likely was some behind-the-scenes talk about the matter between Brown and Smith, for a little over a week after the "Queries" appeared and shortly before Brown would be joining his New York friends, Smith, while visiting relatives in Connecticut, records the somnambulistic expedition of a cousin, who, slightly ill, "rose in sleep, put on only overalls & surtout & walked to his father's — which is 4½ miles distant." The cousin evidently knows he is a sleepwalker, but is unaware of what goes on when it is happening. "This will do for C. B. Brown," Smith writes (*Diary*, p. 454). Though curiosity about the secret powers (and disturbances) of the human psyche was not just a private thing with Brown and Smith, it is worth a guess that publication in the *Weekly Magazine*, almost concurrently with the "Queries," of pieces having to do with somnambulism, ventriloquism, and animal magnetism may well have been suggested — if not actually submitted — by a major contributor like Brown, author of the then featured serialization of *Arthur Mervyn*.[36]

"Somnambulism: A Fragment" is probably Brown's first extant treatment of the phenomenon. Developmentally, it falls somewhere between "Sky-Walk" and *Edgar Huntly*, and, though not published until 1805 when Brown placed it in his *Literary Magazine*, the idea that it may have been a discarded false start on *Edgar Huntly* — as

---

[36]"A Particular Account of a Singular Sleep-Walker," "An Instance of Ventriloquism," "Animal Magnetism" (*WM*, 2 [23 June, 30 June 1798], 250–253, 277–278, 278–281). The ventriloquism and somnambulism items are anecdotal bagatelles of no merit for our purposes beyond their subject, and the one on mesmerism is lifted directly from the *Britannica* (Third Edition, in its first American publication: *Encyclopaedia; or, A Dictionary of Arts, Sciences and Miscellaneous Literature* [Philadelphia: Thomas Dobson, 1798], X, 49–50).

Charles E. Bennett proposes — seems a good enough supposition regarding its status.[37] (The story assuredly could not have been reclaimed from "Sky-Walk," long gone at that point.)

As published, "Somnambulism" makes a self-contained short story — and a moderately good one, at that — told by its narrator, Althorpe, unaware of his somnambulism, which enhances its impact. Althorpe is distraught that urgent business requires the instant — nocturnal — departure of Mr. Davis and his betrothed daughter, Constantia. The youth is fruitlessly in love with her, and,

[37]*LM*, 3 (May, 1805), 335–347. Charles E. Bennett, "The Charles Brockden Brown Canon," Ph.D. diss., Univ. of North Carolina, 1974, p. 209.

While one cannot rule out the possibility that "Somnambulism" was a discarded — or leftover — portion of "Sky-Walk," we have no way of proving that it was, and there are altogether too great — and close — a set of parallels between it and *Edgar Huntly*:

1) Like the Davises of "Fragment," Waldegrave is urged to "postpone his ill-omened journey" (p. 7), and also like them, he brushes aside the narrator's entreaty and resolves to take his leave in the night.

2) As with Waldegrave, Constantia Davis is shot by the pistol of an unknown assassin and falls at the foot of a great oak (an elm in *EH*) set in the middle of a private road. In both, the murder seems totally without motive, and the murderer disappears.

3) The region where it happens, called Norwood in "Fragment" and Norwalk in *EH*, is near the home of Inglefield, who, both times, rushes out with his servants on hearing the shot and has the mortally wounded person taken to his home. In *EH*, Inglefield lives three miles from the narrator's uncle's house; in the story, the Davises are about three miles from the oak when they become aware of being followed.

4) Both narrators, Huntly and Althorpe, are somnambulists, and both are keenly devoted to the slain person.

For what it is worth chronologically, in terms of the proximity of "Somnambulism" to *Edgar Huntly* — in the *Wieland* notations, which probably postdate "Sky-Walk," Brown lists the name Davis next to "2 Dudley," the derivation perhaps of "Constantia." Below it are "Edny," "Wyatte," and "Inglefield," and above are "Lorimer-2" and "Alstrop" (p. 423). "Davis. Dudley" is later repeated on another list (p. 441). A Mr. and Mrs. Althorpe appear in *Arthur Mervyn*.

frustrated at losing the opportunity to advance his suit, he conjures up unseen dangers as a basis for detaining them. But his apprehensions are rejected, as is his offer to guard the Davises on their way. What he could not bring himself to do at the last minute—rush forth and overtake them en route—is accomplished in a dream, where his imagined peril quickly takes the form of an assailant, who, after killing Constantia, is hunted down and shot on the spot by Althorpe. Next day comes word of a shocking coincidence: Constantia had in truth been mysteriously shot at the foot of a familiar landmark, an ancient oak that grows in the middle of the road. It is learned that the Davises had sensed they were being trailed by a shadowy figure who flitted in and out of sight. At first, they assumed it to have been Althorpe—lovelorn—but were calmed on being told it was probably a rustic idiot who liked to roam the countryside and frighten people in the night. At what seems a rather hazardous part of the wood, the figure strangely vanishes. The travelers alight from their carriage, a scream panics the horses, in whose flight the carriage is dashed against the oak, and, as Mr. Davis returns to his daughter, realizing the folly of leaving her alone to seek the servant and horses, a pistol is fired at Constantia.

The key to the story occurs in its prologue, a purported "extract" from the *Vienna Gazette* of 14 June 1784. It tells of a young lady unaccountably shot dead in the road while on a night journey with her father. The perpetrator is found to be a habitual somnambulist much in love with her, who had been anxious about her safety and committed the murder while asleep, "entirely unknown to himself."[38] Unfortunately, this connection lies outside the

---

[38]This telltale phrase, the subtitle of "Sky-Walk," gives one pause. How, in the first place, would Brown have come upon a dispatch in this *Vienna Gazette* from the year 1784, a journal whose back numbers seem not to have been all that accessible? Also, why did he not indicate he was providing a translation of the "extract"—the *Gazette de*

story, though, clearly, the "extract" and title are not indispensible for us to guess that Althorpe's state of mind and pursuit make him a prime suspect. Althorpe points up another weakness of the story when he admits how "astonished" he and his uncle were at their "negligence" in not warning the Davises about Nick Handyside, the idiot prankster (p. 343).

At any rate, while we are left to ponder the bitter irony of the narrator's murdering the girl he loves unknown to himself, the mechanism of sleepwalking, together with its psychological ramifications, is relatively untouched. Brown takes the matter just far enough to show the tortured ego (technically the "id" in this case) attempting to compensate for its practical defeat. All things considered, the potential for horror is still considerable, however; for sleepwalking does more than just release the inner man. He *acts*, often dangerously. Also implied is the response of the pleasure-principle denied, the backlash of man's raw emotional nature. And these energies are not simply worked off passively in the wish-fulfillment of a dream. Nor is it bad certainly that Brown should leave it to us to deduce the volatility of the forces at play here. The point

---

Vienne having been published in French? Possibly Smith might have brought it to his attention, but who would have told *him* about it — some fourteen years after the event? Since the recent researches of a European scholar, Alfred Weber, have been unsuccessful in turning up a copy of the somnambulist item either in the *Gazette* or other journals of the time in which it might have been picked up ("Eine neu entdeckte Kurzgeschichte C. B. Browns," *Jahrbuch Für Amerikastudien*, 8 [1963], 280, n.2), one wonders if Brown may not have simply manufactured it, offering an obscure foreign source as a way of covering his tracks. It is, in fact, rather hard to resist the notion of a put-up job. For not only has it been impossible to turn up a single copy of the *Gazette* for the year 1784, but it is indeed questionable that it was not defunct by then. Weber's source has publication of the *Gazette de Vienne* running from 1757 to 1788, but reports nothing on hand for the year 1784. Moreover, a recent recheck of the card catalogue at the Öster-reichischen Nationalbibliothek discloses that it has holdings only for the years 1757 through 1763 and for 1769.

is he seems somewhat hesitant about exploiting them, in contrast to the way they are dealt with in *Huntly*. Only in the preparatory phase of the story do we get an indication of how the mind under stress plays tricks on itself, as Althorpe's self-induced fears, terrifying to him by their very indefiniteness, are transformed into hard reality. With notable insight he explains, "The strength of a belief, when it is destitute of any rational foundation, seems, of itself, to furnish a new ground for credulity" (p. 337).

If prior to *Edgar Huntly* Brown was not quite sure about what to make of sleepwalking, it might be well to ask where the subject stood with his contemporaries, as a base from which to appreciate how it would be employed in the novel.

V

First and foremost, somnambulism was universally considered a sign of infirmity, a disease centered in the nonvolitional (we would say autonomic) system, which, since it took possession of a person, mind and body, belonged in the twilight realm of dementia. As Erasmus Darwin quaintly put it, "no one in perfect sanity walks about in his sleep, . . . and in respect to the mind, we never exercise our reason or recollection in dreams." Sleep itself is an existential mystery (a semblance of death while the body yet lives), and we are subject to "rather marvellous occurrences . . . in this imperfect state."[39] Significant

---

[39] *Zoonomia; or The Laws of Organic Life* (London: J. Johnson, 1794), I, 199. Darwin's statement that "man in his sleeping state is a much less perfect animal" (ibid.) may have been the root of Brown's "A. Z." query as to whether sleep was "a perfection or defect in the human frame" (see p. 332, preceding).

There is, by the way, almost a duplication of Darwin's wording in Sarsefield's comment on the signs of Huntly's sleepwalking: "None but a man, insane or asleep, would wander forth so slightly dressed, and none but a sleeper would have disregarded my calls" (p. 249).

among marvels of the sub-rational dream life is its salu-
brious aspect, seen in the sleeper's necessary "expenditure
of sensorial power." In the language of eighteenth-century
mechanistic physiology, the Darwinian explanation has it
that if there were a blockage somehow of the carry-over of
sensation from our waking to our sleeping state (ordinarily a "perpetual flow"), with the return of wakefulness the
accumulated trains of sensation, unexpended in imaginary experience, would become confused with those
caused by real "irritation," so that a "delirium" might
potentially "supervene" (ibid., I, 200). In short, the ongo-

With regard to the rather uniform opinion on the status of somnambulism, among other sources making the same essential points
that Darwin does about "disease," some that Brown may have been
acquainted with would be: the article in Diderot's *Encyclopédie, ou
Dictionnaire Raisonné des Sciences* . . . (Geneve: Chez Pellet, 1778),
XXI, 393-397; the *Britannica* article, *Encyclopaedia; or, a Dictionary of
Arts, Sciences, and Miscellaneous Literature* . . . (Philadelphia: T. Dobson,
1798), XVII, 534-537; the entry in John Quincy's *Lexicon Physico-
Medicum*, 11th ed. (London: T. Longman, 1794), p. 611; and Benjamin Rush's "Inquiry Into the Cause of Animal Life," *Medical Inquiries and Observations*, 2d ed. (Philadelphia: J. Conrad & Co., 1805), II,
379-426 (1st ed., 1789-1793). That the ideas about sleep and sleepwalking represented in these writings were to hold sway for some time
we know from Robert MacNish's *The Philosophy of Sleep* (1830; rpt.
New York: D. Appleton & Co., 1834), pp. 145-161. More specific
reference to ideas expressed in the above will be forthcoming.

Among the popular—more nearly mediaeval—accounts of somnambulism, like that by one Erra Pater (*The Universal Interpreter of
Dreams and Visions* [Baltimore: George Keatinge, 1795], pp. 9-10, 12,
20), who deals in "corrupted humours" sending impure "vapours" to
the brain and attributes sleepwalking to an "abundance of blood
swelling, and as it were frothing out, boiling and active spirits" (pp. 6,
10), such activity is looked upon as bordering on the possessed. Apart
from all this, there was, of course, an entire subliterature that traf-
ficked in the strange doings of schizophrenic sleepwalkers like Cyrillo
Padovano, a man of no great learning who could somnambulistically
solve university exercises of extraordinary difficulty that were totally
beyond him when awake and who subsequently lapsed into unseemly
thievery on entering holy orders, climaxed by his plundering the
corpse of the convent benefactress of her jewels and finery ("The
History of Cyrillo Padovano, the noted Sleep Walker," *Massachusetts
Magazine*, 2 [1790], 48-50).

ing pseudosensation in slumber discharges a cathartic function for mental stability. This positive, "medical" analysis, emphasizing restorative action and a return to normalcy, has a bearing on Huntly's homeopathic entry into Edny's other consciousness—noted below (pp. 349-350), along with Darwin's conception of reverie and sleepwalking, states at once wondrous and diseased (Brown speaks of "most wonderful diseases," p. 3), in which we cease to be conscious of existence (I, 220), but without being sensorially incapacitated. (Brown would have agreed that such states "abound" with "instructive phenomena," I, 198.)

We know that Brown had had direct access to Darwin in 1798, probably at the instigation of Smith, who, having read *Zoonomia* toward the end of January, copied parts of it into his diary and made specific reference to two adjacent sections, "Catenation of Motions" and "Sleep" (*Diary*, p. 421). He had been corresponding with Brown at this time, and while there is a good chance he was pretty much in the dark about a recently completed draft of "Sky-Walk"—not the sort of event to go unnoticed had it been mentioned in a letter from Brown (contents not revealed) of 3 January (ibid., p. 413)—the thing he previously had going with Brown about sleep disorders would have been reason enough for him to recommend Darwin on sleep, particularly as his section on "Reverie" also dealt with somnambulism (I, 221-223). At any rate, Brown was sufficiently impressed not only to consult Darwin on his own, but to use his treatment of "Eratomania" (one of the "Diseases of Volition" subject to "maniacal hallucination," II, 363-365) as the basis for a "Man at Home" sketch in April[40] and not long thereafter to cite Darwin's discussion

[40]"The Man at Home," No. XII, *Weekly Magazine*, 1 (21 April 1798), 352-355. Taking up Darwin's paradoxical classification of love as one of the "diseases of volition," Brown first corrects this to a disease of the "understanding" and then embarks on a conundrum-like digression, half-facetiously giving the symptoms of an even more

of "Mania Mutabilis" (II, 356–359) as "explication" of
Wieland's illusional ailment (the "sights" and "sounds"
Wieland accepted as real had actually "originated in sudden madness"; "similar illusions," we are assured, being
by no means "rare"— *Wieland*, pp. 179, 177, 178).[41] Thus,
Edgar Huntly seems to mark at least the third time (possibly the fourth) that Brown would go to Erasmus Darwin
for a species of madness.

Perhaps the first thing to be said about somnambulism
as a manifestation of madness in *Edgar Huntly* is that the
connection is least perceptible to the person who makes
the frontal contact with it, Edgar himself—which is as it
should be for a basic naïf, unschooled in such matters,
who besides harbors an inclination toward the same problem. But, for all that, he is not a bad observer, being
acutely motivated thereto by the identical feeling of guilt

universal, though less recognizably morbid, "disease," in which our
thoughts are "full of deformity" (p. 353). He finally names it (unsur-
prisingly, sleep) and defines the relationship between it and love:
"they are equally deviations from the truth of things and the perfection of our nature." He ends by conceding it is only when carried to
excess that love becomes a "dangerous disease" and offers three cases
in which its outcome was derangement, in two of them followed by
death; e.g., a man whose betrothed marries someone else in his
absence causes him to blow his brains out. The conjunction of sleep
and love-sickness, especially the lunatic turn taken by the latter,
practically compels our consideration of a possible relationship with
"Somnambulism: A Fragment," so directly comparable in subject
matter (see pp. 332–336, preceding). Indeed, one is not a little tanta-
lized by the conjecture that "Man at Home" XII may have been a
prelude to "Somnambulism: A Fragment." (Support here for its place-
ment somewhat before *Edgar Huntly*, which would also strengthen
Bennett's argument for its possibly being a discarded start on the
novel—see p. 333.) Certainly, the two pieces link up rather nicely
through Darwin. (Among other things, Darwin noted that in its
extreme phase love-sickness commonly ended in suicide—as in
"Man"—or revenge—as in "Somnambulism," [II, 365].)

[41]In his "Advertisement" to *Wieland*, Brown's defense against skep-
tics is to suggest an "appeal to Physicians and to men conversant with
the latent springs and occasional perversions of the human mind"
(p. 3). Darwin, to be sure, would qualify.

339

he assumes to be troubling the sleepwalker. In fact, with Huntly reporting what he sees and what he thinks about it, we get objectivity (with an assist from contemporary theory) leaking through the subjectivity, and the disparities are informative.

In that initial scene where Huntly comes upon the half-naked figure digging a pit at the foot of the elm, mad as it may seem, the idea of derangement is not really uppermost in his mind. Indeed, he had had to fight off his own fear of being overcome by "the insanity of vengeance" (p. 7) and is somewhat taken aback to find his flimsy hypothesis realized that Waldegrave's murderer would return to the scene of his crime. During the three initial episodes of noctambulation,[42] Huntly keeps feeding his avid suspicion, determined he will have his man and relieve the "torment" (p. 6) that he has been remiss. Thus, to see Edny digging is to suppose a telltale "grave" and that "his purpose is to explore or hide" (a weapon, perhaps?). Then, as this fellow sits himself down in the pit to cry his heart out, Huntly's case is made. His discovery — somewhat slow in coming — that "this person was *asleep*" (p. 12) after all clinches it. He explains:

> The incapacity of sound sleep denotes a mind sorely wounded. It is thus that atrocious criminals denote the possession of some dreadful secret. The thoughts, which considerations of safety enables them to suppress or disguise during wakefulness, operate without impediment, and exhibit their genuine effects, when the notices of sense are partly excluded, and they are shut out from a knowledge of their intire condition. (p. 13)

Now that Huntly ventures to *interpret* the incident, we are invited to ask: how close is he? If one checks him out,

[42]As our textual note indicates, Brown twice has Huntly erroneously count them as two, as if he were already becoming unnerved by these expeditions (see pp. 452–453).

close enough, it would seem—at least according to the two sources we can believe Brown most probably consulted, the *Britannica* article and Darwin. The *Britannica* writer, using the influential "Transactions" (mainly, case histories) compiled by the Physical Society of Lausanne (authorities also cited by Darwin), stresses that while the sleepwalker does respond to stimuli that had affected him while awake,[43] his actions, as such, are based on totally imaginary data—internalized experience—which bear no necessary relationship to his waking perceptions. Experiments show that objects the sleepwalker deals with are imprinted on his imagination in so lively a fashion that he behaves as if they were physically perceived (p. 536). Thus, the imagination—as opposed to sensory reality—is the controlling force throughout; in fact—bearing in mind Edny's almost nightly replication—one takes note that the imagination is said to be capable of renewing its impressions "with as much force as if they were again acquired by means of the sense" (p. 534). In other words, Clithero Edny may be acting out his guilt, but he is doing so in the terms that his imagination conceives—and dictates—not those of what may actually have taken place to so stimulate him, and certainly not in conformity with Huntly's interpolation. So far the pieces fit, and reinforce Brown's bilevel focus. Also on target in pointing to the imaginary base of Edny's activity and the inner depths from which it springs are Huntly's assertions that his "employment" is part of "some fantastic drama in which his mind was busy" and that "to comprehend it, demands penetration into the recesses of his soul" (p. 14). Discounting for the moment Huntly's posture as Clithero's Chillingsworth, with regard to *comprehension*, what Huntly

[43]In some cases—though it is not the rule—the powers of suggestion can be so great for the sleepwalker (who usually has a very delicate nervous system to begin with) that a tale told the night before may become the substance of his "fit." However, in the instance cited, this theory could not be affirmed, as the patient had a predisposition to dream about the subject of the tale anyway—i.e., robbers (p. 535).

doesn't quite understand is the very real inscrutability of Edny's illness (modern research still has not satisfactorily located its etiology[44]); rather quick to oversimplify, he is confident he can get at the cause and in doing so cure the patient—with, as we have seen, crushing results.

There is much else Huntly fails to grasp. For instance, the point Darwin comes down very strongly on is the complete detachment of the somnambulist: the catenation of ideas which occurs to the sleepwalker and makes him act as he does is subject neither to "irritation" from without nor "recollection," the individual being suspended in a state of intense "reverie." As Darwin defines the condition: "those persons who are said to walk in their sleep,

[44]This according to one of the leading present-day sleep researchers, William C. Dement; see his *Some Must Watch While Some Must Sleep* (New York: W. W. Norton & Co., 1972), p. 79. Others who come to the same general conclusion are Edward J. Murray, *Sleep, Dreams, and Arousal* (New York: Appleton-Century-Crofts, 1965), pp. 274–277; and Rosalind Dymond Cartwright, *A Primer on Sleep and Dreaming* (Reading, Mass.: Addison-Wesley Publishing Co., 1978), p. 119.

Modern sleep researchers, by the way, depart from the eighteenth- and nineteenth-century formulations in several major areas. For example, 1) they rule out the theory that in somnambulism one acts out a dream (it takes place at the deepest stage of sleep, while dreams occur at a shallower level); and 2) they downplay the disease factor (it is confined mostly to young children, who usually outgrow it), save for its extreme form involving convulsions, these generally being symptoms of the far more serious psychomotor epilepsy—something also described by Darwin (I, 223, 225; Dement, pp. 26–28, 79; Cartwright, pp. 117–121).

Interestingly, however, certain contemporary analysts offer the same sort of psychological explanation that Brown gives concerning the removal in sleep of inhibitions on socially unacceptable feelings suppressed during wakefulness. Dement, for example, cites Dr. Roger Broughton's views to this effect: "the episodes [of sleepwalking] may represent the expression of emotional conflicts that are allowed to occur because some psychic barrier is lowered in sleep." But, emphasizing the continued uncertainty about *cause*, Broughton also acknowledges that attacks of sleepwalking "may be caused by some purely physiological abnormality that arises in a 'psychological void'" (p. 79).

are affected with reverie to so great a degree, that it becomes a formidable disease; the essence of which consists in the inaptitude of the mind to attend to external stimuli" (I, 221). Hence, if he is disconnected from recollection and all external stimuli, it is hard to say that Edny's actions are *rationally* joined to what has gone before.[45] Moreover, in making such a connection, Huntly would have him going back over his trauma, but as Darwin observes about reverie, that state consists of "an effort of the mind to relieve some painful sensation" (I, 226). Even sleep becomes "imperfect" when our sensations excite "aversions" (I, 208); we run *from* not *toward* what is painful. The reason for our distraction in reverie is that we are absorbed with a "great sensation of pleasure . . . or in the pursuit of some interesting train of ideas" (I, 220). Manifestly, what we see with Edny is a man trying pathetically to run from his pain and being unsuccessful at it; therefore, the vehement sobs, the burying himself in caves, and desire for self-immolation. Furthermore, despite Huntly's making himself known to Edny, he is quite wrong to assume that Edny is consciously aware of his presence, and is specifically reacting to it, when, for example, he begins to cover up the pit as if "desirous of hiding something from [Huntly's] inspection" (p. 11). He does react to Huntly's calling out to him, but only as something happening within his own medium; so Huntly accurately reports: "Where I stood I could not fail of being seen, and yet he acted as if he saw nothing" (ibid.). And again, after the ritualistic filling of the pit, followed by another spate of weeping — impossible if Huntly had registered upon Edny in the way *he* thought he did — we are told: "He passed me . . . without appearing to notice my existence" (p. 12). All of this is quite consistent with the absorption syndrome of reverie, in which, as Darwin has

[45]One part of the complex unanimously recognized by all, including Huntly (from personal experience), is that the somnambulist has absolute amnesia regarding his seizures.

343

it, we are "inattentive to time and place, and do not distinguish [our internal] train of sensitive and voluntary ideas from the irritative ones excited by the presence of external objects" (I, 220).

In the Lausanne "Transactions," it is said that objects may strike the somnambulist's sight without being recorded in his mind, that he probably fixates what is already sketched in his imagination (op. cit., p. 535). Given these circumstances, an Edny would—as was also thought—be engaged in a motor dream (p. 534), and Huntly's appearance would merely have been something to be assimilated into it. Ironic by their irrelevance are Huntly's alternating perceptions: although he makes a racket charging behind Edny through the thicket, Huntly at first thinks he "regarded it not," and immediately thereafter is convinced that Edny knows he is being followed and prolongs the journey "in order to fatigue or elude his pursuer" (pp. 18-19).

Such, then, was the sort of background available to Brown from his reading; not so, of course, Huntly, whose conduct constitutes a different side of the picture and conforms to yet other determinations, which broaden the overall Gestalt, and invite certain complications. Obviously, the question to begin with is if the *one* sleepwalker is pronounced mad, how can we tell that the *other* is not? To say that we can't may be a glib answer. But Edgar Huntly has been so roundly maligned in previous sections of this essay—and in recent criticism at large—that it should make little difference if one adds madness to the rest of his sins: his blundering, ignorance, narcissism, misconceptions, and, finally, his miserable failure as benefactor— the one thing he wanted most to be successful at. Yet, one has to concede, it seems equally plain that Brown did not want Huntly to be taken as an utter madman. He may find his double in Edny, but that does not make *him* an Edny. Or, put another way, just because madness erupts into sleepwalking does not mean it works the other way around.[46] Maddened, yes, with the panther and the Indians, but those are life-threatening situations, not exactly the norm for Huntly.

Where, then, does this leave us with regard to the sleepwalking? To some extent, it is explained by Huntly's sense of guilt, even by contagion, given his susceptible nature; in either case, however, it is surely the price he pays for an inordinate sensitivity expended on behalf of unmerited suffering. However poorly his conduct may reflect upon the Enlightenment's championing of Progress through Reason and Civilization, Huntly is insistent that benevolence must persevere — and so prevail (p. 111). He represents the Zeitgeist in its most flattering self-image and would frankly be judged by its good intentions, towards which Brown himself was not always ambivalent. When, at the time *Edgar Huntly* was being written, the reviewer of the *Britannica* for the second issue of Brown's *Monthly Magazine* (if not the editor personally, at least the reflector of his public voice)[47] praises the encyclopedia for helping the reader "to survey the history of the human

[46]Nor does Huntly necessarily become an exception to the thesis of disease, which operates so well with Edny. Clearly, though the disease, being mental, may be madness, it may also be something less, so that the difference between Edny and Huntly would roughly be that between a psychotic and a neurotic, the latter being socially functional. John Quincy, noting that the Scottish physician, Dr. William Cullen, places "Oneirodynia" (troubled sleep which includes somnambulism and incubus) "in the class [of] *Neuroses*, and order *Vesaniae*," seems to allow for gradations: Vesaniae he defines as "diseases attended with alienation of the mind, *or* a defect of the judgment" (italics added), *Lexicon Physico-Medicum*, pp. 611, 815.

[47]One thinks Brown may well have been the reviewer, for regardless of how "irksome" it might have become, he intimated that he had to do a goodly share of the reviewing in the magazines he edited. He said that on some occasions he contributed almost all of the "original prose" as well (letters to John Blair Linn, 8 July 1802 and 4 July 1804 in David Lee Clark, *Charles Brockden Brown: Pioneer Voice of America* [Durham, N.C.: Duke Univ. Press, 1952], p. 215; and Dunlap, *Life*, II, 111).

mind in its progress from rudeness to refinement, and to teach him to anticipate the glorious destiny which awaits the full development and exertion of intellectual energy in a more enlightened age" (1 [May, 1799], 135)—"There," one says, in unshocked recognition, "spoke the Age": eternally sanguine, self-congratulatory, and smugly assured of its perfectabilian vision. Whatever of this spirit rubs off on Huntly can be counted as a negative, though that does not cancel the man's inclination to decency. In spite of the rhetoric — painful to *us* — we can scarcely ignore its meaning for the times. For liberal Philadelphians like Benjamin Rush, the power of sympathy (Huntly's forte) was appreciable. Regarded as the most cogent moral agent in the human arsenal, it was the "vicegerent of . . . divine benevolence in our world," and thereby "intended to bind up all the wounds which sin and death have made among mankind."[48] Certain to be exalted by their peers, the Huntlys of Rush's world lived by this credo.

[48]*Essays, Literary, Moral and Philosophical*, 2d ed. (Philadelphia: Thos. & Wm. Bradford, 1806), p. 142 (1st ed., 1798). Also tuned in to cultist sensibility (making him Huntly's literary brother) was Brown's Man at Home, who, as prefix to an account of atrocities perpetrated in one of the "ancient republics," observed, "I have heard of men who, though free themselves from any uncommon distress, were driven to suicide by reflecting on the misery of others" (*Weekly Magazine*, 1 [14 April 1798], 320).

It is important to note that by taking the other view of rationalism in his use of the double and particularly by his instancing the positive outcome of somnambulism, Brown runs directly counter to the basic Lockean and Hartleyan stance, which categorically disallows any idea of an other, subconscious existence, like that evidenced by dreams and sleepwalking. Hartley dismisses the content of dreams as being wild and inconsistent, and having no connection with "Nature"; and the amnesia of sleepwalkers suggests their activity is comparable to that of persons who read inattentively (*Observations on Man*, [London: S. Richardson, 1749], I, 385–387). For Locke, it is an empirical absurdity to suppose that man has a double identity, that, while the body sleeps, his soul can "have its Thinking, Enjoyments, and Concerns, its Pleasure or Pain apart, which the Man is not conscious of. . . ." For the soul to be able to think without retention of its

On the issue of how such virtue was to be converted into "an eloquent narration," its embodiment made fictionally viable as character, Brown would adduce, shortly after finishing *Edgar Huntly*, the simple formula expressed by his didactic "Walstein" of "exhibiting a virtuous being in opposite conditions"[49] (shades of *Caleb Williams*). A start perhaps, but that was theory. As it got worked out for Huntly, the problem Brown actually assigns his protagonist has the more Hawthornian twist that "we go all wrong, by too strenuous a resolution to go all right." When, as Hawthorne pursues the matter, we are required to become part "of a complicated scheme of progress, [this] can only result in our arrival at a colder and drearier region than we were born in."[50] In the events which precipitate and follow on Huntly's sleepwalking, Brown proposes that we look at goodness in a state of nature. The experience of which Young Goodman Huntly's adventures in the strange wood are compounded is that evil can come out of good, and good out of evil.

Evil out of good has received sufficient coverage and need not be further rehearsed. Quite as meaningful is the good evolved out of evil—i.e., what have been the *rewards* of Huntly's bout with sleepwalking? Regarding this point, one of the central ideas in the "philosophic" literature on somnambulism (that based on observation) is that, illness notwithstanding, it takes us beyond our normal capacities; we outperform our waking selves. Something there is about sleepwalking which enables us to accomplish wonders, to do things sometimes with greater intelligence and exactitude than is otherwise possible to us. This, we are

thoughts is to render it much like "a Looking-glass, which constantly receives variety of Images, or *Ideas*, but retains none. . . ." (*An Essay Concerning Human Understanding*, ed. Peter H. Nidditch [Oxford: Oxford Univ. Press, 1975], pp. 110, 112).

[49]"Walstein's School of History," *Monthly Magazine*, 1 (September, 1799), 408; (August, 1799), 337.

[50]*The Marble Faun: or, The Romance of Monte Beni*, ed. William Charvat et al. (Columbus, Ohio: Ohio State Univ. Press, 1968), p. 239.

told, distinctly challenges those who cannot believe nature is full of impenetrable mysteries. At the extremity of such effort, the sleepwalker takes on the impossible. He will rush into self-endangering actions, maybe even kill himself.[51] Much of this, Huntly amply verifies. From the moment he somnambulates into the cave pit, it is more than a wonder he doesn't get himself killed several times over. But, speaking of the impossible, Sarsefield sees him recalled from the dead—twice (p. 242)—little knowing *how many* times his life had nearly been lost, once from bullets of the party Sarsefield was leading in search of him (p. 222). At various points, his "toils . . . appeared . . . less easy to be borne again than death" (p. 216). Nonetheless, as Huntly appraises what he has been through, he calls it a progress "from uncertainty to knowledge" (p. 6), meaning more, obviously, than the discovery of Waldegrave's murderer.

Since it is not possible for the subject himself to report anything that occurs *while* he is sleepwalking, Brown mainly has him disclose the feelings of transcendence afterwards. But, interestingly, he has him doing so beforehand as well. Huntly is so compulsive to be sympa-

---

[51]"Somnambule, & Somnambulisme," *Encyclopedie*, XXXI, 393–397. Examples are given of sleepwalkers who recklessly run through the streets, swim, or walk along the edge of rooftops without fear (p.393). Those who display intellectual achievement are said to have written sermons (accurately corrected) with their eyes closed and musical compositions (pp. 393–394). Images of the precipice and abyss are common—like those which occur in the rambles of Edny and Huntly.

Recitation of the marvels and dangers that happen in sleepwalking are by no means confined to late eighteenth-century accounts. Modern investigators allude to instances of sleepwalkers who have written novels and recited Homer in the original Greek (the latter in the case of an illiterate servant girl), and others who would stride across narrowly separated walls, do their shopping, or commit unintentional murders. J. Kaplan, "Sleepwalking: Fact, Fallacy, or Fancy?" *Today's Health*, 38 (September, 1960), 55. Gay Gaer Luce and Julius Segal, *Sleep* (New York: Coward-McCann Inc., 1966), p. 134.

thetic, so avid to project himself into Edny's condition (immersed as he is in the autoscopic chase), that, feeling himself practically there, he says, "I plunged into obscurities, and clambered over obstacles, from which, in a different state of mind, . . . I should have recoiled with invincible timidity" (p. 23). Everything necessary for Edny's salvation is done at the same fever pitch, to which the neck-breaking terrain of deepest Norwalk is no deterrent. Time and again, Huntly's nervous "perseverence surmounted every impediment" (p. 108). But the most persistent of the impossibilities Huntly tasks himself with, and the one most vital to him—and the novel—is, of course, Edny's rehabilitation.

Mindful perhaps of how the man had scorned his initial effort to impart "consolation" (the "effects" of that "misguided zeal," were acidly declared to have merely "put the seal to [Edny's] perdition," p. 36), Huntly realizes that normal procedures will likely prove futile in such a case, that the opposing effect of reason will probably not suffice to flush out so "inveterate" (p. 110) an emotional defect. So, Huntly significantly decides on a homeopathic therapy.[52] Deliberately casting aside the "antidote" of "reason," Huntly opts to treat a "phrensy" (p. 95) that resulted from an excess of sensibility by offering a treatment cognate with the agent that caused the disease: he wants "to set by

[52]The concept of homeopathic cure was just being developed in the 1790s. Dr. Samuel Hahnemann (1755–1843), its innovator, had published his first essay on the subject in 1796 ("Versuch über ein neues Prinzip zur Auffindung der Heilkräfte der Arzneisubstanzen"), but we have no evidence Brown was acquainted with it. Nor need he have been, any more than Huntly has to be aware that there was a medical hypothesis behind what he was trying out purely on the basis of instinct and common sense. For the record, however, Hahnemann inveighed against the prevailing practice, *contraria contrariis* (the invariable purging and blood-letting), and argued for *similia similibus*: "*In order to cure diseases, we must search for medicines that can excite a similar disease in the human body.*" See Martin Gumpert, *Hahnemann: The Adventurous Career of a Medical Rebel* (New York: L. B. Fischer, 1945), pp. 86–99.

[Edny] in silence, to moisten his hand with tears, to sigh in unison, to offer him the spectacle of sympathy . . ." (p. 106). Fortunately, Huntly thinks better of the enterprise and instead leaves some food beside the exhausted sleeper, an act which he rightly intuits will be taken as a sign of anguish for Edny's well-being—possibly intervention from above—and have a better chance of accomplishing his purpose.[53] At the end, he learns that his strategem has worked, albeit indirectly. A thankful Edny wants him to know "thy efforts for my benefit were not useless. They have saved me from murdering myself . . ." (p. 270).

Would that Huntly had left well enough alone. But, then, he could not know how mistaken he was in thinking Edny was curable, particularly since he had not only recovered from his own sleepwalking, but had stoutly endured its consequences and emerged from the wilderness a new man. Whether or not there was a homeopathic side effect to Huntly's sleepwalking—the imbalancing guilt which immediately instigated it seems also to have been dissipated by it—one of the most sensational applications of somnambulism in Brown's time was its use by Mesmer and his disciples (Puységur, in particular) specifically to cure illnesses. Briefly, Mesmer postulated that just as there were magnetic fields in nature ("mineral magnetism"), so too was there an invisible "fluid" surrounding the human body (like gravity, the emanation from one universal *fluidium*), and obstruction of the flow between its magnetic poles was the ultimate cause of sickness. The way to effect a cure was simply to reestablish the harmonious flow of one's magnetic current, which was usually done by the doctor's moving an iron rod around

[53]Brown goes Darwin one better in proposing a wholly psychological approach to treating the sleepwalker's ills, and in matching distress with distress. In addition to wine, opium, and warm baths, Darwin had urged "exciting the sensitive ideas by good news, affecting stories, or agreeable passions" (I, 440).

the patient's head or affected part, taking note of the direction of the poles and at times possibly massaging them.[54] The breakthrough would come when a "crisis" was induced, which threw the patient into convulsions resembling an epileptic fit or somnambulistic trance, and this was viewed as the secret catalyst in the healing process.

The apex of Mesmer's career spanned six luminous years, from his arrival in Paris in 1778, after rejection in Berlin and Vienna, to 1784 when Louis XVI appointed an investigative commission (whose membership included Lavoisier and Franklin), which would find his practices fraudulent. Surrounded by controversy from the beginning, Mesmer got himself launched through a magnetic restoration of vision for the near-blind son of a prominent banker, and though his disreputable healing methods were frowned upon by the medical/scientific community, he became one of the most talked about men of his age, counted an entire coterie of aristocrats among his advocates, was discussed in the academies, press, salons, and cafes, patronized by the queen, investigated by the police, ridiculed on the stage, burlesqued in popular songs and cartoons, and saw his tubs ("baquets" he called them) hawked in the street. Despite all the clamor, he managed to cultivate a fairly respectable following that furthered his work—lay promoters like Bergasse and independent fellow researchers like Deslon, Puységur, Deleuze, and the Abbé Faria. Chief among his popular adherents and the person most responsible for bringing animal magnetism to the attention of Americans was Lafayette, a member of the mesmerists' Order of Har-

[54]This was but one of several techniques, another of them being a rather social affair, in which patients were grouped around a wooden tub equipped with iron rods and were corded together while the doctor applied the rods to appropriate places and soft piano music in the background abetted the magnetism that streamed through everyone from the conducting tub. Helmut Hirsch, "Mesmerism and Revolutionary America," *The American-German Review*, 10 (October, 1943), 11. Hirsch provides a drawing of the tub treatment.

mony, who not only was made privy to Mesmer's secrets, but also successfully employed them on a ship-boy during his voyage to America in 1784, contacted Washington about the new medicine, lectured to the American Philosophical Society on the subject, and hypnotized a Shaker, whose sect he believed essentially utilized mesmeric principles by its "laying on of hands" for healing.[55]

Brown could not easily have avoided knowing about animal magnetism. The article on it in the *Britannica* which he likely reviewed was printed in the *Weekly Magazine* at a time when he was a major contributor to the journal (2 [30 June 1798], 278–281), and a farce by that name was also regularly performed in New York, Philadelphia, Boston, and Baltimore during the 1790s, notice of which was taken by Brown's good friend, William Dunlap, in 1797 and 1798 (Dunlap, *Diary*, I, 162, 264). But Brown would likewise have known that the royal commission had discredited mesmerism, that Jefferson heartily denounced it, and that, in spite of its former support in high circles, it was commonly regarded as a form of quackery, being so represented in the play. On the other hand, the one strand of mesmeric treatment that seems to have been making headway even after the com-

---

[55]Some works that may be fruitfully consulted for the details of Mesmer's activities, the history of his movement, and subsequent developments in mesmerism are: Christian Bäumler, *Der Sogenannte Animalische Magnetismus oder Hypnotismus* (Leipzig: F. C. W. Vogel, 1881); Alfred P. Sinnett, *The Rationale of Mesmerism* (Boston: Houghton, Mifflin and Co., 1892); Stefan Zweig, *Mental Healers: Franz Anton Mesmer, Mary Baker Eddy, Sigmund Freud,* tr. Eden and Cedar Paul (London: Cassell and Co., 1933); Margaret L. Goldsmith, *Franz Anton Mesmer: A History of Mesmerism* (Garden City, N.Y.: Doubleday, Doran & Co., 1934); Robert W. Marks, *The Story of Hypnotism* (New York: Prentice-Hall, 1947); Robert Darnton, *Mesmerism and the End of the Enlightenment in France* (Cambridge, Mass.: Harvard Univ. Press, 1968); Maurice M. Tinterow, *Foundations of Hypnosis, From Mesmer to Freud* (Springfield, Ill.: C. C. Thomas, 1970); Ernst Benz, *Franz Anton Mesmer (1734–1815) und seine Ausstrahlung in Europa und Amerika* (Wiesbaden: Steiner, 1977).

mission's report, and which came to the fore again when serious interest in animal magnetism would be revived in the 1830s, was that pursued by A. M. J. de Chastenet Marquis de Puységur, who relied principally on somnambulism to bring on the "crises" by which cures were accomplished.

Though we cannot ascertain that Brown was familiar with Puységur's methods, the resemblance between them and aspects of the somnambulism used in *Edgar Huntly* are too suggestive to be ignored.[56] In 1784 Puységur published a record of over seventy patients with a variety of diseases whom he had cured through "magnetic somnambulism," and two years later he came out with a book containing rather detailed case histories and an indication of his procedure. He would use as "doctor" ("medecine") a person with an appropriately suggestible nature and place him in a magnetic sleep ("sommeil magnétique"), making him the intermediary whose powers of empathy established inner communication with a patient so as to diagnose and cure his illness. At first, it was believed that the somnambulist could only produce the cures by sympathetically taking on the disease himself, but Puységur deduced that the symptoms were actually just the associative sensations necessary for the somnambulist to do his job. One of the mystical attributes of the "sommeil

[56]Even if the connection were wholly accidental — and we have no way of knowing that it was, or wasn't — Brown and Puységur seem to have been in touch with similar ideas about a psychosomatic approach to the treatment of illness.

And, on this score, Brown would very likely have known the sort of respect that Rush had for mesmerism. Although he had to "reject the futile pretensions of Mr. Mesmer to the cure of diseases, by . . . animal magnetism," Rush was perfectly willing to accept the efficacy of the psychosomatic principles on which he operated: "The facts which [Mesmer] has established, clearly prove the influence of the imagination, and will, upon diseases. Let us avail ourselves of the handle which those powers of the mind present to us, in the strife between life and death" (*Medical Inquiries and Observations*, 2d American ed. [Philadelphia: Thomas Dobson, 1794], I, 324).

magnétique" was the gift of "clairvoyance," that superior vision necessary to, as it were, see into another person's being and comprehend his ailment.[57] It is at this point that the somnambulistic cure becomes joined to the prevailing eighteenth-century doctrine of benevolence so much insisted on by a figure like Edgar Huntly. As Puységur's disciple J. P. F. Deleuze put it in his book on mesmerism, dedicated to his master (without whom, he said, "magnetism would have been forgotten after Mesmer"):

> In order to have a somnambulist judge correctly the state of a disease, he must in some sort identify himself with the patient. For, the motive which determines him to identify himself with a suffering being, can be no other than the sentiment of pity, or the love of good. It supposes a forgetfulness of one's self, and personal interest must necessarily alter its purity.[58]

One need not place Edgar Huntly's exposure to somnambulism on anything like a mesmeric footing to appreciate its affinities with the teachings of a Puységur. He would be the selfless doctor of Edny's wounded soul, and, though he is no technician, he is well enough versed in the tradition of sympathy to know what kind of faculty he has at his disposal. However else one sees it, what other than the motive of sympathetic healing, the urge while under the curative spell to find his subject, would specifically send him sleepwalking to Edny's cave, and to no other

---

[57] *Rapport des Cures Opérées à Bayonne par le Magnétisme Animal* (Bayonne: Prault, 1784); *Mémoires pour servir a l'Histoire et a l'Établissement du Magnétisme Animal* (Londres: n.p., 1786), pp. 122–124, 336, 399.

[58] *Practical Instruction in Animal Magnetism*, tr. Thomas C. Hartshorn, 2d ed. (Providence, R.I.: B. Cranston & Co., 1837), p. 205. (Original French publication in 1825 [Paris: J. G. Dentu].) Deleuze had directly observed Puységur administering cures in 1787—which, by coincidence, is the date of the action of *Edgar Huntly*.

place?[59] (Having earlier come out of the other end of the cave, where he distinguished Edny seated among the rocks in the chasm below, Huntly remarks, "no motives were imaginable by which others could be prompted to explore this road" [p. 104]—i.e., the route that took him through the cave into which Edny had first disappeared.) Already convinced that mere "words were impotent, and arguments . . . nugatory" (p. 106)—medication was never in the picture—Huntly is the beneficent intermediary bent on alleviation by "the efficacy of [his] presence" (p. 138); he totally identifies with the patient, though not himself possessed of the disease he is trying to cure, which, of course, is not sleepwalking but its cause.

A long shot at best, his mission aborts in impenetrable darkness, and he comes to with the sensation that he exists in a "wakeful dream" (p. 161). But, fortunately, there is carry-over. The spell being broken, Huntly must see to his own "deliverance" (p. 162)[60]—upon which, if sleepwalking is inherently rehabilitative, that property may be assumed to have some residual impact. At least, such was the thinking of those who studied it. In fact, as animal magnetism began to gain credibility in France, a committee of the Royal Academy of Sciences looked into what was being done with it, and—unlike the commission of 1784—determined that persons in whom somnambul-

---

[59]A word of clarification. Although I have cited guilt as the *provocation* of Huntly's somnambulism, that Edny should become the *objective* of it merely instances the transference of guilt regarding Waldegrave to a comparable feeling stirred by the need of getting to poor Edny. A sense of partial responsibility for the one man's death becomes a basis for his wanting to make sure he prevents the death of the other.

[60]It is really just as well he did not reach Edny, considering that even a trained mesmerist would probably have had limited success with a psychotic, particularly as Mesmer and company concentrated mainly on physical defects. Deleuze, however, felt the magnetist should persist even with those somnambulists who—like Edny— "seem to set little value upon their cure" and think they will be better off dead (p. 76).

ism had been induced acquired a wholly new consciousness (MacNish, p. 158). (Simply put: one gets better, or,
depending, better than one was.) A man whose "constitution [was] by no means distinguished for its force" (p.
139), Huntly did indeed draw upon some such new
consciousness — that is, its effect — for survival. Deleuze,
for example, found that the sleepwalker has naturally
aroused in him "a sort of instinct, which enlightens him in
respect to his own preservation" (p. 56) — and, as has been
indicated, the literature on the subject was full of death-
defying exploits.[61] Speaking of the "transition" he had
"undergone" in defending himself against the Indians (for
him something totally "wild and inexplicable"), Huntly
seems to tie it in with his new consciousness, directly
traceable to the aftermath of his sleepwalking. He says:
"all that I had performed; all that I had witnessed since
my egress from the pit, were so contradictory to precedent
events, that I still clung to the belief that my thoughts
were confused by delirium" (p. 194). In any case, we have
to suppose a certain extra dimension beyond the push of
terror which would produce Huntly's euphoric sense of
rebirth after all the "vicissitudes of peril" he had withstood, so that, Jonah-like, he could report:

> The miracles of poetry, the transitions of enchant-
> ment, are beggarly and mean compared with those
> which I had experienced: Passage into new forms,
> overleaping the bars of time and space, reversal of
> the laws of inanimate and intelligent existence had
> been mine to perform and to witness. (p. 239)

[61]See pp. 347–348 preceding. Deleuze's method is more appropriate
for Huntly, since, unlike Puységur, he worked directly with the
affected person, putting him into a somnambulistic state. He held
that in addition to its displaying "surprising penetration," and making
known "the means of curing diseases," somnambulism in itself gives
one "faculties and means of knowledge which we [ordinary mortals]
have not." A sensibility is instilled in the sleepwalker, the "develope-
ment [sic] . . . of which we can have no conception" (pp. 65, 57, 58,
67).

We have, to be sure, followed his passage into a new form, his transition having at times been marked by baptismal "raptures" (p. 180). Historically, the cave has been an archetypal symbol of the return to the womb, a death to the old self and trust that one will be born again better able to cope with the fears that sent one there.[62] But it is especially in the means, the *reversal* of the presumed "laws of inanimate and intelligent existence," that one suspects the presence of something very much akin to the latent mysteries which mesmerists of Brown's time were uncovering in the therapeutic miracles of somnambulism — feats quite unexplainable by the received laws of existence. As Brown let us know, he hoped that his gothic effects (best when dimly understood) would be taken as having a basis in nature; instead of using "Gothic castles and chimeras," he wished to engage "the sympathy of the reader, by means hitherto unemployed by preceding authors" (p. 3). Why not the latest in contemporary medicine?

VI

What the Negro was to Benito Cereno, the Indian was to Edgar Huntly. "Most men are haunted by some species of terror or antipathy," Huntly declares, "which they are . . . able to trace to some incident which befel them in

[62]See, e.g., Carl Gustav Jung, *Psychology of the Unconscious*, tr. Beatrice M. Hinkle (New York: Moffat, Yard and Co., 1916), p. 245. In analyzing various of the mother and rebirth mythologies, Jung observes concerning man's ultimate arrival at the Styx (for his night sea journey): "The wish is that the black water of death might be the water of life; that death, with its cold embrace, might be the mother's womb, just as the sea devours the sun, but brings it forth again out of the maternal womb (Jonah motive)" (ibid.). He notes that the word "gulf" is derived from the Greek *kolpos*, meaning "bosom," "womb," "mother-womb," or "vagina" (p. 305). Moreover, the tomb (Huntly on awakening in the pit felt as if he had been buried alive, p. 162) represents "restitution to the mother," with the hope of rebirth, "by which such burial is rightfully rewarded" (p. 407).

their early years." *He* is Indian-haunted. The fact that his home was "assailed" in "the dead of night" by eight such "assassins" who murdered his parents and infant sibling "in their beds," "pillaged" the house and "burnt [it] to the ground" has produced "lasting and terrific images in [his] fancy" (p. 173). Petrified merely at the sight of Indians (never mind that they be innocently asleep, intentions unknown), Huntly is certain their presence alone means that "pacific" neighboring settlers are in danger of "the most horrid and irreparable devastation," that, in fact, these "implacable foes" will bring on an "exterminating war" (pp. 174, 173). So heated is his anxiety, one may wonder if he is not getting ahead of himself.[63] Yes, they have rifles, but had he not learned the folly of going unarmed into a trackless woodland inhabited by cougars and rattlesnakes? Nor has it been established whether these are resident Indians, and thus harmless, or "wanderers and robbers" (p. 171). He was aware of prior hostilities, yet he knew as well that because of "a long course of injuries and encroachments," the Indians had reason to fear the white man and were justifiably "exasperated" (p. 173).

Partly, the psychological moment is all wrong for Huntly. Here he is crawling out of the Plutonian depths — a phenomenal deliverance — in no shape to meet Indians, and yet he must brace himself to do battle with five of them. Miraculously, he has just saved his life — that, too, doubly (from entombment and the cougar); he

[63]Indeed, he thinks the Indians he sees at the cave mouth may well be the ones who had orphaned him and his sisters (p. 178), whereas he had just finished telling us that *that* band had been pursued, "overtaken and killed" (p. 173)! Unless Brown was simply contradicting himself (as he could have been), or betraying a private bias (equally possible), he would be showing how demoralized Huntly had become under the stress of his situation. We get some evidence for the latter on the basis that when Huntly discovers these Indians are in possession of his rifle, left at his uncle's house (meaning his uncle and sisters would have been killed), he has aroused in him "the misguided fury of a maniac" (p. 185).

is about to exit the devouring cave, nearly "disabled, by hunger and fatigue" and "perishing with thirst," and the first sound he hears is running water, the first sight a flame (symbols of spirit and life-giving), when his prospects darken as suddenly as they have brightened. He sees the naked legs "scored into uncouth figures," the moccasins "adorned in a grotesque manner"; it is an alarming "spectacle" and, nearly hysteric with fear and trembling, he has to assume the hand of demonism: "Had some mysterious power snatched me from the earth, and cast me, in a moment, into the heart of the wilderness?" (pp. 169-171). What a radical change from his normal "devotion to the spirit that breathes its inspiration in the gloom of forests" (p. 94). Gone is the lyric melancholy so lately nurtured by these woods, a jaded nostalgia perhaps for the once-fashionable sentiments of Shaftesbury and Gray,[64] but nonetheless another casualty of Indian shock. No longer could Huntly presume to indulge his fetish of "lov[ing] to immerse [himself] in shades and dells, and hold converse with the solemnities and secrecies of nature in the rude retreats of Norwalk" (pp. 94-95).

While it is good to bear in mind that Huntly's fancy is rich in preconceptions, the paranoia does not mean he has been irrationally carried away. For this breed of Indian will turn his Angst into bloody prophecy. Not only had Indians wantonly destroyed members of his family in "former Indian wars" (pp. 172-173), but he is also to learn that a "sanguinary" brave, inflamed by Old Deb, had made Waldegrave a random reprisal victim (pp. 280-281). His uncle would be the first to fall in combat

---

[64]Cf.: "Even the rude *Rocks*, the mossy *Caverns*, the irregular unwrought *Grotto's*, and broken *Falls* of Waters, with all the horrid Graces of the *Wilderness* itself, as representing NATURE more, will be the more engaging, and appear with a Magnificence beyond the formal Mockery of Princely Gardens."Anthony, Earl of Shaftesbury, *Characteristicks of Men, Manners, Opinions, Times*, 2d ed. (1714; facs. rpt., Farnborough, Hants.: Gregg International Publishers, 1968), II, 393-394.

with the Indians (p. 244), and his own life would be continuously imperiled by them. Moreover, poor nonresisting Edny is "mangled" nearly unto death (p. 269); the girl hostage, after witnessing the slaughter of her family, has been dragged for miles to the cave and is eventually tomahawked (pp. 182, 190); another girl is found dead in the road, scalped (p. 230)—as Huntly would have been were it not for his timely recovery from a swoon (p. 202); hearing a report which suggests one of his sisters has been carried off, he takes it for granted she will suffer the traditional "fate worse than death" (p. 235); and, as the rampage spreads, a farmer is shot in his fields, a house in Chetasco burned to the ground and "its inhabitants murdered or made captives" (p. 250). Considering the record, then, who is to gainsay Huntly if he regards the Indian as the Dark Man of the Forest, a pitiless oppressor and a blight on his soul?

Even among humanitarians like Benjamin Rush — founder of the first antislavery society in America — the Indian was no prize. Disavowing Rousseau and leaning rather more toward Buffon on the status of natural man, Rush accepted as a donnée the inherent depravity of Indians, passing along tales, for example, of their deliberately famishing themselves so as to get "their appetites" keyed up for "that savage species of war, which is peculiar to them." They seemed to him a congenitally stupid race: defects of the "understanding" could be read in their "vacant countenances," and these along with their "long and disgusting taciturnity" seemed "effects of the want of action in their brains from a deficiency of ideas." Their stoicism — admired by some — Rush would interpret as an absence of feeling. Animals that they were, alternately given to hunger and gluttony and all the "vices which are alike contrary to moral and physical happiness," they were — for cause — prone to die young.[65]

[65]*Medical Inquiries and Observations*, 2d ed. (Philadelphia: J. Conrad & Co., 1805), II, 26, 427–428.

So, for the benefit of unnamed dilettantes — parlor "philosophers of Europe" — who "celebrate the virtues of the savages of America" from afar, Rush would ask that romance be tempered with "information" obtained from travelers like Pierre Charlevoix, Louis Hennepin, Jonathan Carver, Bernard Romans, William Bartram, and others "who have resided among them." Such data he would subjoin "to complete their natural history," the substance of which is a litany of Indian "vices"; not very charitable, but a helpful reminder for those who know only the "fashionable" image. *Real* Indians are characterized by: "uncleanness" (they are mainly "strangers to the obligations . . . of . . . the marriage bed"), "nastiness" (they are oblivious "to decency in the *time — place —* and *manner* of their natural evacuations"), "drunkenness" (the farmer who loses a keg of rum will find it "empty on one side of the road, and Indian Tom drunk and asleep on the other"), "gluttony" (they very commonly "stretch themselves on the ground after a full meal, and grunt there . . . till they recover from the effects of their intemperance") — and on the list goes, rounding out to an even ten this "short nomenclature of . . . vices," the others being treachery, cruelty, idleness, theft, gaming, and the debasement of women (*Essays, Literary, Moral and Philosophical*, pp. 256-259). Moreover, the pioneer settler who moves to the woods and becomes a neighbor of Indians soon takes on their grubby habits. Living in revolt against "the operation of laws," he "loves spirituous liquors, and . . . eats, drinks and sleeps in dirt and rags in his little cabbin [*sic*]" (ibid., pp. 214-215).

Brown's Indians share *some* of these traits. With regard to the reputed idleness, for instance, Huntly looks upon them as behaving like beasts of the wild who wake and sleep as the spirit freely moves them; and "if . . . wakeful at an unseasonable moment," he envisions them to be models of placid vacancy (the conventionalized tableau): "they always sit upon their haunches, and, leaning their elbows on their knees, consume the tedious hours in smoking" (p. 174). We also have the example of Old Deb's treachery in fomenting the "depradations" of her "countrymen" and her glorying "in the mischief she had done" (p. 280). As for cruelty, that is as natural to Brown's Indians as the air they breathe. So far as we can tell, it is their sole profession—and delight. Panicked as he is, Huntly may exaggerate their sadism, but the idea that an Indian lives only to "exult in the laments of his unhappy foes" (p. 200) was more than a commonplace of captivity literature; given his experience, it is not unreasonable for Huntly to assume they "longed to feast upon [his] bowels and to quaff [his] heart's-blood" (p. 224).

By no means unique, the attribution of depravity was far from local—in place or time. Not only was it central to the mythology of dark savages (originally born mainly of theology and ignorance), but having been sustained by almost two centuries of captivity and abduction narratives, histories, pseudohistories, journals, biographies, sermons, poems, plays, stories, and novels, its key features were already full-blown in the consciousness of the first Englishmen to found a successful colony in the New World, and that vision came over with them from Holland, already concretely embellished, months before they had so much as laid eyes on such flesh and blood Indians as Samoset and Squanto, without whom none of them would have survived. The sober-minded William Bradford positively knew in advance that America was populated "only [by] savage and brutish men which range up and down, little otherwise than the wild beasts." And, as the Pilgrims contemplated their awesome journey, it was understood that those who should survive the "casualties of the sea," "the miseries of the land," as well as "famine and nakedness and . . . want," and "grievous diseases," would yet have to meet

continual danger of the savage people, who are cruel, barbarous and most treacherous, being most furious in their rage and merciless where they overcome; not

362

being content only to kill and take away life, but delight to torment men in the most bloody manner that may be; . . . cutting off the members and joints of others by piecemeal and broiling on the coals, eat the collops of their flesh in their sight whilst they live, with other cruelties horrible to be related.[66]

No longer awash in benevolence, Huntly the Indian-hater makes no secret of his contempt. This, however, does not necessarily give us a fix for Brown's standing on the Indian question, except that, in so far as prejudice seeps through the calculated sensationalism, he seems not to have been very far from Rush's position. A major objective for Rush was to establish the Indian's place in his anatomy of cultural evolution. Telescoping Condorcet's well-known scheme of social progression in the *Esquisse d'un tableau historique des progrès de l'esprit humain* (1794), Rush has the Indian relegated to the lowest classification on the scale from savage nomad to civilized farmer, the former being, by definition, a rung below the barbarous (*Essays, Literary, Moral and Philosophical,* p. 221). But the Indians Rush represents are generic redmen. Hence, no allowance is made for differences among and

[66]*Of Plymouth Plantation*, ed. Samuel Eliot Morison (New York: Alfred A. Knopf, 1970), pp. 25–26.

Obviously, this is not the place to attempt a survey of attitudes toward the American Indian from 1620 to 1799, especially since there is a goodly number of useful studies on the subject, but some aspects of it will be touched on shortly. Several works that may be consulted for the more comprehensive picture — in addition to those cited in n.17 above — are: Hoxie N. Fairchild, *The Noble Savage: A Study in Romantic Naturalism* (New York: Columbia Univ. Press, 1928); Albert Keiser, *The Indian in American Literature* (New York: Oxford Univ. Press, 1933); Reginald Horsman, *Expansion and American Indian Policy, 1783–1812* (East Lansing: Michigan State Univ. Press, 1967); Richard VanDerBeets, ed., *Held Captive by Indians: Selected Narratives 1642–1836* (Knoxville: Univ. of Tennessee Press, 1973); and Louise K. Barnett, *The Ignoble Savage: American Literary Racism, 1790–1890* (Westport, Conn.: Greenwood Press, 1975).

within tribal groupings and between those who had been Christianized (like the Conestogas) and those who remained pagan, between those who were pacified by treaty or missionary training and those who remained vengeful and bellicose — to say nothing of countless Indians who were corrupted by their association with whites. Obviously, none of these fine points seems to have mattered much. (Since he was not writing a sociological document, Brown, of course, would be less culpable on this score than Rush and other "scientific" writers.) At any rate, the predominant interest of the times was the practical one of how the Indians could be dealt with, and, considering our hunger for territory, that meant keeping a vigilant eye on those most capable of making trouble — or, in other words, the warlike type we find in *Edgar Huntly*. However humane and nonviolent one's outlook (and both Rush and Brown had been raised in Quaker households), it was a fact of life that Indians constituted a clear and present danger to the infant nation, and this is but one of several matters on which Brown would show tacit agreement with ideas set forth by the "plain dealing" French "Counsellor of State" of his *Louisiana* pamphlet, who understood all too well (as some Americans evidently did not) that our Indians were unquestionably the "most dangerous inmates" of the country (far more so than our black slaves who had even greater cause for "enmity"). Trying to reawaken France's waning imperialist ambitions in America (Brown's warning that the nation renounce timidity, stop the political haggling, and look to its security), the wily Frenchman observed how the Indians' "savage ignorance, their undisciplined passions, their restless and warlike habits, their notions of ancient right, make them the fittest tools imaginable for disturbing the states." There being some thirty thousand Indians on our western border "whose delight is war," the French could easily manipulate such a "terrible militia" by judiciously "supplying their fury with arms." Thus, he concluded: "We shall find, in the bowels of the States, a mischief that only wants the touch of a well-directed spark to involve in its explosion, the utter ruin of half their nation."[67]

In sum, not only does Brown concede the shared assumption about generalized Indians (a concession strengthened by the motive to support our mercantile interest in New Orleans), but, seen in this light, and bearing in mind that a majority of Indians sided with the French in the war of 1754–1763 and many with the British in the Revolution, one also senses the political and psychological parameters within which Brown staged a mini-Indian-war in the outlying settlements, a scant thirty miles north of the Capital, and made his hero a participant in the counter-attack, whose success is total.

There are at least two other noteworthy instances in which Brown credits the validity of Indian-phobic tendencies, one indirect and the other direct. The elder Wieland, imbued with religious idealism, feels himself enjoined to bring "the truths of the gospel" to the "North-American Indians"; however, his fears of the peril awaiting him are confirmed by "a nearer survey of savage manners," and he loses heart. Fourteen years pass, and the need to try again comes back to him with "uncommon energy." So he perseveres, in spite of having his "exhortations" "repelled with insult and derision," and withstands "incredible fatigues, hunger, sickness, and solitude," until "the license of savage passion, and the artifices of his depraved countrymen" finally convince him that Christian principles and minimal decency can make little headway with Indians. Moreover, Clara on contemplating the monstrosity of her brother's murders repeats the shibboleth of horror that the only known prototype for such acts, "in the highest degree, inhuman," would be the work of "savages trained to murder, and exulting in agonies" (pp. 10, 11, 174).

In the other reference, Brown openly approaches the

[67]*An Address to the Government of the United States on the Cession of Louisiana to the French* (Philadelphia: John Conrad & Co., 1803), pp. 74–76.

question in his own person. It occurs in his translation of Volney's *Tableau du climat et du sol des États-Unis d'Amérique* (1803), which is laced with footnotes wherein Brown takes Volney to task for a variety of inconsistencies and corrects what he considers misconceptions and errors of fact.[68] Volney, who saw our Indians at firsthand (though superficially), devotes a longish supplementary chapter to their way of life, and it is instantly clear that he has as little use for them as Rush had had.[69] He becomes so defamatory, that Brown feels obliged to explain Volney is "as zealous to depreciate, as Rousseau was to exalt [the Indians'] character." When, in fact, Brown wisely points out that "Volney's abhorrence of Rousseau, and his *man of nature*, has hurried him to the contrary extreme," so that the "two extremes . . . are nearly allied" (pp. 399, 415), one's appreciation of Brown's desire to steer a middle course is abruptly dashed by remarks which betray his own racism. To Volney's statement that the Indian must be "continent and almost chaste from principle, and the danger of his situation," Brown roundly objects:

> This is ascribing to the Indian much more moderation and foresight than he displays on other occasions. Since he is not deterred, by the most palpable and powerful considerations, from the excessive indulgence of other appetites, more immediately and glaringly destructive of his safety and health than this, we cannot suppose him so very wise and provident on this head.

And when, several paragraphs later, he reads that one inducement white men give for joining the Indians is

[68]See our "Historical Notes" to *Ormond* for a summary of Brown's disagreements with Volney, pp. 444–445.

[69]Not two paragraphs into his chapter, he has already recited their "freaks of vulgar drunkenness," their "wallowing in the filth with the pigs," their daily quarrels to the death, and general "anarchy and disorder." *A View of the Soil and Climate of the United States of America*, tr. C. B. Brown (Philadelphia: J. Conrad & Co., 1804), pp. 354–355.

"their licentious indulgences with the squaws," Brown sarcastically asks: "What becomes of the continence and chastity supposed above to be characteristic of the savage life?" (pp. 370–372). Similar reflections on Indian nature have to do with an irredeemable primitiveness, as their inability to negotiate the easy ascent from hunter to domesticating shepherd, when, for example, a people reputedly as untamable as "the Tartars, in the same kind of country, have become pastoral" (p. 394).

Obviously, Brown needed hostile Indians for the purposes of drama. Readers of fiction were looking for conflict, suspense, a life and death clash with Evil, not fairness or the monotony of bliss. However, after one has glimpsed his private opinion, it seems relevant to ask whether Brown was overstepping artistic necessity in his treatment of the Indian; that is, whether gothicizing nature required him not only to blacken his native Americans with unmitigated brutality, but also to make them objects of disgust. It is true that examples of this kind abounded in the available literature, but there are shadings of antipathy in *Edgar Huntly* which suggest that Brown's depiction of the Indian was slanted in ways that go beyond the needs of characterization.

Even allowing for symbolic coloration, in quite a number of instances one can also detect Brown going out of his way to accent the negative (at times even stooping to pettiness)—a process which not only gets turned around, but has fascinating consequences when, to all intents and purposes, Huntly himself becomes an Indian. The simplest case of disparagement comes with Brown's repeated use of the word "savages," notable only because he personally made such a to-do about its connotations. On the one hand, he chastized Volney for insisting on the technicality that North American Indians should properly be called savages to distinguish them from East Indians, yet in *Edgar Huntly* Brown almost never calls *his* Indians anything other than savages, which, according to the definition he belabored with Volney, means he is picking a term reserved for those "we want to stigmatize as wicked and

367

cruel, and [which] is given to men in the rudest state of society, only when we allude to their ignorance or ferocity" (*View*, p. 352). No epithet is reiterated nearly so frequently in *Edgar Huntly*, and all of those substituted for "savages" (with the exception of something like Deb's "countrymen") are more patently pejorative, as with "swarthy band" or "detested guests," allusions these, not to what the Indians do—their being "inexorable enemies," "assassins" and "marauders"—but to what they are (pp. 280, 175, 178, 185, 186, 258).

Or take Old Deb and her "hut." Compared with how the humblest white settlers are accommodated, one would think she had just emerged from the stone age. Her rude dwelling, a match for the "poverty and desolation" of its surroundings, is a windowless affair built of "unhewn logs," from between which the "loosely plastered . . . clay" has mostly been washed away, letting in only such light as manages to leak through the crevices. What passes for a chimney is made of "half-burnt bricks," the door is latched by a "leathern thong," the earthen oven, a "cavity" in the wall, is filled with rubbish, and gives way under Huntly's weight. Until his arrival with the girl hostage "all within was silence and darkness." As for furnishings, a bed is something made of rope stretched across saplings covered by a blanket and resting on stones to keep it off the ground. A board lodged between the bed and log wall makes do for a table and the only other "furniture" is a hoe, a bucket containing some water, roof droppings, drowned insects, and sand, plus a basket or two. All that can be found of food are a few "stale fragments" of bread (pp. 183–184, 188). A sorry scene. Adjoining the hut is a small cornfield, but, unable, or unwilling, to try to live off the land, Deb gains her subsistence mainly by begging (pp. 208–209).

Further wandering in the same general region, devoid of any "token of human residence [or] . . . spots of cultivation" (one does not so much as meet a wild hog [p. 204]), suddenly brings Huntly to the trim cottage of a white frontier family, and the night-and-day contrast between it and Deb's "hovel" is rather spectacular. Approaching, the wayfarer sees cattle tracks in a much-beaten path, a rivulet, good soil, a clover field, apple trees, a cornfield, and then the house comes into view with walls made of planed boards. As for the rest: "A window of four panes admitted the light, and a chimney of brick, well burnt, and neatly arranged, peeped over the roof." He hears "the voice of children, and the hum of a spinning-wheel," and, in spite of his dishevelment, he is hospitably received with food and drink and takes a brief rest (pp. 205–206). Then—lo and behold—comes the revelation that the hut, dilapidated as it was, had not even been Deb's property in the first place, but was put up by an impoverished Scottish immigrant. He was the one who had cleared the land, brought out farming tools, put in a crop, and lived on the "produce" of his fields. After the Scotsman's mysterious disappearance (the best guess has it that he was done in by Indians), his place would be appropriated by Deb and her dogs (p. 210). However much of a shanty the hut may have become, its being more desirable to her than the wigwam she gave up tells us a little of what the Indian's normal life-style was like.[70]

Nor is this the end of it. Any supposition that Brown was not so much trying to denigrate the Indian as to observe the rule that a habitation reflects its inhabitant must overcome the contradiction that Selby's Europeanized son, a gruff and drunken lout, whose "malignant passions" run riot, is domiciled in nothing less than a princely mansion, a house painted white with not just windows, but sashes "supplied, contrary to custom, with

[70]Fittingly, the hut will toward the end be tenanted by much ravaged Clithero Edny, his final refuge before Huntly stirs him up for the last time (p. 285). It is also interesting that, whereas Brown denies the Indian a hut of his own in *Edgar Huntly*, in response to Volney's statement that Indians "have no notion whatever of property in land *or houses*," Brown counters, "Except the hut each one occupies" (*View*, p. 373).

glass." It remains a "model of cleanliness and comfort" even in the face of an attack by Indians (pp. 229, 226). With everything else running true to form, can anyone believe *Indian occupancy* would not have made a difference in the house?

On a related front, we have noted how the Norwalk landscape became miraculously transformed once it was known to have been repopulated by Indians. Not alone will its unspoiled romantic charm disappear, but the fact that Indians are on the loose, looting, razing, hacking, and slaying, immediately converts the area into an absolute wasteland — a location in which one loses all orientation ("I scarcely knew in what region of the globe I was placed." [p. 182]). When Huntly comes into the vicinity of Deb's hut, an environment he had initially been content to describe as perilous and rugged is swiftly downgraded to the point that "no fancy can conceive a scene more wild and desolate." Wherever he looks, he is presented with "only new emblems of sterility" (p. 181). Indeed, desolation works as a sort of leitmotif. Let mention be made of some "sterile" tract amidst the meandering steeps and hollows of this fallen Garden and it becomes almost axiomatic that the place is a breeding ground for "lurking" savages (p. 211).

What does one make of a people who half-nakedly skulk around in the wasteland that is their natural habitat, whose movements are mistaken for those of "a beast" (p. 199), and who are not heard to utter one intelligible word,[71] even in their own incomprehensible language, except for the "mutter" or "shrieks" they emit when mor-

---

[71]Leslie Fiedler some time ago pointed out the phantom-like quality of Brown's Indians, noting that his "aboriginal shadows do not even speak," their function being to "merely threaten." *Love and Death in the American Novel* (New York: Criterion Books, 1960), p. 146. Norman Grabo is also impressed by the Indians' speechlessness: they seem to come "from some nightmare without words." *The Coincidental Art of Charles Brockden Brown*, p. 68.

tally wounded (pp. 191, 201)—persons who, except for a hundred-year-old woman, have no individuality (at least none worth describing), and who have motives only to violence and ghastliness?

Returning very briefly to how all of this stereotyping impacts on the matter of literary integrity, while no one wants to defend the bias in Brown's treatment of the Indian, it can be reasonably argued that if the underlying ill-will reflects badly on the author (which is really the programming of his times), it need not be bad for his novel, as such. For one thing—considered internally—unless one feels the need to read him didactically, the Brown style of hostile Indian promotes a fuller awareness of the context of horror and unreason which awaits man in a state of nature; the agon of Norwalk shows man at war with the more sobering aspects of his own nature (his id, if you will) and raises the moral query as to what the uncertain potentialities of that nature are. At any rate, this is a very old question and we cannot get very much into it here.[72] What rather needs to be dealt with are the where, why, and how of Brown's getting into it. Obviously, his position was neither original nor unique. It takes but the slightest perspective to comprehend that for every patch of seventeenth- or eighteenth-century wilderness that hid a covey of hateful Indians, one could find a settlement somewhere that had its share of Indian-haters—and writers who exploited the hatred. The point

---

[72]It goes without saying that bias has a way of begetting its own counter-action, and, analogously, an important corrective direction is eventually opened up for Edgar Huntly, for he gains new strength by living like an Indian. From his comments on Volney, one can see that Brown himself seems to have been as uncomfortable with extreme positions as anyone else, which is one reason he was so much given to inconsistency. Actually, it was very common for him to be of two minds about most controversial subjects, and the manifestations of it in *Edgar Huntly* which appear in his handling of the double are among the more complicated ones. With the Indians, he could perhaps have been a bit more ambivalent.

371

is Brown was doing no more than following the mandate of history, a cursory sketch of which will show the traditional attitudes he was drawing on.

Having sampled Bradford's anticipation of trial by savages, we are thankfully not obliged to linger over the lurid Indian of Puritan demonology. A more clear-cut line of descent for the Indian section of *Edgar Huntly* lies in the rather substantial subgenre of the captivity narrative. Beleaguered every step of the way, Huntly resembles no one so much as the escaped hostage, which he is in deed, if not in fact. Overshadowing everything else, however, is the unabated horror-mongering of the genre. By its standards Brown seems almost restrained.

A major reason captivity narratives of the early typological stripe had such lasting popularity (those especially of Mary Rowlandson, John Williams, and Jonathan Dickinson, best sellers kept in print by successive generations) was not just that they dealt in explicit gore, depicting the orgiastic delight of Indians meting out torture, but that readers devoured these gruesome tales as factual terrors people like themselves had lived through. There was Mary Rowlandson, herself shot in the side, watching relatives and friends being butchered before her eyes ("the Blood running down to our heels"), children being torn from their mothers, knocked in the head, and "wallowing in their blood." A man running from a nearby house had been felled and was begging for his life, promising money, but the Indians "knockt him in [the] head" anyway, "stript him naked, and split open his Bowels." It was, as Mary said, "a solemn Sight to see so many Christians lying in their Blood, . . . like a company of Sheep torn by Wolves. All of them script naked by a company of Hell-hounds, roaring, singing, ranting and insulting, as if they would have torn our very Hearts out."[73]

[73] *The Soveraignty and Goodness of God, Together With the Faithfulness of His Promises Displayed: Being a Narrative of the Captivity and Restauration of Mrs. Mary Rowlandson*, 2d ed. (Boston: T. Fleet, 1720), pp. 3–7.

Rowlandson's "lively resemblance of Hell" (ibid., p. 8) was written for Calvinist readers of the late seventeenth century, describing an episode in King Phillip's War. Yet those shrill images of the tearing out of one's vitals, used a number of times by Brown, would seem just as contemporary over a century later because essentially the same scenario was being replayed in such items as the "Manheim Anthology" of 1793 (reissued in 1794, 1798, and 1799), the last selection in which, dealing with a Revolutionary battle of 1778 that became known as a massacre by Indians, was set in the Wyoming Valley, about one hundred thirty miles west and north of Philadelphia on the Susquehanna, an area to which Brown's Delawares had removed in the 1740s.[74] Whereas Rowlandson exhibits the rewards of the devout in their constancy and service to God, the Manheim narratives are a mere compilation of barbarities (not all authenticated) published to serve Mammon. Two young maidens are stripped and tied to saplings, and hundreds of pine splinters are driven into their bodies and ignited (pp. 204–205). A suckling infant is ripped from its mother's arms, killed, and scalped on the spot, the mother is shot and scalped, as is her daughter, a hatchet is sunk into the brains of a six-year-old son, and two additional daughters are also scalped—all within ten furious minutes (p. 206). The naked father survives only because, having fainted, he would be rescued by a friend (p. 206). Houses are routinely plundered and set afire, the occupants often incinerated in them (pp. 218–219, 220). As with Brown's hostage girl, there is much dragging about of defenseless women, some out of their homes to be killed (p. 231). Those taken hostage are forced to march long distances with heavy loads and are subjected to unspeakable tor-

[74]"Manheim Anthology," in *Held Captive by Indians: Selected Narratives 1642–1836*, pp. 202–242. Another account of the Wyoming Massacre, yet to be examined, contains material about an Indian Queen of possible application to Old Deb.

tures (pp. 218–220). Mutilation is not uncommon; occasionally, there is word of cannibalism (pp. 221–223). And those battered hostages who manage to make their way back to the houses of friends are—like Huntly—greeted with alarm and disbelief, until they identify themselves and learn they were thought to have been done in some time ago and that members of their family have meanwhile been murdered (p. 226). In isolated instances, counter-atrocities are committed on the Indians, but, as with Huntly, always in self-defense: an exceptionally plucky rural wife takes on a small band of attacking Indians, axes out the brains of one of them, the entrails of another, and splits the head of a third (p. 210). Considering the treatment one might expect at their hands, it was no sin to kill an Indian. One had either to kill or be killed, or both. Like Huntly, no one wanted to be taken alive, and those who were prayed for death. Just to see a "tawny savage" with tomahawk raised was to shoot on reflex (p. 235).

With graphic sensationalism becoming so commonplace as to blur the line between fact and fancy, fiction sometimes had to strain to compete with the nonfiction, some of which had all the earmarks of having already been freely adapted from life. Nonetheless, compete the story-tellers did. Mrs. Ann Eliza Bleecker's *The History of Maria Kittle*, generally agreed on as the first American novel to give any extensive treatment to the Indian, is little more than a fictionalized captivity narrative.[75] Set in the vicinity of Albany, New York, it recounts Mrs. Kittle's abduction and the attack on her family by supposedly friendly Indians, who take an infant son from her arms and dash "his little forehead against the stones," shoot her brother-in-law, and tomahawk his pregnant wife. Thereupon, we are told, as the attacker's "sanguinary soul was

[75]Written in 1781 and originally published in serial form in the *New-York Magazine; or, Literary Repository* from September 1790 to January 1791, it was first published as a book in 1793 and reissued in 1797.

not yet satisfied with blood; he deformed her lovely body with deep gashes, and tearing her unborn babe away, dashed it to pieces against the stone wall, with many additional circumstances of infernal cruelty." When the house was set afire, Maria's daughter, who had hidden herself in a closet, was burned alive.[76]

Borrowing from the captivity narratives' atrocity mill was widespread in eighteenth-century fiction, especially when it purported to be factual. On the less extravagant end of the spectrum are those works in which the Indian's native ferocity is more or less a staple danger that goes with the Territory. Thus, John Filson, who gave rise to the myth-making Daniel Boone legend in *The Discovery, Settlement and Present State of Kentucke* (1784), casts his Indian in the stock role of a natural enemy whose unprovoked killings and general meanness are facts of life — the "daily . . . perils" one expects in wilderness surroundings. If every other member of his scouting party "was plundered, dispersed, and killed by the Indians," it seems to have made scarcely a ripple in Boone's life. Even when taken prisoner, Boone is not especially perturbed at being treated "with common savage usage." It is discouraging but not unusual for his company of pioneers to lose six persons in an Indian attack — one of them Boone's eldest son. Other brutalities — killings, abductions, and tomahawkings — are all duly reported, but not very often do they get much emotional underscoring, other than for Boone to observe that the cruelty was "shocking to humanity" or that a scene of mayhem was "a horror almost unparalleled."[77]

The savagery increases in stories about soldiers fighting in the Indian wars, as does the reaction to it when the source is a person of sensibility, these being ingredients of

[76]*New-York Magazine*, 1 (October, 1790), 563–565.

[77]*Filson's Kentucke*, ed. Willard Rouse Jillson (fasc. rpt. 1784 ed. New York: Burt Franklin, 1972), pp. 53, 8–9, 52, 57, 72, 76, 77. The apparent sang-froid is partly a characterization of Boone and partly the result of Filson's promotional motives.

an anonymous epistolary novel, *The Hapless Orphan; or, Innocent Victim of Revenge* (1793), whose heroine harps upon the Indians' treachery, barbarity to prisoners, and quenchless hostility. But it is on the catch-penny fringes of pulp fiction that captivity motifs were pushed to ever more bizarre variations. Charles C. Holt, who has done a study of short stories of the early republic, summarizes one of the more grisly specimens, "A True Relation of the Unheard of Sufferings of David Menzies, surgeon, among the Cherokees; and of his Surprising Adventures," (published in *The American Moral and Sentimental Magazine*, 21 May 1798): the titular character "is seized by Cherokees and subjected to torture by being turned slowly on a spit over an open fire. The Indians have recently discovered the process of larding, and are interested in experimenting with juices from human flesh. Menzies escapes and survives by eating bacon which has been treated with juices from his own body."[78] In short, the Indians were becoming less and less real—a race of psychopaths.

Brown's *Edgar Huntly* seems to occupy something of a middle ground. This it shares with works like Susannah Rowson's historical novel, *Ruben and Rachel; or Tales of Old Times* (1798), which in the retrospective chapters devoted to Indians revives much of the captivity formula, and in so doing brings out elements of tone and incident that are pitched in the same general vein as those in *Edgar Huntly*. Somewhat paralleling Huntly's recall of the basis for previous Indian wars, which included a recognition of white "encroachments" (pp. 172–173), is the following from Rowson:

> . . . some disagreements having fallen out between the native Indians and the English settlers, the former frequently made inroads on the latter, plundering and burning their habitations, and either

---

[78]"Short Fiction in American Periodicals: 1775–1825," Ph.D. diss. Auburn University 1968, p. 44.

massacreing [*sic*] the inhabitants, or taking them prisoners and carrying them up the country where they often exercised on them the most wanton barbarity; scalping, maiming and disfiguring . . . . But what could be expected from the untaught savage, whose territories had been invaded by strangers, and who perhaps had suffered, from the cruelty of the invaders. . . .

Also somewhat reminiscent of *Huntly* is Rowson's having the "habitation" of Mr. Dudley (this was Rachel's family name) "marked [for attack] by an Indian who had strayed from his companions" because of its isolated situation. In addition, like Huntly, Mr. Dudley, who was away from home when the Indians attacked, mistakenly believes for a time that his wife and daughters have been killed by Indians.[79]

[79]*Ruben and Rachel* (Boston: David West, 1798), I, 142, 146, 147. It need scarcely be said that analogues of this kind do not make a source of *Ruben and Rachel*, nor would the case be much enhanced if one threw in a cave where Rachel's family took refuge during an Indian attack (I, 148). The fact is, Jonathan Carver (whose *Travels* Brown would have known from references to it by Rush and Volney) likewise described a remarkable Indian cave "only accessible by ascending a narrow, steep passage that lies near the brink of the river"; he met a Winnebago queen somewhat like Old Deb, "a very ancient woman, small in stature," who is pleased by the attention Carver paid her; and in phrasing very close to Brown's (p. 200), Carver asserts that Indians have been known to "devour the hearts of those they slay, and drink their blood, by way of bravado" (*Travels Through the Interior Parts of North-America in the Years 1766, 1767, and 1768* [Dublin: S. Price, et al., 1779], pp. 59–60, 29–30, 286). Yet, one would be reluctant to offer Carver as a source. Nor—to cite but one more instance—could one make any claims for *The History of Pennsylvania* by Brown's teacher, Robert Proud, in which there is another variant on Deb, an Indian woman "of eminence," who had "authority, and spoke much in [tribal] Councils." Proud also alludes to a time of rumored Indian insurrection in the vicinity of Philadelphia, followed by a false alarm about three families that had supposedly been all but cut off by Indians, but had actually bolted in panic ([Philadelphia: Zachariah Poulson, Jr., 1797–98], I, 463, 335–338).

What all of this leads up to are two final concerns: what did Brown know about real Indians—what in fact could he have known—in relation to what he wrote about them, especially his Delawares; and, secondly, as we have noticed the relationship of Huntly's encounter with them to traditional usage: what special meaning does Brown give to that experience?

When Huntly begins to learn by bits and pieces what happened in his absence, fearing one of his sisters may have been taken captive, he believes her fate will be "to gratify the innate and insatiable cruelty of savages by

Anyone who has read enough of these accounts soon realizes how pointless it is to cast around for sources, for the captivity literature is so saturated with similar and near-similar materials one is hard put to tie any given event to one unique story. The repetition is doubtless suggestive of prevailing Indian custom, but some also looks very suspiciously as if it were an outgrowth of horrors being liberally pirated about. The excruciating torture by pine splinters, for example, not alone appears in three separate selections in VanDerBeets' *Held Captive By Indians* (pp. 189–190, 205, 241), but it had also been mentioned by Carver, with the difference that, instead of its being applied to white women, as in the other citations, Carver directly heard it told of an Indian who tried to minimize the torment his Indian captors were inflicting on him by telling them how he had subjected *his* Indian victims to the flaming splinter death.

It is because of the chewing and rechewing of incidents—which often makes a pastiche of the seemingly individual tale—that one would tend to be skeptical of accepting Richard Slotkin's suggestion that the so-called *Panther Captivity*—a trifling thing, twelve pages in the longer reprints—was "almost certainly a source" for *Edgar Huntly* (*Regeneration Through Violence*, pp. 256–257). In spite of some superficial correspondences like the discovery of an escaped woman hostage at a cave mouth and her subsequent reunion with her father, there is also a good deal in the story that has nothing whatsoever to do with *Huntly*—e.g., the reason for the woman's capture is the result of an elopement (her father objected to her marrying his penniless clerk); the clerk is burned at the stake, and she lives in the wilderness for nine whole years before being found by the narrator, Abraham Panther (*A Very Surprising Narrative of a Young Woman Who Was Discovered in a Rocky Cave* . . . [Augusta, (Me.): n.p., n.d.], pp. 3, 5, 7, 10, 11). Originally published in 1787, the story was frequently reprinted.

378

suffering all the torments their invention can suggest, or to linger out years of dreary bondage and unintermitted hardship in the bosom of the wilderness" (p. 235). Unmentionable particulars are omitted ostensibly for reasons of delicacy; however, since this encapsulates vintage captivity material (down to the "bosom of the wilderness" cliché — wrong in tone), it could be assumed people were familiar enough with the conventional details. Certainly, Brown knew the tradition better than he knew the Indian. No one would argue with Dunlap's contention that he probably "drew his pictures of [the Indian] from his own fertile fancy" (*National Portrait Gallery*, III, 5). While it is doubtful that Brown had any contact with "wild" Indians, Daniel Edwards Kennedy supposes it was not impossible for him to have met benign ones, citing Samuel Knapp's *Life of Thomas Eddy* (New York, 1834), in which notation is made of a small group of Delawares living at Atsion, just twenty miles from Philadelphia, as late as 1797. Also, since Brown would have visited Hospitality, the country estate of his maternal uncle and namesake, Charles Brockden, about twenty-five miles from Philadelphia in New Jersey, he could as well have met Delawares there (Kennedy, pp. 1146B, 1156).

Indians were no strangers to Philadelphians. In May 1771, the year of Brown's birth, Captain Killbuck, a prominent Delaware, was in the city to talk with Pennsylvania authorities, and in August 1776, White Eyes, another Delaware chief, was presented to Congress and formally thanked for promoting good relations between Americans and Delawares.[80] Regular contacts, official and semi-official, were maintained throughout the 1790s. Volney, for example, recounts having had some "nine or ten visits, in January and February, 1798," with the Miami Chief, Mishikinakwa (Little Turtle), a former foe, who had come to Philadelphia "with a view of obtaining

[80]C. A. Weslager, *The Delaware Indian: A History* (New Brunswick, N.J.: Rutgers Univ. Press,1972), pp. 272, 303.

the assistance of the government, and the benevolent society of friends," in helping him to turn "the attention of his people from hunting and fishing to tillage" (*View*, pp. 356–358).

Much of what Brown gathered from translating Volney was by no means new to him, as was instanced by his corrective comments. For the average Philadelphian of the 1790s, simply reading the newspaper would have told him there were Indians—and Indians, a good many peaceable. Some came on business, as did Little Turtle, and might be regarded as no more than a novelty. In July 1790, all of twenty-eight chiefs of the Creek Nation arrived for treaty negotiations, and, on being escorted to the Indian Queen Hotel, drew the usual crowd of curiosity seekers. Indians were known to travel quite regularly through the states for pleasure, and to be festively received—sometimes with what was thought to be appropriate amusement. A dispatch from Hartford had it that a coachload of Indians passed through town on their way to Boston, where a certain citizen was going to give a ball for them, and "an ox [was to be] roasted (alive) for their entertainment." One even reads of John Bill Ricketts, the Barnum of that time, having fourteen chiefs, squaws, and warriors on display at his newly erected circus, less than a week after its opening. When Indians came to town to pay their respects to the Federal Government, they would frequently put on a war-dance show—to become a long-standing custom—and, at a formal reception, one of their chiefs would express "their gratification at the civilities shown them."[81]

But over against the domesticated chiefs, the decadent plaything and circus types, Philadelphians were hearing

[81] *Federal Gazette and Philadelphia General Advertiser*, 19 July 1790, p. 2. *Bache's General Advertiser*, 22 March 1793, p. 3. *Federal Gazette*, 17 April 1793, p. 3. J. Thomas Scharf and Thompson Westcott, *History of Philadelphia, 1609–1884* (Philadelphia: L. H. Everts & Co., 1884), I, 469. The Indian Queen Hotel, incidentally, is referred to in *Ormond*; see the frontispiece and "Historical Notes," p. 410.

aplenty in congressional debates on the defense budget about the far from pacified tribes on their western frontier, parts of which — Cumberland County, for example — were not that far away. Delegations sent out with a commission to arrange peace treaties were coming back half a year later empty-handed, or with counter-proposals that all settlers be withdrawn from over the Ohio, which would then become a certifiable boundary (*Philadelphia Gazette*, 12 September 1793, p. 2). Such had been the fate of conciliation efforts urged by those wanting a reduction in military expenditure and greater reliance on local militias. Opponents, noting there had been more or less chronic hostilities since the formation of the Republic, indicated that, if the French and British had previously excited the Indians to war, it was against one another, whereas they were now being enlisted in a common cause against the new nation, usurper of their land. The country had a nasty little war in its midst, subtler than formal ones, but no less costly, that had been dragging on from around 1784. Outbreaks had ranged over widely scattered areas. On the thinly settled and vulnerable Georgia frontier, for example, even Savannah was not safe; citizens, feeling themselves constantly threatened there, had to mount regular guard details. The district of Kentucky between 1783 and 1790 had lost over 1,500 men, women, and children killed or taken captive, along with the loss of 2,000 horses and other property amounting to at least $5,000 (no insignificant figures for that day). Pennsylvania was no exception. Supporters of concerted military action, wanting to bring the issue closer to home, cited the accomplishments of the great Indian fighter of the 1760s, Colonel (later General) Henry Bouquet, who with two regiments had taken the war to the enemy and soundly defeated the Indians terrorizing Carlisle, which allowed people to return to their homes. And, as if to enforce the point that these dangers had not gone away, simultaneous with the congressional debate came a report that a Captain Harley, en route with forty-three men to guard the Cumberland settlement, had run into an ambush which cost him his life along with the loss of twenty men, plus valuable equipment (*Bache's General Advertiser*, 4, 5, 7, January 1793, pp. 3, 3, 3). Somehow, no one had to be reminded that Pennsylvania had been the site of a number of pitched Indian battles during the Revolution.[82]

Generally speaking, then, Brown seems to have had the

[82]Hoping to curb British facility in gathering allies among the various tribes (e.g., with the offer of a bounty for white settlers' scalps), Pennsylvania and the Continental Congress, in January, 1777, secured a promise of neutrality from the Six Nations (the powerful confederation of New York Iroquois). The agreement was soon broken, however, and, for about two years running, nearly all of Pennsylvania's western and northern counties were plagued by combined British and Indian raids, culminating in the Wyoming Massacre. This occurred on 3 July 1778, when a force of 400 Tory Rangers and 700 Indians converged on settlements in the Wyoming Valley, near present day Wilkes-Barre. The Indians felt they had a special score to settle with these settlers (people from Connecticut, relocated by the Susquehanna Company), who had since 1754 been driving them off their prize hunting grounds. As the settlement could muster no more than 300 defenders — many unfit for military service — its forces were quickly overcome, and the Indians went berserk — torturing, scalping and butchering everyone they could lay hands on. Though civilians had escaped, news of the massacre produced the "Great Runaway" of settlers back to the Delaware, where, as historians report, the massacre "became more horrible with each retelling until it became the major atrocity story of the Revolutionary War." It would be "represented in the American press as the wanton murder and torture of helpless women and children by Indians under the direction of British officers" (Robert S. Klein and Ari Hoogenboom, *A History of Pennsylvania*, 2d ed. [University Park: Pennsylvania State Univ. Press, 1980], p. 101).

In one colonial counter-attack later that summer, a force led by Colonel Daniel Brodhead moved against the Mingoes, Shawnees, and Delawares, devastating Indian communities and their crops. A similar campaign through Pennsylvania and New York was conducted by General John Sullivan in the next year, and his scorched earth policy followed by the bitter winter of 1779–1780 so weakened the eastern tribes as to render them capable mainly of hit-and-run raids for the balance of the War (ibid.).

right kind (and scale) of action for the right time-frame—
the mid-1780s. Where, however, did his Delawares fit
into all of this? At first sight, not quite accurately, it
would seem, as to tribe, time, and geography. After all,
the Delawares, many of whom had come under early
Moravian influence, were reputed to have been one of the
less aggressive tribes (the Iroquois looked down on them
as "Women," stupid for letting go of their land), and, until
provoked, they had, according to Heckewelder, been very
agreeable and generous—actually naïve—in their initial
relationship with the Whites.[83] Following renegotiation of
the Walking Purchase Treaty (a shameful land grab perpetrated by one of Penn's sons), the Delawares were in
1742 forced to vacate their lands north of Philadelphia,
their unavailing protests being finally stifled by pressure
from the Iroquois, who were angling for political advantage. As a result of successive removes to the Susquehanna and the Muskingum valleys, then to northwestern
Ohio, and eventually the White River—a tributary of the
Wabash—the Delawares were probably to be located in
the latter area in the 1780s, making it impractical for
Deb's kin, even "brothers and sons," to consider an annual
pilgrimage back to easternmost Pennsylvania for the sake
of an old matriarch (p. 209)—over half a year's foot travel
round trip. On the other hand, Brown does—half-
correctly—place the main body of the tribe on "the banks
of the Wabash and Muskingum" (p. 207), and his vaguely
dating their migration as around 1755, (thirteen years
late for the first move and at least twelve too early for the
last), is not the kind of error that makes much of a difference. Furthermore, with Deb, he is giving us the lone
survivor of a departed generation, a crusty old squaw (by
"birth" and "talents" a person of status), sufficiently aged,
in any event, to have spoken for the embittered opposi-

[83]John Heckewelder, *An Account of the History, Manners, Customs of the Indian Nations, Who Once Inhabited Pennsylvania and the Neighbouring States* (1819, rpt. Philadelphia: Historical Society of Pennsylvania, 1876), pp. 76–79.

tion in 1742, exerting "all her zeal and eloquence" to denounce the outrageous treaty, and ornery enough "to remain behind, and maintain possession of the land" (ibid.). Significantly, it had been the stubbornness of one Delaware tribe who resented white "encroachments" (Brown's term) into their country around the Forks of the Delaware, flagrantly exceeding the bounds of the original treaty made with William Penn, that brought about the notorious second walk of 1737 (see n. 12 above). The fact is, continued Delaware occupancy need not have been restricted to isolated individuals, since in return for what was taken from them, the Delawares were given a ten-square-mile tract near the Forks for a reservation. The Huntlys may have been properly surprised to suddenly find murderous Indians in their midst; however, looked at from the Indian perspective, Deb had "succeeded to the government," of the whole region and "the English were aliens . . . who occupied the land merely by her . . . permission" (pp. 208–209). Thus, the insult that an uncle of Edgar's should have established a barnyard and orchard on ground where a former Delaware village had stood (p. 207) readily explains why the Huntly family would be singled out for Deb's special ire.

Several other data are worth mentioning that enhance the relevance of Delaware hostility and white resentment in context with the tensions found in Brown's novel. First, as the Delawares' humiliation in 1742 became an indelible scar on the tribal conscience, their animosity thereafter was assured; so that some of them sided with the French during the French and Indian War and were said to have been among the victorious forces in the battle at Fort Duquesne, where Huntly's uncle had served under Braddock and been wounded (p. 244). They had also been one of the tribes who by an agreement at Fort Niagara in May 1776 joined the British during the Revolution; and, consequently, theirs were among the villages that had been attacked by the expeditions of Colonel Brodhead and General Sullivan. Though these attacks severely weakened the Indians and reduced their ability to fight major engagements, what happened was that Indian warfare did not so much stop as change its character to incidental raids, which, as has been indicated, continued along Pennsylvania's frontier into the 1790s.

Raids against small locally defended communities of just the sort that Brown places at Solebury and Chetasco were quite common in rural Pennsylvania during the 1780s. Still active areas apparently were the Delaware and Wyoming valleys. On one occasion, in 1781, a party of Indians killed an old man and took three prisoners somewhere along the Delaware, and being pursued had to give up their prisoners, with one of the Indians being mortally wounded and a pursuer shot in the thigh. Three weeks later, at Stroudsburg, on the road from Wyoming to the Delaware, an old man and his son were shot and scalped near their house. A second son was shot and left for dead; the man's wife and infant, meanwhile, were carried off and the child's brains were dashed out.[84] Quite

[84]Charles Miner, *History of Wyoming* (Philadelphia: J. Crissy, 1845), pp. 296–297. Miner describes a number of similar small-party raids in the 1780s; e.g., pp. 301–302, 305.

Since these events took place near the area where the action of the novel occurs, and at about the same time, some effort must be made at last to unscramble Brown's geography in *Edgar Huntly*. The allusions made to various places and distances in his mythically named "Norwalk" are sometimes fairly exact, sometimes not.

Though it has not been possible to turn up a "Chetasco," Mary Waldegrave's home at "Abingdon" seems pretty solid. A post village in Abington township, more commonly called "Morestown," Abington was located fourteen miles from central Philadelphia and two miles northeast of the present-day suburb of Jenkintown. Solebury, where Huntly lived, is a township in Bucks County, thirty miles northeast of Philadelphia, bounded on the east by the Delaware River. Huntly gives the distance between his home in Solebury and Abingdon as a good night's walk, and that seems to square with the time it should take to go that distance. A major village within the township was New Hope, a few miles west of which there was a large spring, named "Aquetong" by the Indians, and denoted one of the remarkable features of the township. In the nineteenth century, it obviously, when Brown prefaced his *Huntly* "Fragment" with the statement that his setting was to be "the upper branches of the Delaware," he could be confident of being taken at his word that he was not writing about remote imaginings; for the "truth of [his] incidents," as he said, would be apparent to "men acquainted with the perils of an Indian war." Almost any up-to-date reader would know that "similar events have frequently happened on the Indian borders" (ibid.).

Raids specifically by Delawares were usually reported as having been conducted in response to injuries done them. One of the more bloody of these occurred in March

would become known as "Ingham's Spring," or "Great Spring," which comes close enough to "Big Spring," the translation Brown offers for "Sky-Walk," that being the name he said the Delawares had given to the district where that novel was set. Another interesting part of the landscape was a limestone cave in Durham township near Solebury, the narrow entrance to which is about one hundred yards from the river, and about two hundred and fifty feet up from the level of the adjoining land. The interior consists of three spacious rooms, as it were, the first entered by a descent of thirty feet, with the second and third being on successively lower levels. All told the length of the cavern from north to south is something like ninety yards.

Since the Forks of the Delaware come at Easton and are the point from which Brown would be designating the "upper branches of the Delaware" cited in his preface to the *EH* "Fragment" as the place of Huntly's residence, that kind of reference turns geography upside down, Solebury being thirty miles *south* of the Forks that Huntly is said to be residing *north* of. (It is of no help for Weymouth to be told that Huntly lives "near the *Forks* of Delaware" [p. 149].) Other places named in the "Fragment" preface are equally confusing, as Brown claims that "those who have ranged along the foot of the *Blue-ridge*, from the *Wind-gap* to the *Water-gap*, will see the exactness of the *local* descriptions" (see p. 493 of this edition). The action of the novel never ranges anywhere near *that* far north or west. The Water Gap is all of fifty miles north of Huntly's "natal township" of Solebury, and Wind Gap is about twelve miles north and slightly west of the Forks.

It is rather difficult to account for these discrepancies, since Brown had to have known the general region well enough to understand where he was locating his narrative. It seems doubtful that a clear geographic change would have occurred between publication of the "Fragment" and the novel proper.

386

1782 when a group of innocent Christian Delawares became the victims of vengeful militiamen in search of non-Delaware marauders who had gone on a scalping spree along the Pennsylvania-Ohio border. Aroused to retaliation, the Delawares went in search of the reckless militiamen and were said to have "tortured those they caught with brutal delight."[85] Possibly the most notorious instance of Delaware involvement in atrocities has to do with the role played by Queen Esther Montour in the Wyoming Massacre. She was the half-breed wife of Eghohowen, a chief of the Wolf clan of the Delawares, who became chieftainess on his death; and what she did was to line up sixteen Americans around a huge boulder, since named the Bloody Rock, and to go from one to the other of her prisoners dashing their brains out with a tomahawk.[86] Although Brown's Deb is no Esther Montour, the parallel of a woman leader among the Indians is not without substance. What Deb lacks in the ability to wield a bloody hatchet, she compensates for in putting her relatives up to it.

A concluding word about what the Indian experience meant for Edgar Huntly. It has been seen that eighteenth-century views of the Indian were fairly dichotomized between the Rousseauists, with their ideal of a natural morality in the innocence of the Forest, and those in the opposing camp, who suggested that life among the natives led to degeneracy, a view espoused by Frenchmen like Crèvecoeur and Volney in their antipathy to Jacobinism, but also strongly urged by realistic republicans like Rush. Brown would for the most part seem to have sided with the Indian-phobes, whose every word indicated that to know the Indian was to loathe him.[87] As Huntly beholds

[85]Elma E. Gray and Leslie Robb Gray, *Wilderness Christians: The Moravian Mission to the Delaware Indians* (Ithaca, N.Y.: Cornell Univ. Press, 1956), pp. 73–74.

[86]Chester Hale Sipe, *The Indian Chiefs of Pennsylvania* (Butler, Pa.: The Ziegler Printing Co., 1927), p. 448.

[87]A rather hypocritical stance this for Pennsylvanians, when their

what he has wrought outside Deb's hut—a heap of Indian corpses—he is half astonished at himself and half apologetic. It is only in considering the waste of life—and that only in their death—that he can pause to think better of the Indians, even praise them: here, he muses, are "three beings, full of energy and heroism, endowed with minds strenuous and lofty, [who have] poured out their lives before me" (p. 194). His responsibility they are, but this is still uncomfortably like the old saw that the only good Indian is—yes—a dead one. In truth, Huntly's concern here cannot be taken as much of a redemptive statement. It is bankrupt benevolence. Redemption will come by a different path.

Cooper had bridged the dichotomy by creating good Indians to be balanced off against his bad ones. But, more than that, he had appropriated the nobler aspects of native life for Natty Bumppo and softened the crudities of the Daniel Boone in him with natural morality and Moravian training. Brown did not have so neat a resolution, but he forged another type of accommodation that had its own priorities. Simply put: Huntly not only survived his Indian ordeal, he survived it well, triumphing single-handed over an entire band of Indians skilled in all the nefarious arts of guerrilla warfare, as he was not ("unfurnished with stratagems or weapons, disheartened and enfeebled," in fact, p. 193). Moreover, the way he got the job done was by becoming a better Indian than those he vanquished—better, that is, both in their terms and his own. So, as the occasion called for it, he "imbibed . . . a spirit vengeful, unrelenting, and ferocious" (p. 192). Seasoned warrior that he was becoming, he could take a

history showed that the colony had in 1756 made it official policy to offer bounties for Delaware scalps; and, in addition, when none of them had done anything to prevent the Paxton Boys' massacre of gentle Conestogas in 1763, or to exact punishment for their crimes. Pearce, *Savages of America*, p. 39. *The Paxton Papers*, ed. John R. Dunbar (The Hague: Martinus Nijhoff, 1957), pp. 60–61, 107–108, 194, 207.

sorely wounded Indian (number five) out of his agony by driving a bayonet through his heart (p. 202). Just the slightest bit cocky, he succumbed to a whim and "stuck his musquet in the ground, and left it standing upright in the middle of the road" (p. 203).

Although over-matching his physical superiors offered Huntly no cause for "exultation" (p. 192), that did not rule out pride, rightfully earned. His strength depleted by "anguish, and fear, and watchfulness; by toil, and absti-nence, and wounds" (p. 212), and seeing himself stranded by approaching night on the "southern barrier" of Norwalk, thirty miles from Solebury, he will put his "energies both moral and physical . . . to the test" (pp. 211–212). He disdains to be outdone by lynx or roe, but the need is greatest to measure himself against the Indian; it is the "Mohawk" he would exceed "in patience under hardship, and contention with fatigue." Elevated to the level of transcendence, it is as if Huntly needs this for a high: "I have ever aspired to transcend the rest of animals in all that is common to the rational and brute, as well as in all by which they are distinguished from each other" (p. 212). He feels rather set up by his newfound hardihood;[88] after the dangers he has met, he can sleep in the "rift" of a rock and be utterly "reckless" of rattlesnakes and panthers (p. 217).

Sentiments of this kind make us think back to the cave; and we recall that this is all of a piece with what had gone before. Having climbed out of the void, Huntly felt him-self reduced to savage ravings, which made him eat his linen shirt, want to bite the flesh of his arm, and rend some living animal to pieces (which he almost does), per-haps even tomahawk himself and as he dies madly allevi-ate the pain by swallowing his own blood (p. 164). The same cave that shelters man-eating cougars also harbors

[88]It is amazing how often he tells us he thrives on competitiveness. For example: "There is no one to whom I would yield the superiority in swimming . . ." (p. 223).

killer Indians and he will more than compete with them, he will outdo both in savagery. Experience teaches him that savagery is a two-way street, traveled by animals and men alike, red and white equally. It might repel the man of civilized sensibilities, but in the extremity of desperation, another self of that same man might find his savage nature an imperative of existence. Huntly, of course, protests too much (and too often): "My temper never delighted in carnage and blood" (p. 124). Obviously, that delight is great because he fears it, as he feared the Indian, a prodigy of wickedness. Out in the woods he *was* that Indian; it was by no mistake that the discerning Sarsefield had taken him for one (p. 257).

And so we are back to the ineluctible psychomachy of Huntly's spirit at war with itself. The man is bewitched by that conflict, drunk with it. Edny was *one* of his other selves. Since the doubling impulse is itself self-perpetuating, he will also discover—to his simultaneous disgust and triumph—that the Indian and cougar are yet other selves. The central impetus, however, remains one of renewal through transcendence. To look again at his statement of awakening—"Few, perhaps, among mankind," Huntly boasts, "have undergone vicissitudes of peril and wonder equal to mine. The miracles of poetry, the transitions of enchantment, are beggarly and mean compared with those which I had experienced." He'll settle for nothing less than "passage into new forms, overleaping the bars of time and space, reversal of the laws of inanimate and intelligent existence. . . ." And he had done it; these have been "*mine*," he says, "to perform and to witness" (italics added, p. 239). The ego—that *American* ego—will not be stilled. Whatever the deficits in his relationships with Clithero Edny and the Indians, Edgar Huntly remains the eternal American lured on by the promise of renewal, a quest which even when it fails will not fail him because it can always be renewed—again.

VII

The *Huntly* criticism has grown to be quite voluminous of late, accelerating to over ninety items from 1950 to the present, nearly half the total in dissertations on Brown. Since a survey of the entire corpus, embracing pre-1950 material as well (sixty additional pieces), would take an essay unto itself, the best that can be accomplished here is to sketch some trends and highlight views that give us a sense of how the novel was received historically.

Taking in the first half-century of criticism, which contains only two reasonably comprehensive essays (one by E. T. Channing in 1819 and the other by William H. Prescott in 1834), one finds most of the interest concentrated on scenic effects, plausibility, and Clithero Edny. Brown would not have been flattered at the slighting of his protagonist (one reviewer overtly gives him "the secondary part in the piece"[89]), and he would have been shaken to learn that for all the pains he took with his Indians, they were practically invisible to critics, failing to receive specific mention until 1834, and then only to suffer by comparison with Cooper's nobler species, who are preferred because of their "sentiments of courtesy, high-toned gallantry, and passionate tenderness." For the reader habituated to a softer, more "poetic" strain of romanticism, it was unfortunate that Brown could only bring out their "rude and uncouth lineaments" — following "popular conceptions" — and ignore any "intimations of a more generous nature."[90] The most intelligent comments on scene — and on Brown in general during this period — are those by E. T. Channing, who is much taken with the pace at which Brown drives us through the landscape and

[89]Anon., rev. of Brown's novels, *British Critic*, 3d ser., 2 (April, 1826), 57.

[90]William H. Prescott, "Life of Charles Brockden Brown," in *The Library of American Biography*, ed. Jared Sparks (New York: Harper & Brothers, 1834), I, 159.

with his technique of using it to reflect the inner mood of his characters, especially the gloom, which "oppresses the spirits with an almost inexplicable sadness." This concept is picked up by others — e.g., a reviewer describes Brown as writing "with eyes, that see reflected in the face of nature the same harsh and strongly marked features, which so evidently predominate in his views of human character."[91] This is one emphasis that recurs a good deal in more recent criticism, where, however, it usually gets embedded in more elaborate discussions of atmosphere and symbolism.

Improbability is no great issue — either way, accepted or rejected — certainly not with regard to the panther and somnambulist episodes that were complained of on those grounds. As Channing points out, "The question is not how much of this has happened or is likely to happen; but is it felt; . . . can we never lose the impression [the writer] leaves?" (op. cit., p. 74). Most interesting comments on character gravitate around Clithero Edny, the consummate neurotic, and the mystery of the madness he wills upon himself. His is the "deplorable" history of the "perversion of a noble mind." Readers are disturbed by the unhealthiness of it all: Is he the fit subject for a novel? "We often shudder in contemplating him." Yet, were he absent, the story might not be half as worth following. *With* his adventures the novel is elevated "to a high place in . . . romance-writing"; they indeed show the "force" of Brown's "genius."[92] A likely explanation for the attraction of Edny would seem to lie in the fact that early nineteenth-century critics spoke for a world still very much dedicated to normalcy, one which clung to rational-

[91]Channing, rev. of Dunlap's *Life, North American Review*, 9 (1819), 73. Anon., rev. of the Goodrich Edition of Brown's novels, *Western Monthly Review*, 1 (December, 1827), 490.

[92]*Western Monthly Review*, p. 490. *British Critic*, p. 59. Anon., rev. of *Edgar Huntly, Critical Review*, 3d ser., 3 (1804), 360. Anon., rev. of the Goodrich Edition of Brown's novels, *American Quarterly Review*, 8 (December, 1830), 336.

ism's assurance that man could always improve a bad situation and which resisted any thought that he was not in control of his fate—ideas made stronger by Emersonians and incipient Victorians alike.

There is a long (and relatively lean) middle period in *Huntly* criticism running from the mid-nineteenth to the mid-twentieth centuries; middle in time, but more in the sense of not being high, because while it is an era of maturing judgment, in which the novel (together with Brown) receives increased attention and its basic motifs are being more systematically addressed and placed in historical perspective, the nascence of a full-blown effort to examine the novel in the totality of its richness will not be reached until the third phase, that of post-1950 criticism. Nonetheless, considerable advances in Brown criticism occurred during the middle period. He was achieving respectability and less frequently being condescended to—even by the British. It was suddenly discovered that Brown "paved the way for Fenimore Cooper," that his pit was a source for Poe's in "The Pit and the Pendulum," that he was a pioneering American novelist, and, in *Huntly*, the first to use "rugged scenery, wild animals, and savage redskins."[93] With the major Romantic fictionists, Irving, Cooper, Poe, Hawthorne, and Melville marching after him, Brown acquired a premier niche in our literary history, though—hierarchically—it rightfully placed him a step below that of his successors.

Several matters to be noticed about this stage in *Huntly* criticism—despite its lack of distinction—are that the

---

[93]Anon., "The Pioneer of American Fiction," *The Dartmouth*, 2 (1868), 41–44. J. S. McCowan, "Our First Novelist," *Sewanee Review*, 4 (1895–1896), 174–180. David Lee Clark, "Introduction," *Edgar Huntly* (New York: Macmillan, 1928), p. xiv. Clark, "Sources of Poe's 'The Pit and the Pendulum,'" *Modern Language Notes*, 44 (June, 1929), 349–356. Margaret Alterton, "An Additional Source for Poe's *The Pit and the Pendulum*," *Modern Language Notes*, 48 (June, 1933), 349–356. Harry R. Warfel, *Charles Brockden Brown, American Gothic Novelist* (Gainesville, Fla.: Univ. of Florida Press, 1949), p. 155.

novel is being less reservedly praised (some call it Brown's "strongest work"); somnambulism and the Indian (the latter unidealized) are being appropriately recognized as major motifs; the gothic darkness of Brown's imagination is featured as a strong conditioning force in the novel, as is his "distinctively American" setting; and Brown is credited with a gift for creating "a quick succession of novel incidents and hairbreadth escapes," part of the tonal environment of peril, excitement, and suspense. Also, critics continue to dwell on the sorrows of Clithero Edny. Dissenters make reference to the ragged plotting, wayward invention, the blandness of Huntly as hero, and his tiresome philosophizing; and they again raise the charge of incredibility—though there is nothing as snide as Cooper's choice remark that "Edgar Huntly . . . contains an American, a savage, a wild cat, and a tomahawk, in a conjunction that never did, nor ever will occur. . . ." A majority of the critics would probably have agreed with the mixed verdict of Julian Hawthorne that Brown's novels have "subjects . . . strongly conceived and ingeniously designed, but the execution is apt to be inadequate and crude." (The same type of assessment is current in present-day criticism.) But, regarding *Huntly* in particular, a majority would equally agree with Ernest A. Baker, who suggested the virtue of Brown's execution was to be gauged by its impact, as in "the sense of abject and incomprehensible fear that pervades the book, the formless dread with which we accompany the adventurer into the panther-haunted caves . . . and flee with him through the midnight woods infested with murdering Indian braves. . . ."[94]

[94]Fred Lewis Pattee, *A History of American Literature* (New York: Silver, Burdett, 1909), p. 104. Reuben Post Halleck, *History of American Literature* (New York: American Book Co., 1911), p. 91. Lillie Deming Loshe, *The Early American Novel* (New York: Columbia Univ. Press, 1907), p. 72. John Erskine, *Leading American Novelists* (New York: Henry Holt and Co., 1910), p. 34. Sister Mary Mauritia Redden, *The Gothic Fiction in the American Magazines (1765–1800)* (Wash-

With the very marked advance in critical sophistication over the past thirty-four years, especially in the area of close reading, one would expect that a writer of Brown's vulnerability—his writing plagued with hack-work carelessness, quirky syntax, and outright sloppiness of organization—would have suffered a major decline, the horror of his sins more than his subjects having been made resplendent for all to see. His sins we have surely seen, but also the reverse of a decline. *Edgar Huntly* has ridden the Brown-boom along with the other three major novels. The sudden rise in Brown's stock was augmented by the fact that for critical heavyweights like R. W. B. Lewis, Richard Chase, Harry Levin, and Leslie Fiedler, Brown became a factor in formulating central directions in our literary tradition.[95] If not exactly installed as one of our classic novelists, he was coming close, for as Lewis observed, Brown promoted themes "to be located by later fiction in the very heart of American life" (p. 98). Chase and Fiedler were also among the first to probe the deeper

ington, D.C.: Catholic Univ. Press, 1939), p. 60. Albert Keiser, *The Indian in American Literature*, p. 34. "The Pioneer of American Fiction," *The Dartmouth*, p. 43. George B. Smith, "Brockden Brown," *Fortnightly Review*, NS, 24 (1878), p. 419. John Alden, *Alden's Cyclopedia of Universal Literature* (New York: Alden, 1886), p. 161. Carl Van Doren, *The American Novel* (New York: Macmillan, 1926), p. 13. George Snell, "Charles Brockden Brown: Apocalypticalist," *Univ. of Kansas City Review*, 11 (1944), 137. Martin S. Vilas, *Charles Brockden Brown* (Burlington, Vt.: Free Press, 1904), pp. 37, 39. Arthur Hobson Quinn, *American Fiction, An Historical and Critical Survey* (New York: Appleton-Century-Crofts, 1936), p. 32. James Fenimore Cooper, "Preface" *The Spy*, 2d ed. (New York: Wiley and Halstead, 1822), p. vi. Julian Hawthorne and Leonard Lemmon, *American Literature* (Boston: D. C. Heath & Co., 1891), p. 24. "Introduction" M. G. Lewis, *The Monk*, ed. Ernest A. Baker (London: G. Routledge, 1907), p. xiv.

[95]Lewis, *The American Adam* (Chicago: Univ. of Chicago Press, 1955), pp. 92–98. Chase, *The American Novel and Its Tradition* (Garden City, N.Y.: Doubleday & Co., 1957), pp. 29–41. Levin, *The Power of Blackness* (New York: Alfred A. Knopf, 1958), pp. 21–22. Fiedler, *Love and Death in The American Novel*, pp. 73–80, 129–149.

psychological meanings of *Edgar Huntly*, its historical symbolism, and its broader mythic nuances, which would suddenly open up the latent complexities to be explored by recent critics of the novel.

By their collective reading, the novel becomes a web of basic archetypes. Character relations, language, geography, imagery, narrative action, structure (pick your area) — all have been shown to possess clues to the shared heritage of our inner experience, of which the material events in the novel provide reflective metaphors, some of them bent through a Freudian prism. The cave, for example, is invariably a symbol of the subconscious, and the reasons Clithero gives for killing Wiatte and his devotion to Mrs. Lorimer are taken as Oedipal rationalizations.[96] If this has meant a bringing of Vienna to Philadelphia, most readers would likely concede it has been quite profitably done. Whatever the faults of such criticism, dullness at least is not one of them. But more than that, the psychological interpretation has generated what is probably the most unified body of writing about a novel by Brockden Brown, which is a sign at least of the believers it has made among some rather fastidious readers. Much of the impetus for this phenomenon goes back to Fiedler; his insights have been that influential. Wanting to establish the real locus of theme, he brushed aside the inconsequential problems of disorganization and improbability: "It is a charmingly, a maddeningly disorganized book, not so much written as dreamed, but it convinces

[96]Fiedler, p. 147. Philip Russell Hughes, "Archetypal Patterns in *Edgar Huntly*," *Studies In The Novel*, 5 (Summer, 1973), p. 186. David Brion Davis, *Homicide in American Fiction, 1798–1860: A Study in Social Values* (Ithaca, N.Y.: Cornell Univ. Press, 1957), p. 99.

Other variations are Paul Witherington's, that somnambulism represents man "out of touch with his primitive consciousness," and Paul Levine's, that the wild landscape in *Edgar Huntly* is "a gothic symbol of the unconscious psyche." "Benevolence and the 'Utmost Stretch'": Charles Brockden Brown's Narrative Dilemma," *Criticism*, 14 (Spring, 1972), 181. "The American Novel Begins," *American Scholar*, 35 (Winter, 1965–1966), 146.

the reader, once he has been caught up in the fable, of its most utter improbabilities; for its magic is not the hocus-pocus of make-believe, but the irrational reality of the id" (p. 144).

Fiedler rather briskly touches on a number of motifs, among them "the image of flight . . . revealed as the image of life itself" (in *Huntly* this is raised to its "highest power"); most pertinent, however, is his following through on the practical identity of the id. It is the Indians, he holds, who represent the "projection of natural evil and the id." Symbolic of the instinctual life, they are "living extensions of the threat of the wilderness," and as such bear the burden of "guilt, hatred, and terror bred by our historical relations to them." At the same time, Huntly's new awareness of our blindness to the human capacity for evil universalizes it: "Any man may wake to find himself at the bottom of a pit. *We are all sleepwalkers!*" (pp. 145–148).

While most promising areas of inquiry seem to have been fairly well staked out by the early 1960s, the very fertility of the ideas within that domain led to considerable diversity in their application — and not a few arabesques of ingenuity. A good deal of this occurs in dissertations, where, for instance, notions of the subconscious proliferate and are given a rather strong play. Thus, in addition to the cave, the landscape also becomes a map of the subconscious, Clithero Edny is Huntly's subconscious, the subconscious is a "reservoir of innate depravity," Deb becomes Huntly's mother figure who rules the subconscious, the pit represents a fall into the subconscious, and the operation of the subconscious is signaled by shifts of style.[97] Stated so elliptically, the criticism

[97] Paul Witherington, "Narrative Technique in the Novels of Charles Brockden Brown," Ph.D. diss. University of Texas 1964, p. 57. Kenneth Bernard, "The Novels of Charles Brockden Brown: Studies in Meaning," Ph.D. diss. Columbia University 1962, p. 77. Frederick Stilson Frank, "Perverse Pilgrimage: The Role of the Gothic in the Works of Charles Brockden Brown, Edgar Allan Poe, and Nathaniel Hawthorne," Ph.D. diss. Rutgers University 1968,

sounds more confused perhaps than the characters, but in context the protean uses of the subconscious have their validity.

For this, properly termed the "most introverted" of Brown's gothic romances,[98] does not depend on physical mysteries like spontaneous combustion, ventriloquism, and an implacable pestilence, or the premeditated villainies of high-minded hypocrites and deviant con-men for its terrors; no, in *Edgar Huntly*, the inexplicable resides in man's most intimate self. (The bottom nature barbarities of Brown's Indians, though an aspect of the uncharted wilderness, are anything but mysterious.) Edny and Huntly are underground men, obscured to themselves. Questers both, the one man wants relief, the other enlightenment, but, as David Stineback sums it up, that which was found was not exactly what had been sought: "Edgar Huntly begins as a pursuer of knowledge beyond himself and ends in being pursued by the truth within himself."[99] The pattern of ironic reversals—plus the necessary fluidity of symbolic action—more than accounts for the fascination of the book and the imaginative criticism that has recently grown up around it. The general point on which the most informative of this criticism converges is the interpenetration of the inner and outer worlds, a matter best delineated by Norman Grabo, who notes that the "reciprocity between [Huntly's] mental states and external conditions . . . is such that each seems to inform and symbolize the other," a process that "seems to work both ways at once."[100]

p. 266. Carl W. Nelson, Jr., "The Novels of Charles Brockden Brown: Irony and Illusion," Ph.D. diss. State University of New York at Binghamton 1971, pp. 142, 150. David L. Butler, "A Study of the Literary Style of the Novels of Charles Brockden Brown," Ph.D. diss. St. Louis University 1973, pp. 99–101.

[98]Paul Levine, op. cit., p. 146.

[99]"Introduction," *Edgar Huntly* (New Haven, Conn.: College and University Press, 1973), p. 22.

[100]*The Coincidental Art of Charles Brockden Brown*, p. 56.

Plainly, there is no other book of Brown's (or, for that matter, of any other American's before Poe) in which setting becomes so fully functional. That finally is where critics have found the most inviting symbolism in *Edgar Huntly*, as well as what has been called the "mythological resonance" of its internal relationships.[101] The oneiric ambiance is especially compelling; the misty feeling that everything appears to be a waking dream, a quality which according to Warner Berthoff renders "the central action . . . self-engendering and dissociated," and places it in the realm Henry James reserved for high romance: "experience disengaged . . . disencumbered, exempt from the conditions that we usually know to attach to it."[102] Also effective in defining mood, language recapitulates theme, as with the drama of understanding and confusion being paralleled by light and dark images, mazes and obscurities.[103] The wild has appropriately been characterized as Kafkaesque, enabling Huntly to find truth in darkness; it is "an index to the hero's mind" and symbol of his "developing madness," the locale for "Huntly's monologues of conflict" and the journey which produces "the emergence of the dark self."[104] Fundamentally hostile, the scene of an alien odyssey, Brown's nature—George Toles reminds us—engenders "the intense feeling of [man's] exclusion, of [his] dispossession from his native ground"; the "spectral forest" of Norwalk recedes "even further into a twilight gloom where objects shed both form and feature, and 'the conditions' that are revealed relate solely to the psychic

[101]Alan Axelrod, *Charles Brockden Brown: An American Tale* (Austin: Univ. of Texas Press, 1983), p. 162.

[102]"Adventures of the Young Man: An Approach to Charles Brockden Brown," *American Quarterly*, 9 (Winter, 1957), 422.

[103]Kenneth Bernard, "*Edgar Huntly*: Charles Brockden Brown's Unsolved Murder," *Library Chronicle*, 33 (Winter, 1967), 42–45.

[104]Frank, op. cit., pp. 260, 281. Donald A. Ringe, *Charles Brockden Brown* (New York: Twayne Publishers, 1966), pp. 88, 90. Dieter Schulz, "*Edgar Huntly* as Quest Romance," *American Literature*, 43 (November, 1971), 327, 326.

disorder of the narrator." "*Edgar Huntly*," Toles continues, "was the first novel to divine the immense significance of the concealed landscape for the American imagination."[105]

Brown, we know, intended *Edgar Huntly* to be an authentic American tale. There is an important sense in which his hero is the land, for that is where he learns his identity (as would others, like Natty Bumppo, after him); it absorbs and disgorges him. And there is another equally important sense in which the land is his hero. The transposition is accomplished through a peculiarly American style of symbolism in which things are often best perceived by connection with their qualitative opposites, the concrete person/place by an abstraction that establishes its character. As Edwin Fussell has said of Brown: "He was perhaps the first American writer to suspect that the West might more profitably be defined as a condition of the soul than as a physiographical region."[106] Among his other "firsts," then, Brown was the first of our novelists to image an appropriately symbolic setting for the American Adam's return to the Garden of his origins for the redemption — more literally re-judgment — of the uncovenanted inner man.

In *Edgar Huntly*, Brown mapped the frontier from inside out — our inside. Ultimately, we would say he gave mythic content to a definitive experience etched in our national consciousness.

S.J.K.

[105]"Charting the Hidden Landscape: *Edgar Huntly*," *Early American Literature*, 16 (Fall, 1981), 133–134. William Hedges takes the view that Brown's "sense of place is apt to be virtually non-existent" ("Charles Brockden Brown and the Culture of Contradictions," *Early American Literature*, 9 [Fall, 1974], 108). However, the point he misses is that place is usually an affective entity for Brown — something known by how it is felt, or what it means when translated into attitudes. Thus, to deal with the question of its existence, one must start from the premise that the world outside is largely a perceptual construct, maybe only marginally "real" — a matter elucidated by Toles, who observes: "Nature in *Edgar Huntly* can never be experienced (or even conceived of) objectively" (p. 134).

[106]*Frontier: American Literature and the American West* (Princeton: Princeton Univ. Press, 1965), p. 9.

TEXTUAL ESSAY

Commenced not long after he had completed *Arthur Mervyn, First Part* early in February of 1799, and finished by the end of the spring, the third of Brown's novels to be published that year made its appearance some months later on an undetermined date. A portion of *Edgar Huntly* — including some of the most exciting episodes — had earlier appeared in another form in the April number of the *Monthly Magazine*, which Brown had that same spring begun to edit for the New York printers, Thomas and James Swords. This initial issue of Brown's first magazine was published in mid-May, and soon thereafter, so far as we can determine, Brown delivered the manuscript for the three-volume first edition to Hugh Maxwell in Philadelphia. The July number of the *Monthly Magazine* carried a notice that the novel was in press. In late July and throughout August the *Philadelphia Gazette and Universal Daily Advertiser* ran more extensive advertisements for Volume I, together with a subscription notice which contained the three paragraphs that served as the preface to that volume. Both the contents of the advertisements and the use of these paragraphs suggest that the first volume was probably ready for sale some time in August, but there is no further evidence about the date of its actual release or about the publication of the other two volumes.[1]

---

[1] See Historical Essay, pp. 295–303 for more details. Kennedy, p. 1182, cites a letter of 29 May 1799, from William Johnson, which

No manuscript or other pre-publication documents have survived, but some of the variants between the text found in the *Monthly Magazine* (M) and that printed in the first edition (A) no doubt derive from these pre-printing forms of the novel. The provenance of these variants and of those occasioned by the resetting of two formes of the first edition, as well as the relations of the early texts, constitute the major problems that must be solved before an editor can choose copy-text, decide whether to adopt certain variants from the other early texts, and make emendations.

I

Fortunately, the first volume, which comprises Chapters 1–10, does not present any major problems.[2] It is a duodecimo in half-sheets collating $12°$: A^2 B–X^6 Y^4 (Y5–6 = A1–2?). The presumption would be that this volume was printed by the more usual work-and-turn method rather than by "two half-sheets worked together," and if uniformity of basic procedures for all three volumes may be assumed, this presumption seems confirmed by the aberrations in Volume II, which are confined to the half-sheets K and M.[3] The 1801 title page, which creates the second issue, is a cancel. It is likely that this "Second

dates the issue of the April number as mid-May, some two weeks late. *Note*: references to works already cited in the Historical Essay appear in short form here.

[2]Type displacement creates the erroneous reading 'called ,' in some copies where others have 'called.' (105.14).

[3]Whatever the causes behind the existence of the three states of quire K and two of quire M, the various aberrations should have been reflected in quires L and N if two half-sheets were worked together. Even if some irregular pairing of half-sheets is postulated for argument's sake, the regularity of quire L and the fact that the odd half-sheets K and M were printed differently from one another—with different type and on different paper—indicate that each had discrete problems confined to its own forme.

Edition" was occasioned by the fact that the Conrad syndicate — 'Conrad & Co. No. 30, Chestnut Street, Philadelphia: M. & J. Conrad & Co. No. 140 Market Street, Baltimore: and Rapine, Conrad & Co. Washington City. 1801'–in that year replaced Thomas Dobson, Asbury Dickins, and (presumably) the printer Hugh Maxwell as publishers.[4]

The same basic patterns define the 1799 and 1801 issues of Volume II (Chapters 11–19), which collates 12°: A^6 B–T^6 X–Y^6. In this volume, however, half-sheets K and M survive in three and two typesettings, respectively.[5] State *a* of K survives in sixteen copies in America, nine of the first issue and seven of the 1801. State *b* is extant in only one copy, at the University of Kentucky, and it carries a 1799 title page. Likewise, all eleven copies of state *c* belong to the 1799 issue. The variations in reading amongst the three states of quire K (pp. 109–120) are not inconsiderable and suggest something of the quality of Maxwell's work throughout *Edgar Huntly*, as may be seen by consulting the apparatus (pp. 482–483).

The priority of the three states of quire K and the two of M in Volume II is the most difficult of the bibliographical questions posed by the first edition, but various kinds of physical evidence settle the question for state *c* of quire K as well as the two states of M and also indicate the proper order of K's *a* and *b*. As might be expected, the variant readings and even some instances of type damage and displacement throughout the volume provide inconclusive evidence. The readings are of course reversible.

---

[4] On 29 August 1801 in his *New York Weekly Museum*, John Harrisson advertised the novel as "just received, and for sale" in his shop, and the same advertisement appeared in several subsequent issues during the remainder of the year and the first half of 1802 (17 October, 24 October, 28 November 1801, 2 January, 9 January, 22 May 1802).

[5] Aside from the major variation discussed below, type displacement in this volume has created the readings 'rom' and 'damgerous' in some copies where others have 'from' and 'dangerous' (167.7, 174.31).

And the damage and displacement, while tending to suggest the order argued here, are compromised by the uneven inking and general sloppiness of the printing. To be useful this kind of evidence requires the assumption of a direct temporal relationship between the various half-sheets in any given copy; such a relationship may in fact exist, but it would be risky to rely on as primary evidence, especially when only one copy of state *b* survives.

State *c* of quire K, however, resembles the second state of quire M, found only in copies at the American Antiquarian Society (MWA), Princeton University, and Dickinson College, in having physical features that immediately set it apart from the rest of the half-sheets of this volume and the other two. Whereas the first state of quire M was, like the remainder of the novel, printed with an english font on unmarked laid paper,[6] these three copies exhibit wove paper and a small-pica font in this half-sheet.[7] These characteristics quite separate these examples of quire M from the composition and printing which produced the other half-sheets found in these three exemplars, with the notable exception of quire K. All three copies also contain state *c* of quire K, which is characterized by a wove paper that is of a yet different stock, less coarse and less bulky, than the paper of quire M. This second wove paper is nevertheless quite distinguishable from the laid paper found in the other quires of Volume II

[6]The subscription notice run in the *Philadelphia Gazette* specified that *Edgar Huntly* was to be "comprised in three volumes large duodecimo" and printed "on a new type and superfine paper" (see p. 297; also p. 301).

[7]The type could be pica; because the spacing between lines precludes a twenty-line measurement as the basis for identifying the body, the size has to be estimated by comparison against the examples in H. D. L. Vervliet, *Sixteenth-Century Printing Types of the Low Countries* (Amsterdam: Menno Hertzberger, 1968), and in W. Turner Berry and A. F. Johnson, *Catalogue of Specimens of Printing Types . . . 1665–1830* (London: Oxford Univ. Press, 1935). For the identification of type size we have relied on Philip Gaskell, "Type Sizes in the Eighteenth Century," *Studies in Bibliography*, 5 (1952–53), 147–151.

(with the exception of state *b* of quire M, of course) and, more importantly, in the other two states of quire K. The type is also different, though less obviously so than that of quire M: it is an english font but is distinguished by the unique presence of ct ligatures, which must be traceable to a different pair of cases or at least a different compositor. Moreover, the distance of 6 or more millimeters separating the headline from the first line of text in state *c* of quire K contrasts with the virtually uniform 5 mm distance found in the other quires of this volume. Because the remaining half-sheets of Volume II and all those of Volume III (with the single exception of its two-leaf preliminary quire) are printed on the laid paper found elsewhere in Volume II, and throughout Volume I as well, it seems clear that the half-sheets comprising states *c* of K and *b* of M were printed out of sequence, presumably after the main stock had been exhausted with Volume III's last half-sheet of text but before its preliminaries had been wrought off. The discrepancies in paper together with those in type and in headline distances are about as conclusive as one could hope. Any attempt to argue the priority of either state *b* of quire M or state *c* of quire K requires such complicated and incredible hypotheses that the physical evidence alone is sufficient to show that in both cases new formes were composed and additional copies of the half-sheets struck off after the normal process of composition and printing had run its usual course.

The discrepancy in headline distance that helps set state *c* of quire K apart from the printing process which produced the remaining half-sheets of Volume II — and indeed the forty-two half-sheets of Volumes I and III — proves to be the crucial evidence for ordering states *a* and *b*. Other facts are inconclusive, though suggestive. For instance, since state *b* survives in only one example, at the University of Kentucky, whereas state *a* is represented by sixteen known copies, this fact could be taken to suggest that state *b*, like state *b* of quire M, was set up and run after the normal printing had occurred, in order to meet a similar or identical problem. Although this conjectured procedure is probably accurate (see following), the evidence is, like that of the variant readings, reversible and inconclusive. One could also argue that state *b* was an original but short-lived typesetting that, owing to pie or other eventualities, produced relatively few copies before it had to be replaced. Because the types and papers in states *a* and *b* are identical with those found in the remaining quires (except state *c* of quire K and *b* of M, of course), no obvious evidence exists like that found in these odd examples to establish the priority of these states vis-à-vis one another.

Nevertheless, the distance between the headlines and text in each page of state *b* is, like that of *c*, 6mm or more, whereas that of state *a* conforms to the pattern exhibited almost without exception throughout the some 250 pages of Volume II.[8] What this distance apparently represents is a set number of scabbords (or "scaleboards," as Caleb Stower calls them), or of reglets or leads, of set thickness placed between the headline and the first line of text. Which one of these three kinds of material served to create the "white" in this book can only be inferred (see following), but the compositor's general procedure would have been similar in any case and is outlined by Philip Luckombe, who follows John Smith in these instructions for setting the second page of a book with scabbords:

> The Running title being set, we put a suitable distance between that and the Matter; and therefore consider the Bearings off of our letters in the Running title: for if it consists of all Capitals that have no descending letters amongst them, and runs throughout the work, three Scabbords of a middle size, will

[8]The exceptions are the 4.5 mm measurement in sigs. L1^v, L6, R1, and T2^v, the 5.5 mm in M6^v (first state), and the 6 mm in N5^v; the probable causes of these few discrepancies are touched upon below. Sigs. K2^v and K4 measure 7 mm, K3 and K3^v 6.5 mm, in state *b*.

be sufficient to separate the Running title from the Matter; whereas four thick Scabbords will make no more than a proper distance, where Running titles are in Italic, or mixed with it; and withal have descending letters among them. But in this case, as in others, we have regard to proportion, and make a difference in distances, agreeable to the size as well of the Letter as Page.

The crucial role played by the compositor's personal judgment in setting his first running title is obviously of some interest in this account. Another function of the individual compositor is indicated by Joseph Moxon in his definition of the scabbord: "Scabbord is that sort of Scale commonly sold by some Ironmongers in Bundles; And of which, the Scabbords for Swords are made: The Compositer cuts it Quadrat high, and to his Length."[9] Whether scabbords, reglets, or leads actually produced the white space between the headlines and the text of *Edgar Huntly*, what is remarkable, given these procedures, is the uniformity of the headline distances found throughout the three volumes, which exhibit a total of only nine pages

[9]Philip Luckombe, *The History and Art of Printing* (London, 1771; rpt. London: Gregg Press, 1965), p. 383; Joseph Moxon, *Mechanick Exercises on the Whole Art of Printing*, ed. Herbert Davis and Harry Carter, 2d ed. (London, 1683–1684; rpt. London: Oxford Univ. Press, 1962), pp. 38–39; John Smith, *The Printer's Grammar*, (London, 1755; rpt. London: Gregg Press, 1965), pp. 109–110; Caleb Stower, *The Printer's Grammar* (London, 1808; rpt. London: Gregg Press, 1965), pp. 92–93. Stower's description of the use of leads or reglets parallels Luckombe's of scabbords; see below. It is not entirely clear that scabbords or reglets were placed between the text lines, since Philip Gaskell, *A New Introduction to Bibliography* (London: Clarendon Press, 1900), p. 46, also mentions "typemetal" and "cards" for this purpose in his general discussion. See the paragraphs below for some brief consideration of this and related questions and, for a more detailed discussion of the technical questions, S. W. Reid and James F. Caccamo, "The States and Issues of Brown's *Edgar Huntly*," *PBSA*, 75 (1981), 326–339. We wish to thank the Bibliographical Society of America for permission to reprint material from this article.

that vary from the standard of 5 mm — if states *b* and *c* of quire K and *b* of M are excepted. In part such uniformity was probably owing to measures of economy. To avoid having to assemble leads, scabbords, or reglets anew and to save cutting scabbords or reglets for each page as they set — that is, to save wasting time and rather precisely wrought and expensive material — Maxwell's compositor(s) probably had sets of spacing material that they transferred from forme to forme as the printing proceeded. Indeed, they probably had many sets, to take care of formes at press or standing by.[10]

The procedure described by Luckombe for using scabbords or for using leads or reglets described by Stower, seems to have been fairly settled in Maxwell's shop for the printing of *Edgar Huntly*, and the uniform following of another pattern in the one extant copy of state *b* of quire K suggests that it was composed and imposed out of sequence, during a separate process in which a 6-mm distance was decided on as the standard, though in fact two pages (K2^v and K4) exhibit a 7-mm distance otherwise unprecedented in the entire edition. The few deviations from the standard of 5 mm elsewhere in Volume II and at scattered points in Volumes I and III seem to be isolated and momentary compositorial aberrations. No such explanation can be offered for the invariable deviation in state *b* of quire K, which obviously represents a deliberate decision carried out sedulously in this forme, but not car-

[10]That this would have been quite as mechanical a process as is sometimes believed to have prevailed in the use of skeleton-formes in a shop of the earlier centuries seems doubtful. Maxwell was a generally careless rather than methodical printer, and only the grossest inducements — such as those postulated here — can be supposed to have led to some measure of efficiency in his shop. The few aberrations from the standard prove this general rule, for the uniformity of headline distance is remarkable given the generally poor quality of his work. In fact, it may be conjectured that the sets behind sigs. L1^v and L6 of Volume II could have been reused in R1 and T2^v, leaving only two additional aberrant sets, one in M6^v and one in N5^v, for all of Volume II.

ried through the remainder of the volume or indeed in Volume III. The theory that state *b* precedes state *a* requires belief in an implausible string of coincidences: (1) that a deliberate decision to change the headline distance was made for the tenth forme but abandoned in the very next and thenceforth, with a return to the previously ruling norm; (2) that this decision was carried out by changing the sets of leads, scabbords, or reglets that were used in this forme and that these twelve new sets were never used again, not in the forme that printed half-sheet L or in any subsequent formes; (3) that by an extraordinary coincidence this same forme later needed resetting and still later a second resetting; (4) that in the first resetting the compositor just happened to return to the standard headline distance (if not to the very sets of leads, reglets, or scabbords) generally used throughout the remainder of the volume but momentarily rejected in the original forme of quire K; (5) that the second resetting (state *c*) returned to the odd headline distance of the aberrant first (state *b*) rather than conforming to the more recent distance and indeed to the rest of the half-sheets in the volume. This series of deviations and coincidences of course stretches credulity. It is much more plausible to conclude that state *a* was set up in the normal way with the continued use of some of the lead, reglet, or scabbord sets from preceding formes and that the odd state *b* came later, after the norm for the headline distance had been forgotten and perhaps after the lead, reglet, or scabbord sets had been dispersed, with state *c* following it still later.

The element of coincidence in the first but implausible theory, particularly as it concerns the conformity of state *a*'s headline distance to that in the rest of the volume, becomes only less credible as further information on the scabbords, reglets, and leads available to Maxwell comes forward for examination. The evidence is rather technical and does not require elaboration here. Suffice it to say that whether scabbords, reglets, or leads were used, the printing process would have involved specially assembling sets of them for the pages, or cutting them to order, or both. That different sets of assembled material lie behind the different headline distances in states *b* and *c* is certain, and the general procedures that must have been employed in assembling and working with these various sets make any argument for the priority of either of these two states highly improbable. At this distance it is of course impossible to determine exactly how the assembling of such material would have produced the spacing below headlines observed in the first edition, though some fairly plausible conjectures are possible and support the order of states argued here.[11]

Whether or not these conjectures definitively account for all the phenomena observed is perhaps debatable, but that does not affect the main conclusions. Nor is the larger question of the occasion of the resettings of quires K and M crucial to ordering them. Why this happened, particularly why two resettings of quire K occurred, is not at all clear. State *b* of quire M, with its obvious disparity, suggests a hasty process, perhaps to make up for an underprinting of this half-sheet. Clearly the composition and printing of it and state *c* of quire K seem to have taken place after Volume III had been printed, if the evidence of different paper may be trusted. Yet this does not seem to be a case of a publisher reaching the bottom of a pile of edition sheets (or half-sheets) and calling for additional examples to make up the last few copies. The odd states all appear in 1799 copies, none in 1801. Only the earliest states of both quires K and M turn up in the 1801 issue, as well as the 1799, and this fact suggests that these were at the bottom of their respective piles, as they should have been if they were first printed and the piles left alone unturned. In the event of underprinting, we could understand the relative rarity of state *b* of quire M and state *b* of K but would have to suppose that a supervisor noticed the underprint long before many copies were

[11]For more on these matters, see "States and Issues," pp. 333–338.

released, or that some accident to the formes late in each run occasioned the resetting of both quires M and K but that this resetting was delayed until after Volume III had reached completion. The former supposition fits the facts for state *b* of K, the latter for state *b* of M and perhaps *c* of K. But the entire set of suppositions is rather complex, is surely speculative, and is fortunately unnecessary to establish the priority of states *a* of both quires K and M.

The priority of state *a* of K is of course crucial to choosing copy-text, but because of the light the other two states may shed on the reliability and habits of Maxwell's compositors, there remains the question of the copy for states *b* and *c*. Most of the errors are in state *c*, clearly the most corrupt of the three, but since it consistently returns to the readings of *a* instead of following *b* when errors in the latter are not obvious ones (e.g., at 154.15, 154.22, 154.38), state *c*'s independence of *b* seems assured. Indeed, each is apparently a page-for-page and line-for-line reprint of state *a*, rather than a resetting of manuscript copy, and thus their errors in punctuation, spelling, and wording provide a useful index to the composition of the entire set of volumes (see following).

The third volume (Chapters 20–26) presents no problems of textual significance,[12] but the various issues do raise some curious questions of publishing history. Those 1799 copies that contain "The Death of Cicero, A Fragment" collate $12°$: π^2 A–U^6; "The Death of Cicero" occupies half-sheets R–U, R1 serving as a part- or section-title, with a new sequence of pagination (pp. *1–2* 3–48). Sig. π1 contains the title (verso blank), and π2 is blank in those copies that have it (several lack this leaf). This gathering was presumably printed last (see Stower, p. 162) and consists of wove, not laid, paper; the paper appears to be of the same stock as that used for state *c* of quire K in Volume II and may thus provide a rough dating of that

---

[12]Again type displacement creates readings in some copies: 'agumented' for 'augmented', 'o' for 'of', 'mya ssociates' for 'my associates', 'me$_\wedge$' for 'me.' (224.19, 229.5, 253.15, 289.9).

alternative typesetting. In both the 1800 and 1801 issues the single title-page leaf is a cancel. The 1800 title page mentions "The Death of Cicero," which is ignored not only on the 1799 title but on the 1801 as well.

The occasion of the 1801 issue of this volume was presumably the same as that of Volumes I and II, but the implications of the 1800 issue for dating the actual printing of the third volume are unclear. By late 1799, apparently, Maxwell had moved his shop from Letitia Court (located between Front and Second Streets off what is now Market) around the corner to 25 North Second Street, where he took over the premises so quickly vacated by William Cobbett in early November upon the election of his enemy, Thomas McKean, to the governorship and on the prospect of Benjamin Rush's libel suit against him reaching a hearing.[13] From the fact that the 1799 title to Volume III continued to give Maxwell's address as Letitia Court, it follows that the printing of the volume must have been completed some time prior to Maxwell's decision to relocate: that is, before the early weeks of November. But though Maxwell's move thus provides a kind of *terminus ad quem* for the production of the three volumes, it does not fix the date of the printing of the final sheets precisely nor account for the survival of the 1800 title page with Maxwell's new address. Of course, Maxwell's move would itself have provided sufficient occasion for the new title page. But the fact that neither of the other two volumes survives in 1800 issues is curious, as is the wove paper in the 1799 preliminary gathering of the third. We might explain these facts by speculating that Maxwell became aware of his impending change of address just as he was finishing Volume III and

[13]Pierce W. Gaines, *William Cobbett and the United States 1792–1835* (Worcester, Mass.: American Antiquarian Society, 1971), pp. xvi, 242; Lewis Mumford, *The Life and Letters of William Cobbett in England & America* (New York: John Lane, 1908), I, 111–112; George Spater, *William Cobbett: The Poor Man's Friend* (Cambridge: Cambridge Univ. Press, 1982), I, 105.

at that point decided to print up an 1800 title for more-or-less simultaneous issue of this volume only. This scenario would put the completion of the entire set, begun in June or early July (see pp. 300–301), in late October or early November, and it would help fix the date of state *c* of quire K as well. However, the 1800 title leaf is a laid paper that differs not only from the wove of the 1799 but from the stock of the remainder of Volume III. Hard evidence for simultaneous issue is therefore wanting, and since a six-month period of production seems unlikely if not economically disastrous, the precise dating of the three volumes, particularly the last, remains conjectural at best.[14]

Equally uncertain is whether the two extant copies that lack "The Death of Cicero" represent a separate 1799 issue.[15] The fact that *Edgar Huntly* ends on Q6 and that "The Death of Cicero" begins on R1 makes it entirely possible that Maxwell originally sold copies without the four quires that contain "The Death of Cicero." If Brown's statement that "Maxwell has projected the printing of Huntley [*sic*] on too large a scale" may be taken to refer to its three-decker format rather than the number of copies to be printed,[16] it could suggest that Maxwell ended up adding "The Death of Cicero" to fill out the volume. On the other hand, it would be a very poor printer indeed who could not cast off and calculate the scope of his copy and divide it into three equal portions. Moreover, the fact that the paper on which "The Death of Cicero" is printed seems to be identical with that containing the text of *Edgar Huntly* would appear to indicate that half-sheets R–U were printed before the 1799 preliminary quire (and before state *c* of K and *b* of M in Volume II). Since the

[14]Maxwell had produced *Arthur Mervyn, First Part* (a shorter work, but not so much shorter) in the space of three months or less earlier in the year.

[15]These two copies are housed at Yale University and the American Antiquarian Society.

[16]Dunlap, *Life*, II, 97.

413

edition was issued in sheets, rather than bound, there is no way to be sure that the two odd copies are not in effect defective. At this distance it is impossible to determine whether or not these two examples represent a separate issue, though the evidence now at hand would seem to discourage that view. All we can tell is that there are extant three issues of Volume III and possibly a fourth, that there are two issues of Volumes I and II, that none of these issues itself occasioned variation in the text, but that in the 1799 issue of Volume II quires K and M exist in three and two states, respectively, with many variants, and that fortunately the order of these typesettings can be determined with some confidence.

II

Because it is a textual question involving lost manuscript "copy," the relationship between the text that occupies the last half of Volume II and that printed in the *Monthly Magazine* during April of 1799 is less susceptible to determination. However, examination of the variants between these texts makes it necessary for us to eliminate one and possible for us to reject a second of the three hypothetical genealogies that present themselves: (1) that M was set from Brown's manuscript and in turn, after he had annotated an example of it, served as copy for A; (2) that each was set independently from the very same manuscript, which Brown revised for A after the Swordses had returned it; (3) that M was set from a fair-copy manuscript which the Swords shop discarded and that for Maxwell's purposes Brown made another fair-copy from his draft, producing revisions and corrections in the process.[17]

[17]A fourth alternative, that he recopied the Swords manuscript copy, is unlikely under the circumstances and at any rate amounts to the same thing as the third alternative in its implications for choice of copy-text and, to a large extent, choice of variant readings.

The evidence for discarding the first of these hypotheses is remarkably extensive, given the circumstances, though it is naturally of various weights. Variant readings indicate that this hypothesis is untenable, and this conclusion receives some support from external considerations which, while not entirely persuasive on their own, are nevertheless not irrelevant. The analogy of *Arthur Mervyn, First Part*—where the installments of the novel published in the *Weekly Magazine* during June, July, and August of 1798 served as copy for what became the first nine chapters of Maxwell's first edition—might encourage the belief that Maxwell used M in a similar way for *Edgar Huntly*, and the general desirability of printed as opposed to hand-written copy would lend some support to this view. However, the situations are not really comparable. The manuscript of *Arthur Mervyn, First Part*, much of which Brown sent in installments from New York to Philadelphia, was apparently not retrievable by Brown when its publisher James Watters died of that city's yellow-fever epidemic late in the summer. There is no evidence that Brown revised this portion of *Arthur Mervyn, First Part* when— after Maxwell had, in December 1798, first proposed book publication—it was reprinted in January or February of 1799. But there is some evidence that the installments sent from New York were rushed into the mail, perhaps in the form of Brown's original and only manuscript, since he missed at least one deadline and since the completion and publication of *Wieland* was his chief preoccupation at the time.[18] In the case of *Edgar Huntly*, however, the situation was different, for as editor of the

---

[18]For details, see the previous volumes in this edition: especially, Norman S. Grabo, "Historical Essay" and S. W. Reid, "Textual Essay," in *Arthur Mervyn or Memoirs of the Year 1793: First and Second Parts*, ed. Sydney J. Krause, et al. (Kent, Ohio: Kent State Univ. Press, 1980), pp. 452–456, 480–481; also Alexander Cowie, "Historical Essay," in *Wieland . . . Carwin the Biloquist* (1977), pp. 319–323, and Russel B. Nye, "Historical Essay," in *Ormond or The Secret Witness* (1982), pp. 307–309.

Monthly Magazine Brown presumably had more control over the copy he submitted to his printers and was surely in a better position to provide against the anticipated publication of his work in book form. Indeed, *Edgar Huntly* and the *Monthly Magazine* were Brown's only real literary employments during most of 1799, and the latter, after its initial issue had been gotten together, was not sufficiently taxing to keep him from taking a two-week trip to Philadelphia in mid-May (probably in part to deliver *Edgar Huntly* to Maxwell) or a ramble through Connecticut in June (see page 301). The closer analogy, in fact, seems to be *Alcuin*, a manuscript of which Brown apparently retained for future use when sending Elihu Hubbard Smith another manuscript that provided copy for the Swords booklet, which eventually appeared concurrently with the independent printing of the dialogue in the *Weekly Magazine*.

Had an example of M served as copy for A one might expect some shared error to filter through, particularly given the rate of error exhibited elsewhere in A and the unlikelihood that Brown, of all people, would have assiduously corrected M's text while revising it. In fact, there are no such common errors that constitute reliable evidence. The closest thing to one is the reading 'had began' (at 202.36) found in both, but this particular example is not necessarily "incorrect" by his time's standards, and it must certainly be discounted as evidence not so much because of the likelihood of independent misreading of Brown's small hand as because of his notorious sloppiness in matters of tense, which can be documented *ad nauseam* in his other novels.[19] Other possible errors are few and less convincing: 'preparation' (185.6) is not very offensive in its context and is, at any rate, an instance of Brown's most common grammatical fault, his disregard of number,

[19]See the textual note on 202.36 and the Textual Essay in *Ormond*, p. 352, n.17; also, for example, *Wieland*, 232.6, 238.20; *Ormond*, 130.1–2, 141.30–31; *Arthur Mervyn*, 416.10.

whereas 'this' and 'into' (195.4, 171.14) are even less certainly wrong and less infelicitous. A few shared spellings—'shrowded', 'died', 'commiseration' (172.23, 195.31, 206.15)—are frail evidence; though the first is the only -*ow*- in A, which has three examples of -*ou*- elsewhere, it and the other two are clearly acceptable alternatives of the time, and two of them (not 'died') may even have been dominant then.

In short, there is nothing reliable to support the view that A derives from M. On the contrary, there is much evidence against it. The most obvious reading, perhaps, is A's ellipsis in the following sentence:

The company, attracted by this dialogue, crowded round the girl, whom her father, clasping in his arms, lifted from the ground, and pressed, in a transport of joy to his breast.

(196.6–9)

Here M has the more predictable 'clasping her', but A's construction is undoubtedly Brown's, as can be seen from parallels, in this novel and others, too numerous to list.[20] It is, of course, possible that A omitted M's 'her' by chance, but a deliberate rejection of M's apparently correct construction for the awkward one it prints, however genuinely authorial, seems unlikely. The evidence here suggests a compositor working directly from Brown's manuscript and, in this case, reproducing faithfully what he wrote (or did not write). He was not so successful when he set 'when' earlier (170.32), producing a possible reading but one that, as the context shows, clearly represents a graphic error for the 'where' that M's compositor correctly deciphered. A similar instance of variation deriving from misreading of Brown's small hand is found near the very end of Volume II, where each man has independently and

[20]See the textual notes in *Wieland*, 100.30, and *Ormond*, 12.8, and the readings referred to there; also *Arthur Mervyn*, 113.11, 152.3.

417

differently rendered what must have been a difficult, because uncommon, word in his MS copy (211.31): though A's 'cultivable' is probably superior, M's 'culturable' is not so bad as to require correction, and both quite evidently derive independently from Brown's autograph. It may be, also, that A's 'energis' ('energies' in M) two pages later represents a similar problem with manuscript (212.20), though it could well be an outright error of Maxwell's workman.

Beyond these substantive variants, which must necessarily depend on context, judgment, and knowledge of the author for their value, A has a few spellings that indicate its independence of M. The most frequent and consequently most useful of these is the variation between M's 'footsteps' and A's 'foot-steps' throughout the last half of Volume II. Sometimes this word occurs at the break between lines in one text or the other and is therefore ambiguous as evidence. In general, though, M is uniform in spelling 'footsteps', whereas in its three volumes A has three times as many 'foot-steps' as it does 'footstep(s)' (twenty against seven). Although thus tolerant of the joined form while preferring the hyphenated, Maxwell's shop is surprisingly consistent in spelling six 'foot-steps' where M has 'footsteps', and in so setting one form that falls at a line-break in M. It is difficult to prove that the seven joined forms found elsewhere in A derive from Brown's manuscript, for, though invariable in their spelling, only four instances of the word survive in his manuscripts, all spelt as 'footsteps'. But it seems probable that Maxwell's shop would have reproduced some of M's spellings had it served as copy, since in setting *Arthur Mervyn, First Part* his men retained all five such forms from the *Weekly Magazine* while elsewhere producing their preferred hyphenated form — which is, incidentally, unique to Maxwell's books amongst the first editions of Brown's novels and pretty certainly represents the printer's as opposed to the author's style.

Other variant spellings are not so numerous, but they support the inference to be drawn from this word. A has two -*e*- spellings of 'steadfast' where M has -*ea*-, but it elsewhere has one -*ea*- and two -*e*- forms. Maxwell's tolerance though not preference for -*ea*- spellings—which, again, four uniform spellings in his manuscripts suggest was Brown's own preference—is also exhibited in the first nine chapters of *Arthur Mervyn*, where his men reproduced both -*ea*- spellings from the *Weekly Magazine* while elsewhere setting one -*ea*- and two -*e*- forms. The -*ea*- spelling would appear to be a specimen of the Swordses' styling for the *Monthly Magazine*, judging from Brown's other works published in that periodical (as opposed to *Wieland*, which the Swords shop spelt uniformly with -*e*-). Again, if it were set from a copy of M, A should have reproduced at least one of these -*ea*- forms but in fact failed to do so. Something similar happens in the one case of A's 'attendents' which varies against M's 'attendants', for A actually is ambivalent about the spelling of this word (setting three -*a*- and two -*e*- forms elsewhere), though Maxwell's shop earlier in the year had reproduced six -*a*- spellings from the *Weekly Magazine*, while setting six -*a*- and five -*e*- forms in the following chapters of *Arthur Mervyn*. The -*a*- spelling could represent the Swords brothers' styling for the *Monthly Magazine*, (if Brown's other works published there, together with *Wieland* and *Alcuin*, which they also printed, may be taken as evidence), but in any case it seems to have been the acceptable spelling, and it is never reproduced—as we might have expected it to be—in A. Neither does A reproduce the single instance of M's 'tranquility', though otherwise exhibiting ambivalence toward the -*l*-/-*ll*- spellings of this word, nor retain the single instance of 'suspence' found in M, though it has two -*c*- spellings elsewhere as well as eight -*s*- spellings (in *Arthur Mervyn*, Maxwell's shop follows its printed copy in both -*l*- spellings and the single -*s*- form of these words). This evidence, though variable and not overwhelming in

419

quantity, is qualitatively of some value in supporting the view, which rests largely on the substantive variants, that A was typeset from a manuscript independently of M.

Some mild support for this view also comes from other accidentals, though in these cases we have only the evidence of A and M themselves. The most blatant is the rare spelling of 'tom-hawk' (initially 'Tom-hawk'), which occurs throughout A in contrast to M's more conventional 'tomahawk'. This very unusual spelling — certainly not the ordinary form, according to standard sources, and with its hyphen unprecedented in them — would have been typeset six times in *Edgar Huntly* before Maxwell's men would have encountered M's more predictable 'tomahawk', assuming seriatim composition. Nevertheless, the fact remains that A's compositor(s) invariably set this unusual form, though exhibiting fixed principle and regularity in almost no other aspect of the text. Less pervasive, certainly, but equally anomalous is A's 'uncerimoniously', which could be the survival of a sixteenth-century form or a simple manual error but probably represents a graphic error where M has the conventional medial -*e*- (184.13). In yet another respect the text of A is remarkable if M served as copy for the last half of Volume II. M is characterized by a certain, almost uniform, styling of parenthetical phrases, which it assiduously (though not invariably) punctuates fore and aft. The first of many examples that comes to hand involves the phrase 'at least' (170.29), which M surrounds by commas, while A omits them (see also 193.33). More frequently, it is only the initial point that A omits, whereas M supplies both in its more precise and conventional treatment of a passage. M's style almost certainly derives from the Swords shop, and to believe that A repeatedly rejects it in favor of a system (or lack of one) that probably reflects Brown's own free-wheeling usage is to persevere in an inference against logic and probability. Likewise, in specific passages, A fails to set a point and thus produces an ambiguity that probably reproduces Brown's own, where M more precisely clarifies the passage; styles a series of indirect quotations in a way that is more awkward and less conventional than M's, though probably more faithful to Brown; produces a typical Brownian "inaccuracy of punctuation" where M sets the passage more "correctly"; and sets two points that either produce a complex but plausible sentence where M has a smooth and predictable one, or result from a thorough alteration of the syntax of the passage such as Brown would have undertaken only in recopying his manuscript (198.17, 196.12-13, 196.22, 174.29-30). These bits of evidence, together with that already cited, constitute a rather formidable case against A having been set from an example of M annotated, however much, by Brown.

The evidence, cumulative as it is, may be less conclusive perhaps than could be hoped, but it approaches being so because of its consistency. The texts of M and A are apparently collateral. And they are both authoritative not only because they are independently derived from Brown but also because A obviously contains revisions introduced after the manuscript copy for M had been turned over to the Swordses (presumably in early April) and before Brown delivered the manuscript for the whole novel to Maxwell (probably in May). These revisions generally concern detail and description and are of no real consequence for the plot or characterization. Most are either additions or expansions. The clause inserted at 191.13-14 and the long passage added at 202.28-34 are exceptional in their relevance to and clarification of the action and its significance. By and large the additions elaborate on something already latent in M's text, as when A adds 'the *well-pole*' to 'the *worm-fence*, and the hayrick' as a further sign of the presence of white farmers on the borders of the wilderness, or by inserting the phrase 'of a leopard' not only creates a parallelism but also provides an echo of Edgar's earlier encounters with the panther, or cougar, or tiger (204.6-7, 212.12). The most extensive concerns the interior of old Deb's hut — its bread, its bucket, its hoe — which Brown alters by rearrangement and additions (184.5–10). Something similar happens later, where Deb's agrarian economy is more fully described, her 'hoeing and grinding' of corn more elaborately detailed, and the critters she traps—'rabbits and apossums'—identified (208.8–10). The wilderness facing Edgar and his female companion during their escape from the Indians is altered a bit in A by means of expansions that complicate the difficulties through which they must struggle (181.31, 181.34–35, 182.21, 182.22–23). In some of these cases omissions of M's text necessarily accompany A's additions and expansions (e.g., deletion of 'withes' at 182.22, or of the axe and spade at 184.9). One or two other deletions of words seem to be for stylistic reasons or for clarity. Only one cut is of any definite weight: A omits M's description of Edgar's fusil as rusted and bruised, and given the developments in the plot later, the propriety of this excision is apparent (185.22). Still another change may have been motivated by concern with a different kind of propriety, for the resting place of his female companion's head, which is Edgar's knees in M, becomes the rude bed in A (184.33). But this alteration, like the two curious deletions involving the pipe-smoking of the first Indian that Edgar encounters (174.34, 177.20), may represent mere simplifications of the narrative.

That A and M are collateral authoritative texts seems clear; whether they are independently derived from one manuscript or from collateral manuscripts is less certain and, fortunately, less consequential. For the question whether they were set directly from the same manuscript or from different manuscripts descending from a common draft affects only those variants—mostly accidentals but some substantives as well of a particular kind—that might be viewed as indifferent alterations created by Brown in the course of retranscribing these chapters to create copy for A. If such retranscription occurred, then the ancestry of the prints would generally shift the weight in favor of A's forms, whereas if both descend from a common ancestor, then M and A would have exactly identical authority and choices would have to be made strictly on the basis of the texts' respective accuracy and the nature of the variants—both elusive qualities so far as such readings are concerned.

The evidence for the two possible genealogies is almost equally elusive: graphic or other kinds of errors found at the same points in both M and A and also traceable to an identical unreadable manuscript would support the hypothesis of common manuscript copy, whereas minor variations that appeared to result from the process of retranscription but not to have called for deliberate revision would indicate that Brown followed this course in making printer's copy for A. Errors of the first sort are, quite simply, not to be found in M and A. Yet this negative evidence is not entirely decisive because the probabilities of their presence are low. Of the second kind there are certainly some instances, but here distinguishing authorial variation from transmissional is no easy task. The most convincing cases would be those changes that are so indifferent as not to have been calculated or to have required alteration by an author simply looking through a finished manuscript with a view to revising it. Such are A's 'dawn of day' for M's 'the dawn of the day', its 'into' for M's 'in', its 'in' for 'in a', and its lack of paragraphing at one point (186.38, 178.26, 212.14, 171.17), but each is to some extent (the first perhaps the least) open to interpretation as an error of either A or M.[21] Less open to this objection is the alteration of M's 'hares' to 'rabbits'; however, since Brown soon adds the phrase about 'rabbits and apossums' to define the quarry of old Deb's 'snares', this substitution could be regarded as a minor accompaniment to revision (207.34, 208.9–10). Somewhere between these two poles lies perhaps the best evidence: A's 'measure', 'looks, occasion', 'overhear', and 'subjected', where

---

[21]For instance, A's phrase 'in miserable plight' (212.14) does seem to be an instance of Brown's frequent ellipsis—a parallel is 'in quality of servant' (*Ormond*, 107.30)—but though it could represent Brown's alteration during retranscription, M's 'in a' could be a simple error.

M reads 'measures', 'look, occasions', 'overheard', and 'subject' (172.4, 208.18, 208.23, 213.8). These are more likely to be authorial rather than compositorial variants, and the argument seems hardly credible that all represent deliberate revisions such as Brown would have inserted in a retrieved manuscript that had already provided suitable copy for M. Related to this group are clarifications and minor improvements of infelicities that would be noticed more readily by an author transcribing a manuscript rather than looking it over: the transposition of 'partly', while not entirely satisfactory once the problem is grasped, does help cure a subtle ambiguity (188.21), as do the addition of 'But' (192.4) and the substitution of 'but' for 'and' earlier (183.28). These difficulties require considerable concentration to be detected, and this is true too of A's rather fussy substitution of 'precarious' for M's 'ambiguous' (184.31), the omission of M's redundant 'merely' and misleading 'but' (208.36, 209.11), and of some other alterations that might be cited but also might represent either genuine revision or the errors of the compositors of M or A.[22]

Although these readings are by their nature not decisive, the utter lack of conflicting evidence cannot help but suggest that Brown in fact transcribed his draft in order to supply Maxwell with copy for the last half of Volume II as well as the remainder of the novel. Indeed, external considerations would support such a conclusion even if internal evidence were entirely lacking. It would seem improbable that Brown would have wanted to depend on getting his manuscript back from his printers before proceeding to finish his novel. Such a manuscript, marked up for printing and handled by the Swords compositors, would have been difficult to work with and would have made difficult copy for Maxwell. Many pages probably would have required recopying anyway, particularly those where the revisions discussed earlier (pp. 421–422) were to be made. The time saved by such a process would have

---

[22]For example, 173.26, 181.31, 181.35, 193.25–26, 197.33.

been in the end negligible and hardly worth the trouble to Brown. It is more likely that he adopted a procedure which he apparently followed when publishing *Alcuin* in New York and Philadelphia the previous year and which is suggested by his earlier remarks about wholly transcribing a "hasty and inaccurate" draft and spending as much time doing so as was consumed in making the draft in the first place, presumably owing to the introduction of some alterations in the process.[23] We might even conclude that, given their nature, many of the changes introduced in A were not so much the cause as the natural effect of the transcribing process.

One final and relatively minor question of genealogy concerns the three paragraphs "To The Public" which occupy the second leaf of the preliminary gathering of Volume I. These also served, as two paragraphs, for the opening of the subscription notice dated 9 August which appeared the next day in the *Philadelphia Gazette and Universal Daily Advertiser* and was repeated five more times during the remainder of the month. The text is so short that it is impossible to ascertain beyond cavil whether Andrew Brown and Samuel Relf, the publishers and printers of the *Gazette* (G), used an example of A's preliminaries or Brown's manuscript (or a transcription of it) as copy, or indeed whether they first set up the subscription notice and Maxwell printed his preface from that. As to the last possibility, however, the evidence is remarkably consistent (given the circumstances) that this rather odd procedure — which would have required the printer and publisher of the book to relinquish part of his manuscript copy to newspaper printers he was employing — was not in fact followed. There is no shared error and only one genuine substantive variant between A and G, but though wrong, G's 'The' (3.6) is so plausible a reading that it would probably have passed Maxwell's men, particularly in the rush to bring the printing of Volume I to a conclu-

---

[23]See Dunlap, *Life*, I, 107, quoted and discussed in "The Bicentennial Texts: A Note," in *Wieland*, p. xx.

425

sion. Moreover, A's erroneous 'Peurile' looks very much like the kind of minim error it commits elsewhere, rather than a simple transposition of G's correct 'Puerile', and its unusual 'seldome' is more likely to represent a somewhat antiquated spelling of Brown's manuscript than an alteration of G's normal 'seldom' (3.18, 3.6). Perhaps as telling are the differences in punctuation. A's repeated use of the semicolon where G has preferable colons accords with its text of the novel itself, but since M's text confirms that many of these semicolons in Volume II are in fact derived from Brown, it seems very improbable that A's variants can be regarded as changes of G's more predictable points that Maxwell's men perversely introduced. Likewise, the comma at 3.20 is more in accord with Brown's general style and is probably his own rather than A's addition to the unpointed text of G; this is perhaps the case with the semicolon at 3.21, though it could conceivably be a substitution for G's comma.

In short, the evidence, such as it is, indicates that A's preface is textually independent of G, as one might have expected under the circumstances. Whether the opposite is true is less clear. G's 'The' is an outright substitution that cannot be traced to compositorial difficulty with Brown's manuscript, and its 'Puerile' is an obvious correction that along with G's punctuation could just as well have been set from an example of A's preliminaries as from manuscript. The question is relatively academic, fortunately, since A's less stylized text would have to be preferred to G's, were they independent and collateral. However, in view of the advertisement of 30 July and its implication that Volume I was nearly ready for publication, the odds are that Maxwell never turned a manuscript over to Brown and Relf, either before or after he had set up his preliminaries, and that the opening paragraphs of G's subscription notice were printed from an example of Maxwell's own typesetting for A.[24]

[24]The fact that the preliminaries were apparently set up and machined last suggests of course that Maxwell had completed the printing of Volume I by about this time. See Historical Essay, p. 302.

IV

The genealogy for *Edgar Huntly* suggested here, then, begins with a manuscript draft of the whole novel from which descends a partial transcription that served as copy for M and a separate and complete transcription that supplied copy for A. With the possible exception of G's text of the preface, this first edition, together with M where it exists, is the only authoritative text of the novel that has survived. The Minerva Press issued a second edition (without the preface) in London in 1803 over the imprint of William Lane and A. K. Newman, but it lacks authority. The first English edition of *Edgar Huntly* (E) begins a new sequence of chapter numbers with each volume of the three-decker (as does *Arthur Mervyn*, also issued in a new Minerva edition that same year). To compensate for Maxwell's uneven division of the novel, Lane and Newman moved the last chapter of Volume I to the beginning of their second volume and the last two of A's Volume II to the third volume of E. The Minerva edition obviously had no access to M, for where M and A vary, it either follows A (with the exception of typographical errors) or produces a third variant which demonstrates quite clearly that M was not consulted (see esp. 170.32, 184.7). Similar evidence shows that the printer's copy contained state *a* of reset quire K of Volume II, though the lack of variant readings in quire M leaves the question of E's copy at this point in doubt. The compound variants, where E disagrees with both A and M when the latter corrects the text of the former, are but an indication of the misguided and nonauthorial "correction" which A's text underwent in the hands of Lane and Newman. Although making the usual kinds of errors incidental to reprinting (e.g., at 188.25), the Minerva edition contains a number of alterations that are clearly beyond the province of the compositors. Two of these exhibit outright misconstruction of the text (236.17, 212.20), the latter being particularly interesting because it shows the editor's sensitivity to things distinctively American and his feeling that he needed to make Brown pallatable to the English public. At other times E seeks to correct Brown's frequent violation of agreement or his less frequent ellipses (e.g., 27.32, 46.17, 207.19), or alters diction characteristic of Brown: 'adventure' becomes 'venture', 'unintermitted' becomes 'unremitted', 'mistreatment' becomes 'ill-treatment', 'to be' becomes 'of being', 'immured' becomes 'concealed' (22.13, 27.26, 153.38, 167.27, 263.34). These changes are in character and frequency like those introduced in the Minerva *Arthur Mervyn*, and their lack of authority is unmistakable.

It is possible that like the 1803 *Arthur Mervyn* E was reissued in 1821 by Newman alone. Advertisements to that effect ran in the *Port Folio*,[25] but no 1821 copies have been located, and the presumption has to be that if any such copies in fact appeared they were a reissue of the nonauthoritative 1803 impression and nothing more. However, *Edgar Huntly* stands alone amongst Brown's novels in having reached a second English edition after this period; that is, as late as 1831 Colburn and Bentley published a reprint of E both as part of their Standard Novels series and as a separate volume. The novel also appeared during the nineteenth century in America together with Brown's others in the succession of derived collected editions that began with S. G. Goodrich's in 1827. Along with *Wieland* it has enjoyed the distinction of two editions prepared by twentieth-century scholars, but neither is as responsible in its text as those of Brown's first published novel. Both rely for copy on the convenience of one of the nineteenth-century American editions, with predictable results. David Lee Clark's three volumes of 1928 in Macmillan's Modern Reader's series follow "closely" the 1857 Polock edition, which is "carefully collated" with A but altered by reference to it only when a

---

[25]*Port Folio*, 11 (1821), 241; see Reid, "Brockden Brown in England," *Early American Literature*, 9 (1974), 188, 193, n.2.

change is "more conducive to a better understanding of the sentence." David Stineback's 1973 single volume, part of the Masterworks of Literature Series, uses the 1887 McKay, collates it with A, and aims to preserve the general texture but also modernizes the spelling and regularizes the punctuation of one of those two editions (it is unclear which). Finally, there is the AMS Press's 1967 facsimile reprint of the copy of A at Indiana University, comprising states *a* of the reset quires, which makes the text of the first edition more available but introduces modern print where its heavy reproduction has sufficiently obscured the original.

V

Where E offers the only early text other than A, choice of A as copy-text is straightforward, though how its text is to be emended remains to be decided. Where the reset quires of the second volume offer variant readings,[26] the first typesettings, states *a* in both cases, must provide copy-text, and the others simply lack authority, though they are useful as rough indexes to the accuracy of the transmission elsewhere in the first edition. Where M offers an authoritative collateral text, A must still provide copy-text, but the situation is more complex and the usefulness of M in supplementing the testimony of A requires careful consideration.

If both the *Monthly Magazine* and the first edition are descended from authorial fair copies, technically they are equally close to Brown's inscription, but A is nevertheless superior in that it derives from a manuscript which presumably contained his later changes. Insofar, then, as we can postulate second thoughts on Brown's part, A obvi-

---

[26]Other cases of internal variation in A are (as already explained) of a different character, and in these cases the present edition reproduces the correct readings, which apparently have priority, and the apparatus is based on these correct readings.

ously represents the more reliable text. It must of course be the copy-text for the revised passages (e.g., 202.28–34), for M cannot bear witness to the forms of such revisions any more than to their wording; and when A and M exhibit truly indifferent variation in accidentals, the readings of A must generally be respected as probably deriving from Brown's later manuscript and therefore presumably reflecting it. However, the situation by no means warrants adoption of A's possible errors in the face of correct readings in M. Because many of the variants in substantives and most in accidentals could represent either Brown's alteration, or an error in A, or an error in M, the respective accuracy of A and M is a definite factor in determining the extent to which A's readings should be relied on where M offers acceptable alternatives. Examination of these texts, particularly A, is clearly necessary.

In M and A we have texts of very different natures. M's is a sophisticated text produced by accomplished printers as part of a magazine that the Swordses quite evidently "styled" to some extent. The careful punctuation of parenthetical phrases has already been mentioned, and other features of the text exhibit the same tendency to be tidy. Confirmation of this general assessment comes not only from other works published in the *Monthly Magazine*, but also from the first editions of Brown's *Alcuin* and *Wieland*. In addition to the Swords 1798 booklet of *Alcuin*, there survive two independent texts and part of a third, and the variation amongst them shows clearly the care for details of punctuation and spelling that was exercised in the Swords shop during the production of the pamphlet. In this case, however, we have to reckon with the editorial supervision of Brown's friend, Elihu Hubbard Smith, who published the booklet. Yet *Wieland*, which the Swordses also printed in 1798, exhibits a similarly clean though less fussy text, and this evidence as well as that of the *Monthly Magazine* itself makes it quite clear that M's text of *Edgar Huntly* is a conscientious but somewhat sophisticated one produced by very capable printers.

On the other hand, in Maxwell's first edition we do not

have to contend with the kind of uncertainty that characterizes a sophisticated though conscientiously produced text like M's. Yet A's freedom from this sort of error is owing not so much to the faithfulness as to the thoughtlessness of the printing. Maxwell's text is naïve but careless, as the obvious errors throughout amply testify. The most telling indictment of Maxwell's work is the resetting of quires K and M of Volume II. In these pages there are four genuine errors in wording, besides seven literals (e.g., 'diffierent', 'constiution'). These four variants are, however, all simple errors: 'lighted' for 'alighted', 'consequence' for 'consequences', 'it' for 'its', 'as' for 'us' (154.15, 154.18, 155.7, 155.28). More frequent are the changes in the forms of words—spelling ('pretensions' for 'pretentions'), hyphenation ('winter blast' for 'winter-blast'), division ('everyland')—and still more pervasive the alteration of punctuation, which involves the omission or addition of commas, the omission of the period, and the confusion of the two.

This same basic pattern is exhibited in the reprinting of the first nine chapters of *Arthur Mervyn, First Part*, which Maxwell's shop set up from the *Weekly Magazine* earlier in the year.[27] In the process of reprinting some ninety pages, Maxwell produced sixteen verbal errors, including three

[27] Although it was apparently a small shop and may therefore have been subject to some turnover in personnel, there is reason to believe that at least part of *Edgar Huntly* was typeset by one of the workmen who set the first nine chapters of *Arthur Mervyn, First Part*. The most telltale bit of evidence is the spelling 'conciousness' (47.36–37), which parallels the two changes from 'conscious(ness)' to 'concious(ness)' in the eighth chapter of *Arthur Mervyn*. Also of interest is the tendency to set initial *in-* instead of *en-* spellings, as in 'injoyment' (68.16), which duplicates the preference for such forms that is quite evident in the many changes of the *Weekly Magazine's en-* spellings in *Arthur Mervyn*. Then there is the fondness for hyphenated compounds exhibited in both. Were these forms not so distinctive, the assumption of identical personnel—as distinguished from the general working environment of Maxwell's shop that was ultimately responsible for his sloppy work—would be risky, but these telltale traces of a compositor's hand suggest that at least one typesetter (Maxwell himself, perhaps) remained in this shop through much of 1799.

omissions, two changes of tense, one of number, one involving initial *th-/h-* ('his' for 'this'), and nine others that involve a single word (e.g., 'affected' for 'effected', 'no' for 'know', 'he' for 'we'). In addition, there are nine literals, a paragraph change, more than thirty alterations of spelling (including twelve of *en-* to *in-*), a dozen changes of word hyphenation (in all but two, the hyphen is added), and numerous changes involving the addition or (less frequently) omission of commas and the interchange of commas, semicolons, colons, queries, and periods.

These alterations during the reprinting of *Arthur Mervyn* provide a general guide to the kinds of error Maxwell's shop was likely to produce, and in *Edgar Huntly* itself the reset quires give more specific evidence of his workmanship. Both ranges of evidence confirm impressions drawn from obvious errors in the first edition. But even more pertinent testimony comes from the last hundred pages of Volume II, where M often supplies evidence from identical rather than analogous text. Here, however, the possibility of Brown's having altered his manuscript and of transmissional changes in M make the testimony more suspect than might be hoped. Nevertheless, agreement of M and A indicates the kinds of errors Maxwell was not prone to making. And in the disagreements involving wording, minims, spelling, and punctuation we have some specific evidence that helps confirm general impressions of A's inaccuracies. Even if we allow for styling by the Swords shop, for instance, M helps confirm what may be gathered from most of A about confusion of queries, commas, and periods, not only when M supplies the correct form but also when, as at 201.4, it errs and shows the inherent difficulty which Brown's small hand posed for distinguishing the last two.

Extrapolation from these various ranges of evidence is a delicate business, of course, because we cannot blithely assume a uniform manuscript throughout. For instance, the rate of obvious error seems to be especially low in the latter part of Volume II, whether because Brown had already worked the rough spots out of the text when transcribing it for M or for some other reason. Certainly there seem to be many more errors involving punctuation, the apostrophe, and similar details in Volume III than earlier, and generally less in Volume I than in the succeeding two. And of course neither the evidence of *Arthur Mervyn* nor the reset quires can give us much information about graphic errors; rather, in trying to assess the kinds of difficulties Brown's manuscript presented Maxwell's men, we have to rely on variation between M and A and on whatever can be inferred from the remainder of the text or from such errors in other novels. Nevertheless, the various kinds of evidence so far examined do offer greater insight than is normally obtainable into the nature and extent of the errors of A.

These errors survive, of course, not only because of the difficulties of Brown's manuscript and the incapacities of Maxwell's typesetters, but also because the proofreading was so shoddy. As with *Arthur Mervyn, First Part*, Brown was not available to proofread his novel because he was in New York—this time actually editing the *Monthly Magazine* rather than launching it. The extent to which he entrusted the onerous task of proofreading to his brother James is indeterminable, but James and Maxwell appear to have borne the burden, so far as it was borne at all. For whatever reason, whether Maxwell's chronic carelessness or his inability to employ a proofreader arising from his "indigence,"[28] the proofreading of this book failed to correct not only literals and similar typographical blemishes disconcerting to a printer, but also more serious faults. As examination of the reset quires and of M's collateral text indicates, many of the latter, though wrong, give readings plausible enough to be passed in proof by a nonauthorial reader working without benefit of copy. Although we shall never know for certain what kind of proofreading A underwent, it seems clear that Brown did not see proof,

[28]The word is Brown's; Dunlap, *Life*, II, 99.

and there is reason to believe that proof was not always scrupulously read against copy by someone else.

VI

Yet the text present in A is by no means irredeemable, especially since it appears to be a naïve one. As already suggested, the survival of M's independent text tells us something about the accuracy as well as inaccuracy of A, insofar as we can presume relative uniformity in the manuscript and the printing process. When A's readings are confirmed by M's, we have in effect recovered the text of their common ancestor, Brown's draft, from which the readings were passed to the two transcriptions that provided copy for either M or A. The agreement of these texts makes emendation very difficult indeed, despite the merits of the readings. Thus the curious 'had began' (202.36) mentioned earlier demands respect, and weighty reasons would be required before it could be emended; external evidence in fact supports both this particular form, despite its jarring ring to modern ears (see the Textual Notes), and therefore the significance of M's agreement with A as well. Furthermore, such agreement has implications beyond those questionable readings that occur in the second half of Volume II. The unusual 'fastnesses' in both M and A (207.22) verifies the authenticity of the word earlier (124.11) and virtually rules out emendation, even though M does not exist for this portion of the novel. Likewise, the awkward phrase 'wait their forthcoming' (190.1-2) discourages any inclination to make an easy change to 'await' in the earlier 'wait his departure' (23.14), and the use of 'were' (210.12) prevents alteration of A's 'were' in an identical context in Volume I (29.25). This last example illustrates the wider usefulness of M's text, for the sentence exhibits lack of agreement amongst both subject and verb and pronoun and its referent. Indeed, the existence of M forestalls emendation of the general violation of such agreement throughout A, not just the specific kind found in the latter half of Volume II and confirmed there by M. Moreover, M not only confirms A's 'scored into', as against E's 'scored with' (171.14), or its redundant 'pondered upon' (193.30); it also supports analogous forms, such as 'echoed to' and 'spurn at' (20.34, 67.17). Were no 'wait' present in both A and M, their similar 'rise' (175.9) would indicate that the earlier 'wait' (23.14) came from Brown's pen. In questions of tense, number, punctuation, and similar "inaccuracies of grammar, orthography, and punctuation,"[29] the *Monthly Magazine* text helps define the limits of emendation in both general and specific ways.

When, however, M's text varies from A's, the editorial problem is much more acute. In some cases, choice of copy-text helps resolve the dilemma. With variants in accidentals like A's 'achievements', 'clothing', and 'expense' as against M's 'atchievements', 'cloathing', and 'expence', where both forms are acceptable and the evidence of Brown's extant manuscripts is too scarce to define his usage, the readings of A must stand as probably reproducing those of its manuscript copy. Fortunately, this is true both because of the possibility that Brown himself was ambivalent about these matters, and therefore could have indeliberately varied the spellings when retranscribing the novel to supply Maxwell with setting copy, and also because M is the more carefully styled text and is more likely to have altered Brown's manuscript to bring it into conformity with the Swordses' notion of normality or correctness. This general guideline covers a large portion, perhaps a majority, of the accidentals variants between M and A. Likewise, with merely indifferent substantives A's variant must generally stand as probably

[29]See Dunlap, *Life*, I, 107; Brown to Bringhurst, 20 May 1792, quoted in Herbert R. Brown, "Charles Brockden Brown's 'The Story of Julius'; Rousseau and Richardson 'Improved'," in *Essays Mostly on Periodical Publishing in America*, ed. James Woodress (Durham, N.C.: Duke Univ. Press, 1973), p. 40; see "The Bicentennial Texts," p. xx.

reflecting Brown's later manuscript, and identifiable revisions of substantives presumably introduced by Brown during the course of transcribing his draft for Maxwell must obviously be chosen above M's forms, even though these may also be authorial.

Yet genuine problems of selection between the variant readings of M and A arise wherever A errs, or appears to have erred, while M offers a reading that not only has authority but also seems to be authorial. A trivial example is A's dittography at a page break (187.17), where M preserves the reading that must have been in both of Brown's manuscripts; a less trivial example is A's graphic error 'when' for M's 'where' (170.32). Not all cases, however, are so obvious, though the principle is the same. When, for instance, A has 'they [old Deb's dogs] . . . attended her person or guarded her threshold, agreeable to her directions', whereas M offers 'agreeably' and other examples show that M's reading conforms to Brown's usual usage and suits his idiom, it is more likely that A has altered the text and thus smoothed out a distinctively authorial form than that its 'agreeable' represents an unplanned authorial revision reflecting indifference (see 207.31 and the Textual Notes), and this principle for emending A by reference to M thus extends to all A's acceptable readings, whether accidentals or substantives, that may nevertheless be errors for M's form. The heart of the dilemma is the question of revision, particularly the unmeditated kind that can occur during a transcription. Variants that could be either A's error or its reproduction of an authorial alteration have to be decided on their merits and on the probabilities that either A or M has erred or that Brown would change such a reading. Here the entire range of evidence gathered from M's identifiable normalizations, the reset quires in Volume II of the first edition, Maxwell's resetting of *Arthur Mervyn*, and those revisions that are more definitely assessable plays an important role. If A preserves a form that seems to be distinctively authorial, we can usually infer that M has normalized or that Brown has revised; in either case A's reading must stand, and the problem is relatively straightforward. The nature of the reading and the descent of the texts combine to support A's variant. On the other hand, when the variants are indifferent so far as content and meaning are concerned, when A's form is the more conventional and could be either its error or an unmeditated change introduced spontaneously by Brown during transcription, when M has the less predictable reading and that reading seems to conform to Brown's idiom, then the odds favor adopting M's variant as at least preserving an authorial form, if not certainly as a correction of A's error.[30] These general guidelines result in the adoption of a majority of the variants found in A, the more naïve though certainly corrupt text, but they also lead to alteration of its text by reference to M in some cases.

VII

In the remainder of the novel where there is only a single authority, selection of readings of course presents no problems, but emendation does. Essentially the situation is like that in any single-text work, where the merit of the individual readings is the crucial factor, but the implications of M's text, the reset quires, and the reset chapters of *Arthur Mervyn* are not irrelevant even here. Aside from those obvious errors that would require correction in any case, A has a number of readings that, though possible, appear to be defective and seem to require emendation in light of the various evidence that Maxwell's shop was subject to making certain kinds of error. For instance, several of M's readings suggest a disposition in A to mis-

[30]This guideline is perhaps an adaptation of the classical principle of the *lectio difficilior* (as well as the distinction between "good" readings and true ones), but the genealogical situation and the criteria for assessing the nature of the readings are more narrowly defined.

read Brown's small hand, especially his minims, and this fact — together with other supporting evidence, including similar errors elsewhere in A — encourages emendation of several such readings where the context and Brown's own usage suggest that A is in error. Likewise, quire K of Volume II and the reset chapters of *Arthur Mervyn* reveal tendencies to substitute similar words (e.g., 'as' for 'us', 'he' for 'we') and to confuse singulars and plurals,[31] and both these tendencies help support certain emendations of errors of these kinds. The confusion of the comma and the period, which sometimes probably derives from Brown's small hand, is often obvious, but in those fewer cases where it is not, the text of M and Maxwell's resetting of the two quires of *Edgar Huntly* and of nine chapters of *Arthur Mervyn* all testify to A's being vulnerable to this particular error of punctuation, while to various extents they also confirm that the printer of A was prone to adding commas freely and making transpositions.

By no means, however, does this mean the floodgates are open to all sorts of tinkering with A's text. As already pointed out, the agreements of M and A are as important as their variations in defining general limits to emendation and precluding the alteration of certain kinds of forms that may seem at this distance to require "correction." Even when such evidence is not abundant, the absence of such errors in the reset chapters of *Arthur Mervyn*, in the reset quires of A, or in the rest of A itself raises some doubt about the propriety of a proposed alteration, and often Brown's style in *Edgar Huntly* or his other works discourages emendation even if the general acceptability of a given form cannot be demonstrated. Thus presumptions of error in negatives (e.g., 47.29, 93.9, 145.19), in constructions involving 'to be' (e.g., 109.34, 167.27), in omissions, and in various accidentals receive little support from examination of such general evidence, and the incli-

---

[31]This is in addition to the problems inherent in Brown's habit of representing his final -*s* (see the Textual Note on 186.28).

nation to emend is inhibited unless the merit of the particular case alone is decisive. Likewise the doublet 'Walcot' /
'Walton' toward the end of the story finds a precedent in
the 'Marguerite' / 'Philippine' confusion in *Arthur Mervyn*
and is retained here as representing Brown's own indeci-
sion.

Certain special cases of accidentals illustrate these general observations and require consideration. Of the some
two hundred accidentals emended, a number involve the
forms of two words already mentioned, 'attendant' and
'footstep(s)'. The various instances of each must be treated
as a class rather than individually. There are six examples
of the first word in the copy-text, half of them spelled
'attendant(s)', the remainder 'attendent(s)'. For one of the
latter M has the alternative -*a*- spelling, and the variation
poses an immediate problem of choice as to which should
be adopted. Of course this is exactly the kind of error
Maxwell's shop was prone to making, and in fact the -*e*-
spelling occurs in no first editions of Brown but Maxwell's. The most interesting evidence comes from *Arthur
Mervyn, First Part*, where Maxwell's shop also varied the
spelling, reproducing all 6 of the -*a*- spellings found in the
Weekly Magazine, but setting an equal number of -*a*- and
-*e*- forms when working from manuscript. We cannot
prove that Brown actually favored -*a*-, since we have
records of only one example of the word in his
manuscripts — spelled 'attendant'. But the *OED* and other
authorities do not allow the -*e*- spelling, and it is a fair bet
that a compositor in Maxwell's shop was more likely to err
by setting 'attendent(s)' when faced with a manuscript
than when working from print. Since M offers the variant
-*a*- in one instance, there is no choice but to adopt it as
representing what Brown actually wrote and to reject A's
-*e*-, and this decision, based as it is on the premise that A
is in error, must naturally extend to its other -*e*- spellings
and result in a kind of regularization of the form of this
word throughout the novel.

The case of 'footstep(s)' is very similar, though it is

more acute because it involves unavoidable decisions on hyphenated forms that fall at line breaks in A. Again the first edition is variant, having seven 'footstep(s)' and twenty 'foot-steps', besides four forms ambiguously divided and hyphenated at breaks between lines. Again M offers an alternative spelling to A's, in every instance having 'footsteps' where A invariably hyphenates the word six times in the latter part of Volume II.[32] Again this is the kind of form Maxwell's shop was prone to change. More specifically, the reset chapters of *Arthur Mervyn* (where nine hyphens are added to the *Weekly Magazine* text) exhibit a tendency to divide compounds, and this evidence confirms that of the generally heavy hyphenation displayed throughout A. In fact, in hyphenating 'foot-step(s)' Maxwell's books are again unique amongst Brown's first editions, and again in Maxwell's edition of *Arthur Mervyn* his compositor follows the 'footstep(s)' of printed copy uniformly against personal preference but reverts to 'foot-step(s)' once Brown's manuscript begins to serve as setting copy. It is a fair presumption, then, that as with 'attendent(s)' the first edition's unique 'foot-steps' reflects a Maxwellian preference rather than Brown's own, although we have only four instances in his manuscripts — all spelled 'footstep(s)' — to help define his usage. To adopt the spelling found a majority of the time elsewhere in the copy-text when faced with the hyphen at line breaks in A and the variant 'footsteps' in M (181.38–182.1, 194.8) is to accede to what is almost certainly compositorial styling under the illusion that the copy-text is sacrosanct. But if the unhyphenated form must be adopted here, as it must, on the premise that M preserves Brown's usage in the face of Maxwell's preference for hyphenation, then majority rule — the fact that Maxwell sets three times as many 'foot-steps' as he does

[32]In one case the word falls at a line break in M, but in view of its uniform treatment of the word elsewhere and the Swordses' scrupulousness in such matters, there is little doubt about the significance of this hyphen.

'footstep(s)'—can hardly be invoked to decide A's other two hyphenated forms at line-breaks.[33] Nor can any of A's hyphens, representing as they apparently do the printer rather than the author, continue to stand in the face of M's presumably more faithful spellings, and if these are dismissed from the text, then almost half of A's preferred forms have been rejected as Maxwell's errors and there seems no choice but to emend the remainder, rather than leave them in the text with the implication that they somehow reflect the authentic inconsistency of the author when they actually represent the evident variability and accidents of the printing process.

In most other cases, however, the evidence for emendation, though it exists, is less persuasive that A's spellings should be altered, and thus this edition generally declines to adopt similar plausible emendations. The present text does follow M's 'musquet' rather than A's unique 'musket' (172.10)—the first instance of the word and apparently a momentary spelling by A's compositor which he immediately abandoned in the face of the manucript's consistent but less conventional usage—and its 'burthen' instead of A's 'burden' (203.3)[34]—a spelling very like those just discussed in being unique to Maxwell's editions of Brown and more clearly contrary to his usage, which A faithfully reflects in seven other instances. It also corrects spellings that can be defined as wrong in Brown's time, many of them involving double consonant errors apparently produced by Maxwell's shop. But this edition retains A's variant spellings 'steadfast' and 'stedfast', its 'tranquility' and 'tranquillity', 'suspense' and 'suspence', 'clothing' and 'cloathing', and its 'timerous', 'achievements', and similar forms despite variants in M that receive mild support from Brown's manuscripts. Such support is far from decisive in these cases, while the variation in *Edgar Huntly*

---

[33]For the general principles that cover such specific cases, please see "The Bicentennial Texts: A Note," in *Wieland*, pp. xxi–xxii.

[34]This decision consequently dictates emendation of the only other instance of 'burden' in A (292.31).

itself and the evidence in other works are not substantial enough to indicate that A is in fact in error. Of special interest is the unusual 'tom-hawk', unprecedented elsewhere in Brown and in works cited by the *OED* and *DAE*. M's invariable 'tomahawk' is of course the most usual form, but not a single such spelling appears in A, and therefore, according to the guidelines developed above, M's form is more likely to be Swords styling whereas A's unconventional form very probably reflects that of its copy. A's incorrect capitalization of the word five of the first six times it appears probably exhibits the printer's temporary misapprehension that this is a proper name, and it thus suggests that he was not imposing a previously learned spelling on Brown's manuscript. Although there is some chance that the hyphenation is Maxwell's and that Brown's manuscript in fact had 'tomhawk', because A is invariant in this respect this inference must remain wholly speculative and the copy-text's 'tom-hawk' must remain in the text. With one exception the same principle applies to A's other hyphenation and word-division: much of it is likely to be the compositor's rather than Brown's — including 'loco-motive', 'some-what', 'daylight', 'deep laid', and 'dwarf oaks' for M's 'dwarf-oaks' — but M as well as A has forms such as 'Red-men' and 'night-fall', and there is nothing for it but to retain the copy-text's division even when it is inconsistent, as in 'daylight' /'day-light'.[35] That one exception involves the treatment of 'Norwalk', which in its second, third, and fourth occurrences has a hyphen that is thereafter dropped. This appears to be analogous to Maxwell's tendency to hyphenate proper names (e.g., 'New-York', 'Elizabeth-town'), but unlike these and others 'Nor-walk' finds no support in collateral sources, and as a temporary imposition of compositorial styling similar to 'musket' and 'burden' these three hyphenations are emended in the present edition. Otherwise, this edition is rather pertinacious in preserving a

[35]159.33, 217.13, 215.15, 74.9, 181.35, 172.35, 212.18.

number of seemingly odd forms of proper names. Whenever there is a reasonable chance that A's spelling reproduces Brown's, it stands here even though external evidence does not verify A's precise form and only shows that the components in question were variable. However, in one or two cases where A's spelling appears to represent an unacceptable form as well as the kind of compositorial error found elsewhere in the first edition—e.g., the graphic error 'Salsbury' in the first instance of this name, or the transposition 'Powels-hook' for 'Powles-hook' (23.20, 292.8)—a correction appears in present text.[36]

Beyond the spellings of A, a small proportion of which qualify for emendation under these guidelines, there are the more vexing problems of its punctuation. These problems range from pointing that affects syntax and sense, through the pervasive ambiguities involving discourse, to the almost typographical formalities of successive dots and dashes. One of the more troublesome features of the text for the modern reader is its casual and almost indiscriminate use of the comma and semicolon. This practice, however, not only prevails throughout A but also finds confirmation in M's text despite the greater meticulous-

---

[36]For instance, Jedidiah Morse's *New Gazetteer of the Eastern Continent* (Charlestown: Samuel Etheridge, 1802), sig. Qq2^r, his *American Universal Geography*, 6th ed. (Boston: Thomas & Andrews, 1812), II, 591, and the *OED* list A's -*u*- as a possible alternative to the more usual -*er*- and -*ar*- spellings of 'Jagunaut' (60.38), though never in conjunction with its -*aut* ending. This might be a case of minim error, but it also could well represent Brown spelling the name phonetically or memorially and thus producing a rare combination of the two elements; hence, A's form is retained. Likewise various sources show a good deal of uncertainty, or rather controversy, about the spelling of 'Lennilennapee' (207.4), but though A's form is itself unprecedented, so far as we know, it has enough in common with various other spellings to have a claim to adoption. On the latter point, see William Rawle, "A Vindication of the Rev. Mr. Heckewelder's History of the Indian Nations," *Memoirs of the Historical Society of Pennsylvania* (Philadelphia: M'Carty and Davis, 1826), I, 265. On 'Powles-hook', cf. *Clara Howard* (1801), 111.6.

ness of the Swords shop, and the conclusion seems inevitable that in this respect A's text reflects the manuscript of Brown, who like earlier writers employs such points to represent rhetorical pauses more than syntactical relations.[37] By and large A's system is quite satisfactory given its premises, and although one or two emendations have proved necessary to eliminate misrepresentations of Brown's meaning, the vast majority of such punctuation stands in the Bicentennial text as it does in A, despite the fact that modern standards would demand "correction" in run-on sentences, complex series, and compound subjects.

A related problem is the presence (or less frequently the absence) of commas where neither sense nor the time's usage would seem to require them. Whereas the vast majority of A's punctuation is satisfactory and must stand even though it may not reproduce Brown's own in every case, some of it appears to be genuinely erroneous. The nine reset chapters of *Arthur Mervyn* exhibit more than one hundred additions of this point, but only thirty omissions. M's text is of some help here, for though it is more styled in ways already explained, sometimes when A has yielded to a similar temptation to smooth out Brown, M appears to retain pointing less conventional and more characteristic of him. Thus while the copy-text must prevail in virtually all situations where its reading is doubtful but nevertheless acceptable, in a relatively few cases, particularly in Volume II, A's treatment of commas seems so defective on its own terms as to require correction.

In another respect, however, A frequently appears to be genuinely in error—the handling of queries. A few instances involve the semicolon, as M's correct reading at 189.14 suggests, and such confusion may in fact reflect the difficulties of Brown's small hand. Certainly these few instances are not confined to either passages of discourse,

[37]A telling example of this is Robert Lowth's own usage in his *Short Introduction to English Grammar* (London, 1762; rpt. Menston: Scolar Press, 1967).

whether direct or indirect, or to the internal dialogue of Clithero, Edgar, and Sarsefield, which constitutes most of the narration of the novel. However, it is in such internal dialogue, the ethical meditations of one of the three speakers whose accounts of their experiences occupy so much of the three volumes, each in its turn, that the defects of A's punctuation are most clearly evidenced. Usually analysis can show whether a statement in such a passage is declarative or interrogative, and the compositors of A provide the right point in most cases. However, in other instances, proportionately small but nevertheless numerous, the period appears in place of the query. This could have been owing to a shortage of the sort in Maxwell's typecases, for the demand for the query was great, but since the situation is sometimes reversed, it is probably true that Brown's manuscript was somewhat deficient in this respect (as the first edition of *Ormond* suggests) and that the printer sometimes committed an error as part of his general effort "to mend things . . . either wrong or else ill digested" (Stower, p. 213). At any rate when Brown's meaning is ascertainable, as it usually is in such cases, emendation of a straightforward kind is obviously necessary. In some cases it is possible that an exclamation was called for, but as these are less in evidence and also less ascertainable, very few exclamation points have been adopted in lieu of the query or period, which generally serve very well.

Passages of direct or indirect discourse present similar problems, though they are more troublesome because of Brown's free-wheeling methods of rendering dialogue. Again the lack of the query is the most frequent situation, again Maxwell appears to be styling the manuscript to some extent (see, e.g., 142.5–8), and again this appears to have led to an occasional creation of a question where a simple declaration was meant. In one passage of indirect discourse (196.22), M's text confirms this general assessment, but the most difficult of such passages are those involving continuity, where successive questions are

445

strung together with commas, semicolons, or, once, a dash. By and large A's system is adequate for rendering such passages as well as other discourse, and it provides the general basis for the relatively few emendations of queries in discourse that the sense demands.

Indeed A's system of rendering discourse is like that of most other first editions of Brown in following a loose set of conventions that presumably reflects its manuscript copy, representing both direct and indirect quotations by a fluid use of the paragraph, dash, successive dots, colon, and comma (as well as the period). Again the line between direct and indirect discourse ranges somewhere from fine to nonexistent. As with those passages just discussed involving continuous or successive questions, this edition adopts the dominant system of the copy-text in treating all discourse,[38] emending A in accordance with its own usage only where it appears to have failed to represent Brown's manuscript accurately on its own terms. In fact, there are very few such alterations, for the first edition is consistent in treating both kinds of discourse in a freehanded manner, and even the use of double quotation marks to represent isolated statements by minor characters enjoys the support of M (196.2–5) and seems to work quite satisfactorily within the larger system, though one minor change (at 26.11) in conformity with this subsystem proves to be advisable.

The least important aspect of A's punctuation is its alternate use of dots and dashes not only to introduce or conclude discourse but to represent a shift or pause in thought or narration, whether dramatic or subtle. The variation between three hyphens in Volume I and the one-em dash in Volume III and between the number of dots throughout all three volumes seems to be typographical rather than textual, compositorial rather than authorial. Most of these dots appear in the first volume, and

---

[38]For the general principles in handling discourse, please see "The Bicentennial Texts," p. xxiii.

along with the three hyphens they suggest a printer trying unsuccessfully to reproduce a feature which is commonly found in Brown's manuscripts. In fact, in his surviving manuscripts Brown, like many other writers, frequently uses quick successive strokes of the pen to represent pauses, and these look as much like short dashes as dots, though they are on the baseline, and cannot be imitated exactly by either of the two typographical devices. The number of such strokes is arbitrary and variable, particularly at the ends of paragraphs, where they usually fill out the remainder of the manuscript line. This would account in part for the variability in number at the ends of A's paragraphs, just as in mid-paragraph passages the number of dots the compositor set would have been influenced by his need to justify his lines more than by Brown's inscription. By the time they reached Volume III Maxwell's men, like the Swords compositors earlier (see 196.12), had apparently given up trying to imitate this feature of the manuscript copy too precisely and, already having dropped the three hyphens altogether, resorted to the solid one-em dash exclusively a third of the way through the volume.[39] Throughout the volumes of the first edition the number of dots ranges from eight to three, the norm being four (including the period in this count), and there is no real distinction between the use of these devices to set off discourse or to represent pauses or shifts. Certainly the number appears to have no rhetorical or syntactical significance. Since nothing but distraction would be achieved by reproducing these dots and dashes slavishly, even were that possible, this edition (without further notice) regularizes them in accordance with the first edition's prevailing norm, preserving its distinction

[39]That is, if we except the two cases of a very different kind in which, as earlier, dots stand for names not supplied (289.24, 132.14). Although the number of dots in these cases may also inaccurately reflect Brown's manuscript, the function of the dots is different. There seems to be no practical alternative to substituting three-em and two-em dashes, which at least approximate the spacing of the first edition.

between dashes and dots but setting all instances of the three hyphens as one-em dashes and all the dots as three spaced ones, while retaining the additional periods at the ends of sentences.

The text of *Edgar Huntly* offered here, then, is basically that of A with some variants adopted from M where it exists and with additional emendations introduced where the context, Brown's usage, and whatever we can learn about the printing of A from the evidence available combine in one way or another to indicate that A is in error. Because A is a naïve but corrupt text, some fifty changes of its substantives and two hundred of its accidentals have proved to be necessary. One-fifth of the substantives and a smaller proportion of the accidentals come from M and are incorporated in the text that occupies the last hundred pages of Volume II and the first few of Volume III of the first edition (pp. 170–213). The remainder, though some of them are drawn from E, represent editorial attempts to correct presumed errors in the wording and particularly in A's defective punctuation and other details. These range from the most obvious botches and typographical faults to features involving diction and syntax (26.22, 54.9, 65.37, 100.13), and from attempts to choose between possible corrections of impossible readings (26.22, 84.2, 220.38) to the adoption of two obvious changes from state *b* of quire K[40] and the alteration of the duplicated chapter number 'XIV' with the consequent renumbering of succeeding chapters. However, this edition allows to stand a number of readings that may seem faulty to a modern reader at first blush, including 'set', 'confide . . . on', 'fastnesses', 'conscious to', 'had began', 'participating' (106.16, 115.21, 124.11, 152.19, 202.36, 259.23), and the spelling and punctuation already discussed.

The appendixes that follow contain reports on the vari-

[40]As already explained, in other cases of internal variation within A, the correct readings presumably have priority and are included in the copy-text for this edition.

ants from the copy-text in the present edition, on the substantive variants in E, G, and M, on all variation between A and M and within the reset quires of A, and on similar matters. A statement of the general textual principles of this edition, as well as of the handling of "silent" changes and of other matters connected with the apparatus, appears in the first volume of this series.

S.W.R.

APPENDIXES

TEXTUAL NOTES

NOTE: In these discussions of readings adopted by this edition, either by emendation of the copy-text or retention of its reading when emendation is possible, citations of passages in *Wieland* (*Wie.*), "Carwin" (*Car.*), *Ormond* (*Orm.*), and *Arthur Mervyn* (*AM*), refer to volumes in the Bicentennial Edition. Citations of *Clara Howard* (*CH*), "The Death of Cicero" (*DC*), and *Jane Talbot* (*JT*) use the page and line of the first printings. Those citations not preceded by an abbreviation are to the present volume of *Edgar Huntly*. The following sigla identify the editions discussed.

G: *Philadelphia Gazette and Universal Daily Advertiser*, subscription notice (10 August 1799 *et seq.*), without authority
M: *The Monthly Magazine* (April 1799), I, 21–44
A: *Edgar Huntly; or, Memoirs of a Sleep-Walker* (Philadelphia, 1799), copy-text
    A^a: first state, quire K or M, Vol. II
    A^b: second state, quire K or M, Vol. II
    A^c: third state, quire K, Vol. II
E: *Edgar Huntly, or Memoirs of a Sleep-Walker* (London, 1803), without authority

11.6 low] A's 'low' seems preferable to the 'slow' of E, by virtue of the contrast with the later 'louder' and the fact that the phrase 'at wide intervals' appears to take care of questions of timing.

25.17 two] The inconsistency between this statement and the preceding references to three observations (beginning at 10.21,

17.32, 23.8-9) might suggest an error by the compositor. But the lapse (if it is Brown's lapse, and not a discrepancy meant to reflect on Edgar's state of mind) seems almost certainly to have been authorial, since a little later in the same chapter Edgar again refers to the 'two preceding nights' (30.27-28).

26.22 dejection. On] A's phrase 'on discovering how he had been employed,' can go with either the preceding or the following clause. However, that Brown deliberately intended an ambiguity as well as an impossibly complex run-on sentence appears to be an untenable defense of A's reading. The first edition must be in error, and given the use of the semicolon after 'uttered' (26.24) and such frequent errors elsewhere in A, it seems likely that one of the commas, after either 'dejection' or 'employed', represents a misreading of a period. Since Clithero could well have been alarmed and dejected on being awakened rather than becoming so only after being told about his sleep-talking, since 'he would . . . had uttered' dearly begs for the introductory phrase, and since a graphic error involving Brown's initial *O-* seems more likely than one involving his *H-*, we have ended the sentence with 'dejection', quite contrary, incidentally, to the judgment of E's editor.

36.21 in] Although it would be tempting to alter A's 'in' to 'at' in parallel with 'shudder at', the point seems to be that Clithero will shrink during his punishment, and 'in', though unusual, should be allowed to stand.

46.24 The] A's 'Her' is such irredeemable nonsense that it cannot even be attributed to Brown's general imprecision and awkwardness. The obvious correction seems to be 'The' (adopted by E) in view of similar errors both here (cf. 252.29) and elsewhere (*Car.*, 268.18, *Wie.*, 90.27; see the textual notes there).

47.8 render] This is an egregious example of Brown's ellipsis and his tendency to let previous but distant words, in this case 'union' (47.6), serve as the object of a verb; though A might be in error, it is probably faithful to Brown's manuscript here. Cf. *Orm.* 12.8.

47.29 no considerable] With such a construction, it is tempting to postulate the omission of the prefix 'in-', but the succeeding sentences appear to confirm A in its awkward reading. The evidence of the context is far from decisive either way. Yet general considerations tip the scale against emendation (see the Textual Essay, pp. 438-439).

50.24 sinister] A's 'sinister influences' appears to be correct and presumably carries the connotations of something unlucky, unfortunate, or unfavorable, rather than malicious or corrupt.

54.9 Still] 'Sill' is obviously an error; ascertaining the correct form is another matter. Either 'Sure' or 'Still' (adopted by E) seems most likely to fit the context and explain the origin of the error. The former assumes misreading, of which there are sufficient examples in A, but it is not entirely appropriate to the speech of Mrs. Lorimer, whereas 'Still' would be a simple typographical error and does seem appropriate not only to this lady but to the indirect mode of discourse that Brown uses here and elsewhere.

60.19 ingenuous] Either A's 'ingenious' or E's 'ingenuous' fits the context and Sarsefield's character, and both receive support from other details: 'ingenious' from Sarsefield's general character and experience—e.g., his being a 'scholar' and a 'surgeon' (60.36, 61.4)—as well as from such phrases as 'fiery and energetic', 'impassioned boldness', and 'acuteness of his penetration' (60.22–23, 60.23, 61.29), the latter equally from his general character and from the phrase 'harmless deportment' (61.23). Graphic errors involving minims are not unknown in A, as readings in M testify (e.g., 170.32, 184.13), but the immediate context is the decisive issue: 'noble and ingenuous' are (as 'but' shows) meant to contrast with Sarsefield's 'various and boisterous pilgrimage' and the traces it has left on 'his sun-burnt and rugged features' (60.19).

65.37 man;] Like an earlier example of ambiguity in a complex sentence resulting from A's erroneous comma (26.22), this conundrum has to be decided not only by reference to the context but also to the first edition's demonstrable proneness to certain kinds of errors. In this case it is rather clear that 'whether once dead or not' goes with the subsequent clause and that the preceding short clause is emphatic, while the lack elsewhere of compositorial confusion between Brown's miniscule and majuscule *w* suggests that A's error involved the punctuation alone.

66.10 denounced] The form 'pronounced' would be more predictable, but A's reading has all the qualities of Brown's idiom. A very similar instance occurs at *Wie.*, 197.26.

70.7 here] The point of view has evidently shifted to the house of the 'banker' (70.5), and in its 'here' A reproduces, though a bit awkwardly, Brown's inscription. Cf. *Wie.*, 227.30.

73.2 Those] A's 'These' appears to be an error occasioned by Brown's small hand, as the following relative clause and indeed the construction of the whole sentence suggest; 'Those' seems to be the obvious emendation. Cf. *AM*, 340.7; also *AM*, 445.4, *Wie.*, 84.30, 136.1, 222.16.

83.8 lightning. Armed] Although the punctuation and capitalization produce a sentence fragment, it is clear that the fragmentation is intended by Brown, as is particularly evident from the sentence itself and the violent change of thought represented by the dots in its midst: Clithero begins to say what he did with the 'pointed implement' and then digresses to identifying it and how he came upon it; only after the next paragraph does he resume his account of the action itself, and only at 83.36 does he begin to complete his incomplete thought.

84.2 widely] That A's 'widley' is defective there can be no doubt; but whether 'widely' (adopted by E) or 'wildly' remedies the defect is another question. Either is surely suitable, but the emphasis seems to be less on Clithero's state of mind and body than on the career of his arm, both here and later (85.22), and the types of literal errors found elsewhere in A (54.9), in quire K, and in *Arthur Mervyn* support the adoption of 'widely'.

89.17–18 can no otherwise] Although this sounds slightly askew, A's reading is unlikely to be an error for Brown's 'cannot', which he usually writes as one word; the rhetorical flavor of A's reading is appropriate to the general flavor of Clithero's account (cf., e.g., the inversion at 87.33–34).

93.9 voluntary] Although driven by compulsion, Clithero is rightly described in A as 'the voluntary minister' of Wiatte's vengeance on his sister, and the temptation to emend to 'involuntary' must be resisted. Clithero is fully conscious of what he is about, though in a frenzy, and Edgar's previous observations show he was acting according to 'a just intention', even though it is based on 'a double mistake' (92.18–20).

97.36 intention] The context shows that 'intention', adopted by E and all later American editions, is what Brown meant, and A's 'attention' appears to be another example of the kind of Maxwellian error observable in the resetting of quire K and of *Arthur Mervyn, First Part* (see Textual Essay).

98.21 seemed as] The construction begs for the 'as' added in E and later American editions; though A's mere 'seemed' may be an example of Brown's ellipsis, it is probably an instance of the kind of omission Maxwell's shop made in resetting the first nine chapters of *Arthur Mervyn* (see *AM*, 20.4, 21.1-2, 87.9-10).

100.13 had certainly come] Brown's general liberty with tenses leads to toleration of almost any apparent lapse. But aside from the egregiousness of this particular case, there are good reasons for believing that A's 'came' is in fact an error, despite the roughly analogous 'had began' that both A and M reproduce independently (202.36). Robert Lowth's *Short Introduction to English Grammar* (1762; rpt. Menston, England: Scolar Press, 1967), acknowledges the frequency of *had began* in classic English authors though deprecating it (pp. 85–90), and also accepts, with slight reluctance, the use of *sung, drunk,* and so on in the imperfect past, but it shows no such wavering insofar as *came* and *come* are concerned (p. 80). Furthermore, the presence in A of similar graphic errors related to Brown's small hand indicates that it has erred. More specifically, the fact that a page change occurred between the setting of 'had certainly' and 'came' suggests that the compositor lost touch with the context and could easily have misread the manuscript when returning to it after performing the various tasks usually associated with concluding a page. In spite of the general argument against alteration, these particular circumstances seem to indicate that emendation (as in E) is required.

106.16 set] This is still a rural idiom and therefore appropriate to Edgar; it would have to stand even if it did not survive through the eighteenth century as an alternative to "sit" in literate language—which it did, as the *OED*'s citation of Jefferson shows.

115.21 confide implicitly on] This may seem to be an error of A's, and graphic errors involving Brown's minims may encourage emendation. But the phrase has a hoary ancestry that comes down at least to 1700, and it should be retained as another example of Brown's uncanny instinct for the ancient English. Cf. 29.5, 147.16.

123.26 eminently] The degree, not imminence, of the danger is in question here, and A's reading seems to be correct.

124.11 fastnesses] A perfectly sound reading, this recalls an ancient use of the word (according to the *OED*, sense 5) that is accepted by E. Cf. 207.22.

138.35 confided] Again the temptation to emend A, either by altering the verb or by inserting 'I' before it, should be resisted; this is another instance in which a previous subject—the 'I' at 138.34—serves for a remote verb.

145.26 those] With the arrival of Chaledro, the point of view shifts immediately—and apparently anticipatorily—to identification with 'this monk' (145.29), and this suggests that not only this particular instance of A's 'those' but also the one at 146.14 comes from Brown, and that E's 'these' should be rejected.

152.19 conscious to] This sounds like Brown's idiom, as another example at 159.6 suggests. It must be retained on this and general grounds (see Textual Essay, pp. 438-439).

153.32 funds] Since there is no evidence that Weymouth's father is dependent upon his friends for support and, furthermore, since it seems unlikely that Weymouth himself would seek support from such people, the obvious conclusion is that the reading 'funds' found in the 1887 American edition is in fact a correction of A's erroneous 'friends', which may be owing to graphic similarity.

170.32 where] Although it is possible to retain A's 'when' and force its sentence to produce a plausible but unsatisfactory reading, M's 'where' is obviously the correct variant of what appears to be A's graphic error: the point is not that the fire enables Edgar to reach a desired position, but that from this 'station' he is enabled to view the fire and, therefore, by changing his station eventually to catch sight of the Indians (171.11-12). The probable origin of A's error makes M's 'where' preferable to E's plausible 'whence', though its deliberate alteration supports the view that A is in error.

173.26 lately] The emphasis in this passage is clearly upon the element of 'time' (173.24) and upon the fact that long-standing friction had recently come to a head and was 'expected' (173.28) to erupt into violence shortly. M's 'greatly' is probably an error of memory encouraged by similar sounds, though it is possible that A's 'lately' is an afterthought of Brown's incorporated during transcription of the manuscript behind A. Certainly, A's reading does not appear to be an error for M's. Cf. 197.33.

174.29-30 and, . . . calamities,] That A's compositor has erred twice and thus produced a complex but perfectly plausible passage where M has a more predictable one ('and$_\wedge$ . . . calamities.') is a scarcely credible proposition. It is much more likely that M has smoothed out Brown's construction. Of course, it is possible that A's passage represents Brown's revision during transcription of its copy and his decision to idealize or further rationalize Edgar's action, but whether revision or faithful transmission of a passage corrupted by M, it must stand on the principles outlined in the Textual Essay.

178.26 into] There is not much to choose between A's 'into' and M's 'in'. M's reading could be an unusual one derived from

Brown, but it is not clear that it represents Brown's idiom. Hence, A's reading seems preferable either as a correction of M's error (perhaps involving eyeskip to 'the') or as an unconscious revision during retranscription.

181.32–33 roughnesses] Although this plural could represent M's error, it is, like 'remembrances' (186.28), an unusual form that has the sound of Brown's idiom (see, e.g., 20.33). On the other hand, A's 'roughness', while it could represent an inadvertent revision by Brown during the process of retranscription, is more likely an error (perhaps a normalization, perhaps encouraged by a kind of eyeskip). For these reasons and others already explained (see the Textual Essay), we adopt M's less predictable form.

186.28 remembrances] A's 'remembrance' is a predictable reading, whereas M's 'remembrances' has the ring of Brown's idiom; though 'remembrance' could possibly be an inadvertent revision, it is unlikely that Brown would have been disturbed by this plural any more than by the earlier 'roughnesses' (181.32–33). A's predictable form probably represents either a graphic error such as is not uncommon with Brown's hand, in which a short downstroke often makes the plural (cf. *AM*, 332.7), or a simple printer's error, to which Maxwell's shop was somewhat prone (see 154.18, for the error made in resetting state *c*, and *AM*, 86.18). See the Textual Essay for discussion of this general problem.

186.38 dawn of day] It is barely possible that this is A's error for M's 'the dawn of the day', but that A's phrase represents two unconscious omissions is certainly less likely than that M's conventional reading is a deliberate alteration by the Swords shop, particularly since similar constructions in *Ormond* (72.9–10, 107.30, 287.17–18) and other examples of Brown's ellipsis suggest that A's phrase is authorial. The odds therefore favor A's reading, either as a minor stylistic alteration made by Brown during the course of retranscription or as an original reading corrupted in M.

189.5 numbers] The singular 'strength' paired with A's 'number' suggests that A may have erred through anticipation; M's 'numbers' is a somewhat surprising idiom in this context and probably derives from Brown, whereas A's 'number' seems more predictable and probably represents a printer's normalization that should be rejected. Cf. the contrasting situation at 210.1–2.

189.35 was as] Although it is possible that A's 'was as' is in fact an error for M's 'was', the likelihood is much greater that M's reading represents eyeskip or A's reading simple revision during retranscription.

193.25–26 hardships] There is no ascertaining whether A's 'hardships' (retained by E) or M's 'hardship' represents Brown's final reading. M's might be explained as an error induced by the singular of 'pain', but A's plural also could be a corruption influenced by the parallel 'strategems' and 'weapons'. In two similar instances, A has the singular, once coupled with another singular (60.21–22) but once with a plural (213.7). Since A's reading might derive from unconscious revision and may be just a mite less predictable than M's in this context, we adopt it.

197.33 tranquilized] Either A's 'tranquilized' or M's 'realized' is a possible reading, though each makes completely different sense of the passage. A's is straightforward and makes 'these men' (197.26) the antecedent for 'their' in this clause, as it is for the preceding and following instances of 'their' and for the two earlier occurrences of 'them'. It is also more desirable in that it suits the contrast with 'Other enemies might be abroad' and means that the men's fears might have been sufficiently relieved by Edgar's exploits for them to turn their attention to the welfare of their own families rather than that of their neighbors, and this meaning receives some support from Sarsefield's later revelations that Edgar's three killings had helped reduce the number of the largest band of savages from twelve to two (251.20–26, 255.20–21). M's 'realized' is more convoluted since it makes only this 'their' take 'families' as its antecedent and accounts for the withdrawal of these men by suggesting that some dire events had made the apprehensions of their families a stark reality, thus employing an early sense of 'realized'. (The realization of the fears of the men cannot of course be in question.) M's reading could be a memorial error for Brown's 'tranquilized', resulting perhaps from the similar endings and sounds (173.26), or just possibly Brown may have revised the entire sense of the passage by changing this word in the course of transcription. In any case, 'tranquilized' does not appear to be A's error for 'realized' or some other (presumably less original) word, and therefore it must be adopted.

199.16 this] A's 'the' does not seem to be as genuine as M's reading (cf. 73.2, 193.31); since this is the kind of error to which A was prone, on the evidence of reset quire K and the first nine chapters of *Arthur Mervyn*, A's more predictable form (retained by E) should be rejected in favor of M's original 'this'.

202.36 had began] The agreement of A and M in this rather odd-sounding reading makes emendation difficult unless we can assume independent error, and we cannot in view of a similar form in *Ormond*, 235.30–31. This form, then, appears to be Brown's, and although Robert Lowth's *Short Introduction to English Grammar* deprecates such forms, it is clear from his citation of numerous examples in authors like Milton, Addison, Prior, Pope, and Gay that such constructions had a certain currency in the eighteenth century.

207.31 agreeably] It is almost a formula in Brown that a character will act in a certain way 'agreeably' (as M has it) to his own or another's 'direction' (cf. 147.14–15; *AM*, 364.3), 'maxims' (*Orm.*, 25.32), 'conceptions' (*CH*, 30.11), 'advice', 'wishes' (63.12; *JT*, 32.26, 257.13), or whatever. M's reading appears to be authorial and original, A's 'agreeable' a more conventional one that modifies 'they' (the wolf-dogs) rather than 'attended', as is intended. Hence (see Textual Essay), we adopt M's form as preserving Brown's instead of A's, which is unlikely to represent his unconscious revision and probably is Maxwell's alteration (cf. *DC*, 37.6, later in Volume III, the only other example of such a form we have been able to locate).

210.1 suspicion] Although 'doubt' might offer some slight support for the singular here as an instance of parallelism, the salient fact is that A's 'suspicion' is more unusual than M's 'suspicions'. Were the situation reversed, there would be some argument for adopting M's form, but in this case A's reading must be selected as representing either an inadvertent revision of Brown's or a correction of M's normalization.

210.21 wolfs] Brown almost certainly wrote the 'wolfs' preserved in M, a form that survived into the eighteenth century (*OED*); although A's ordinary 'wolves' may be a revision, it may also be a normalization of Brown's own form, and retention of M's original reading seems in order (see Textual Essay).

210.23–24 visit . . . rarely] There can be no question about the originality of M's 'made her visit to Solebury more rarely', a construction sufficiently awkward yet sensible to come from Brown rather than from the conventionally minded Swords compositor. The question is whether A's predictable 'visit . . . rare' results from Brown's revision during transcription or from A's deliberate or unconscious smoothing out of his idiom. It is a question that cannot be answered definitively. But M's reading is so like similar verbal phrases (e.g., 20.34–35, 67.17, 240.1) and so effective in maintaining the contrast with the second half of the sentence, that it should be adopted on these specific grounds as well as more general ones (see the Textual Essay on other instances of these kinds of error in A, in resetting quire K, and in *Arthur Mervyn*).

214.15 thus] Although A's word is possibly an error for 'this', as the less predictable reading it is more likely to be Brown's own and must stand.

220.38 halloos] A's 'hollows' seems to be incorrect, as the references to voiced sounds earlier (219.22, 219.28, 220.1) show, and other minim errors in A, especially those verified by superior variants in M (170.32, 184.13), encourage emendation. This could take the form either of 'hallows' or of 'halloos', but even though the former would involve only *o/a* confusion, the appearance of 'hallooed' at 163.11 suggests adoption of the latter.

230.22 locks] Although A's 'looks' makes a possible reading, it also makes a redundant one; the obvious point is, that the fact that the girl had been scalped revealed that she had been assaulted by Indians. Cf. 236.26, 236.30.

245.22 my Uncle's] By any standards, A is in error. Edgar falls asleep 'at Huntly farm' (127.37), and has 'disappeared by night' from there (243.21–22). Whether he or Maxwell's compositor was confused by the intervening 'Inglefield's' (244.7), or some other cause is to be sought to account for this error, is unclear. But A's 'Inglefield's' requires correction in order to bring it into accord with the action Brown had in mind.

252.29 thither] It is impossible to be certain whether A's 'hither' or the 'thither' adopted by subsequent American editions is correct. The absence of such errors elsewhere in A, at least obvious ones, as well as Brown's general imprecision would support A's reading, but the facts that his small hand was subject to *th-/h-* confusion and that Maxwell earlier in 1799 produced a similar error when setting from print (*AM*, 23.21) supports the view that A errs. The subsequent sentences show that the point of view has yet to shift to Deb's hut, and consequently we have chosen to emend. Cf. the textual note on *Wie.*, 11.7 and references there.

255.28 starting] Although the sense here is obviously the

'startling' present in all later American editions, the similarity of the words and the continued use of 'start' as a transitive to mean 'startle' suggests that A, and E as well, has reproduced Brown's word.

259.23 participating] The awkward 'participating' found in A and retained by E appears to come from Brown, who elsewhere uses the word in this sense. Cf. *AM*, 186.20.

286.2 effected] The referent for 'This' seems to be not just Clithero's 'belief' but the overthrowing of that belief: Edgar seeks to 'dissipate', 'cure' and 'restore', not just have an impact on Clithero (286.5–6), as his subsequent actions show. Brown knew the distinction between 'affect' and 'effect', which was established by his time (see Johnson and *OED*), and A's 'affected' appears to be a minim error (cf. 153.32, 220.38, 217.35) to which other printers were subject, though this specific case is probably owing to Brown's small hand or to a tendency of Maxwell's shop to confuse these two words (cf. *AM*, 28.13). See also *Wie.*, 179.35, *Car.*, 248.10.

LIST OF EMENDATIONS

NOTE: This list contains all instances of alterations of the copy-text, except for the silent changes specified in the note on the Bicentennial Texts in Volume I of this edition. (See the Textual Essay for the treatment of the copy-text's press-variants.) Each note gives the reading of the Bicentennial text before the bracket, followed by a siglum identifying its earliest source (either one of the editions examined, or the present editors) and then by the variant reading(s) of the copy-text and of the other editions between it and the source of the adopted reading. This information is provided for both substantives and accidentals; for a complete history of substantive variants among the editions examined, see the Historical List. In those portions of the novel where they exist, the texts of states *b* and *c* of quire K and *b* of quire M in the first edition's Volume II (153.4–157.24, 163.1–167.31), of the *Philadelphia Gazette and Universal Daily Advertiser* (p. 3), and of the *Monthly Magazine* (170.21–213.8) are reported in the same fashion as the complete 1803 edition, with one exception: where it is impossible to compare the emendation and the rejected reading of the main textual tradition with the reading of the *Monthly Magazine* because it has an entirely different version of the passage, the symbol "*var.*" shows this fact. Throughout the list an asterisk (*) before the lemma indicates that the Textual Notes discuss the emendation. A wavy dash (~) represents the same word appearing before the bracket and occurs only in the recording of variants in punctuation or other accidentals associated with that word, when the word itself or its forms is not the variant being noted; the inferior caret (‸) shows that punctuation is absent. Three dots (···) mean that the note omits one or more words in a series, and a vertical stroke (|) marks the break between lines. When the reading of the lemma is a possible compound and is ambiguously hyphenated between two lines in the present edition, a dagger (†) precedes the entry; the reader may consult Part B of the following appendix for more information on such word-division. "B" following the bracket identifies readings adopted for the first time in the Bicentennial Edition (that is, readings not appearing in the editions examined). Preceding the list are the sigla which identify the editions examined and cited in it.

G: *Philadelphia Gazette and Universal Daily Advertiser*, subscription notice (10 August 1799 *et seq*), without authority

M: *The Monthly Magazine* (April 1799), I, 21–44

A: *Edgar Huntly; or, Memoirs of a Sleep-Walker* (Philadelphia, 1799), copy-text

    A^a: first state, quire K or M, Vol. II

    A^b: second state, quire K or M, Vol. II

    A^c: third state, quire K, Vol. II

E: *Edgar Huntly, or Memoirs of a Sleep-Walker* (London, 1803), without authority

3.18	Puerile] G; Peurile A
5.25	sentiments. In] B; ~$_\wedge$ In A; ~; in E
6.3	this?] E; ~. A
11.12	sympathy. Every] B; ~$_\wedge$ Every A; ~; every E
13.25	nefarious] E; nefareous A
15.17	certainty?] E; ~. A
15.28	me,] B; ~$_\wedge$ A; ~ — E
16.3–4	surprise?] E; ~. A
16.8	them?] E; ~. A
17.11	artifices.] B; ~? A–E
18.38	out.] E; ~$_\wedge$ A
19.18	rocks.] E; ~$_\wedge$ A
19.19	Norwalk] E; Nor-walk A
22.26	Norwalk] E; Nor-walk A
23.20	*Solebury*] B; *Salsbury* A–E
26.11	these,] B; ~$_\wedge$ A; ~ — E
26.11	pity"] E; ~$_\wedge$ A

* 26.22   dejection. On] B; ∼, on A; ∼∧ on E
26.32   After] B; after A-E
30.5   answered] E; Answered A
32.24   unfolded,] E; ∼ ; A
33.1   repetition] E; repeti- | tition A
34.11   Norwalk] E; Nor-walk A
36.25   light?] E; ∼. A
36.28–29   aggravate] E; agravate A
39.29–30   attendant] E; attendent A
40.34   freest] E; free- | est A
* 46.24   The] B; Her A; the E
47.36–37   consciousness] E; conciousness A
48.5–6   consumed] E; consumeed A
48.17   highway] E; higway A
50.16   indelible] E; indellible A
52.12   purpose?] E; ∼. A
* 54.9   Still] B; Sill A; still E
56.25   it?] E; ∼. A
57.7   preliminaries?] E; ∼. A
58.26   arms.] E; ∼∧ A
* 60.19   ingenuous] E; ingenious A
60.33   ∧He] B; (∼ A; — ∼ E
61.17   Philopoemen] E; Philoepamen A
61.29   acuteness] E; accuteness A
64.21   exhibited] E; exibited A
64.23   exclaming,] B; ∼∧ A; ∼ — E
65.24   uneasiness.] E; ∼∧ A
* 65.37   man;] B; ∼, A-E
66.2   opinion?] E; ∼. A
69.3   perils?] E; ∼. A
70.10   account] E; acccount A
71.11   exclaimed,] B; ∼. A; ∼ — E
* 73.2   Those] B; These A; these E
74.17   Wiatte] E; Wyatte A
77.3   one?] E; ∼. A
77.7   infallible] E; infalible A
79.3   breathe?] E; ∼. A
82.28   lineaments] E; linaments A
82.35   emissary] E; emisary A
* 84.2   widely] E; widley A
84.12   lineaments] E; linaments A
84.13   Negligently] E; Neglegently A
85.5   future.] E; ∼? A
86.37   articulated.] B; ∼, A; ∼ — E

87.12	miscreant.] E; ~∧ A
87.27	enemy;] B; ~. A; ~: E
90.18	distinguished?] E; ~. A
92.22	decisions!] E; ~? A
92.31	infallible] E; infalible A
92.38	it?] B; ~. A; ~ — E
93.3	menacer?] B; ~. A; ~! E
95.11	himself?] E; ~. A
95.32	Norwalk,] E; ~. A
95.35	was it] B; it was A–E
96.8	dells?] E; ~. A
* 97.36	intention] E; attention A
* 98.21	seemed as] E; seemed A
98.27	necessary] E; neccessary A
98.28	footsteps] E; foot-steps A
100.9	footsteps] B; foot-steps A–E
100.12	boldly] E; boldy A
*100.13	come] E; came A
101.36	subjected] E; sujected A
104.15	Clithero.] B; ~? A; ~! E
105.20	ground.] E; ~∧ A
106.14	footsteps] B; foot-steps A–E
107.22	task;] E; ~, A
109.11	occasioned] E; ccasioned A
109.25	footsteps] B; foot-steps A–E
110.8	life?] E; ~. A
110.15	malice?] B; ~. A; ~; E
111.19	Lineaments] B; Linaments A; lineaments E
111.34	be∧] E; ~, A
112.13–14	necessary] E; neccessary A
115.1	Inglefields;] B; ~, A; ~: E
115.10	sacred?] E; ~. A
115.11	violence?] E; ~. A
115.22	heard?] E; ~. A
119.38	attracted] E; atracted A
120.27	sufficient] E; sufficent A
124.17	defence.] E; ~, A
124.35	tom-hawk] B; Tom-hawk A; tomahawk E
125.17	footsteps] B; foot-steps A–E
†127.30–31	tom-hawk] B; Tom-	hawk A; tomahawk E
130.10–11	complacency] E; complacensy A
131.10	man?] E; ~. A
131.19	gratification?] E; ~. A
131.26	vision?] E; ~. A
134.25	change.] E; ~∧ A

135.26	footstep] E; foot-step A
137.5	unoccupied] E; unocupied A
137.6	footsteps] E; foot-steps A
137.14	which‸] E; ~ , A
137.26	employment] E; employ- | A
140.21	foreboding.] E; ~ , A
142.5	dollars.] E; ~ ? A
142.8	it.] E; ~ ? A
142.29	expect] E; except A
148.4	remittance‸] E; ~ , A
148.12	affair.] E; ~ ‸ A
151.33	friend's] E; friends' A
152.31	The] B; the A–E
153.3	equity,] E; ~ . A
*153.32	funds] B; friends A–E
154.31	fortune?] E; ~ . A
157.16	indeed] Aᵇ; ineed Aᵃ
157.21	benefit] Aᵇ; benfit Aᵃ
160.23	excluded?] B; ~ . A–E
160.33	clothed. A] B; ~ , a A; ~ —a E
160.33	trossers] B; trossars A; trousers E
160.35	wanting.] E; ~ , A
161.12	ground.] B; ~ , A; ~ : E
161.13	tom-hawk] B; Tom-hawk A; tomahawk E
162.18	dreams.] E; ~ , A
162.27	effected,] E; ~ . A
163.33	footsteps] E; foot-steps A
163.37	agonies,] Aᵇ; ~ ‸ Aᵃ
†164.23–24	tom-hawk] B; Tom-hawk A; tomahawk E
165.8	pit?] E; ~ . A
165.11	safety?] E; ~ . A
166.2	verge; when] B; ~ , when A; ~ . When E
166.16	tom-hawk] B; Tom-hawk A; tomahawk E
168.23	temporary] E; temporary A
168.26	occurred] E; occured A
169.38	footsteps] E; foot-steps A
170.11	likely] E; likly A
*170.32	where] M; when A
172.10	musquet] M; musket A
172.18	view] M; vew A
174.10	from] E; fom A
174.13	the] M; thc A
174.25	footsteps] M; foot-steps A
179.1	and‸] M; ~ , A
179.7	footsteps] M; foot-steps A

180.9	impediments.] M; ~∧ A
*181.32–33	roughnesses] M; roughness A
†181.38–	footsteps] M; foot- | steps A
182.1	
182.5	ocean.] M; ~∧ A
183.3	occurred] M; occured A
184.2	stretched] M; srtetched A
184.8	sand;] E; ~, A; *var.* M
184.10	visible.] M; ~∧ A
184.13	unceremoniously] M; uncerimoniously A
185.4	footsteps] M; foot-steps A
*186.28	remembrances] M; remembrance A
187.1	and∧] M; ~, A
187.17	The] M; The | the A
*189.5	numbers] M; number A
189.14	suggested;] M; ~? A
189.35	station.] M; ~∧ A
194.8	footsteps] M; foot- | steps A
195.5	approach] M; aproach A
196.22	contest?] M; ~. A
196.30	zeal,] M; ~∧ A
*199.16	this] M; the A
203.3	burthen] M; burden A
205.12	footsteps] E; foot-steps A; foot- | steps M
205.18–19	attendants] M; attendents A
*207.31	agreeably] M; agreeable A
*210.21	wolfs] M; wolves A
*210.23	visit] M; visits A
*210.24	rarely] M; rare A
210.34	barked.] B; ~, A–E, M
211.4	footsteps] M; foot-steps A
211.27	footsteps] M; foot-steps A
212.20	energies] M; energis A
214.6	hopeles] B; hoples A; hopeless E
215.7	attendant] E; attendent A
215.23	speedily] E; speedly A
215.37–	mountain?] E; ~. A
216.1	
217.35	extremities] E; extremeties A
220.10	myself?] E; ~! A
220.13	stream?] E; ~. A
*220.38	halloos] B; hollows A–E
221.8	armed;] B; ~, A; ~: E
227.4	endured,] E; ~. A

227.17	pails-full] B; pail's-full A; pails full E
227.34	signals.] E; ~∧ A
229.28	occurred] E; occured A
229.29	Selbys] E; Selby's A
230.6–7	distance;] E; ~, A
230.19	closely∧] E; ~, A
*230.22	locks] E; looks A
231.8	imagined] E; immagined A
231.22	last] B; least A–E
231.24	face;] E; ~, A
231.31	inured] E; innured A
231.37	led] B; lead A–E
232.26	miles∧] E; ~, A
234.21	retaken.] E; ~? A
234.23	Yes] E; yes A
235.22	friend?] B; ~. A; ~ – E
237.18	occurred] E; occured A
239.38	soul.] E; ~, A
240.18	footsteps] B; foot-steps A; foot-	steps E
241.25	forgotten?] B; ~! A; ~, E
244.3	too?] E; ~! A
*245.22	my Uncle's] B; Inglefield's A–E
246.14	relation,] E; ~. A
246.16	Huntly,] E; ~; A
247.2	Solebury; some] B; ~, some A; ~. Some E
249.36	occurred.] B; ~, A; ~: E
250.13	warriors] E; wariors A
251.6	footsteps] E; foot-steps A
251.16	emerge] E; immerge A
252.8	footsteps] E; foot-steps A
252.17	footsteps] E; foot-steps A
*252.29	thither] B; hither A–E
252.34	distinguished] E; distinguised A
257.32	moment's] E; moments A
258.38	led] B; lead A–E
261.16	insanity] E; insantiy A
262.4	speak?] E; ~. A
262.25	calamity!] B; ~. A; ~:– E
262.34	astonished] E; astonised A
263.25	hither?] E; ~. A
265.11	Clithero?] E; ~. A
265.15	life?] E; ~. A
265.18–19	promontory;] B; ~, A; ~: E
267.17	fury,] B; ~. A; ~ – E

267.19	moment's] E; moments A
267.33	Walcot's] E; Walcots A
273.15	death;] B; ~! A; ~ — E
273.16	elm;] B; ~! A; ~ — E
274.8	gratitude,] E; ~ A
276.35	reverse!] E; ~? A
277.28	occurred] E; occured A
278.19	other!] E; ~? A
278.26	condition,] E; ~; A
278.31	information] E; informntion A
279.25	privilege] B; previlege A–E
280.14	friend!] E; ~? A
281.36	consumed] E; ~, A
284.13	out.] B; ~? A; ~; E
284.26	subsistance?] E; ~. A
285.8	deportment,] E; ~; A
285.11–12	employer's] E; employers A
*286.2	effected] E; affected A
287.10	footsteps] B; foot-steps A; foot- | steps E
287.35	tone:] B; ~; A; ~ — E
288.38	me;] B; ~? A; ~ E
290.3	inexpressible] E; enexpressible A
290.27	intelligence?] E; ~. A
292.8	Powles-hook] B; Powels-hook A; Powel's-hook E
292.31	burthen] B; burden A–E

NOTE: Chapter Headings: The Bicentennial text corrects A's duplicated chapter number 'XIV' in Volume II and renumbers succeeding chapters accordingly. It omits the title repeated before each heading.

END-OF-LINE WORD DIVISION

NOTE: The two following lists provide information on the word-division of divisible compounds that are hyphenated at the ends of lines in the copy-text or in the Bicentennial Edition. List A contains, in the form of the established text, such compounds which are hyphenated and divided at the break between lines in the copy-text. A double dagger (‡) precedes the notation if the word happens to be similarly hyphenated in the Bicentennial Edition (see List B for more information on such words). List B contains all examples of possible compounds hyphenated at the break between lines in this edition which are meant to be hyphenated in the established text; the absence of such compounds hyphenated in this edition shows that they are meant to be unhyphenated in the established text. A dagger (†) precedes the notation if the word is an emendation (see the List of Emendations for further information) and a double dagger (‡) precedes it if the word happens to be similarly hyphenated in the copy-text (see List A of this appendix on such words). Both lists omit words with hyphens between capitalized elements (e.g., North-|American) and those that are clearly mere compositorial syllabication (including syllabication of compound words falling elsewhere than at the point of word-division).

A. Word-Division in the Copy-Text

3.15	diseases	14.25	thoughtful
11.33	methought	15.17	Henceforth
12.6	himself	15.30	myself
13.12	half-clothed	17.1	myself

18.26	sometimes	111.23	needlessly
19.6	bedewed	112.38	carefully
23.15	whithersoever	113.3	day-light
26.34	house-keeper	114.1	workmanship
28.5	sleep-walker	115.11	without
28.23	workmanship	115.25	groundless
29.31	somewhat	118.14	forever
31.32	suitable	120.15	somewhat
32.37	homewards	123.36	afternoon
35.20	otherwise	125.2	cat-o'mountain
36.4	yourself	126.1	fellow-creature
36.23	understanding	126.13	withdrawn
37.38	thenceforward	126.38	headlong
42.28	herself	127.6	hind-legs
46.28	son-in-law	132.15	blameless
50.9	play-fellow	134.22	understanding
51.31	themselves	140.2	moon-light
64.9	bed-side	140.4	methought
66.14	something	145.32	fishermen
68.18	helplessness	149.1	unfavourable
70.21	fear-inspiring	161.29	Overpowered
72.24	landlord	163.18	headlong
74.33	homeward	166.4	myself
76.21	whatever	168.4	myself
81.1	forebodings	170.6	sometime
84.8	without	172.25	somewhat
84.10	methought	175.39	likewise
86.1	bed-clothes	178.31	re-entrance
87.35	myself	‡181.38–	footsteps
89.6	likewise	182.1	
89.31	mankind	182.11	herself
92.2	foreseen	‡183.38–	bedstead
94.29	footsteps	184.1	
95.6	himself	185.35	Defenceless
‡97.6–7	Afterwards	187.1	overtaken
98.11	footsteps	‡189.11–12	mankind
99.4	myself	190.2	forth-coming
100.11	without	193.21	bloodshed
103.30	endless	194.8	footsteps
104.26	overgrown	195.9	something
‡107.9–10	re-emerged	198.14	without
107.16	himself	202.11	overpowered
107.19	himself	207.18	countrymen
109.4	fearlessly	207.23	Norwalk

207.37	farm-house	247.4	Norwalk
208.31	whatever	249.23	Norwalk
209.11	sometimes	249.34	without
211.24	themselves	252.36	themselves
212.8	Thenceforward	253.3	overspread
213.6	forebodings	253.6	Norwalk
217.19	South-east	254.14	tom-hawk
219.26	overheard	255.23	withdrawn
223.20	fruitless	267.9	needless
227.33	bed-chamber	273.19	likewise
228.12	without	275.13	withdrawn
229.17	Somewhere	276.20	methought
231.38	without	283.8	to-morrow
234.5	withdrawn	284.10	otherwise
237.29	stair-case	‡287.27–28	withdraw
238.12	ink-stand	287.35	themselves
240.31	himself	288.13	whoever
241.2	unforeseen	291.22	madman
244.17	prepossessions		

B. *Word-Division in the Bicentennial Edition*

9.35–36	wide-spread	183.17–18	half-burnt
14.6–7	ever-flowing	192.10–11	re-load
27.37–38	self-possession	204.6–7	*well-pole*
72.10–11	by-standers	217.7–8	over-arched
96.14–15	mid-summer	233.11–12	Grist-mill
‡107.9–10	re-emerged	236.20–21	window-light
†127.30–31	tom-hawk	248.4–5	bed-side
†164.23–24	tom-hawk	268.21–22	common-room
181.6–7	half-stifled		

HISTORICAL LIST OF
SUBSTANTIVE VARIANTS

NOTE: This appendix lists only substantive variants from the Bicentennial text in the editions examined. Accidentals—including accidentals variants of the readings—are not, as such, listed; thus the report that two texts agree in having one of two readings (e.g., 'apprized' as against 'surprised') implies only that they both have the same word (e.g., perhaps in the spellings *apprized* and *apprised*) and not necessarily the identical form. Also not listed are variants in chapter headings (see the Textual Essay) and such features as are silently emended throughout the Bicentennial Edition (e.g., mere turned letters), whether they are in the copy-text or another edition (see "The Bicentennial Texts: A Note," p. xxiii, in Volume I of this series). By the same token, as the purpose of this report is to list the genuinely substantive variants which constitute the evidence for decisions on genealogy and authority ("The Bicentennial Texts," p. xxiv), this list does not report as variants impossible readings created by pulled types or other merely typographical faults (e.g., 'rom' and 'fom' for 'from' at 167.7, 174.10) either in the copy-text or in the other editions. Nor does it record a second time examples of foul-case, mechanical transposition of letters, or other similar "literals" which appear in the copy-text and are correct in other editions. Reports on such readings appear in the Textual Essay (when they involve press-variation), in the List of Emendations, and in the appendixes that follow. However, whenever there is a possible or ambiguous reading that falls in any of these classes (e.g., 'hoples' at 214.16), the variation is reported here in the usual way. Moreover, the main list includes variation in Volume II's reset quire K (153.3–157.24), in the preface (p. 3), which was also printed in the *Philadelphia Gazette and Universal Daily Advertiser*, and in that part of the novel (170.21–213.26) which first appeared in the *Monthly Magazine* (there are no substantive variants in quire M of Volume II, 133.1–144.22). Where in this part of the text A and E differ in some particular word and the entire passage in M varies to such an extent that the texts are not comparable, the symbol "*var.*" shows this fact. Throughout the main list, each note gives the reading of the Bicentennial text before the bracket, followed by the variant reading(s) and then by the sigla for the editions having that variant. A wavy dash (∼) represents the same word appearing before the bracket and occurs when variation involves punctuation associated with that word but the word itself is not the variant being noted; the inferior caret (∧) shows that punctuation is absent. Three dots (···) mean that the note omits one or more words in a series. When a lemma is a single word which has been divided at a line break in this edition and which consequently occupies two lines, the page-line reference locates the reading by citing only the first line. In a given entry, the editions are cited only when they vary substantively from the reading of the Bicentennial text given in the lemma (i.e., omission of sigla implies agreement). The following sigla identify the editions cited.

G: *Philadelphia Gazette and Universal Daily Advertiser*, subscription notice (10 August 1799 *et seq.*), without authority

M: *The Monthly Magazine* (April 1799), I, 21–44

A: *Edgar Huntly; or, Memoirs of a Sleep-Walker* (Philadelphia, 1799), copy-text
  A^a: first state, quire K, Vol. II
  A^b: second state, quire K, Vol. II
  A^c: third state, quire K, Vol. II

E: *Edgar Huntly, or Memoirs of a Sleep-Walker* (London, 1803), without authority

3.6	That] The G
8.23	an] a E
11.6	low] slow E
12.29	no longer of] of no longer E
13.18	denote] betray E
13.20	enables] enable E
19.23	glimpses] glimpse E
20.25	lofty] the lofty E
22.13	adventure] venture E
26.22	dejection. On] ~, on A; ~∧ on E
26.22	employed, he] ~. He E
27.26	unintermitted] unremitted E
27.32	was] were E
28.2	a change] an alteration E
32.31	an] a E
33.14	than] that E
35.2	an] a E
37.11	regard] consider E
40.13	became] grew E
43.10	unostentatious] without ostentation E
43.14	those] these E
46.17	depends] depend E
46.24	The] Her A
49.6	an] a E
49.13	ties] tie E
49.27	a] an E
51.10	my mind] it E
53.15	represented] represent E
54.9	Still] Sill A
54.26	an] a E
55.7	that] which E
56.18	an] a E
60.19	ingenuous] ingenious A
61.5	Scotsmen] Scotchmen E
61.20	Apennine] Appenines E
62.34	more] most E
62.37	alteration] alterations E
62.38	an] a E
67.3	incident] accident E
67.15	the lady] his sister E
67.27	near at] at E
67.30	shall forthwith] forthwith E
68.27	an] a E
70.6	recovered. It] ~, and E
70.10	this late] so late an E
71.11	an] a E
72.7	nigh at] at E
73.2	Those] These A–E
74.8	theme] result E
74.34	an] a E
75.3	wicked. An] ~, a E
75.9	an] a E
80.8	or] or a E
80.31	now] not E
84.2	widely] widley A
86.25	the lady] Mrs. Lorimer E
86.32	the lady] Mrs. Lorimer E
87.26	is] and E
88.3	merely made] made E
88.8	and] and the E
89.1	in] to E
89.23	them] it E
89.36	an] a E
91.5	romancers] romances E
92.32	the lady] Mrs. Lorimer E
92.33	the brother] her brother E

93.18–19	journey, and ⋯ situation,] journey, E	137.26	employment] employ- A
93.32	to] for E	142.3	at] in E
93.35	heard of] learned E	142.7	kindred] relation E
95.30	this] the E	142.29	expect] except A
95.35	was it] it was A–E	143.27	beside] besides E
97.36	intention] attention A	145.14	ate] eat E
		145.19	or] nor E
98.8	road] rode E	145.26	those] these E
98.12	had] have E	146.14	those] these E
98.19	stair] stairs E	147.8	an] a E
98.21	seemed as] seemed A	147.19	in this] on this E
		150.1	an] a E
100.13	come] came A	151.32	you] you that E
102.3	was] way E	151.33	friend's] friends' A
102.25	an] a E	153.32	funds] friends A–E
103.32	an] a E	153.38	mistreatment] ill-treatment E
104.3	an] a E		
104.11	But this] This, however, E	154.15	alighted] lighted A[b]
106.1	His] this E	154.18	consequences] consequence A[c]
107.8	hither] here E	155.7	its] it A[c]
109.34	to be] of being E	155.23	union] a union A[c]
110.31	these evils] their influence E	155.28	us] as A[c]
		156.15	has] have E
111.29	intrusion] instruction E	158.5	The] this E
114.17	were] was E	162.15	at] to E
118.8	thus to] thus E	165.4	an] a E
120.27	was] were E	165.6	into] in E
121.1	of] of of E	165.18	An] a E
122.37	former] foregoing E	165.21	An] A E
123.30	the] my E	165.22	by] by my E
124.14–15	ruggedest and most] most rugged and E	167.27	to be] of being E
		168.13	conjecture] suppose E
127.35	an] a E	168.30	the] a E
131.8	This] these E	168.36	now] no E
132.9	devoted] diverted E	170.1	an] a E
133.3	Beside] besides E	170.2	an] a E
135.28	run to] reach E	170.5	of which] that E
136.3	was] were E	170.5	sensible] sensible of E
136.25	circumstances] circumstance E	170.32	where] when A; whence E
		171.14	into] with E

172.4	measure] measures M		rye bread. An axe, spade, and hoe, completed all the furniture of this habitation M
172.15	an] a E		
173.26	lately] greatly M		
174.13	post,] ‿∧ M		
174.30	calamities,] ‿. M, E	184.6	and a] a E; var. M
		184.7	the bucket] which E; var. M
174.34	fire.] ‿, and smoking his pipe. M	184.8	sand;] ‿, A; var. M
176.21	without abruptness] hence lessen her surprise E	184.9	an] a E; var. M
		184.31	precarious] ambiguous M
176.36	as I] I E	184.33	herself ⋯ bed] her head upon my knees M
177.20	precipice,] ‿,and tranquilly employed in smoking, M		
		185.22	The] It was polluted with rust, and had received various bruises, but the M
177.26	reach ⋯ could escape] escape E		
178.17–18	torments] torment E		
178.26	into] in M	186.28	remembrances] remembrance A–E
179.21	an] a E		
180.22	an] a E	186.38	dawn of] the dawn of the M
181.31	creeping vines] oak-bushes M		
181.32–33	roughnesses] roughness A–E	187.17	The] The the A
		187.25	the gift] it E
181.34–35	cedars ⋯ moss,] trees M	188.21	formed ⋯ partly] partly formed by a cavity M
182.21	pit. At another we] pit, or M		
		188.25	possible] impossible E
182.22–23	branches ⋯ or] withes and branches of the oak M		
		189.5	numbers] number A–E
		189.35	was as] was M
182.38	spaces] tracts E	190.5	an] a E
183.28	but] and M	190.8	an] a E
183.32	Of] and of E	191.13–14	The ⋯ ear: He] He M
184.5–10	the stale ⋯ furniture] a cedar bucket, replenished with brackish water, and the reliques of a loaf of	192.4	But I] I M
		193.11	an hand] a hand E
		193.25–26	hardships] hardship M
		193.31	this] the E
		195.4	this] his E

195.29	an] a E
196.7	clasping] clasping her M
197.33	tranquilized] realized M
199.16	this] the A–E
199.27	an] a E
202.28–34	these! But ⋯ universe!] these! M
204.6–7	cultivation, the *well-pole*,] cultivation, M
204.23	farther] further E
205.21	an] a E
205.25	chimney∧ of brick,] chimney, of brick∧ M
206.2	started] sprung E
206.24	shirt] a shirt E
207.3	tribe] tribes E
207.19	upon] upon the E
207.31	agreeably] agreeable A–E
207.34	rabbits] hares M
208.8	plucking ⋯ among] hoeing and grinding M
208.8–9	corn; bruising ⋯ stones,] corn∧ M
208.9–10	snares, for ⋯ apossums,] snares, M
208.14	An] A E
208.16	directions] direction E
208.18	looks, occasion] look, occasions M
208.23	overhear] overheard M
208.36	were] were merely M
209.11	insensibly] but insensibly M
209.26	an] a E
210.1	suspicion]

	suspicions M
210.21	wolfs] wolves A–E
210.23	visit] visits A–E
210.24	rarely] rare A–E
211.17	an] a E
211.31	cultivable] culturable M
212.12	boundings of a leopard] boundings M
212.14	in] in a M
212.20	maze] maize E
212.20	energies] energis A
213.8	subjected] subject M
214.6	hopeles] hoples A
214.33	direction] quarter E
214.37	farther] further E
215.11	an] a E
216.12	an] a E
216.29	an] a E
217.31	but] still E
218.8	were] was E
219.8	farther] further E
219.33	an] a E
219.36	this] the E
220.38	halloos] hollows A–E
221.32	precipitation] a precipitation E
221.36	endlong] headlong E
221.37	an] a E
222.20	the] for E
225.11	upward] upwards E
225.28	river. It] river, which E
226.1	an] a E
226.13	an] a E
226.21	or a] or E
227.17	pails-full] pail's-full A
227.24–26	had ⋯ accomplished.] at that moment any

	further attempt at discovery seemed vain: still E	252.29	thither] hither A–E
		252.31	gained] reached E
		252.36	to] on E
228.10	Is't] Is it E	253.6	hastening] hasting E
228.10	Damn] D--n E		
229.20	an] a E	253.11	thus precluded] precluded E
229.29	Selbys] Selby's A		
230.20	an] a E	253.36	carried] was carried E
230.21	an] a E		
230.22	locks] looks A	253.37	in the arms of] by E
231.37	led] lead A–E		
232.14	an] a E	254.7	intelligible] intelligent E
232.14	by] for E		
233.13	saw before me] saw E	255.3	an] a E
		255.5	had ceased] was over E
234.14–15	did ⋯ belong?] the house belonged. E	256.12	disinvolve] extricate E
234.21	said ⋯ had] say she has E	257.17	and] and we E
236.17	acquainted with] informed of E	257.32	moment's] moments A
236.30	were] was E	258.15	an] a E
236.31	An] a E	258.16	ate] eat E
237.12	were] was E	258.27	was] were E
237.13	or] nor E	258.38	led] lead A–E
237.14	an] a E	259.6	an] a E
237.16	noise and] noise, E	259.9	an] a E
238.13	This] Such an E	260.2	Long-room] long room E
241.7	Thus] Thus it should seem as if E	261.10	that] this E
241.9	should have been] were to be E	262.15	Unhappy?] ~ , E
		263.15	numbered] counted E
242.16	could not] cannot E		
242.22	an] a E	263.34	immured] concealed E
244.3	my sisters] sisters E	264.27	in] in the E
245.22	my Uncle's] Inglefield's A–E	265.16	a sound] sounds E
245.23	which] what E	266.11	of my] of E
246.35	were] are E	267.5	suggested] caused E
248.3	in] on E	267.14	is] be E
248.20	was] were E	267.19	moment's] moments A
251.12	an] a E		
251.16	emerge] immerge A	267.33	Walcot's] Walcots A
252.14	elude] escape E	269.24	not] but not E

270.10	an] a E			Lorimer's E
270.12	was] were E		277.37	Clithero] he E
270.19	it] them E		285.11–12	employer's
270.25	was] were E			employers A
270.29	ate] eat E		285.25	an] a E
272.29	discussion]		285.28	what] what more E
	discussions E		285.29	but] than E
273.6	was ⋯ mode] were		286.2	effected] affected A
	but two modes E		287.33	purpose] ideas E
273.9	This] The latter E		288.37	could] and E
273.10	the] a E		289.24	an] a E
274.14–15	the lady] Mrs.		292.8	Powles-hook]
	Lorimer E			Powels-hook A;
275.20–21	the lady] she E			Powel's-hook E
275.35	the lady] Mrs.		292.17	women] servants E
	Lorimer E		292.31	active] inactive E
275.37–38	the lady] Mrs.		292.33	council] counsel E
	Lorimer E		293.14	an] a E
276.27	the lady's] Mrs.		293.28	an] a E

Variants in Volume II
of the First Edition

Note: This list records variants among the three states of quire K and two of M in Volume II of the first book edition which were found in examining twenty-two copies and are discussed in the Textual Essay. (See the Record of Collations and Copies Consulted below.) Since in each instance the present edition's reading is that of one of these states, the list takes the form of columns. The first column contains the reading of the first state (*a*), which generally (though not always) is found in the Bicentennial text, the succeeding columns those of the other states. The citations preceding these columns refer first to the present edition's pagination and lineation and second (in parenthesis) to those of the first edition.

Variation in Volume II, quire K

		state a	*state b*	*state c*
153.4	(109.1–2)	acknowledge∧ that,	~∧~ ,	~ , ~∧
153.25	(110.11)	Europe∧	~∧	~ ,
153.31	(110.19)	father,	~ ,	~∧
153.32	(110.21)	maintenance	maintainance	maintenance
153.38	(111.6)	shock,	~ ,	~∧
154.15	(112.7)	alighted	lighted	alighted
154.18	(112.11)	consequences	consequences	consequence
154.22	(112.17)	guize	guise	guize
154.25	(112.22)	exercised	xercised	exercised
154.33	(113.10)	every land	every land	everyland
154.38	(113.18–19)	pre-|tentions	pre-|tensions	pre-|tentions

482

		state a	state b	state c
———	113.dir	[*omitted*]	K₂	K₂
155.5	(114.4)	winter-blast	winter blast	winter blast
155.7	(114.6)	its	its	it
155.14–15	(114.17)	condemned.	~ ·	~ ,
155.18–19	(115.1)	knowledge∧	~ ,	~∧
155.23	(115.7)	union	union	a union
155.28	(115.15)	maintain	maintain	mantain
155.28	(155.15)	us	us	as
155.32	(115.20)	drudgery∧	~∧	~ ,
155.32	(115.21)	constitution	constiution	constitution
156.12	(117.2-3)	diffi-|cult	diffi-|cult	dffi-|cult
156.20	(117.14)	needle.	~ ·	~∧
156.21	(117.16)	expenses∧	~∧	~ ,
156.24	(117.20)	not,	~ ,	~∧
156.31	(118.9)	moment,	~∧	~ ,
156.32	(118.10)	condition∧	~∧	~ ,
157.1	(118.20)	account∧	~∧	~ ,
157.15	(119.19)	away∧	~∧	~ ,
157.16	(119.20)	ineed	indeed	indeed
157.18	(120.1)	different	different	diffierent
157.19	(120.2)	money,	~ ,	~∧
157.21	(120.5)	benfit	benefit	benefit

Variation in Volume II, quire M

		state a	state b
163.1	(133.1)	walls,	~∧
163.7	(133.9)	passing	pssing
163.19	(134.5-6)	received,	~∧
163.37	(135.7)	agonies∧	~ ,
167.10	(143.14)	scull	skull

Variants Between the First Edition
and the *Philadelphia Gazette*

NOTE: This list includes all variants found through collation of the paragraphs 'To The Public' which constitute the preface to the first edition (A) against the opening paragraphs of the subscription notice published in the *Philadelphia Gazette and Universal Daily Advertiser* (G) for the first time on 10 August 1799. Not recorded are A's omission of G's headings, G's omission of A's signature initials, and similar features of format and design. Since in each instance of variation the present edition's reading is either that of A or of G, the apparatus takes the form of columns. The first column contains the reading of the first edition, which almost always is found in the Bicentennial text. The second column presents the reading of G, which in one case supplies the reading adopted here. The citation preceding these columns refers to the page and line of the present edition where one of the variant readings will be found. The use of the wavy dash ($\sim$), the inferior caret ($_\wedge$), and the vertical stroke (|) conforms to the practice followed in the List of Emendations and explained in its headnote.

	First Edition (A)	*Philadelphia Gazette (G)*
3.5	[¶] America	[no ¶] America
3.6	seldome	seldom
3.6	That	The
3.7	operate;	$\sim$:
3.13	sources;	$\sim$:
3.16	claim;	$\sim$:

	First Edition (A)	*Philadelphia Gazette (G)*
3.18	Peurile	Puerile
3.20	hostility,	~∧
3.21	western	Western
3.21	wilderness	Wilderness
3.21	suitable;	~ ,
3.21	and,	~∧
3.22	these,	~∧
3.23	part,	~∧

VARIANTS BETWEEN THE FIRST EDITION
AND THE *MONTHLY MAGAZINE*

NOTE: This list includes all variants found through collation of the latter part of Volume II of the first edition (A) against the fragment which first appeared in a slightly different form in the April number of the *Monthly Magazine*. Not recorded are readings created by press-variation in the first edition (see the Textual Essay for reports of these), M's omission of A's chapter headings, A's omission of M's headings, and similar features of typography, format, and design. Since in each instance of variation the present edition's reading is based on either that of A or of M, the apparatus takes the form of columns. The first column contains the reading of the first edition, which generally but not always is found in the Bicentennial text. The second column presents the reading of M, which in some cases supplies the reading adopted here. The citation to the left of these columns refers to the page and line of this edition where these variants occur. The use of the wavy dash (～), the inferior caret (ᴧ), and the vertical stroke (|) conforms to the practice followed in the List of Emendations and explained in its headnote. A reprint of the text of the introductory paragraphs which precede M's '*Edgar Huntly: A Fragment*' concludes this part of the apparatus.

	First Edition (A)	*Monthly Magazine (M)*
170.21	any∧	∼,
170.22	hand∧	∼,
170.23	gleam,	∼∧
170.23	faint,	∼∧
170.25	vivid	vived
170.25	vivid,	∼∧
170.29	or∧ ··· least∧	∼, ··· ∼,
170.32	when	where
171.17	[no ¶] No	[¶] No
171.25	mountain∧	∼,
172.4	measure	measures
172.10	musket	musquet
172.17	discovered∧	∼,
172.18	vew	view
172.21	that∧	∼,
172.28	tract,	∼∧
173.13	and∧	∼,
173.19	band,	∼∧
173.26	lately	greatly
174.10	fom	from
174.13	post,	∼∧
174.13	thc	the
174.23	wilderness,	∼∧
174.25	foot-steps	footsteps
174.29–30	and, ··· calamities,	∼∧ ··· ∼.
174.34	fire.	∼, and smoking his pipe.
174.35	me∧	∼,
175.39	like- | wise	likewise
177.20	precipice,	∼, and tranquilly employed in smok-ing,
178.24	grasp.	∼:
178.26	into	in
179.1	and,	∼∧
179.7	foot-steps	footsteps
180.9	impediments∧	∼·
180.24	hazard∧	∼,
181.12	assunder	asunder
181.17	I∧	∼,

	First Edition (A)	*Monthly Magazine (M)*
181.18	proceeded$_\wedge$	~ ,
181.31	creeping vines	oak-bushes
181.32–33	roughness	roughnesses
181.34–35	cedars with their ragged spines and wreaths of moss,	trees
181.35	dwarf oaks	dwarf-oaks
181.38–182.1	foot- | steps	footsteps
182.5	ocean$_\wedge$	~ .
182.11	her- | self	herself
182.15	Meanwhile	Mean- | while
182.21	pit. At another we	pit, or
182.22	branches	withes and branches
182.22–23	oak rebounded in our faces or	oak
182.28	overtaken,	~ $_\wedge$
183.3	occured	occurred
183.10	logs$_\wedge$	~ ,
183.28	but	and
183.38–184.1	bed- | stead	bedstead
184.2	srtetched	stretched
184.5–10	the stale fragments of a rye-loaf, and a cedar bucket kept entire by withs instead of hoops. In the bucket was a little water, full of droppings from the roof, drowned insects and sand, a basket or two neatly made, and an hoe, with a stake thrust into it by way of handle, made up all the furniture	a cedar bucket, replenished with brackish water, and the reliques of a loaf of rye bread. An axe, spade, and hoe, completed all the furniture of this habitation
184.10	visible$_\wedge$	~ .
184.13	uncerimoniously	unceremoniously
184.25	sunrise	sun- | rise
184.25	sunrise,	~ $_\wedge$

	First Edition (A)	*Monthly Magazine (M)*
184.31	precarious	ambiguous
184.33	herself, by my advice, upon the bed	her head upon my knees
184.34	without	with- | out
185.4	foot-steps	footsteps
185.14	me$_\wedge$	~ ,
185.22	The	It was polluted with rust, and had received various bruises, but the
186.12	offspring	off- | spring
186.15	savage,	~$_\wedge$
186.16	hatchet,	~$_\wedge$
186.25	or$_\wedge$	~ ,
186.28	remembrance	remembrances
186.29	misfortunes$_\wedge$	~ ,
186.32	meditations$_\wedge$	~ ,
186.35	watch$_\wedge$	~ ,
186.38	dawn of	the dawn of the
187.1	over- | taken	overtaken
187.1	and,	~$_\wedge$
187.11	tom-hawk	tomahawk
187.17	war.	~$_\wedge$
187.17	The | the	The
187.36	and$_\wedge$	~ ,
187.36	end$_\wedge$	~ ,
188.2	door$_\wedge$	~ ,
188.21	formed ⋯ cavity partly	partly formed ⋯ cavity
189.2	and$_\wedge$	~ ,
189.5	number	numbers
189.6	strength,	~$_\wedge$
189.11–12	man- | kind	mankind
189.13	foreseen	fore- | seen
189.14	cowardice$_\wedge$	~ ,
189.14	suggested?	~ ;
189.26	captive$_\wedge$	~ ,
189.35	station$_\wedge$	~ .
189.35	was as	was
189.37	and,	~$_\wedge$

	First Edition (A)	*Monthly Magazine (M)*
189.38	it∧	~,
190.2	forth- | coming	forth-coming
190.13	mean- | while	meanwhile
190.16	stedfast	steadfast
191.11	withdraw	with- | draw
191.13–14	The ball entered above his ear: He	He
192.2	tranquility	tranquillity
192.4	But I	I
192.6	spirit∧	~,
192.13	expiate,	~∧
192.21	and∧	~,
193.13	but∧	~,
193.15	tom-hawk	tomahawk
193.21	blood- | shed	bloodshed
193.22	fire-arms	fire- | arms
193.25–26	hardships	hardship
193.33	or∧	~,
194.8	foot- | steps	footsteps
194.11–12	undergone	under- | gone
195.4	myself	my- | self
195.5	aproach	approach
195.9	some- | thing	something
195.14	and∧	~,
196.7	clasping	clasping her
196.8	joy∧	~,
196.12	here? ···	~ ?∧
196.12	you? ···	~ ?∧
196.13	you?∧	~ ?—
196.22	contest.	~ ?
196.30	zeal∧	~,
196.37	was∧	~,
197.33	tranquilized	realized
198.11	clothing	cloathing
198.14	with- | out	without
198.17	Besides∧	~,
198.17	fusil,	~∧
198.27	styptic,	~;
198.35	and,	~∧
199.5	expense	expence
199.12	troops,	~∧
199.14	and∧	~,

	First Edition (A)	*Monthly Magazine (M)*
199.16	the	this
199.17	great,	~∧
199.26	nothing	no- | thing
200.19	friends;	~ :
200.37	stedfast	stead- | fast
201.4	uncocked.	~ ,
201.9	light;	~ :
202.11	over- | powered	overpowered
202.21	enterprise	enterprize
202.24	timerous	timorous
202.26	achievements	atchievements
202.26	experience,	~∧
202.28–34	these! But what ⋯ universe!	these!
202.36	moon-light	moon- | light
203.2	tom-hawk	tomahawk
203.2	cavern;	~ :
203.3	burden	burthen
204.6–7	cultivation, the *well-pole*,	cultivation,
205.12	foot-steps	foot- | steps
205.15	myself	my- | self
205.18–19	attendents	attendants
205.25	chimney∧	~ ,
205.25	brick,	~∧
205.29	myself	my- | self
205.30	myself	my- | self
206.1	tom-hawk	tomahawk
206.8	thing∧	~ ,
207.23	Nor- | walk	Norwalk
207.31	agreeable	agreeably
207.33	themselves	them- | selves
207.34	rabbits	hares
207.37	farm- | house	farm-house
208.8	plucking the weeds from among	hoeing and grinding
208.8–9	corn; bruising the grain between two stones,	corn∧
208.9–10	snares, for rabbits and apossums,	snares,
208.18	looks ⋯ occasion	look ⋯ occasions

	First Edition (A)	Monthly Magazine (M)
208.23	overhear	overheard
208.31	what- | ever	whatever
208.36	were	were merely
209.11	some- | times	sometimes
209.11	insensibly	but insensibly
209.19	likewise	like- | wise
209.27	haunts∧	~,
210.1	suspicion	suspicions
210.7	who∧	~,
210.21	wolves	wolfs
210.23	visits	visit
210.24	rare	rarely
210.38	countrymen	country- | men
211.4	foot-steps	footsteps
211.23	and∧	~,
211.24	them- | selves	themselves
211.27	place∧	~,
211.27	foot-steps	footsteps
211.31	cultivable	culturable
211.32	*township*	*town- | ship*
212.8	Thence- | forward	Thenceforward
212.12	boundings of a leopard	boundings
212.14	in	in a
212.16	however	how- | ever
212.20	energis	energies
212.20	energis∧	~,
212.22	achievements	atchievements
212.24	sure-footed	sure- | footed
213.5	suspense	suspence
213.6	fore- | bodings	forebodings
213.8	subjected	subject

NOTE: The following paragraphs were prefaced to the text of the "fragment" published in M.

Mr. Editor,

The following narrative is extracted from the memoirs of a young man who resided some years since on the upper branches of the Delaware. These memoirs will shortly be published; but, meanwhile, the incidents here related are of such a kind as may interest and amuse some of your readers. Similar events have frequently happened on the Indian borders; but, perhaps, they never were before described with equal minuteness.

As to the truth of these incidents, men acquainted with the perils of an Indian war must be allowed to judge. Those who have ranged along the foot of the *Blue-ridge*, from the *Wind-gap* to the *Water-gap*, will see the exactness of the *local* descriptions. It may also be mentioned that "*Old Deb*" is a portrait faithfully drawn from nature.

E. H.

RECORD OF COLLATIONS AND
COPIES CONSULTED

Edgar Huntly; or, Memoirs of a Sleep-Walker
(Philadelphia, 1799): A

The following copies of Volume I have been examined and collated (by different operators) at least twice by machine: OKentU – Spec. Coll. PS. 1134.E3.1799, v. 1; 1799a, v. 1; 1799b, v. 1; 1799bb, v. 1; Spec. Coll. PS.1134.E3.1801, v. 1; 1801a, v. 1; 1801aa, v. 1; InU – PS.1134.E3 (AMS Press facsimile reprint); uncatalogued 1801 copy owned by Miss Pamela Burr. The following copies of Volume II have been examined and collated (by different operators) at least twice by machine: OKentU – Spec. Coll. PS.1134.E3.1799b, v. 2; 1801, v. 2; InU – PS.1134.E3 (AMS facsimile); NBu – RBR/Am.1/B7/1799b, v. 2; PSt – uncatalogued copy; OAU – Spec. Coll./813/B8772e, v. 2; KyU – F.B8123e.1799, v. 2; ViU – uncatalogued copy, v. 2; NjP – Ex.3643.7.33.11, v. 2; NNHi – PS.1134.E23.1799, v. 2; MWA – uncatalogued copy; uncatalogued Burr copy. Quire K only in the following copies has been collated (by different operators) once by machine: NN – *KD.1799, v. 2; NNC – B812B81/Q/1799, v. 2; NNSL – Z/B, v. 2; NcU – PS.1134.E3, v. 2; PPL – Am.1799.Bro, v. 2; DLC – PZ.B14E, v. 2. Quire K in the KyU copy was collated at least four times by hand against state *a*. Quire K in the following copies has been collated (by different operators) once or twice by hand against state *a*: OKentU – 1799b, v. 2; NjP; MWA; NNHi; CSmH – 8124, v. 2; MH – *55-1244, v. 2; PCarlD – R.B.813.B877, v. 2; the last three were machined against the first once. Quire M in the

494

following copies has been collated once by machine: NjP; PCarlD; quire M in the NjP copy has been collated against state *a* by hand three times (by different operators), the MWA copy twice. The following copies of Volume III have been examined and collated (by different operators) at least twice by machine: OKentU — Spec. Coll. PS.1134.E3.1799, v. 3; 1801, v. 3; NNHi — PS.1134.E23.1799, v. 3; DeU — Spec. PS.1134.E33.1801, v. 3; MWA — uncatalogued copy; OAU — Spec. Coll./813/B8772e, v. 3; NjP — Ex.3643.7.33.11, v. 3; InU — PS.1134.E3 (AMS facsimile); PSt — uncatalogued copy; ViU — uncatalogued copy; uncatalogued Burr copy.

Philadelphia Gazette and Universal Daily Advertiser
(10 August 1799): G

The opening paragraphs of the subscription notice as published on 10 August 1799 have been collated against A's preface (by different operators) three times by hand and once by machine against identical notices of the 17th, 20th, 22nd, and 31st of August.

Monthly Magazine, Volume I (April 1799): M

The text of "Edgar Huntly: *A Fragment*." has been collated (by different operators) against that of A five times by hand, and the gatherings of the following copies containing this text have been collated (by different operators) at least twice by machine: OKentU — Per. Spec. Coll. *Monthly Magazine*, v. 1, c. 1; c. 2; c. 3; v. 1-2, c. 1.

Edgar Huntly, or Memoirs of a Sleep-Walker. A Novel. In Three Volumes (London, 1803): E

Five different operators collated this edition by hand against A. Two copies of E were collated (by different operators) twice by machine: PSt — Rare Books Room PS.1134.E3.1803/the; NjR — X.PS1130.C4E.